The Sixth Prophet
by Thomas Knapp
Copyright 2014, all rights reserved

Cover art by Jorge Rivas
Edited by Patrick Coyle and Ray Kremer

Chapter One

A damp cloth wiped across Rumil's forehead, and the cool residue made her cringe. Her face contorted in discomfort, and she finally recognized that she was no longer on the shuttle... and had no idea what happened, or what prompted her to leave it.

A rich, hypnotic female voice floated into Rumil's ears, muttering words she couldn't understand, and a pair of small hands pressed against her chest; pushing her back down as she tried to sit up.

Rumil groaned, and weakly pushed at the hands holding her down, while the voice spoke again, this time in her head in a telepathic query.

You are awake now?

"Yes..." Rumil muttered, her head throbbing painfully, but not from the buzz that normally accompanied any sort of psionic display. Dazed from the pain, it took some time for Rumil to realize that if she couldn't understand her attendant's speech, it was likely the attendant wouldn't understand Rumil either.

While still not terribly sure how to telepathically communicate, she hoped she managed to express that she was indeed conscious. She tried to open her eyes, but only registered a pair of dark blurs barely visible amidst the bright white light that filled her vision.

You received a great deal of head trauma when you fell from the sky, the soothing voice whispered. *Do you remember what happened?*

That she didn't. The last clear memory she had was emerging from the fold Justin had programmed. Then there was a haze... and then she was here... wherever 'here' was.

Here, take this. It will clear your head, the voice spoke again. Rumil felt a pair of fingers touch her lips, and when Rumil opened her mouth in compliance, a small hard pill rolled onto her tongue. Swallowing, she waited for it to take effect.

To her surprise, the throbbing pain in her brain began to break up and dissipate almost immediately. Opening her eyes again, the image cleared to the point that she realized the bright blur was actually from a light above her reflecting off a white background. The two dark blurs slowly became more humanoid-shaped as the clarity of her vision continued to correct itself.

Finally, one of the attendants came directly to Rumil's side, and helped her to sit up slowly. By then, her sight was keen enough to get a good, clear look at the person aiding her. The woman was so slight of frame, her facial features appearing so delicate, that Rumil was irrationally afraid that the girl would break into pieces if she bumped into something. Despite her apparent youth, she had bright, shimmering silver hair that reflected light almost like a mirror. Her eyes twinkled, and for a moment, Rumil was certain that they changed color from green to blue as she turned her head towards the other figure in the room.

That was when Rumil noticed the girl's ears, which possessed a sharp point several Tackems long and pressed tightly along the hairline. As Rumil was transfixed on the attendant's lobes, the second figure, a much older-appearing woman approached, placing one dry, wrinkled hand on Rumil's forehead. Like her younger counterpart, the elderly attendant had the same gleaming hair and almost color-changing eyes.

Fascinating… the other woman remarked telepathically. *I had sensed no mind talent within you at all before you woke up. Most peculiar…*

Yeah… I haven't been able to make sense of her abilities either, Justin declared as he emerged from around the corner, into the open entry of the ward. He was wearing the bottom half of his body suit and the legs panels of his armor, but that was it. His rib cage was wrapped in bandages, and he had his left arm hanging somewhat limply at his side, using the right to apparently keep it from moving.

You were not given permission to leave your ward! The older woman chastised.

I've never been one to know what's good for me, the Kiros Knight shot back playfully.

The younger attendant made a breathy sound similar to a sigh as the older woman began examining Justin, likely to determine if the Kiros had done any further damage to himself. *You are fortunate that you were not nearly as injured as your friends,* the younger lady stated simply while Justin yelped from the less than gentle prodding of the elder.

"How long was I out?" Rumil asked verbally to Justin.

Justin shrugged at the question. "Not sure. All I know is that I woke up about a cycle ago, and that these people don't seem to have any concept to measure the passing of time. We could have been unconscious for staryears for all I know."

"Where's Timothy?"

Justin froze at the question, and then appeared as if he was expecting it. "Perhaps I should explain something to you…" he began, but then paused as if he wasn't at all sure as to how to proceed.

For a brief moment, it was as if every cell in Rumil's body swelled with dread. "What's wrong? What happened? Timothy's… not… dead, is he?"

"No! No! Trust me, he's not dead." Then his mental voice added, *Although he might have been better off…*

Something about the tone of that last telepathic comment suggested to Rumil that she was not supposed to have heard that.

*And what is **that** supposed to mean?* Rumil demanded mentally, trying to get Justin to recognize she had heard his added thoughts on the matter.

Justin blanched again. *You heard that?*

You better believe I did… Then Rumil added vocally, "Now, you better explain yourself."

At that moment, the older attendant interjected. *I really wish they'd choose one speech or the other. I do despise only having half of the conversation.*

There was another man with us— Rumil began, but was interrupted. It was clear even to the attendants who she was referring to.

The pale man? He is alive, but his mind is badly hurt, the older attendant explained. *He spent too much energy to make sure that you survived the fall.*

Rumil blinked repeatedly, trying to remember just what had happened, but her memory was still fuzzy.

Sensing Rumil's confusion, Justin said, "You don't remember the crash? I guess that isn't a great surprise, you smacked your head pretty hard on the navigation console. Sorry about that, I didn't react fast enough when your harness broke."

I need to see him… Rumil demanded, turning her body so that her legs dangled over the edge of the bed she had been laid down in. *Where is he?*

The younger attendant pursed her lips. *I suppose if your friend is well enough to walk around, then you are as well. Ghadri, is it acceptable for me to escort this young lady to her companion?*

Ghadri appeared to be the name of the older attendant, as the older woman nodded. *If the pain in her head has cleared, I don't see what further harm could come of it. Be careful with her, Micha.*

The two women exchanged partings in their verbal tongue, then Micha took Rumil by the right arm and helped the blonde woman to her feet. Then, with a disapproving glare towards Justin, Micha asked, *I assume you wish to accompany us as well?*

Justin nodded solemnly. *It might be a good idea.*

Keeping her hand on Rumil's arm as a guide, Micha escorted Rumil out of the ward and into the short hall, dimly lit from a series of mounted candles. Similar open, arched entries were spaced at alternating intervals along its length, leading into the five other wards along the hall ahead of them. Micha released Rumil once they reached the last ward on the right, peering around the corner before speaking a soft request to whomever was inside. Turning back outside, she motioned for Rumil and Justin to follow.

Be quiet, there are several healers at work here, and they need their full concentration, Micha warned sternly, glaring at Justin specifically. Justin cringed apologetically for what must have been some incident during an earlier visit.

Rumil wasn't sure what she expected to see inside the ward, but it certainly wouldn't have been close to the sight before her now. Timothy was covered in nothing but a thin sheet that extended from his ankles to just below his chest, his arms hanging limply down both sides of the narrow table he was stretched across. The Solarian's head was resting on a thin pad, gently raised against a small lip on the end of the table.

His face was peaceful, his eyes closed, but Rumil felt a loud static crackle in the back of her mind. Instinctively, she mentally located the source. Timothy's own mind was in complete disarray, the normally powerful psionic presence torn and ruptured.

She was suddenly slapped on the shoulder, and Rumil jerked when she realized that Micha had been the one to strike her. *Do not interrupt our healers. They know what they are doing.*

Rumil finally noticed the eight men with the same long pointed ears as her escorts at the head and base of Timothy's table, four on each side. Like Timothy, their eyes were closed, concentrating heavily on their patient, clearly trying to repair the extensive damage to Timothy's mind.

She was in a daze while Micha and Justin escorted Rumil back out of the ward, and towards her own. "What's wrong with him?" she whispered to Justin, somewhat afraid of using any sort of telepathy that could potentially affect Timothy's healing.

Justin replied, "Psionic power is limited by the strength of the mind wielding it, much like how the body is limited by the strength and stamina of the person. Sometimes, an Erani can overdo it, and use more psionic energy than he should, and the mind instinctively tries to compensate by drawing energy from the body. It's why Erani can become physically weak from an extended psionic battle." The Kiros bit his lower lip before continuing softly, "Most Erani have the sense to stop when they feel their minds beginning to tax their body, but for those that don't, it continues to drain on the physical form… eventually causing bodily functions to shut down. This is what doctors call 'psionic shock.' If left unchecked, psionic shock can burn out brain synapses, cause paralysis, and even shut down vital functions."

"What are you saying?"

"I'm saying he passed out shortly after he dragged you to safety from the crash. I was barely able to restart his heart as it was," Justin admitted. "The medical staff here seem convinced they can restore him fully… but I can't imagine how that's possible. I think we're going to have to accept the fact that Timothy is not going to be the same."

Rumil shook her head in disbelief. "I refuse to accept that. Timothy doesn't strike me as someone who's just going to give up, and if these people think he can recover, then I'm going to trust them."

Returning to her ward, Rumil sat down slowly onto her bed, kicking absent-mindedly as Justin continued to explain his position. "You obviously don't understand how much energy Timothy had to expend to do what he did. He not only slowed down a shuttle in complete free-fall, but also altered its trajectory to keep us from a nasty head-on collision with a planet. By Bannor, I have no idea where he found the power to do that."

Rumil blinked, "You didn't help him?"

Justin scowled at the accusation. "*Fifty* of me couldn't have helped him. As it was, it was all I could do just to make sure we weren't torn apart upon impact."

Rumil didn't even need to feel the state of Justin's mind to sense the frustration, guilt, and perhaps even a twinge of jealousy tainting the young Kiros Knight. "He'll be fine, Justin," Rumil stated with slightly more confidence than she felt.

"He better be," Justin replied darkly, then staggered back towards his own ward, shrugging off Micha's assistance angrily. Perhaps it was best that Rumil couldn't recall the crash, he already blamed himself enough as it was.

He knew that he should have checked the programmed coordinates once again before activating the fold – Timothy could have bought them enough time. And that had only been the *start* of Justin's mistakes. Instead of firing the retrorockets to slow their descent, then deploying the atmospheric wings for control, Justin had done exactly the opposite. The shear from the reverse thrust put too much pressure on the wing joints, causing them to completely tear from the shuttle's hull. Without the assistance of guiding wings at such tremendous velocity, the engines became imbalanced, sending the shuttle into a vicious tumble and causing Rumil to have her unpleasant meeting with the edge of console in front of her.

And after that, Justin had been ready to blow a hole in the shuttle, and try and teleport everyone to safety. Fortunately Timothy, while focusing on stopping the ship, carefully reminded him that a jump into unfamiliar surroundings from an unstable vessel wasn't a terribly good idea. It was only after Justin regained consciousness that he thought of an even more compelling problem: blowing a hole in the shuttle would have then totally destroyed any structural integrity on the vessel, causing everything to completely fall apart and incinerate before they could teleport away.

Then Timothy, during all this chaos, was the only one who actually did something. In the time between appearing above this Creator-forsaken planet until their impact with the surface, the difference between the Solarian and himself became painfully clear, and not just in terms of psionic power. The more Justin thought about it, this was his first real test in a serious life-or-death situation, and he had failed rather miserably. Rather than focus on the situation and fall back on his training, he lost his cool, and made one dumb mistake after another, mistakes that very nearly got all three of them killed, had Timothy not pulled some godly amount of sheer mental will out of some unknown source.

And now Timothy's mind was in pieces, for the mistakes Justin had made. That, in the end, was the major issue that was not sitting well in the young Kiros. He slapped a knee in frustration, instantly regretting it when his battered body objected to the quick, harsh movement.

Something is troubling you. May I ask what it is? Micha's telepathic question prompted her appearance at the entry to his room.

No, you may not, Justin replied sourly. *You wouldn't understand.*

Micha blinked, then frowned disapprovingly. *I cannot understand disappointment, or guilt? Both of those emotions are weighing heavily on your mind. I would have to be completely brain-dead not to catch them tainting your aura.*

Justin regarded the slight woman warily. *Where I come from, people like myself have great duties, and high expectations for how I act and perform said duties. When tested, I did not perform well. I guess I just expected better out of myself.*

Micha nodded, getting to the heart of the matter a little too quickly for the Kiros's tastes. *You somehow feel that you should be in your friend's place. How very… peculiar… to wish harm on your own person.*

Justin did not take such a flippant remark candidly. *It was **my** errors that put him where he is now! I'm not **supposed** to feel guilty about that? I acted like I was some untested rookie!*

Micha blinked as if trying to understand just what was so wrong with the situation Justin presented. *But you are still alive, are you not, as is your friend? You will heal, as will he. You will both learn from the experience you have had.* The fey-looking woman then smirked before adding, *What you learn, however… that is another matter.*

Before Justin could reply, Ghadri stepped into the ward, holding in both hands a large, battered book with a plain brown leather cover that Justin recognized all too quickly. As he marveled as to how it possibly could have survived the crash, the elder woman commented, *Some of the men cleaning the site of your crash found this among the remains. I asked the woman you call Rumil, and she claimed that it was yours.*

Justin reached out, and graciously accepted the book. Its continued existence was nothing short of divine intervention. Placing it in his lap, looking down on the beaten, weathered tome, he blankly rubbed his hand across the front cover, feeling the rough, leathery texture under his hand. In a way, it represented the very reason he was sitting where he was.

Perhaps we shall let you have some time alone… Ghadri stated politely, gently escorting Micha out of the ward. Justin didn't do anything that suggested he acknowledged their departure, his gaze transfixed on the book in his lap.

He slowly opened the cover, hearing the binding crackle as he did so. For a book that could be close to nine hundred staryears old, judging from the archaic script and dialect, it was in remarkably good condition. The paper used was still firm, the ink still bold. Possibly, the book had been restored or copied, but eventually he found himself reading the text rather than continuing to analyze its condition.

He eventually recognized what he was reading as largely similar to what he had studied in his Knighthood training. With a sigh, he began half-heartedly flipping through the pages, looking for just what was so different from what he had known Bryan Honore to have written.

He found it at the start of the third stanza. The text was completely new to Justin, radically different from how he recalled that section to begin.

Flipping forward curiously, he discovered the section that he had been taught was the third stanza was actually the fourth in the book he currently held. He turned back to the third section, wondering now just what was so threatening that the early leaders of the Erani sects had decided the entire movement needed to be purged from memory. He carefully took in every word, as much from his desire to read it closely as trying to understand the occasionally archaic words and phrases. By the time he was halfway through the section, his eyes narrowed, his eyebrows furrowed, and his lips pursed in disbelief. He almost couldn't believe what he was reading… He looked over the book once again, once again trying to confirm its age… but it still appeared to be genuine from his scrutiny.

He lifted his head, staring as if his vision could bore through the walls separating the wards. Finally, with a hoarse, incredulous whisper, he muttered, "There is no possible way…"

* * * * *

Justin figured it had been around four cycles later when next he stepped outside his ward, smiling tightly at Ghadri. She looked him over, then tapped him roughly in the side through the loose shirt he had thrown over his head. Justin cringed slightly from the soreness, but managed to keep his smile firmly in place. To Justin's immense surprise, the people of this planet were well versed in psionic ability, especially in medical prowess, able to discern the proper course of action to heal the bodies of even alien origin.

You are healing well, the old woman remarked, *although you could heal faster if you didn't insist on roaming about.*

Justin raised his hands defensively. *I just wish to check up on my dear friends, and then I will return to my bed. Is that acceptable?*

Ghadri scowled as if she didn't believe him for one demitick, but eventually acquiesced. *Don't dawdle in there too long. The mind may be healed, but he still needs to regain the energy he had lost. It's enough that woman refuses to leave…*

I understand. I will not be long. Justin then took his leave of Ghadri, and proceeded the short distance to Timothy's ward. As Ghadri had warned, Rumil was still in the bench she had pulled over to Timothy's bedside, the place that became her perch once she had been cleared to walk about freely.

"Any change?" Justin asked, but it was rather pointless. While Timothy was still unconscious, it was clear that his mind was once again intact, and regaining its old vitality rapidly… and then some.

"Not yet… still asleep," the blonde remarked sadly, surprising Justin by absent-mindedly brushing a lock of Timothy's long black hair out of his face, the tenderness in that endearing action very unlike what he had expected out of her.

"I still can't believe they actually repaired his mind. That sort of damage usually damns a person to a pitiful life. Erani doctors could never have done what these people have. It's eased my mind a great deal," Justin admitted ruefully.

Rumil smirked. "I told you to trust them. Sometimes it takes just a little faith."

Justin was about to deliver a retort on being lectured on the power of faith by an Arcadian, but it died short. She detected his blank expression, and her face furrowed in confusion before she demanded, "What is wrong with you *now*?"

Justin shook his head as much to clear his head as to indicate a response. "Nothing… just still a little dazed."

Rumil frowned at Justin's antics, returning her attention towards Timothy's motionless form. She sighed forlornly, and with another subtle caress, this time on his bare left shoulder, she asked rhetorically, "I wonder how much longer he's going to be asleep."

"I had been hoping for a few more tenth-cycles, but that is proving to be impossible…"

The sound of Timothy's grumpy voice so stunned both Rumil and Justin that they initially didn't register that the Solarian had spoken. Finally, Rumil managed to demand accusingly, "How long have you been awake?"

Despite her angered query, Justin could sense the relief in her mind, as well as see the elated tears working slowly down her cheekbones. It was likely Timothy also sensed those things, but his voice didn't reflect it as he commented dryly, "As long as you and Justin have been prattling."

"How long were you sleeping, then?" Rumil asked next, now lightly confounded.

Timothy made a slight shrugging motion with his shoulders. "Hard to say. I just remember wanting more sleep as you two started talking."

That's when Justin noticed Rumil's psionic presence beginning to wane as if it had just finished whatever task it had been doing. Could Rumil have been accelerating Timothy's healing process? If so, had she even realized she was doing it? The more he pondered the idea, the more it brought up questions he wasn't sure he wanted to try and answer without consulting the Solarian who had her attention.

Justin then declared, "I think I'll inform our handlers that Timothy has woken up…" and waited for either of them to acknowledge that he had even spoken. When neither did, Justin slowly slipped out of the ward.

Rumil looked down on the prone Solarian with a slight, relieved smile. "Don't you remember that you're supposed to be invincible?" she teased softly.

"Sorry to disappoint," Timothy deadpanned, "I'll try to do better next time."

"Don't be funny. You had everyone quite worried, even if they tried to pretend otherwise," Rumil scolded.

"Odd, I thought you had faith in my full recovery."

12

"That doesn't mean I can't be worried," was the retort, her voice cracking slightly. "I don't have many friends, as you might guess. I'd rather not lose one of them until I absolutely have to."

"So, I'm a friend now?" Timothy remarked, raising an eyebrow.

Rumil blushed. "As close to one as I've ever had."

The former hacker's blush deepened as Timothy gently moved his hand over hers, and replied, "I could say the same thing."

An awkward silence followed, broken when Ghadri stepped inside, followed closely by Justin. *So, you are awake now,* the old woman remarked.

It would appear that way, the Solarian shot back, rolling his eyes at the overly obvious observation.

Perhaps now your lady friend will actually eat her meals in the dinner hall like everyone else, Ghadri added.

Timothy's eyebrows rose playfully. "You haven't been dining with our hosts?"

"Bannor take her, she would barely move from that bench long enough to relieve herself. It was so cute when she'd fall asleep, and put her head on your thigh while she drifted off." Justin crowed, "By Bannor, she just about growled at Micha when the girl tried to move the both of you to change your linens."

"I already said I was worried about you…" Rumil said, turning her head in the hopes that no one would see just how red her face was turning.

As much as I am certain this conversation is completely enthralling, I do request that I have some time to look over our patient, Ghadri interrupted. *I would also suggest to all of you that you enjoy your rest while you have it.*

Chapter Two

"Mr. Rio… I'm bored."

Dewin felt his eye muscles spasm from the statement. In the nine cycles since he and his crew had scattered and went into hiding, he had heard that protest, in only a small variety of forms, ten to twenty times a day.

He drummed his fingers on the padded armrest of his chair, trying to keep his voice calm as he remarked without pity, "Yes, I am aware you are bored, Orion. But I told you that I would have to lay low for some time. You should not have come with me."

Of course, he knew that Orion would never leave his side – the Ubek's code of honor prohibiting such an act – but it had been worth a try.

A demitick later, the giddy squeal of a toddler rung through the four-room safehouse that Dewin had procured for himself. "And speaking of people who should not have come with me…"

Dewin let the statement die off, lest he say something he'd regret later. Had he been aware that he would eventually be responsible for a small entourage, he would have found a larger hideout. When he told his contacts to keep tabs on Justin's family, he had not expected these same contacts to drop them onto his lap three cycles later.

Jonathan Feroz burst into the living area from the adjoining hall, skidding to a stop less than a Tack from colliding with Orion, wearing nothing but a smile. The child grinned at Dewin mischievously, and Dewin covered his ears in anticipation of what was about to follow.

"Jonathan Feroz! Get back here and take your bath this instant!" Julianne bellowed. Dewin had another of those moments where he regretted rescuing Justin as an infant, not so much because of his current situation, but to have spared the Kiros Knight moments such as these.

"You can't make me!" Jonathan yelled back.

"So you think, young man!" his mother challenged, then in a softer voice barely audible asked, "Fiona, can you collect the little demon while I finish drawing the bath?"

This prompted the final member of Dewin's little group to make an appearance. When Dewin first met Julianne's primary servant, she had not struck him as a typical Erani. At first he thought it was merely because she was unusually plump for one of that race, but when he politely took her four-fingered hand, he understood the cause of his first impression. Fiona was a Demodian-Erani half-breed, likely the reason she had been relegated to a life barely above slavery.

"Jonathan, please do not make a fuss," Fiona requested. "If you take your bath, I promise I'll read you your favorite story for your bedtime."

The toddler beamed, but asked suspiciously, "You mean it? All the noises and all?"

Fiona smiled, and replied, "Noises and all."

Jonathan hopped in place twice, giggled, and then disappeared back down the hall. "Mommy! I'm coming!"

Orion laughed heartily, slapping his armrest with such force that Dewin was certain it would break. "The child has spirit, and he knows how to get what he wants!" the Ubek crowed, clearly amused.

"If he were my brat, I'd have paddled him by now," Dewin grumbled.

"This is young Jonathan's first trip ever off-planet," Fiona contended. "It is expected that he would be abnormally excited. He actually is rather well-behaved under normal circumstances."

"Must you defend the little terror? He's not your child."

Fiona flushed slightly. "I sometimes… mistakenly think he is."

Dewin raised his eyes in a silent query. Fiona glanced down the hall, where sounds of water splashing and childish laughing could be heard. "I've spent most of my life in the Feroz family since my father was a servant to the Feroz family as well. I've known Justin and Julianne since we were all children. I was one of Julianne's escorts during her wedding. I was there when Jonathan was born. He spent as much time in my arms as his mother's."

Dewin decided he shouldn't have been terribly surprised at Fiona's attachment to Jonathan. Being half-bred, she likely was sterile, unable to have children of her own save through very expensive genetic conjunction, which as he recalled, the Kiros faith absolutely abhorred and prohibited.

"As much as I'd love to hear this story further... I don't," Dewin finally snapped. Truth be told, he felt a certain degree of empathy for Fiona and the life she had been relegated to, without her choice, but that was tempered by his disgust that she remained in her subservient role, not even thinking that she could be free of that life.

The splashing stopped, apparently indicating that the bath had been completed. Jonathan confirmed this less than a tick later when he shouted, "Fiona! I'm getting ready for bed now!"

"I'll be there in a moment, little one!" Fiona called back, and smiled in apology to Dewin and Orion. "I shall have to take my leave now, sirs." She bowed politely then retreated into the hall. Dewin sighed ruefully, turning his attention to the news report on the GalNet that had been playing in the background.

Moments later, he heard the most unusual noises coming from the hall, no doubt sound effects of the story that Fiona had promised her young charge. Curiosity overcame him just long enough for him to stand up, and make the short walk to the bedroom that the Feroz family had acquired for themselves. He stood just to the left of the doorway, and just slightly poked his head around.

Fiona was speaking in a silly nasal voice, trying to sound malicious. However, the humor she was no doubt feeling was inflecting in her voice, creating a sound similar to a small mammal being run over by a large street roller.

He had obviously stepped in during mid-story, but when Fiona cackled, "It is belly burps for you, young hero!" he decided he probably didn't want to hear what came before. Fiona ripped down Jonathan's blanket, lowered her mouth to the boy's bare navel, and made a unique sound that actually did loosely resemble a belch.

Fiona pulled away, and couldn't help but laugh along with the excited giggling of the toddler. She sighed, and pulled the blanket back up to Jonathan's neck. "Well, young hero, we shall continue this story later. However, you must set up camp for tomorrow."

"Do I have to?" Jonathan protested, even as his words betrayed a small level of fatigue.

"Yes, you will need all your rest if you are to become a big, grown-up hero."

"Like my daddy?"

Fiona smiled, and placed one last kiss on Jonathan's forehead, "Just like your father." She leaned back into her chair, and then began to hum a hauntingly soothing melody that would have had the ability to put anyone to sleep of its own merit, but it possibly could have carried a slight psionic suggestion as well. Even Dewin felt his eyelids getting heavy, and barely managed to cover his ears and step away from the door before he himself passed out on the floor.

Dewin stumbled back into the main room, and didn't notice that they had another guest until Orion spoke up, "Mr. Rio, you have a visitor. I think he wants to collect on his part of your deal."

The visitor in question was everything that a Demodian was supposed to be: long hair trimmed neatly at the shoulders, violet eyes gleaming confidently, thin yet broad-shouldered, legs with powerful and tight muscles, and hands with four long, almost bony, digits. His posture was straight, his facial features proud and regal… but his clothes were another matter.

At one time, the royal purple uniform must have been truly impressive, but now the material was faded almost to lavender, and the silver jewelry used to trim the uniform was slightly tarnished and thin, despite what must have been great effort to clean it. It was a telling indicator as to how far the native Diviners of the Demodians had fallen.

"My Excellence, the Diviner of Villium Temple, requests your presence as soon as it is feasible," the uniformed retainer enunciated clearly. "As I recall, this was per the terms of your agreement."

Dewin nodded solemnly. He had not wanted to come to Demod in the first place, let alone make any deals with the old relics who represented the last fading remnants of the failed Demodian religion. However, circumstances had forced his hand.

Once the shuttle carrying Justin and the two fugitives had disappeared from the face of the galaxy, the Kiros turned their attention toward the entire Blood Hawks organization, contrary to Timothy's assurances. The Kiros scoured their region of the Galactic Rim in a manner the pirate leader could only describe as "unprecedented," forcing him to call for a full-scale lockdown of all activity, and for all members to go underground until further notice. Unfortunately, the widespread message allowed the Kiros to track and close in on Dewin's flagship.

Soon after, Dewin had received a well-timed communication from his ancestral home planet. How the Diviner of Villium could know that

Dewin was in dire straits, he couldn't explain, but he wasn't willing to acknowledge any supernatural perception on the Diviner's part. He had terribly few options however, and accepted the Diviner's offer of asylum in spite of his reservations. Thus, his crew escaped to the Galatic Rim while the Diviner provided interference, and Dewin and Orion departed quietly for Demod.

Dewin still wasn't sure what the religious leader wanted in return, and hadn't been inclined to ask since he arrived nine cycles ago. The inevitable meeting had been weighing on his mind though, and in a way, he was glad that things appeared to be moving forward now. At least this way, it wouldn't keep bothering him.

"Actually, we might as well see what the Honorable One wants right now," Dewin commented passively, grabbing a light jacket from the closet next to the door. "Or was there a specific time in which he expected guests?"

"Normally, there is," the retainer replied. "However, I received the impression that you were allowed audience with *her* at your leisure. If you wish to meet with her, then we can leave immediately."

The correction of the Diviner's gender caused Dewin's eyebrows to lift in query. Traditionally, women had never been allowed such lofty positions of faith even if they carried the "gift," as Demodians called it. Clearly, if that fundamental tenet of the practice had been abandoned, things were truly in as poor shape as he had suspected.

"Very well, then let's do so," Dewin replied. "Just get it over with."

"As you wish, sir. I have a hover waiting outside. Just follow me." The retainer then turned on his heel sharply, and Orion opened the safehouse door again to allow both Demodians to exit.

Like the retainer, the vehicle in question must have looked truly impressive at one time. However, the elongated hover designed for bearing figureheads of state and religion was now bearing the years of its use instead. The trim showed the beginnings of rust, the upholstered interior was faded and split, and the shuddering suggested that it needed some considerable tuning of the magnetic propulsion panels.

He almost offered to let Orion crawl underneath to do some maintainence work. Then he remembered that he had no desire to assist the temple any more than was absolutely necessary.

The retainer opened the passenger's side door, and bowed

respectfully as Dewin stepped inside the covered vehicle. The pirate leader rolled his eyes at the gesture and closed the door, pulling it out of the retainer's hand.

The uniformed Demodian scowled slightly, but didn't comment, striding purposefully around the front of the vehicle and climbing into the driver's seat. His head was straight and his demeanor proud all the while, though he served as little more than a chauffeur.

"Must be rather demeaning," Dewin remarked. "You couldn't have signed on for this."

"I do what I must for the glory of the Diviner, Mr. Rio," the retainer retorted as the vehicle jerked violently before moving forward. It picked up velocity once it hit the smoother surface of the main roadway, and turned eastward, where Dewin assumed the Temple of Villium was located.

Villium was one of the few temples remaining in operation on Demod. Due to Erani influence, the native Demodian religion had been in steady decline, especially as the natives were drawn to the perks and advancement of the Erani people, leaving behind the old ways that shunned such unnatural tools. It was a classic case of an obsessive tradition finally becoming outdated and abandoned. As far as Dewin was concerned, that was precisely the way things should be.

Now, only five Demodian cities claimed any support of the Diviners, and of those five, it is highly unlikely that all of them held the "gift," an ability that Dewin understood little about. Something told him he was going to learn more than he ever wanted to by the time he left Demod.

Villium itself was little more than a ghost city. The roadways were about the only thing that looked relatively maintained, and probably only because planetary commissions were responsible for them. The rest of the city – buildings, sideways, pedestrians, shops, alleys, trash – all looked like they had seen much better days. Dewin could have counted the number of vehicles and people moving about on both hands... even with hands that were each short one finger.

"Villium is just the place to be, isn't it?" Dewin quipped.

"You may be a guest of the Diviner, but I am growing increasingly intolerant of your remarks," the retainer warned. "I am taking you to her out of courtesy... I could just as easily make you walk."

The uniformed Demodian then flashed Dewin a close-mouthed

grin, but it wasn't exactly the type of grin that inspires friendship. Something told the pirate leader that the threat wasn't a completely idle one. Dewin slumped back in his seat, and went silent.

Fortunately, he didn't need to stay silent for very long. The Temple of the Diviner was soon filling his vision, and it was a memorable sight. Not memorable in a beautiful, breathtaking manner… more like an eyesore, "what happened here?" manner.

In short, it was ugly. The crumbling, clay-walled, tiered monstrosity was built in an era before hypersteel and fiberwall, and clearly not very well maintained since. It was comprised of several staggered levels in a pyramid shape, and while it was true that each successive clay level was less dingy, the increasing wind erosion made up for it. Fortunately, the clay chosen for the temple had faded with age, because Dewin was rather certain its original colors would have been extremely hard on the eyes. Dirty red, dusty cream, and off white were still preferable to gaudy red, sickening cream, and blinding white.

The roadway led directly up to the rusted double doors at the front of the temple, and the hinges groaned in protest as they were pulled inward. Normally, the doors would open in time for any vehicle to pass through without so much as slowing down, but this time, the hover carrying Dewin had to come to a complete stop as the doors jerked and squealed apart.

They never opened fully. The retainer proceeded forward the moment there was enough of a gap for the vehicle to pass through cleanly. The frustration and indignity was painfully clear on the older Demodian's face as he stopped the hover a final time, the machine shuddering violently as the power drained away, and it dropped to the ground roughly. Dewin's head whipped forward, then fell back again to smack the somewhat tattered and under-padded headrest, and he grit his teeth painfully from the impact.

The retainer mumbled something incoherent before jumping out of the vehicle, and said, "Come this way, Mr. Rio."

Without waiting or looking back, the retainer took up a brisk pace across the parking garage. Dewin jogged quickly to catch up, falling into step with the almost marching Demodian. The elder man stopped abruptly in front of a rather moldy and mildewed wooden door, leading to some form of antiquated lift. Pressing the button that was supposed to call the lift to their level, nothing happened for half a tick. The retainer punched the button seven more times, each with increasing force, until the glowing button stuck in a depressed state, blinking rapidly.

The elder Demodian growled fiercely, the sound echoing through the empty garage. This was followed by a string of curses that Dewin never could have expected from a religious man, coupled with a combination of at least eight kicks and five punches on the lift door. Then as abruptly as the violent outburst occurred, it stopped. The retainer's face that had been contorted in the embodiment of frustrated anger just demiticks ago, shifted to its typical neutral expression. Almost pompously, he straightened his slightly ruffled collar, and smoothed his uniform coat and pants. After two more deep breaths, the retainer turned towards the stairway just down the wall, and said, "Follow me, Mr. Rio."

Once again, Dewin didn't immediately fall in behind the man, but this time it was out of concern for his continued safety. Finally, with a nervous exhale, Dewin did as requested, this time keeping a slightly more comfortable distance.

The tower seemed large from outside, but Dewin decided he had no real understanding as to just how tall the temple was until he climbed it from the inside. The pirate leader had always thought he was in rather good physical shape, but by the fifth tick, he was definitely starting to feel the weight in his legs and lungs.

"How many levels are there until we reach the Diviner's meeting hall?" Dewin asked as calmly as he could.

"Seven, if I recall properly."

"And what level are we on?"

The retainer glanced down to the last stairwell door they had passed. "I do believe we just passed level five."

Dewin nodded appreciatively. They didn't have that much farther to go.

Then the retainer added, "However, the meeting hall is being cleaned and renovated. You will be meeting the Diviner in her chambers… on the tenth level…"

Dewin could not quite contain the groan that slipped through his throat, and that caused the retainer to smirk ever so slightly. Dewin also noticed the elder Demodian slightly pick up his pace as they continued up the steep stairwell. The pirate couldn't help but think the retainer was trying to annoy him.

They had to stop for a few ticks just before the seventh level of the temple. The tower had narrowed enough at that point that the stairwell simply ran along the outer wall, and there were some open-air windows that allowed for a view of the ragged city of Villium. From that vantage point, the city almost seemed normal, with the setting Demod sun casting a glaring light into the window, shrouding some of the haggard buildings, but not enough to hide the disturbing lack of activity on the surface.

Without speaking, the retainer pressed on, pausing just briefly for Dewin to realize they were to supposed to be moving. The pair passed the eight and ninth levels in silence, the turns coming more frequently as each level narrowed further, and finally, the retainer stopped at their destination at the top landing of the stairwell. A single, acid-carved metal relief door bearing words in the native Demodian tongue, and the traditional symbol of the Diviners; a formless humanoid figure sitting cross-legged with his head and arms turned upwards towards the heavens.

"This leads to the foyer of the Diviner's personal chambers. You will wait there until the Diviner is ready to meet with you," the retainer ordered. "When your business is completed, you are to return to the parking garage, and I will return you to your domicile."

The retainer turned about stiffly, then began walking down the very steps he had climbed. For a moment, Dewin pondered saying something in parting, but by the time he decided to actually do so, the retainer had disappeared from vision.

Taking once last appraising glance at the acid-carved doorway, Dewin opened it slowly, having to apply increasingly more force against the rusted hinges, then stepped inside.

Unlike the rest of the temple, the foyer for the Diviner's chambers was neat, clean, and vibrant. Rich purple translucent tapestries, lined with gold gilding, covered every wall. The floor was covered in three different shades of gray stone tile, each bearing silver etchings of the symbol of the Diviner. In each corner of the foyer were rather crude bronze sculptures of Demodian figures, likely past Diviners of the temple. The ceiling carried a mural of Demod's history, from "recent" events like the arrival of the first Kiros missionaries, to older events like the rise of the "gifted" Diviners, to the mythical event that started all recorded history in motion, the Great Cataclysm of Demod.

Dewin hated such mythological stories. The Great Cataclysm was told to every Demodian child, even those raised in the Kiros tradition; a myth of a time where Demod almost became no more. It would be so easy to refute the myth for what it was, had not every other culture of the

Galactic Alliance shared a similar story from the same period. Perhaps something truly catastrophic occurred some time before common record, but not necessarily something grandly spiritual.

A giggle drew his attention, and he cast his eyes back down. From the hall on the other side of the foyer, partially covered in the violet tapestries, a young girl leaned into the room. She wore a silvery tiara across her forehead, framing the thin red curls of her hair, and dressed in what appeared to be a pearl white gown that extended all the way to her toes. She couldn't have been any older than twelve staryears by Dewin's reckoning.

"What are you doing?" the girl said, her voice at that annoying pitch just between soprano and alto.

It almost made Dewin's toes curl to hear it, but he managed to reply, "Just looking at the decorations."

The girl emerged fully into the room, tilting her head at nearly a perfect right angle up at the ceiling. Dewin was momentarily concerned she was either going to snap her neck or fall over, until the young girl said cheerfully, "I like the paintings too. They're pretty." After a moment, she asked, "Do you know what they mean?"

"Yeah, I guess," Dewin answered. "They're just stories though. Probably mostly pure fiction."

"I see," the girl remarked thoughtfully. "But who is to say that fiction isn't just the interpretation of what people perceive to be reality?"

Dewin blinked. That struck him as a terribly odd thing for a child to say. "Where did you hear that?"

"From many people. I've also read it in books."

At that moment, an exquisite specimen of womanhood, dressed similarly to the child, emerged into the foyer and exhaled in relief. Dewin was so overwhelmed with her radiance that he barely managed to reach the conclusion that this must be the Diviner that he had heard of.

"Taesha, you worried me when you suddenly bolted out of the chamber," the woman said, then seemed to notice Dewin for the first time. "Oh, I am sorry! I apologize for the unconventional meeting."

Dewin bowed respectfully, dropping to one knee before her, and kissed one of the woman's long, majestic hands. "No apologies are necessary. It is a pleasure to meet you at last, Madam Diviner. I am here per your request."

The woman blinked three times, before throwing her head back, emitting peals of marvelous laughter. The sound caused Dewin to smile despite himself, and he was certain that this woman was more than a mere Diviner, but some form of magical enchantress. "Oh, dear sir… I do believe you are mistaken," she finally managed to sputter. "I am not the Diviner of Villium. I must inform you that you have already met her."

Dewin's smile disappeared, and his eyebrows furrowed in concentration. "I've already met her? But I've only met one other girl…" His voice died away in dawning comprehension mixed with just a little bit of terror.

He released the woman's hand, and turned his upper body so that he could turn his head towards the little girl he had been speaking to. With a grin that could only be described as impish, the girl was holding out her hand, palm down, and chirped, "It is good to see you, Mr. Rio. Do I get a kiss too?"

For several ticks an uncomfortable silence hovered within the foyer as two women waited for their visitor to absorb the information just given.

Dewin was fairly certain he wasn't having a nightmare. Just in case, he closed his eyes tightly, and slapped himself. After confirming that fact that he was indeed awake, he felt it safe to ask, "You're the Diviner?"

The girl giggled, and answered, "I am the one with the gift. I had figured my retainer had warned you."

"Not entirely…" Dewin muttered.

The girl laughed good-spiritedly, and shook her head. "That dear man does have a tendency to… leave out some things." She then gave a somewhat awkward bow, and said, "For the sake of proper introductions, I am Taesha, the Diviner of Villium temple."

Then, with a great deal less certainty, the little girl turned to the older woman next to her, and whispered, "Was that good mother— I mean, Allouette?"

The older Demodian simply nodded her approval. Dewin vaguely remembered an archaic law of the Diviners: since they had lived so many lives, and were marked as religious leaders from the beginning of time, they had no true parents. This young girl was most likely still getting used to calling the woman who had borne her by her given name.

Encouraged by the affirmation, Taesha grew increasingly confident. "I am glad that we are finally able to meet, Mr. Dewin Rio. I have been anticipating this meeting for some time."

"Why do you say that?" Dewin asked. Despite the increasingly sinking feeling in the pit of his stomach, his curiosity refused to be anchored.

"Ever since the gift came to me, the energies I have read have drawn me to others with the gift. To you, namely."

Dewin rolled his eyes. "I think your energies have led you astray, little girl."

Taesha smiled knowingly. "Come with me, please." She led the way into the chamber hall with a motioning finger.

Of course, Dewin wanted to go exactly the other way, back down the stairs and into the parking garage. However, something told him that he had yet to fulfill the agreement he made with the Diviner. With a nervous sigh, Dewin stepped into the hall as well, nearly running into the little girl waiting just past the shrouded exit.

Regarding Dewin thoughtfully, Taesha took slow, deliberate steps down the hall. "Have you ever wondered about your sense of timing?"

"Excuse me?" Dewin asked.

"You've always had the ability to arrive just when you want to, to step into a scene at just the right time. People think you plan your entrances, when in reality, they just happen."

Dewin's right eye flinched. "Good sense, observation, and a little luck. That's all it is."

"Tell me about Canasa," the girl almost ordered with a devious smile.

The pirate leader gaped. That event was never broadcast, and most people in the Galactic Core didn't even know the planet existed. "How did you...?"

The young girl's grin broadened knowingly. "I read the energies that radiate off you. They are inexorably bound to that place, for reasons I cannot completely glean. Something very profound occurred there, something that won't let you go."

"I met someone there... someone that makes me question my immediate future whenever I'm in the same room with him."

"And why is that? What makes him different?"

Dewin shrugged. "Possibly the fact that he killed almost my entire crew single-handedly. Or maybe the fact that I had at least ten clear shots at him that either bounced, warped, or fizzled harmlessly. Or maybe when he tossed me like a mortal spear into a stash of packing crates."

"Or maybe the fact that you sensed he was going to be trouble before the skirmish even began," Taesha grinned knowingly.

That struck a little too close to home for Dewin's tastes. "Now you're just guessing."

The girl shook her head energetically, then stopped halfway down the hall, in front of another tapestry-covered doorway. "Of course I'm not guessing. Getting you to remember Canasa allowed me to follow the path of energies you took to remember it. That is my gift, the ability to see the memories of those whose energies I sense and follow. I suspect, however, that yours is slightly different. Come inside."

Reluctantly, Dewin did as he was asked. The room they entered was dark, illuminated only by the shrouded light coming from the hall. "Do sit down in the center of the room."

"I'd rather not," the pirate declined.

"Perhaps you are not as far removed from your old Kiros upbringing as you have convinced yourself to believe."

"And what would lead you to that conclusion?"

Taesha shook her head playfully. "You forget that I can read the energies that surround you and how they interact."

She plopped down, cross-legged in the center of the darkened room. "I know what the Kiros say about us. That we're deluded, lost souls at best, and malicious, cunning liars at worst. Our practices are antiquated, obsolete, and dare I say, blasphemous."

Dewin smirked. "Don't worry, I value the words of the Kiros precious little more."

Taesha acknowledged this. "That might be true. I merely saw the negative energies that radiated from you when you saw me sit down. I'm not completely accurate… unfortunately."

It was rather dark, so he couldn't be completely certain, but the occasional sobs and jerks of the little girl's chest implied to Dewin that the child was trying not to cry. As much as he was wary of children, as much as some children absolutely abhorred him, the little girl in the room with him had shown signs she certainly wasn't normal… and Dewin knew how it felt to be different…

* * * * *

Arria Rio smoothed her son's forehead, and her voice was soothing and understanding. At the time, Dewin hadn't thought much about how hard it had been for both his parents; all he had known was that he was one of merely a handful of Demodians surrounded by legions of Kiros.

"Sometimes young boys can be mean, Dewin." The normally elegant woman looked tired and stressed, yet her voice reflected none of that.

"It wasn't a boy," Dewin corrected between sniffles. "It was Miranda. She called me a four-fingered freak."

"Oh," Arria said with a sheepish bob of her head. "Well, young girls can be mean too, and say things that are very hurtful. Often, they say such things because they are afraid of anything different. As long as you don't fear what you don't fully understand, and don't let those differences make your decisions for you, you'll never ever have to worry about being like them."

"How does that help me?" Dewin asked. "I want to be like them!"

His mother sighed slowly, then said, "I wish there was something I could say that would make the mean and nasty words go away… but I can't. I know it's tough, being picked on by little kids that don't know any better. The only thing I can tell you, and this may seem strange, is to remember how these things made you feel. Someday, you might have to face someone different from you, and hopefully, you'll remember the lesson someone else was supposed to learn."

* * * * *

"If my mother wasn't already dead, I'd curse her for this conscience she gave me," Dewin muttered. The memory of his mother – and of what the Kiros had done to both her and his father, after the events

27

that led to his departure from their service – reminded him that the score still wasn't exactly even yet. Perhaps… just perhaps… turning to the "blasphemy" of the old Demodian religion would be just another stab at his old superiors.

He could force himself to believe that.

Finally, he dropped to his knees, and placed his left hand on the girl's shoulders. From the way they were trembling underneath his fingers, and from his closer position, he could tell that the child was indeed trying not to cry. Dewin licked his lips nervously, then said with a great deal of uncertainty, "Now… come on… don't be like that. I'll do it. Just tell me what you need me to do, all right?"

Something told him he just got played… probably when the tears instantly stopped, and she clapped rapidly in considerable cheer. "Good!" she squealed happily. "Just sit down, right there, just like I am, facing me."

His face contorted disapprovingly, Dewin nonetheless lowered himself to the floor, crossing his legs, his body protesting as he brought his feet under his knees. He had to adjust himself several times to find a comfortable position. "All right… now what?"

She didn't respond, at least to Dewin, right away. "Mo—Allouette, can you close the door now?" Taesha asked. From his position facing away from the doorway, Dewin couldn't see what the older Demodian woman was doing – only that the room was suddenly bathed in almost absolute darkness.

"This helped me concentrate as I was just coming into my gift," Taesha explained. "When you first begin exploring your abilities, it helps to be able to block out all outside influences. You need to be able to focus on yourself and only yourself. Only by knowing yourself, and the energies within you, can you explore the energies without."

The girl moved so silently that Dewin hadn't even realized she had moved until her voice tickled his ear. "Sight, hearing, touch, smell, taste… they are all powerful senses, so powerful that they can overwhelm and shroud the senses that define and shape our energies. You need to ignore them, even abandon them, in order to pull inward, to see the self beyond what you experience in your flesh. Focus on my voice for now… but be prepared to even turn me aside. First, you must find your center, the core of your being, the point in which everything you are originates. The easiest way to do that is simply to empty your mind, and let your mind take you where you need to go. If you actively seek your center, you will never find it. It is something that can only be found without searching, almost by accident."

The girl's breath on Dewin's ear started to feel lighter, but he wasn't terribly certain if that was because she was speaking softer, or if he was truly losing touch with his senses. "Each breath should become deeper, longer… let your unconscious take care of your body, you won't be needing it. Let yourself slip into a trance, black upon black."

"I feel like I'm about to fall asleep," Dewin finally mumbled. He suddenly became aware of a lush, smoky smell in the room, but it was so strong he wondered why he hadn't smelled it before.

"Yes, this is where you need to be," Taesha replied approvingly, her voice barely audible, even though she had to be Tackems from the pirate's ear. "Not awake, yet not asleep. This is where your center is found. Let it find you…" From there, if the girl said anymore, Dewin didn't hear it, and he wasn't sure if he would have wanted to.

He had heard others speak of experiences where they felt outside of their body, looking down on themselves as if from above. While he somehow felt like that was the case, it wasn't exactly the sensation he would describe. To him, it seemed as if he were looking at himself from the inside.

He heard the Diviner's voice again, but in his current state, he wasn't sure if she was really talking, or he was only thinking she was talking. "Can you feel the energies around you? They tie you to everything you've experienced, everyone you've met. You can connect with anyone or anything you know by following those energies that have twined and bound you."

Dewin opened his eyes, or he thought he opened his eyes… because what he saw was not what his eyes would normally behold. The room was still dark, but he could see small strands of light, bearing a deep forest green hue, spinning about him. To his right, several strands were looping around and through another set of light blue strands, which congealed into a small ball, an aura with a discernibly humanoid shape silhouetted inside. He tried to blink, but it didn't appear he could, suggesting that he was seeing something beyond normal sight.

"Good. You have come into your gift quickly. You are indeed a rare talent. This is the sight in which you can see the core of things. It is a shifting point, a limbo between the physical and the metaphysical," the light blue ball declared. He had assumed that it had been Taesha, but the voice that spoke to him was far deeper, fuller, and more mature than could have been possible from the little girl. "This is the outer realm of our spirits that are born into new bodies in the constant cycle of reincarnation, until we have finally found the path of our predecessors to the perfect state of Tallah. But you can still press deeper... abandon this sight, become one with the very energies that you see... let them lead you where they do."

It was just then that he saw one deep forest green strand approach from had what appeared like an extraordinarily great distance. He focused on that strand as it circled through his aura, and as if revitalized, it started rushing back outward. Not wanting to lose sight of it, he followed...

Dewin got the sense of incredible distance, beyond anything he had ever traveled. Considering he had seen one end of the galaxy to the other, that was saying a lot. Suddenly, in that extensive distance, it looped with a brilliant white strand, and out of curiosity, Dewin latched onto that other thread of energy, following it back to its source.

He wasn't sure what he was expecting, but the hideously misshapen and crackling ball of white energy wasn't it. The ball twisted and distended in several directions before shuddering and rippling randomly. He instinctively knew just where he had been led and with whom he was in contact – and that something was terribly out of place.

In the periphery, he sensed several other energies working with the wayward and warped strands, working to fix the extensive damage. Following their movements, he fixed the strand he was linked with into the brilliant ball of energy.

Immediately, he sensed mild displeasure from the other presences working. He gained a sense that he was more in the way than helping, and that the other energies had things well in hand. In what he hoped was an apologetic acknowledgement, Dewin withdrew from the aura, and snapped back to his own physical form.

Apparently, his eyes had been closed the entire time, because they snapped open, his face beaded with sweat, his body trembling. He felt like he had run a full thirty TackMets, yet he had not moved even the slightest from his spot in the center of the deeply dark room.

Once again, he felt Taesha's breath on his ear. "You are merely beginning to explore the gift you were born with. Return with my retainer tomorrow, and we shall venture further into your remarkable talent."

*****

Over the next three cycles, Dewin didn't come to understand just what he doing any better… but whatever it was, he was beginning to do it with more comfort and considerably less apprehension.

On one level, he was still extremely skeptical. Even when he would return to his safehouse, his mind would race about what he would see, and how it defied all general knowledge and common sense. Yet, on another, it all seemed to make perfect sense. Despite all the things he had encountered in his life, despite the advancement of intelligent life throughout the galaxy, in the grand scale of things, there was so much unknown, even to the most brilliant of minds. Who was to say that this path of enlightenment that Taesha was leading him on wasn't one way to explore knowledge beyond the limits he had accepted? It certainly was worth the attempt.

Besides, it got him out of the living arrangement straight out of his nightmares.

Regardless of the direction he took when he began his meditation, it always seemed like he ended in the same place. He had come to the conclusion that the broken ball of white energy was the very man who had indirectly sent him to Demod. Justin had apparently used the coordinates Dewin had given him, and Timothy had been injured rather badly in the process, judging from the sensations in Dewin's meditations.

When he told Taesha about that, she nodded, "Your energies are drawing you to this Timothy for a reason."

"What reason would that be?" Dewin asked.

The young Diviner shrugged. "That, I couldn't begin to say. At one time, long before history was of record, the people of the gift could see the grand plan of all things as if it was laid out before them. The reasons for everything that fueled everything could be found in something as simple as the smallest insect. All things were bound so tightly that a connection with anything could lead to the forces that governed all, and enlightenment was but a simple journey."

Her eyes reflected a regret that could not have been born of her short life. "Then, when the Great Cataclysm ravaged our land, something changed. The universe ripped, and never completely healed. What was once an easy path became a tedious, tiresome journey... so much so that it now takes several lifetimes to complete. And as time passes, it only gets harder, and the ability to read the energies of beings becomes weaker. Even now, it is impossible to follow the paths of multiple beings, and even for me, a prodigy among my kind, I can barely follow the energies of one person. In my last life, I was terribly afraid that I'd never be able to find the path to Tallah."

Then she seemed cautiously hopeful. "Then I felt your gift... so strong, beyond anything I had ever felt. I'll admit my reasons for bringing you here were selfish. I think you can take the step I cannot. You can blaze the way, and maybe... I can follow."

The problem as Dewin interpreted it seemed unfounded. Granted, he had little experience to base his opinion on, but it didn't seem like much of a stretch to do exactly what she felt was impossible. However, he wanted to make sure that he was following her request properly. "You think that Solarian... boy... holds the key to your enlightenment?"

The girl shrugged. "Not necessarily... but something keeps drawing you to his energy. At best, he holds a key you seek for your own path, a path that I can then follow. Perhaps through his energy, you will find another energy that will lead you one step closer to our goal. And even if not, it would make for good practice."

Less than ten ticks later, they had taken up their increasingly familiar positions in Taesha's meditation chamber. When her mother went to shroud the doorway, Taesha waved her off. "Actually, I think it's time that our friend Mr. Rio started to learn how to meditate with small distractions."

The scant light slipping into the chamber would barely be qualified by Dewin's standards as a small distraction. Personal weapons fire fell into that category. Jonathan Feroz fell into that category. A little bit of light did not. It took next to no effort for Dewin to drop into the now familiar trance, and begin yet another foray across the great expanse towards Timothy's aura.

Timothy's energy had been steadily healing, and now as Dewin sensed his approach, the Solarian appeared to be whole again. Dewin still gathered a sense of deep slumber, but this was a more traditional sleep rather than the coma of cycles before. Due to the Knight's improved condition, it allowed Dewin to sense the myriad linking strands around Timothy's energies.

Thus came the moment of truth. It was one thing to carry his own energy to another… he supposed it could be a different task altogether to ride someone else's energy to yet another, potentially unknown, destination.

Dewin decided to try something simple, seeing how a great number of his strands were linking to soft, golden threads of energy radiating from nearby. The link led to a gentle golden aura, carrying the silhouette that he instinctively identified as Rumil's. From Rumil's aura, he hopped across another link, this one to a powerful, almost angry, crimson red ball of energies, bearing relief and frustration in almost equal proportion. It took nary a demitick to decide this aura was that of Justin Feroz, and that he didn't want to linger long in case the Kiros Knight would be able to sense Dewin's presence.

Not wanting to go back along the brilliant white that linked Justin to Timothy, he decided to follow Justin's energies to another link, this time to a smooth tangerine aura that was completely foreign to him. Feeling emboldened by his increasing success, he prepared to make yet another jump along this unidentified person when he noticed some strands of this being suddenly tearing away from the central aura as if grabbed by an unseen hand. It didn't appear to link with anything else, instead just fizzling into nothing.

Confused by this, and somewhat disturbed by this peculiar behavior, Dewin decided to take a step back towards those he was more familiar with and see if something similar was occurring to them. Sure enough, once he knew what he was looking for, Justin, Timothy, and Rumil were also being subjected to the unseen force that seemed to be slowly siphoning off the periphery of each of their respective cores.

Curiosity set in, and Dewin decided to investigate. Pulling back to his link with Timothy, determining the Solarian's energies to be the strongest, Dewin waited for the invisible force to snatch a few strands of Timothy's aura then jumped onto the wayward strands and let himself drift along with them.

Dewin was instantly flushed with foreboding, surrounded by a mindless malevolence that would have made him shiver had he been in tune with his physical form. It had no shape, no aura, just an all-encompassing dread that seemed to get stronger the longer Dewin hung to his current perch. The pirate tried to pull back from whatever he was approaching, but whatever it was held him fast, pulling his essence inexorably towards it. His sense started to spin, as if he was beginning to whirl down the drain of a washbasin, his energies overwhelmed and washed in increasing despair. He felt himself weakening, slowly losing the will to fight the shapeless void he was now falling into. Since his adulthood, he had never thought of things as being black and white, but this deepening horror was rapidly changing that perception. Whatever this feeling was, it was evil… pure, unadulterated evil… and something told Dewin that it hadn't even come close to its full strength.

His path was suddenly jarred with a searing pain that shot through his center. With a scream, Dewin realized he had been ripped back into his physical self, his thighs clenched together, crunched against his damaged groin. It felt like a sharp shoe had struck him directly in that tender area, and the pain had broken his trance. Once again, his body was trembling, but not from any side effect of his meditations, but from an almost paralyzing, mind-numbing fear.

He fell on his back in a mixture of terror and discomfort, and with a flash, Taesha was kneeling over him, brushing hair and sweat off his forehead. "I apologize deeply, but I couldn't think of anything else to do. You weren't responding to any of my prompts."

"I couldn't even if I wanted to," Dewin explained. "I need to leave."

Taesha nodded acceptingly. "So we shall do this again next cycle?"

Dewin sighed, and shook his head. "You don't understand. I have to leave, as in this entire planet. I'll return when my business is finished."

"Why?"

"What I saw just now… I need to help stop it. That may sound terribly out of character, but I figure if this… thing… remains unchecked, I won't have much to pirate when it's done. Besides, I still owe a few people a few favors."

Apparently, the young Diviner did a short reading, since she offered no further protest to Dewin's claim. "You must do what you must," she conceded, her voice nonetheless reflecting her disappointment.

Fortunately, the lift was working, so Dewin didn't have to trudge down the insanely tall staircase to reach the bottom levels. As the lift slowly descended, Dewin opened his comm unit, and patched through to his somewhat irksome companion.

"Orion… No, it isn't, just someone really good at imitating my voice," Dewin grumbled with a roll of his eyes. "Listen, it's important, I need you to bring in the crew and get the *Gallan* ready for departure. I want to be able to take off the demitick I return to the safehouse… The Feroz family can stay, but we need to go, as quickly as at all possible… I didn't ask you to think, Orion, I asked you to do. Now get to it." Just before he slapped the comm unit closed, Dewin added, "Make sure the fold drive is in top shape and at full operation. We have a very long trip ahead of us." With that, Dewin terminated the connection and waited for the jerking lift to stop at the parking garage.

It did half a tick later… somewhat. It jammed about five Tackems or so before completely touching the garage floor, leaving Dewin to force the doors open and skip down the remaining distance.

He was then impeded by the progress of a young Erani man, likely Solarian from his complexion, with neatly-groomed and coiffed sandy brown hair. Dewin pointed back towards the lift, and commented, "You'll probably want to use the stairs."

"Actually, I am here to see you, Mr. Rio."

Dewin's eyes narrowed. "I am growing increasingly disturbed by the number of people who know me on sight."

The Solarian laughed. "Think nothing of it; I am merely well informed. I actually come to ask a question for a concerned friend."

Dewin snorted derisively, then spat, "Then ask it and move. I am in a hurry."

The man bowed in apology, and replied, "I come from the High Priest of the Solarian Faith, Horace Hightower. I was informed by some of the High Priest's contacts that you could be found here, and that apparently you were the last to have seen a former Knight of Solaria by the name of Timothy Honore. The High Priest is merely concerned that his old friend has disappeared from even his extensive network."

At that point, Dewin felt a deep repulsion for this man from what Dewin now knew as his center. It was not a unique experience for him; a feeling that bubbled up whenever he met someone of significant deviancy, and had always been a warning that any meaningful interaction was not advised. Dewin had always prided himself on being a good judge of character even before his newfound self-exploration, and felt even less inclination to distrust that instinct now.

"I'm sorry, we parted ways in a rather hasty retreat from Kiros, as I suspect you already know," Dewin replied. "I do not know where he went from there."

The man sighed, as if not surprised by the answer. "That's unfortunate, but hardly unexpected. If you have any ideas, feel free to contact the High Priest directly." The man handed Dewin a small card with several private communication protocols typeset on it, then graciously moved aside so that Dewin could proceed.

The pirate leader moved on, but not without one more quick parting glance at the Solarian who had offended Dewin's extra sense with his presence. Something told him that he would have to take measures to ensure his vessel and crew were not followed.

Meanwhile, Horace Hightower did not even spare the slightest glance back towards Dewin. He figured the pirate leader would find a means to evade any pursuit, but that was of little consequence. "Well, if you do not know, I am certain there are some that do," the priest muttered, looking up at the ceiling of the garage as if his eyes could see through the multiple levels of the temple. "But unlike you, I am in no haste. As it stands, things are progressing exactly as they should."

Chapter Three

Timothy grunted in frustration. He was clearly not used to being bedridden.

"You've probably never been so badly hurt before, either mentally or physically," Rumil reminded him, pushing him back down onto the mattress after the tenth declaration of his suitable health. "While our medical overseers are saying you are improving remarkably fast, you are still by no means fit to be roaming about. The last thing they want is a relapse."

"I said I'm fine," the Solarian Knight protested as he felt his head touch the padded headrest and pillowing.

"If you were 'fine,' then I suspect I would not be able to push you around like I have been," the former hacker noted. "You will have plenty of time to catch up on all your exercises and training regimen once it is deemed you can handle them."

"Then perhaps he has time to speak with me?" Justin asked from the ward entrance.

Rumil turned a sour glance in his direction, obviously not pleased with the Kiros's intrusion. "Our dear healers haven't even deemed him fit to walk around freely, much less whatever you have planned for him."

"I am quite certain a little discussion is not going to strain me greatly," Timothy said with a light hint of exasperation.

Rumil pursed her lips tightly, wishing Ghadri or Micha were present to back her up. As it was, the blonde relented and said, "Fine, get in here and say what you have to say. I'll be watching you like a bird of prey so that you don't stress him unnecessarily… as your presence is prone to do, Feroz."

Timothy caught sight of the book under Justin's arm and gleaned the meaning of the Kiros Knight's visit. "Actually, Rumil, could you give us some time in private? I suspect that Justin wishes to discuss topics that would bore you senseless."

Justin narrowed his eyes suspiciously, and countered, "Why would you say that? I think that she would rather like—"

Timothy interrupted him with an angry glare. "It would probably be best if we discussed this alone."

By that point, Rumil was catching on that something was amiss, and scowled. "Oh no, you don't. You are not keeping me out of the loop anymore."

It appeared Timothy was not going to be cooperative. He looked petulant, and was unwilling to further the discussion… at least while Rumil was present.

Finally Justin rolled his eyes, and asked, "Why don't you just step outside, and I'll fill you in later?"

With an exasperated half-scream, Rumil jumped to her feet. "Fine… be that way, 'Timmy.'" As the hacker stomped outside the ward, she muttered, "Sometimes I wonder why I bother with that chauvinistic, incorrigible, Solarian male…"

She sulked just outside the open doorway as Justin began to speak in a whisper, but as the discussion inside progressed, she noted that their voices were gradually increasing in volume, as if they were forgetting the conversation was supposed to be secret. Starting with incoherent voices, the volume finally increased enough for Rumil to comprehend what was being said.

"Why haven't you told her yet?" Justin almost accused.

Timothy's voice still sounded weak, causing Rumil to grow slightly concerned despite her anger towards him. "I'm still not certain that she's who Bryan Honore is referring to."

"Oh, stop it! I've only read the thing once, and it's already clear as water to me. The man who wrote this book might as well have been looking directly at Rumil when he wrote it," Justin contended. "Everything about her is in there!"

That statement piqued Rumil's attention, almost to the point that she stepped right back into the ward to once again demand an explanation. However, doing so would probably prompt Timothy to go silent again, so she decided to wait to see what else he would say.

"She doesn't believe in that book you're holding. She can barely stand to be associated with anything related to either Erani sect. How do you think she'd react to hear us make that sort of claim? Besides, as I said, the book itself proves nothing, just that it's someone bearing Rumil's description," was Timothy's reply.

"But you believe she is…" Justin led, as if trying to make Timothy admit it at least to himself.

"I'd like to think so," Timothy somewhat sheepishly replied. "But I don't want to push that sort of burden on her until she is ready to accept it."

Finally deciding that the conversation didn't appear to be answering any of the questions forming in her head, Rumil prepared to make her entrance once more when Ghadri approached from behind her.

The Netrian Elder Councilor has arrived. I suspect he wishes to speak with the three of you, the elder woman stated with a hushed mental tone. *It is not proper to keep a Councilor waiting, so I suggest you get your companions ready for his visit immediately.*

Rumil had learned that the planet she had crashed on was divided into seventeen provinces, each led at the highest level by a lifetime appointed official referred to as a Councilor. The longest-tenured Councilor was titled the Elder Councilor, and was the closest to a head of state the planet had. As it stood, the Elder Councilor came from the province of Netrian, where Rumil and her friends currently resided.

Ghadri mistakenly judged the scowl on Rumil's face, because the fey-looking woman chastised, *The Elder Councilor is a respected and venerated leader of my people. I expect a more suitable reaction from you when you meet in person.*

Rumil didn't have the desire to explain that her ire had less to do with the Councilor's arrival so much as his timing. She didn't even have the opportunity, as Ghadri whirled about hurriedly and disappeared out of the ward hall, into the central wing of the medical building.

Rumil's next breath almost came out as a hiss. She strode into the ward purposefully, and declared, "I suppose the both of you heard that, right? Their leader is in the building, and apparently wants to speak with us."

Micha then strode in, the waif-like young woman almost skipping into the ward with glee. *The Netrian Elder Councilor is here! I can hardly believe it!* her mental voice chirped like a songbird. *I am so anxious… I've never met him before! Oh, right, I almost forgot why I am here!* Trying to sound more professional, but only marginally succeeding, Micha added, *I am here to see if you are suitable in mind and body to meet with our Elder Councilor, Timothy. Do cooperate this time.*

I may be sore from my ordeals, but that is partially because I have not been allowed to work it away, Timothy announced with an accusing glare towards Rumil as he gingerly sat up and slowly pulled himself off the bed. *As for my mind, I am glad to say that I am as sound as I was before the crash.*

He backed up that statement with a short display of his psionic abilities, in the form of a sudden, violent, and prolonged burst of air that nearly lifted Micha and Rumil off their feet. Rumil clutched mightily at the bedpost next to Timothy to keep from falling over, and Micha had to hastily construct a psionic shield to stay upright. Only Justin remained unmoved due to the mental shielding he had already prepared. His earlier conversation with the Solarian led him to the suspicion that Timothy would do something to that effect if his caretakers continued to restrict him.

The ease in which Timothy gathered such force proved conclusively to Justin that Timothy was indeed on par with where he was before the fateful crash. However, the speed of the Solarian's recovery to that point, as well as the speed in which he focused that energy, prompted Justin to reach a frightening conclusion: Timothy had not yet reached or demonstrated his full ability.

Any further pondering on the idea was abandoned when the sound of small brass instruments heralded the entrance of another person into the ward hall. The surprisingly meager psionic presence that followed the horns nonetheless carried a sturdiness that only came with a great number of years. Justin quickly came to the conclusion that this was the Netrian Elder Councilor that Micha and Ghadri had been going on about, for what he estimated to be several cycles.

Roughly a tick later, the procession of heralds began to march past the ward, lining along both sides of the hall. Micha suddenly burst into frantic activity to straighten anything that might have been knocked out of place in Timothy's psionic outburst. She whirled about hysterically, still trying to gauge if the ward was suitable for the official's entry.

If she had found anything, there was no time to correct the problem, as the Netrian Elder Councilor swept into the ward with a flurry of his long, billowing green capes. As Justin had suspected, the man was rather old in appearance, yet moved with a vitality that didn't quite mesh with his likely age. His flat-lipped smile was barely visible from the thick jowls on his cheeks, and his nose looked crooked, as if it had suffered a nasty bump recently.

To Justin's surprise, outside of the three layers of capes tied to his neck and back, the man held no other indicators of his status. His shining onyx hair, highlighted with streaks of gray, bore no crown or other adornment. Nor did he wear any special jewelry around his neck, face, or fingers. Even his orange robe, tied tightly around his body, matching trousers, and brown slipper shoes didn't appear to be of any special manufacture.

The Councilor's appearance also wouldn't be the last surprise he had for the impromptu visitors. The old official touched his nose gingerly with the tip of one finger, and said in somewhat broken Basic language, "I am sorry for… a delay. I had a… small accident on the way here. We had to stop… little bleeding before I could… go further."

"You know Basic?" Rumil gasped, especially since there had been no indication that the native people of this planet knew much of anything about the large galaxy that dominated much of their night sky.

"Our first… friend taught me… I learned on after he went away… as good as I could," the Councilor replied, clearly becoming increasingly uncertain of his mastery of the language compared to the three that could speak it quite fluently.

All three of us are capable of hearing and speaking telepathic communication as well, Timothy's mental voice echoed through all the listener's heads. *At the moment, it appears the easiest and most efficient way of conversing.*

As if grateful for the reprieve from further embarrassment, the Elder Councilor's face and telepathic voice reflected that relief. *Thank you for your understanding. When I had learned that more visitors had come from the galactic sphere, I had quickly crammed as much of your Basic language I could in an attempt to impress you or communicate if telepathy proved ineffective. From what I have been told, not all beings in the galactic sphere can utilize the ability.*

And you were told correctly, Justin added with a slight bow of respect. *But either by genes or inexplicable fluke of nature, the three of us can indeed accommodate you in that regard.*

If anything, they are accommodating us, Rumil remarked, partially to correct Justin's comment, as well as to demonstrate her abilities to communicate. *Remember, we are the aliens here.*

Not… entirely, the Councilor answered cryptically, turning to Justin with a somewhat familiar eye. *So, you have come back to us.*

So it would appear, Justin said warily. *From what I have been told, I had come from some place unknown bearing these stellar*

41

coordinates. I was naturally far too young to remember any of it.

The Elder Councilor finally smiled warmly, as if taking sympathy on the somewhat distraught Kiros. *Well, if it is any consolation, I remember you quite well, as well as the two who brought you into this mortal coil.*

Suddenly, the old man frowned, seemingly recalling a not too fond memory. Dabbing at the bottom of his eyes to catch any potential tears, he continued. *I wasn't terribly sure what I would do or say if I ever met the child who was born of their union. In some ways I still harbor resentment that in the end, she chose her mate over me.* Then with a sigh, he added, *Listen to me, I sound like some melodramatic old man who doesn't remember what it's like to be young.*

The Councilor took a deep breath, clearing his head and collecting his rampant thoughts. *I can't say with any real certainty, since my people don't have any words to describe great amounts of time, and I'm not terribly sure of the math involved in your galactic calendar, but I would figure it to be around twenty of your staryears ago.*

Well, considering I'm twenty-two staryears, it would have to be longer than that, Justin interrupted.

Justin! Rumil reprimanded. *Can you at least let him finish his story before you start nitpicking?*

Justin flushed, and hastily apologized.

It is quite all right, the Elder Councilor said. *He crashed in much the same way you did, and we nursed him back to health.*

So he was part of the Locator Project, I would assume? Timothy queried.

Forgetting that she was supposed to mentally project her words, Rumil asked, "The Locator Project?"

"About thirty staryears ago, both the Solarians and Kiros began searching the Galactic Rim and beyond for Mydor, the home planet of the ancient Se-Lan race. As I am to understand, the Kiros titled the mission 'The Locator Project.' After the Baramak Slaughter, both sects terminated the effort, forced to address internal issues," Timothy explained softly to Rumil as the Elder Councilor continued his account.

The man did not mention why he came, or any mission he had, at first. It took many – years? – after he crashed before he openly discussed much of anything with anyone.

The Locator Project, at the time at least, was a very secretive mission, Justin said mentally. *The officers sent on the search were required to keep it under the strictest confidence. I can see no other reason why a member of the Kiros sect would talk about it than if he had finally given up on returning home.*

"I'm more interested in the fact that both visits to this planet have resulted in crashes," Timothy whispered in an aside to Rumil, who nodded slightly in agreement.

He never spoke of this 'Locator Project' you speak of, the Elder Councilor corrected. *As far as I know, he never spoke of why he had come to anyone. However, he had accepted that we simply didn't have the means to help him. Of course, I suspect that the attachment he had developed towards my daughter helped him adjust to that...*

The old man then regarded Justin with a critical eye. *You don't nearly resemble my dear daughter as much as I may have hoped, but I can hardly fault you for that. I haven't seen her or heard from her since the three of you salvaged the crashed vessel, and returned to his home. We may not have any words for the passing of time... but we certainly feel it as it happens.* The Councilor's face turned into one of an almost desperate plea. *How is Casia? Has she been well?*

For the first time, Justin heard his birth mother's name. Enthralled by it, and desperate to know more about her, he didn't have the will to even attempt to fashion a lie. *I'm sorry, as I have been told neither she nor my father survived the flight back to Kiros. I was the only one to make it back to galactic space. I didn't even know her name until now.*

The old Councilor turned pale as a Solarian, as if one of the very reasons for his life had been crushed at that moment. Somewhat surprisingly, the man seemed to turn the blame on himself. *I knew I should have forbidden her to go. I was certainly no expert on the machination James had arrived in, but even I could tell that it was not nearly what it used to be.*

Was James... my father's name? Justin asked, although he figured as much judging from context.

You didn't even know that? the Councilor asked in amazement.

Justin's face dropped forlornly. *I didn't even know that the family that raised me wasn't even my birth family until just recently. I've had a lot to catch up on.*

It almost seemed like the old man had forgotten his own sorrow.

Instead, a gentle determination fell upon the Councilor's face. *I had assumed that your knowledge of my daughter surpassed mine… but clearly that is not the case. You probably have barely any idea who I am, either.* With a regretful smile, the Netrian Elder Councilor extended his right hand towards Justin. *Come with me… talk of my dear Casia should not be restricted to these walls. I suspect that more suitable introductions are in order as well.*

Taking the older man's lead, Justin fell into step behind, starting to leave the ward. Timothy appeared about to ask another question when Rumil pinched him on the arm to break his attention. "And what was that for?" the Solarian accused.

"Let them be. There are some things that Justin needs to sort out." she replied, clearly sympathetic to the Kiros Knight.

"That may be… but I'm more concerned about what could possibly be so important that a man who, by that account, had given up on returning to Kiros suddenly decided that he needed to get back at all costs."

Rumil asserted, "And that concern can still be asked in a few tenth-cycles. Right now, let Justin have this time."

Timothy didn't entirely agree. On one hand, he wanted to give Justin as much time as necessary to learn about the family the Kiros man never even knew he missed. On the other, Timothy had a very ominous feeling as to what would have prompted an agent of the Locator Project to attempt a very risky space flight in a crash-damaged vessel, and if he was right… then time could be one thing everyone had precious little of.

* * * * *

Justin hadn't been granted the right to move around much, thus the central reception area of the medical center was something that was rather foreign to him. It was a rather sophisticated design considering the simple materials used, with a raised ceiling in a octagonal wood frame and glass windows secured into it, allowing for the sun to provide much of the light the room needed. However, as Justin had personally witnessed, they still relied on candles to provide illumination during the night.

One extremely delicate-looking man staggered past, using both arms to carry a large, thick, hide-bound book about as big as his torso towards where three women behind a long desk were dutifully scribbling notes on reams of paper. Justin wasn't allowed any more time to take in the scene as the old man leading him gently tugged on his shoulder, requesting him to keep moving.

I do believe the arboretum would be a wonderful place to sit and talk, the Elder Councilor declared, more to inform Justin than to make a suggestion. Sliding the main doorways manually, the pair stepped outside under the noonday sun, then turned right onto a small cobblestone path that lead along the east side of the facility.

The arboretum was a delicate balance of brightly colored flowers of blue, violet, red, and yellow, tall hardwood trees with leaves in full green bloom, and grass remarkably blended with broad- and thin-leafed varieties. There was one small clearing in the refuge, lined with a circle of flowers, with another ring of short evergreen trees, and a final circle of the taller hardwoods. In the center was an antique-style wooden bench, painted white, with an ornate back that wrapped forward to form a very inadequate cover from rain or sun.

The Councilor took a slow gait to the bench, Justin following, with both taking a seat on the smooth wooden surface. The elder man regarded his surroundings appreciatively, as if forgetting Justin for a brief moment.

Well, I suppose I might as well start with a simple introduction, he finally said. *I am known as the Netrian Elder Councilor, but in your case, it is only fitting that you know me by the name that your mother knew me. You may call me Pius.*

You sound so certain that I am... your grandson... Justin began. He was still grappling with the fact that the man he had known as his father wasn't, let alone that he was now talking with a suspected grandfather he had never met.

We have had only one visitor from the galaxy... and you claim to have been found with coordinates from this very place. Simple deduction would conclude that you are the son of my daughter. Unless you are lying...

Justin shook his head in denial. *That is the story as I have been told it. The man who raised me confirmed that I am not his son, and that I was found in an escape pod from a fold from beyond the Galactic Rim. A pirate claimed to be my rescuer, and gave me the coordinates that pointed*

45

to your planet.

Would any of them have reason to lie?

Once again, Justin looked torn. *At one time, I would not even be able to fathom my 'father' telling even the slightest falsehood. But, as I look back, everything about our relationship was a lie... and I'm ashamed to say this, but I should have realized it sooner. There have been instances in the past where he demonstrated he was a magnificent liar. As for the pirate... well, that should be all you need to know.*

Pius pursed his lips thoughtfully, then ran his tongue over them. *The man who raised you... his name wouldn't be... Joseph, would it?*

Justin asked, *How did you know that?*

When I heard your name after your crash, it's why I assumed that Casia had actually survived. The man who likely was your true father was named James Feroz, and as I understand, he had a brother by the name of Joseph.

Justin's face lit up with dawning comprehension. *James Feroz... he had volunteered for the Locator Project about twenty-five staryears ago. He was declared lost in space before I was ever born. My dear old 'dad' would tell me wondrous stories about my 'uncle,' who would have been the true heir to the command of the Knighthood, but felt his duty to his faith could not have been ignored. Could he have even suspected that he was the uncle... telling stories about the father?*

It's possible, Pius remarked. *The fact that he took you into his care seems that he sensed something special about you. People at the top of Galactic societies were rarely the most benevolent, according to James. I suspect that's why he had little trouble settling down when he deemed it impossible to return to his homeland. Perhaps it was what prompted him to volunteer for what sounds to be a very dangerous mission in the first place. He always struck me as a man who had a certain level of disdain for those who felt themselves naturally higher than others.*

If he was so content here... then why did he try to pilot a damaged shuttle back to Kiros? Justin asked, genuinely curious. Then, realizing for the first time, he added with a hint of anger, *And... why did he bring his wife and son with him?*

Pius quickly answered. *In response to the latter question, James* **had** *told Casia to stay. Sadly, she didn't listen. Possibly not understanding the danger, she snuck aboard the vessel, carrying you with her. She had told me that she did not want you to suffer a severed family* *like she did. I thought nothing of the statement... and thus said nothing. It has now proven to be a tragic mistake.*

A severed family?

Pius looked down at his feet. *When Casia was a child, her mother was called to help cure a terrible plague that was ravaging the Covell Province far to the north. My wife had promised to return... and never did. We later learned that she had fallen to the plague itself. It stung Casia terribly. Surely when she heard James make a similar promise, she decided that she wasn't going to be stung like that again.*

Justin nodded in understanding. He had a hard time acknowledging that any Kiros would have willingly dragged a woman and a child into such a dangerous and deadly trip. Then, the question of why James Feroz felt the need to take that trip came up again.

As for your first question, that I am not certain about, Pius said, his face twisting into a few thoughtful expressions. *The change in James occurred when we made our first pilgrimage to the Old Capital.*

Remembering that Justin would have no idea as to the place he had just mentioned, the Councilor paused slightly, then explained further. *There is a small central continent along the equator of this planet that is considered planetary territory, in other words, no one province lays claim to it. On that small land mass are the ruins of our ancient people.*

We weren't always this... undeveloped. At one time, we held a knowledge that allowed us to do what you now do, travel the galaxy and have great feats of technology. However, a mysterious war that we have little knowledge of anymore ruined that once great society. We've never recovered from that.

Anyway, people of this planet occasionally take pilgrimages to that Old Capital when we can make the time. It serves to remind us of what we once were, and no matter how high you may rise you can always fall to folly. James accompanied Casia and myself on this pilgrimage, and then we beheld the Great Seal.

Warning signs flashed through Justin's mind. The Kiros Knight asked, *What is this Great Seal?*

Pius shrugged. *I am not terribly certain, to be honest. Some say it was a focusing point for the old society's power. Some say it was a warning. Still others say that it harbors a great evil. No one knows for sure. The knowledge is almost completely lost.*

Justin stood up swiftly, all his other potential questions forgotten. Now, he only had one, which Pius had just demonstrated he didn't know the answer to. Not that it terribly mattered, as Justin was afraid he already knew.

We need to see the Great Seal at once. Let's just say it's extremely urgent.

That would take some time to arrange, as there is usually a season for the pilgrimage... Pius began, then flattened his lips thoughtfully. *But it shall be as you request. Perhaps you would understand better what had startled him so...*

* * * * *

"I don't terribly need a spotter," Timothy stated simply, and then resumed his handstand pushups.

"Well, just two cycles ago, you could barely move. I just want to make sure you aren't overdoing it," Rumil said from her position, cross-legged and behind Timothy's back. She was almost mesmerized by the display; a perfect synergy of balance and strength. Of course, the fact that his royal blue bodysuit left precious little to the imagination certainly helped keep her attention.

With one powerful push of his arms, Timothy vaulted onto his feet. In the dim light of the ward, Rumil could barely make out the slightest of smiles on Timothy's face. "You certainly have been showing a lot of concern for me as of late," he remarked.

His voice carried a hint of suggestion that she had never heard from the Solarian before, and it somewhat disconcerted Rumil. Taken off guard, she managed to mutter, "Well, as I said, I don't have many friends... I have to be careful with the ones I do have, right?"

In three strides, Timothy closed the distance between them, lowering himself to his knees so as to look her directly in the eye. Once there, he said, "Really? What if I told you that I don't think you are being honest with me?"

Rumil's eyes bulged. She had never seen Timothy look this way. His normally stoic features now seemed vibrant, his mouth turned upward in a smile that sat on the border between merely suggestive to downright naughty. His eyes gleamed in a manner that she could only describe as...

passionate.

Suddenly nervous, she had to gulp down a breath of air to keep from choking on her own tongue. "Why... would you think I'm... not being honest?" she managed to say, fortunately without any significant stammers.

"I've been privy to some of your thoughts, and before you ask, I didn't need to probe your mind to sense them either. Like right now for example. I could feel your eyes on me, and knew what you were thinking."

His face was steadily drawing closer, and she instinctively leaned back at the shrinking personal space, until she realized that she might like where this was headed. "And... what would that be...?"

She could feel his breath on her lips when he said, "That what could be the harm in pushing aside proper and improper, right and wrong, decent and indecent, for just five ticks..."

"Okay..." Rumil whispered, her voice suddenly hoarse. "Not *exactly* what was on my mind... but I suppose it's close enough."

There was a small part of her that was wondering just where this was coming from, and that perhaps things were moving just slightly too fast. Perhaps Timothy was still not completely together, and was going to do something he would regret later... which would make her regret it as well. That was quickly followed by the equivalent of a mental slap across her own head. It didn't help logic's case that her body was practically humming as the Tackels between their lips slowly turned into Tackets, and she started counting down into the single digits...

Then the coughing of a certain Kiros Knight utterly broke the mood. Had it been a sheet of glass, Justin would have shattered it like a hydraulic hammer.

Rumil instinctively looked over Timothy's shoulder towards the entrance to the ward, her eyes bulging furiously, with her face flushed almost blood red in a combination of anticipation, embarrassment, and righteous anger.

Justin fought back all but one short chuckle, then said with false innocence, "Dear me, I'm not interrupting anything, am I?"

"Not anymore," Timothy answered, his voice flat, and his demeanor stoic once again.

Meanwhile, Rumil was still trying to slow her heart to a passably normal rate, insanely jealous of – and somewhat disturbed by – her Solarian companion, who seemed able to turn his emotions on and off with a switch.

"What can we do for you, Justin?" Timothy asked as he stood up and turned to face his Kiros counterpart.

Similar to Timothy's abrupt change in demeanor, Justin seemed to be able to flip from silly to serious in the blink of an eye. "Micha was bouncing around happily, giggling that she was finally granted the time to go on her first pilgrimage. Coupled with Ghadri's recent declaration of your full health, I suspect we will be on our way shortly."

Timothy didn't need to respond to that, both of them understanding just where this pilgrimage might lead. All Rumil knew was that it somehow tied together with the arrival and sudden departure of Justin's biological father over twenty-two staryears ago and a mysterious planet called Mydor. Nonetheless, she clearly sensed the increasing anxiety that seemed to taint both men whenever they discussed their impending trip to wherever they were headed. Whatever they were expecting, it didn't appear to be good.

"Let me guess… you think it would be best if I stayed here?" Rumil anticipated with a displeased tone.

Timothy replied, "Actually… I was thinking it would be for the best if you were with us when we made this trip."

Rumil, expecting some sort of quip from Justin, was somewhat surprised when no such jibe came. Things must be truly dire for that to happen, and that must be why Timothy wanted her to come along – he was still trying to be the protective Solarian that had promised to keep her safe. Deciding it was better than the secretive, somewhat withdrawn Timothy that had been present around her recently, Rumil decided not to make any further comment other than an accepting nod.

Micha then literally skipped in, possibly even using her own impressive psionic talents to aid her, since her lithe, graceful form lingered in the air slightly longer than it should have with each swift hop. Not even trying to contain her glee, the young woman chittered happily. *As I understand, you three are accompanying me on my pilgrimage, right? I am so excited I can barely think straight… I mean, I've never actually had the opportunity to go on one… I just can't wait for my tasks to be completed!*

Just how long will this trip take? Justin asked.

Micha regarded the question warily, as if uncertain as to how to answer. *It takes as long as it will take.*

"No set concept for the passing of time, remember?" Timothy whispered into Justin's ear.

"Yes… but that doesn't mean they don't comprehend it," Justin shot back, quickly formulating another way to ask the same question. *How many changes of clothes should we bring?*

Micha seemed to understand that question much more clearly. *Well, unless we stay a great long while, I don't see any reason why you shall have to bring more than one.*

Really? Is it that short of a trip from here? Rumil queried.

Actually, it is quite far… but we will be allowed to teleport ourselves the distances between each landmark.

Why don't we just teleport directly to the Great Seal? Timothy asked.

Micha regarded the Solarian like he had just asked her if she could breathe underwater. *That simply is not done. Each landmark carries great significance for the destination at the Old Capital. To truly understand the significance the Great Seal has, it's important for us to visit them.*

"Let's just do it their way," Justin said, anticipating that Timothy was going to attempt to take the location of the Great Seal directly from Micha's mind. "We don't need to be making any undue enemies by totally disrespecting their traditions."

The baleful look Timothy shot him suggested that Justin had assumed correctly. On one hand, he understood Timothy's desire to skip all the middle steps, but at the same time, Justin recognized it wouldn't do much good. Besides, he was very curious about learning more about the apparent land of his birth.

Rumil felt a question pop almost out of nowhere in her head. She had no idea where it came from, but felt a powerful urge to ask it nonetheless. *Is everyone attending the pilgrimage expected to teleport themselves along the path?*

Micha blinked, then replied. *There has never been a pilgrim who has been unable to teleport across the landmarks, as far as I am able to recall. It's always been assumed that everyone is capable. Those who cannot simply do not go until they are able. Why do you ask? Are you incapable of such a task?*

51

Timothy interrupted before Rumil could reply. *She has less confidence in her mental prowess than she should. She comes from a people who normally don't have her gift, you understand, and it understandably makes her unduly cautious.*

I see, Micha nodded. *Well, the distances between the landmarks are not far. You should be quite all right, Rumil dear. Anyway, I must finish my tasks. The sooner I am finished, the sooner we can go.*

Once again, the fey woman bounced out of the ward, humming a light song that quickly died on the air as she disappeared down the hall. At that point, Rumil shouted, "Are you out of your mind?"

Timothy countered, "Justin told me not to shun the customs of these people, so I figured that acknowledging the fact that you did not have the ability would run counter to what they practice."

"Except for the fact that Rumil can't teleport," Justin reminded them. Then remembering that she had apparently picked up several tricks while on Solaria, added, "She can't... right?"

"Perhaps she could, given time," Timothy remarked. "However, I highly doubt we have that sort of time in which to teach."

"So then, you're just going to have her ride your fold path?" Justin asked.

"Not unless you want to." Timothy replied.

Justin shook off the offer with his full body language, shaking his head and waving his hands in refusal. "I doubt I'd have the energy to shift two people several times to our destination, especially if it's half a planet away."

"What if we discover that's a problem?" Rumil asked.

"Don't worry, we'll think of something," Timothy answered confidently.

"The last time you two thought of something, we very nearly didn't live to tell about it," she reminded him.

Justin stepped in, reverting to his playful self. "Oh, come on now. What could possibly go wrong this time?"

Rumil groaned, and rubbed her temple with her right hand. He had to be doing it on purpose at this point.

So, I assume we are ready? Micha asked impatiently, a small pack presumably carrying a change of clothing slung over her shoulder.

As ready as we are going to be, Justin replied, his voice displaying his eagerness to get on their way.

Timothy was just as keen to start. *I do request that we don't dally about at the monuments you wish to visit. I would like to make as much haste towards the Great Seal as possible.*

Justin glared at Timothy for the relatively tactless comment. *Micha can take as long as she needs for her to complete her pilgrimage.* Trying to soothe over Timothy's words, he added to Micha, *We do not wish to rush what is obviously an important trip to you. My friend occasionally suffers from a rather irritating impatience.*

Rumil fought back a short laugh, considering that in her experience it was generally the opposite. Caught in her reminiscence, she didn't realize they were moving until Timothy gently grabbed her by the shoulder, and motioned for her to follow the rest of the party outside.

Night was beginning to creep in on the medical facility, and looking back, Rumil could see several of the building's attendants starting to light the candles that would at least give some illumination to those still working inside.

However, the planet's primary wasn't quite gone yet, as she turned to face the rest of the group and was temporarily blinded as a slight bit of glare crossed her eyesight. Blinking repeatedly to attempt at clear out the hazy shadows that danced across her eyes, she finally regained enough clarity to behold the three breaking out of their huddle.

"I explained to Micha that you weren't feeling too well, and that you probably wouldn't have the energy to teleport all the way to the Old Capital on your own," Justin said, somewhat pleased of himself. "So if you feel at all tired, you'll let Timothy help you the rest of the way. Understand?" Justin winked conspiratorially.

Rumil breathed a slight sigh of relief. Every potential problem solved, no matter how minor, was one less thing that could go tragically wrong… especially lately.

Well, I suspect you will need the location of our first stop, correct? Micha concluded, and without waiting for an answer, telepathically placed their destination in mind. In an aside to Rumil, she added, *If you start to feel drained, let us know. The last thing you should want is to wind up like your friend Timothy was.*

Of course, Rumil responded, and felt Timothy's hand fall on her shoulder firmly in anticipation of the first leg of their journey. Suddenly, Rumil was concerned, not for herself, but for Timothy. Not even a ten-cycle ago, he was comatose, supposedly perilously close to death. Now, he was taking on the apparently heavy burden of teleporting two people along an undetermined distance.

"Same goes to you," Rumil whispered in Timothy's ear.

"What does that mean?" the Solarian asked.

Rumil sighed, "Let me know if you start to feel tired yourself. We don't need you winding up like you were."

"I'll be fine. I feel good as new, as a matter of fact," he reassured her. Then, he added slyly, "There's that concern of yours again. Too bad there's also an audience."

Rumil flushed bright red then turned to Justin and Micha, who were watching with a mild level of amusement. "Enjoying the show?" she accused the pair, then waved them off with a flip of her wrist. "Get moving now, we'll be right behind you."

Micha rippled slightly and disappeared in a bright flash, Justin following right behind. Timothy waited for several demiticks, then let his other hand slip gently around Rumil's waist. Once he felt she was ready; the Solarian whisked them away to their destination.

When they had emerged, Micha and Justin had already begun to move, climbing up the loosely piled and flattened rocks, staggered to form a makeshift staircase up a hill covered in withered brown grasses. Micha turned around and noticed that Timothy had not released Rumil, asking, *Is she well?*

I was worried about this. The teleport was a little much for her. She is still coming to her abilities, Timothy answered. Rumil, deciding to help with the ruse, slumped against the Solarian, and nodded weakly. She decided that her current position would be a nice added bonus to their further travels.

Micha nodded in understanding. *If you feel that you can carry the both of you, Timothy, then that will be acceptable. However, remember that you yourself are just recovering from some severe drain on your mind as well. I will require us to stop if I sense you are starting to wane.*

Understood, Timothy agreed, and pushed Rumil to a standing position. "Are you sure you can walk?" he asked wryly.

"Oh, I don't know," she replied melodramatically. "I may just faint in your arms. Then you would have to resuscitate me."

Timothy grunted, clearly not amused. "As much as I would love to see just where you are going with that line of discussion, I am afraid to say that now is neither the time nor the place."

Rumil growled, and pushed herself away. To think that men accused women of mood swings… no lady held even a slight comparison to the sudden and drastic shifts in the demeanor of Timothy Honore. Gathering her slightly bruised dignity, she stomped off after Micha and Justin, who were already nearing the top of the ravaged hill.

Just what is the significance of this place? Justin asked.

From the most ancient of records we have, this was the place that our ancient peoples formulated the first of many weapons that would spell the doom of the old society, the fey woman replied. *From my understanding, there is some debate as to how this landmark should be preserved… but the large consensus is that there isn't much to preserve anyway.*

Upon reaching the top of the hill, and looking down at the scene below him… Justin understood just what she had meant. It was a scene of ugly and horrific desolation, as if someone had stomped everything flat and barren, then baked the battered earth until it hardened into a black glassy surface. There were the occasional remains of what might have been buildings or vegetation, but it was so battered by time or whatever had caused the obliteration that he could not easily tell.

This looks like the examples of the first thermo-nuclear detonation devices that my father's people built over two thousand staryears ago, Justin commented, noting how the intense heat of those weapons could actually melt sand and dirt into a similar liquid state. Of course, in the current age, they had mass destructive weapons like fusion bombs that would disintegrate matter into nothing but wisps of energy before they ever had a chance to congeal into glass. Perversely, many people considered that "progress."

I have no knowledge of what you mention, Micha stated in a small degree of awe. *I am truly impressed that your kind could possess such terrible things, and still manage to resist the temptation to use them.*

Rather than correct her, Justin merely allowed her to keep her assumption, offering a short prayer of apology to the four billion victims that had fallen to the most recent temptation of others to use "such terrible things." Justin began to appreciate just why people of this world were asked to visit this monument en route to the Old Capital… he had never actually been to Baramak, and had only seen pictures of the destruction that had rained down on that colony world.

In just this short visit, he had come to realize that images, no matter how clear, no matter how they were generated holographically to increase the "realism" of things, no matter how descriptive a book's passage can be… nothing can compare or fully convey the impact of looking upon them firsthand. In looking down upon the site below for mere demiticks, he came to fully realize some things about his history, and the legacy of the society he grew up in that he had never thought of before.

Justin heard a gasp from just to his right, and realized that Rumil and Timothy had caught up with him. The gasp had come from Rumil, her hand flashing up to her mouth, her eyes transfixed on the black desolate landscape below. He sensed her psionic forces, that had been barely there just a demitick ago, begin to flare and build rapidly. The blonde woman's eyes glazed over, and sensing that Rumil was about to have another one of her episodes, moved to aid her. Timothy moved to the other side as Rumil fell to her knees, now clutching her head in what appeared to be a significant amount of pain.

What is happening? Micha asked fearfully. *Why are her mind energies surging so intensely? Is this normal?*

For her… yes, Timothy answered.

* * * * *

Like many of her nightmares, it was dark.

It wasn't a complete, utter blackness, since she could occasionally see her hands in front of her, but it was certainly dark enough to make her curl her tiny limbs tight against her body in fear.

Then the sounds of explosions began to fill her ears. At first, they were but soft rumbles from what had to be a great distance away. As they grew closer, Rumil began to shiver in fearful anticipation, covering her eyes at the concussive detonations began to physically shake the darkened prison she was sealed into. She was tossed to her left, and when she dropped her hands to brace her fall, pain flashed from her sore wrists all the way to her shoulders. Because of that, her arms buckled and Rumil made a nasty connection with the hard metal floor of her black container.

She started sobbing from the collective pain in her extremities and her chin, but those were soon forgotten as the explosions seriously began to rock the container, the blasts muffled by what sounded like large amounts of earth and rubble. Whatever was happening, it was almost right above her.

Curling up on her side, Rumil covered her face with her hands and rocked slightly, crying uncontrollably as the assault on the surface continued. Whenever she would think it was almost over, a new barrage would rattle her prison and cause her to shudder in fear and pain. Finally, after a great number of ticks, the barrage began to die away off into the other direction, and Rumil slowly pulled herself back to a sitting position, taking her hands off her eyes.

Mere Tackets away from her face, looking directly at her, was a phantom image of a red, inhuman head, its cat-like eyes bloodshot and angry, its scaled skin rippling with what she figured was malicious intent. A mouth of ichor-stained fangs filled her vision, then it laughed, a grating, evil burst of simply malevolent mirth.

Rumil screamed, and scampered as far away from the ghostly image, smacking against the wall of her chamber. Whirling around, overwhelmed with the terror of a little child, she pounded against the metal, and screamed repeatedly, "Let me out!"

* * * * *

"Let me out! Please, let me out!"

Timothy had wrapped his arms around Rumil's shoulders, even as she fought to squirm out of his grasp, screaming the entire time. "Rumil, what do you mean?"

"Someone… anyone… please…" She began to sob then flailed wildly once more, her hand coming in contact with the Solarian's fingers. The feel of warm skin seemed to finally snap her out of the trance that had overwhelmed her mind.

57

Rumil buried her head into Timothy's shoulder, and tried to explain what she had seen, but her gulps and sobs rendered much of it incomprehensible. Not sure what else to do, Timothy just rubbed her back, making soft hushing sounds.

Perhaps it would be best if we just moved on, Justin commented. *Unless, of course, you need more time here.*

No, I think the point has been made, Micha answered. *We do have other places to visit as well.*

They allowed Rumil to gather some semblance of her wits then slowly worked their way back down the stone stairway to their arrival point. Checking once more to ensure that Rumil was willing and able to continue, Micha provided their next destination.

Each stop carried a story of the ancient conflict that eventually destroyed the once advanced civilization that dwelled on the planet. The ruins of a battleground, the time-battered hulks of what appeared to be massive spacecraft, an ancient graveyard, and other points of interest. However, the monuments began to become less significant to any of the four as they drew closer to their goal, the Old Capital and the Great Seal within. Their last stop had actually been so swift that Micha only barely recalled what had been there, and only because she had learned about it before ever taking the trip.

Finally, the four travelers emerged just outside the city limits of the Old Capital. Unlike the other landmarks along the way, it appeared that the city itself was at least recognizable as such. Granted, it was in great disrepair, blackened and scarred like the battlegrounds they visited, but there were still discernible ruins, including the metallic frames of buildings and crater-ridden roadways weaving through the chaotic destruction.

It would be best if we proceeded with caution. As you may guess, there are many dangers that lurk in ruins such as these, Micha warned.

With that notice in mind, Micha took the lead through the streets of the ruined metropolis. As Rumil peered up at the increasingly larger skeletons of ravaged metal, then down at what must have been a very deliberate street design, she thought to herself how they bore some remarkable resemblances to the circular, intricately planned Erani cities like Jun or Centris.

Because she was looking up at the scenery above her, she almost stepped into a crater in the roadway. Fortunately, Timothy once again had his eye out for her, pulling her away from what promised to be a nasty drop. He didn't chide her, just motioned for her to continue after Micha and Justin, who were steadily proceeding down the cracked and potted roadway, although they too spent a great deal of time musing over the ruins that now surrounded them. Some skeletal remains of living beings could occasionally be seen through the rubble, but Micha quickly warned them to keep their distance. *The remains of the Old Capital have not been maintained and are very fragile, especially what is left of those who fought here.*

The four continued their slow progression through the Old Capital, and after around one half of a tenth-cycle, the city just seemed to stop. The roadway turned into a jagged, churned mess, and the buildings were reduced to piles of melted and twisted metal before becoming flattened into a gray, lifeless, rocky plain.

This is the Dead Grounds along the Great Seal. We are not sure if the destruction was related to the Seal, or if it came about before or after. However, it is clear that this land underwent great upheaval, and we believe the Seal has some connection to that. Not even the wind blows, no rain falls, and no vegetation grows. It is likely why things are as well-preserved as they are.

Rumil felt a sense of terrible foreboding that she had only known once before, but now intensified many times over. Glancing quickly at Justin, she noticed his frame starting to shiver, and each step he took was with increasing nervousness. Micha appeared similarly affected, although like Justin, she seemed to have been expecting it and was able to maintain her pace, slow as it was. Timothy showed no outward sign of such dread, but continued to linger behind Micha and Justin, having no apparent desire to take the lead.

They traversed the Dead Grounds in utter silence. Both Timothy and Justin were now certain of what they would find, while Rumil took up the rear of the party, taking in the sights of what had to have been an epic battle, possibly fought thousands of staryears ago. She had never believed the stories the Erani told of the mythological Archangel War, which they claimed almost destroyed the entire galaxy. Now, looking upon the Dead Grounds, she began to wonder if there indeed might have been some truth to it. Could such a devastating conflict have been fought here?

We're here, Micha then said, stopping at the ridge of a giant crater about a full TackMet in diameter. She pointed down the steep, nearly vertical decline, and her three friends gingerly stepped to the edge.

Completely filling the bottom of the crater what appeared to be pure obsidian at first glance. However, with a slight tilt of her head, Rumil thought she saw ripples of a deep blood red color along its glossy surface. As she stood transfixed by the sight, the ripples seemed to take recognizable shapes, illuminating horrific carvings of misshapen beasts, many holding other creatures in their mouths, as well as several circles of unfamiliar symbols and runes that spiraled towards the center of the humongous disc.

Rumil suddenly felt a bone-numbing chill that swept through her frame, like a polar wind had stripped her skin of any heat. Despite the unnatural cold that seeped into her veins, beads of sweat were starting to form on her forehead.

Finally, it was Justin who broke the silence. He turned to Timothy and asked nervously, "I don't know much about the one on Solaria... but don't you think this one is... well, a little... bigger?"

Timothy nodded, "Considerably bigger."

"That's what I was afraid of."

Rumil was already quivering with unexplained fear... she didn't need cryptic discussions adding to the intrigue. "Spill it... right now. What are you two whispering about?" she grumbled.

"I had suspected that this very thing would be waiting for us, but I wanted to make sure," Timothy answered solemnly. "As you may have now guessed, we crashed on a planet the Erani call Mydor, the home planet of the ancient Se-Lan race."

He then pointed to the Great Seal. "And that... is the Second Gate."

Chapter Four

Rumil's gaze fixed onto the onyx reflective circle, which both Timothy and Justin seemed to agree was one of the hellish gates that their people had vowed to destroy. Her first rational impulse was to reject the very concept.

However, a deeper part of her wasn't nearly as convinced. She had felt this same dread feeling once before, although with considerably less intensity on Solaria as she had passed the monument that Timothy claimed was the remains of another such gate.

"It doesn't add up though," Justin answered. "The Se-Lan left Mydor because it could no longer sustain life. Yet, this planet seems more than up to the task."

"No, we've merely *assumed* that's why the Se-Lan left their homeworld," Timothy answered. "No record among either of our people can claim direct knowledge to them or their reasons for any of their actions, and even the Prophet Trashal acknowledges that his visions in that regard were not quite as clear as the others he received."

"I'll submit myself to your superior knowledge on the topic," Justin acknowledged. "You've clearly been giving this considerably more thought over your life than I."

Rumil never heard the Solarian's reply. A small thread of sunlight suddenly broke through the thick cloud cover above, casting light on the center of the seal and causing the blood red reflection to reach her eyes. In the center of the circle, seemingly beneath its surface, was an etching of a horrific visage, a head crowned with horns and a mouth filled with clenched fangs. While crudely drawn, it was an image with which she was all too familiar.

Rumil grasped the sides of her head as it began buzzing uncontrollably, more furiously and painfully then it ever had before. She had come to hate what these moments revealed, and she had no reason to think that this most recent episode would be any better.

The images that filled her mind were as painful to look at as they had felt just before imposing themselves on her vision. They seemed disjointed and occasionally shifted uncomfortably, as if one vision was being imposed on another. At times they meshed almost perfectly, yet at others they clashed against each other painfully.

They centered on the very spot she was standing, at the ridge of the giant crater looking down on the Great Seal. In one vision, the land around her was fresh and lively, save the scorched remains in front of her, while in the other it was the wasteland that she had trudged through on her way here. In both, the seal wasn't there. In its place was a swirling maelstrom of red and black energies, from which the beginnings of a small army of red- and brown-skinned, reptilian creatures began to emerge from the pool, their stained talons digging into the sides of the crater, pulling their hideous, deformed bodies toward the top of the depression on all sides.

Directly on the other side of the crater, a lone figure stood, his arms outstretched, looking down at the rising demonic swarm. The figure was also disjointed, as it belonged to two different people standing on the same spot. Rumil couldn't discern the muddled features of either man, though she felt a nagging sensation that she should recognize one of them. Noise from behind caused her to whirl about and see an agonizing mess of beings forming into ranks. Like the figure on the other side of the crater, the visions seemed to be vying for attention, and she couldn't clearly perceive either.

At that moment, the first line of demonic forces reached the top of the crater, and charged forward, passing through Rumil and engaging with the confused mass in a muddled and disjointed melee. For almost a full tenth-cycle Rumil watched the twisted dual-battle in front of her, and finally reached what she figured was as rational a conclusion as any.

The mixed visions were indeed two separate visions, one from the past, and one either recently past, or even the future.

Then, another sound from the crater caused her to turn back once more. An absolutely enormous red-scaled hand, almost as large as Rumil's torso, grasped the crater's edge. It was followed by the other… then a third… and then a fourth.

With all four arms, the creature pulled itself up slowly, and Rumil knew what was going to emerge from the pit even before it even did. Had she not been utterly petrified with terror, she might have scoffed at the predictability of it all.

The grotesque creature then threw itself clear of the crater with one great heave of its arms, landing less than three Tacks to Rumil's right, and extended to its full height. Despite the fact that she had seen this hideously frightening creature in her nightmares and visions several times before, it was only now that she came to understand the scale of the evil she had foreseen. It was at least five times as tall as Rumil was, with four arms almost twice as thick as both of her legs put together. Its own legs ended in three-pronged hooves as large as her head, with rippling muscle texture that threatened to burst through a leathery hide covered in minute scales.

Suddenly, the creature turned its head downward to Rumil. She squeaked fearfully, as its eyes focused right on her, as if it could clearly sense, or even see, her presence. Its forked, green tongue flicked out of its fanged maw, as if licking phantom lips. Then with a serpent's quickness, it lunged down, its teeth snapping, looking to devour the young lady.

With an agonized scream, the vision abruptly ended and Rumil jerked to a sitting position, then realized that she wasn't where she had been, and took a little time to piece together her new surroundings.

She was back in her ward room, in the medical facility where she has spent far too much time already. Timothy, Justin, and Micha were the closest to her, with Timothy on her right side, the other two on her left. Ghadri, and several other medical staff she didn't recognize, formed a second level of observers around her bed.

You scared us. You were entranced for a good long time, Micha sighed gratefully.

At the same time, Justin spoke. "You had all of us scared, especially when you didn't snap out of it within demiticks like you usually do."

That's the worst vision I've ever had, Rumil said telepathically for the benefit of all. *This one seemed triggered by that Gate, or Great Seal, or whatever you all want to call it.* Finally, she turned her gaze angrily towards Timothy, and said vocally, "You seem to have an idea what's happening to me, and I want to know... now."

Timothy exhaled uncomfortably, and nodded in agreement ever so slowly. "I suppose it can't be helped any more. You've proven what I've suspected as convincingly as you possibly could."

Justin turned about to the others in the ward. *Could you give us some time in private? Rumil is perfectly well, and it would be most appreciated.*

Ghadri seemed reluctant to leave her charge, but Micha somehow managed to convince her, and the remaining onlookers slowly filtered outside after them. Once Timothy felt the three were sufficiently alone, he asked Justin, "I assume you have the book on you?"

"It's in my pack. Give me a moment." The Kiros gestured with his hand towards the leather satchel that he had acquired for their trip. He took three quick strides over to the ragged bag and fished through it.

Meanwhile, Timothy said nervously, "I know that you put little weight in the religious doctrines of my kind, but I'm hoping that recent events have allowed you to at least approach what I'm about to tell you with an open mind."

Justin approached with the rough leather-bound book with discolored time-worn pages, and gave it to her. Rumil scowled at the Kiros, and accused, "You know what he's prattling about too, don't you?"

"The passage in question I have marked right there," Justin stated, dodging her question. "I had always wondered why the Solarians' prophet had written his prophecies in Basic language, rather than the native Erani tongue that the prophets previous had used. It wasn't until I read this that I understood."

Rumil, realizing that she wasn't going to get a straight answer from either of them, decided to just play along. She turned herself so that her legs dangled over the edge of the bed, and took the book from Justin with a slightly impolite snag. She instantly noticed the bright red rectangular bookmark just protruding from around the center of the book. With a disgusted sigh, she opened it to the prompted point.

Justin had been correct, as the language used was indeed an antiquated form of Basic. The Galactic Alliance had taken great pains over the ages to make sure there was a sense of continuity in the accepted language of the galaxy, and judging from the mostly comprehensible language in front of her, it was largely successful.

Third Stanza

I do not pretend to understand the will of the Creator God that made us all. I do not understand why he gifted me with his blessing, or why he stayed silent for so many staryears. Nor do I understand why he moves beyond our kind for the next to be blessed with his vision.

Everything we have come to expect with the laws

passed down since the Lawmaker our Master of Creation seems to neglect. The next prophet in the line is not one of us, one of his celestial descendants, but of the lesser races, of the soulless Arcadian people.

"Gee, wonderful man..." Rumil mused sourly.

Timothy, seeming to understand just what she was referring to, replied, "Bryan Honore was a blatant racist for much of his life, who frequently struggled with the issues of those not descended from the Se-Lan race, something that recent editions of his prophecy conveniently smooth over."

"That's not what's important," Justin cut in, pointing back at the page. "Keep reading."

Perhaps that is the point. The next prophet is everything we're not, with hair as bright and colored as the Kiros sun, and eyes of emerald. Among her kind, I suppose she would be lovely, with a form not at all like the lithe, supple forms of our kind. She will bear the marks of anguish on her wrists and legs, like the burns I have suffered in the service of our Creator.

She will know no mother or father, and of her escorts, the sons of the sects, one will know no mother, the other will know no father. And indeed, the Sixth will be a woman, again a slap in the face of all we have known to be true since the times of the Historian.

I cannot comprehend what this means... and that is my own failing. Perhaps that is the point. Perhaps that is why the Sixth is coming.

Rumil slammed the book shut, and shook her head rapidly. "No... no... No! You cannot possibly expect me... When did you two come up with this?"

"We didn't," Timothy denied. "That book is as direct a copy to the original text of Bryan Honore as anything you will find outside of Solaria."

"If you recall, I got this big thing from Dewin," Justin reminded a demitick later. "I can't imagine, after what has happened to him, that he'd fashion some bogus story for the benefit of faithful."

She scrutinized each Erani Knight, as if she could see on their faces any semblance of deceit or intentional falsehood. Finally, she threw the book at Justin and rose to her feet, her posture rife with indignant fury. Turning a baleful eye towards Timothy, she asked, "So… how long have you known about this then?"

"I haven't known anything," the Solarian answered.

"Do not play your word games with me!" she finally snapped. "You've known all along, haven't you? Since when? Since my first little episode on Solaria? Or maybe when you were sent to chase me around? Or maybe even earlier than that, say, in a little adult club in Iomet? That's why you've been so intent on maintaining my safety? So that I could be your little 'prophet' to take back home to torment your dear old daddy!"

Timothy shook his head in denial, but even as he did so… Rumil could see it, his hidden desires were suddenly clear to her, even if he didn't realize them himself. "It's sad… I actually believed you. You actually had me convinced that you were different. But in the end, you were planning to use me just like everyone else."

The Solarian didn't even get a chance to say anything in his defense before she punched him, directly under the chin, causing his head to snap backward painfully. Timothy staggered a couple of steps, and tried to clear the stars from his eyes.

"You better pray to your 'Creator God' that I only end up hating you when I'm done fuming," Rumil spat in parting before bolting out the door at top speed, with the beginnings of tears trailing her retreating form.

"Well, she took that well," Justin quipped after a short awkward silence.

Timothy narrowed his eyes towards the doorway that Rumil had darted through. "I notice she didn't try to attack you," he commented while rubbing his chin absently.

Justin wasn't sure if Timothy was simply playing dumb, or was truly without a clue. Judging from what he had seen, however, Justin highly doubted it was the latter. Nonetheless, he decided to say, "If you can't figure it out, you are truly blind. I suspect you hurt her far worse than I ever could hope to."

For a brief moment, Justin wasn't sure just what Timothy was about to do as he looked back to the doorway, looking as forlorn as Justin had ever seen the Solarian. "Probably..." he finally muttered, then coughed. It seemed to jolt him out of his funk, and he straightened his form, brushing invisible dust from his clothing. "Unfortunately, I can't waste time worrying about Rumil at the moment. There is a much more pressing concern."

Justin nodded, "Like how we're going to get off-planet. If this book I have means anything, we can't count on that Gate staying closed." Justin twitched the prophecy in question with a raised wrist to emphasize the point.

"Looks like you might be following in your father's footsteps," Timothy said. "Hopefully our patch job will be a little more successful than his was."

"Ah... I don't see why something like that will be necessary," commented the melodious drawl from just outside the door.

Timothy slapped his face with his left hand. "That isn't..."

Justin, who could see their surprise visitor, replied, "No, it is. For good or for ill... it is."

Timothy slowly turned about, as if dreading and anticipating the person he would see in the entry. Leaning against the arch frame, arms crossed, tapping his boots together playfully, his smirk was as infectious as it was irritating, and Justin found himself grinning stupidly at the Demodian pirate captain.

"Wonderful place you two decided to crash in," Dewin said with a bright, knowing smile. "Although generally, when you have coordinates for a planet, folding directly to those coordinates are a bad idea." He strode inside the ward, kick-stepping past Timothy. "So, you want off this rock, and I think I know why."

Timothy snorted in disbelief. "You do, do you?"

Dewin suddenly cringed and started rubbing his arms as if a sudden chill had rushed over him. "There's something... evil... on this planet. I could feel it during my meditations all the way on Demod. Elders take me, I can feel it now, even without so much as even trying."

Justin's eyebrows twitched curiously. "Meditating on Demod now?"

"A necessary evil," Dewin retorted. "Although, I'll admit, my time spent since we parted ways has been rather enlightening. So, I can safely assume you think that this dark sensation that has been tugging at me is one of your dastardly Gates?"

"There's no assuming about it." Timothy scowled. "If you were so in tune with your 'inner self,' you'd see little doubt about it, either."

Dewin shrunk back from the brooding Solarian. On the surface, Timothy looked merely miffed. However, the Demodian's newly discovered extra senses were acutely aware of the tumultuous anger bubbling underneath Timothy's exterior. Recovering as quickly as he could manage, Dewin made his next point. "All right, so you've found this Gate. Then what? In case you two don't remember, your list of charges with the Solarian Armed Forces is increasing with each day, and I suspect the Kiros aren't going to be welcoming Justin back anytime soon."

Timothy seemed unperturbed by that analysis. "I have connections of my own."

"Oh, I'm sure you do. As a matter of fact, I suspect I met one of them before I rushed off here. He claimed to be working under a Priest Hightower. Now, I know you put about as much value on my advice as a street vendor selling ten-cycle old ravule cuts, but I would recommend you keep a wide berth from that angle."

"I wasn't talking about Hightower," Timothy sneered. "He's too close to the Solarian center of influence to be of any significant help."

Dewin shrugged at Timothy's assertion. "Very well. I'm not going to argue with you, but my experience tells me that your news will not be well received. By your god, I'd be amazed if you lived long enough to tell it. The two of you have really stirred the zealots of the galaxy into action since you disappeared."

"Then what is your plan?" Justin asked, more to prevent Timothy from asking the same question in a more unfriendly manner.

"I'll be honest: I don't have one. I'm still not terribly sure what we're dealing with. I just wanted to warn you that whatever we need to do, we probably will have to do it ourselves."

Suddenly, the pirate leader looked about, then asked, "Where's Rumil, by the way?"

The mention of the woman's name caused Timothy's facial features to contort in equal parts anger and regret. "She ran off just before you arrived. I suspect she has some things to sort out."

* * * * *

However, Rumil was not much in the mood to sort anything out. She was far too busy bemoaning the shattered trust that she had so fully given. She followed the arboretum path aimlessly, kicking dirt and pebbles with each step.

So, this is where you have been, the rich, wise mental voice of Ghadri echoed in her head. Rumil turned about to see the delicate elder woman stride gracefully to her side. *Your companions have been looking for you. More visitors have come, and they are getting ready to return to where you came from.*

Rumil sighed. *I don't want to go back.*

Ghadri seemed genuinely confused by that almost wistful response. *Why?*

Because I'm tired of my world... I'm tired of my life! the blonde woman ranted. *I'm sick of being used for someone else's desires.*

I don't understand, and I don't wish to pry. Perhaps you can tell me what's truly bothering you.

Ever since I can remember, someone has used me for their own gain. Never once has anyone been interested in me just for me. The fool thing about it all was that I actually believed this wasn't the case. That damned... Solarian actually convinced me. He had me believing again, then I come to find out, all he ever wanted was a little plaything he could use for his spirituality issues! Rumil was truly on a roll now, her face slowly turning red to match the heat in her telepathic voice. *He preached all about being honest, about being worried about me, wanting to keep me safe, and all of it was a lie! He wasn't worried about Rumil, he was worried about his precious little Sixth Prophet!*

Ghadri seemed to ponder that for a moment. *It sounds to me that you aren't actually upset about being used... but of the person using you.*

Rumil flailed her arms. *Oh, come on! Why should I care one whit about Timothy? He's been playing me for a fool this entire time! He can rot in his Bannor for all I care!*

Are you trying to convince me, or yourself? Ghadri asked

knowingly. The older woman placed a hand on Rumil's shoulder, and led her deeper into the garden. *Dear, you can't fool me. Even Micha, as oblivious as she can be, could see it. Neither of us could bring ourselves to move you on the occasions you fell asleep watching over him. Even in sleep, we could see the feelings you had.*

Those feelings are gone, let me assure you.

Ghadri shook her head. *Do you, or even did you, feel this same way about everyone you claim has used you in the past? If so, I'm amazed you haven't burnt yourself out emotionally by now. No, dear, I suspect that your friend was far different than anyone else you met, and that difference is what is making this betrayal so hard to accept.*

He was... emphasis on 'was,' Rumil replied, unrepentant.

Ghadri queried further. *What made him different?*

I don't know... it probably started when he saved me from a rather unpleasant fate at the hands of some drunken goons, Rumil answered thoughtfully. *He was willing to set aside his mission... but now I know why that was...*

Really? He's been your bodyguard of sorts since then?

Well... no... Rumil said, her rant coming to a screeching halt. Actually, she hadn't seen Timothy again for a couple staryears after the events in the Sultry Siren. Okay, so Ghadri made a roundabout point. However, Rumil wasn't about to let Timothy off the hook just yet. *But even if he didn't even have any designs at the time—*

Everyone has designs, dreams, and plans. Everyone has interests. Just because we have them, doesn't mean we'll act upon them... or even think they are at all feasible... or even that the plans are at all bad. I've seen terrible intents prove to create something very good, while even the best of intentions turn very sour. Ghadri gathered her next thoughts, and then continued. *What I am trying to say is no one is different in that regard. The judge of a person's character is not in their plans alone.*

Rumil silently regarded the older woman's words. Maybe she had overreacted slightly, but could anyone really blame her? She was sick of everyone trying to control her and her life, even if they come packaged with the blessing of some higher power.

"Well, there you are!" the familiar voice of Dewin Rio called out from down the path. He quickly caught up to the pair, looking quite pleased with himself.

"I suppose I shouldn't be surprised," Rumil stated. "You have the uncanny knack to show up precisely when you're needed… or precisely when you aren't wanted."

"Oh?" the pirate replied, seemingly unperturbed. "And which is it this time?"

She failed to fight back a slight smile. "A little bit of both."

Dewin smirked, and said, "Well, I just wanted to inform you that your two Erani friends seem pretty desperate to return to the galaxy proper."

"I see." Rumil began. "And I assume that we'll be leaving as soon as possible?"

"Timothy and Justin are actually about ready to take a shuttle back up to the *Gallan* right about now," Dewin explained. "The crew is now just waiting on us." At that moment, the sound of a propulsion engine echoed through the garden, and the white cloud streak of a lifting craft shot through the sky on the other side of the facility.

"Just when did you get here?" Rumil asked, thinking she should have heard the Blood Hawks' arrival.

"Less than a couple ticks before you three popped in from the 'Gate of Bannor' you visited. I was still in post-flight checkdown when you arrived, apparently." Dewin then looked up at the dissipating flight trail, and remarked, "Speaking of which, we should probably get moving, and hopefully we'll meet the shuttle as it comes back down for us."

With a hint of reluctance, Rumil nodded. She gave her partings to Ghadri, and solemnly followed Dewin out of the arboretum. The pirate captain then queried, "What happened with you and Timothy?"

Rumil paled. "How did you know something happened? Did Timothy tell you?"

"No… he just seemed colder and more irritable than usual. The only person I can imagine that would be able to do that is you."

"It's frankly none of your business."

Dewin shrugged. "That's what the Solarian said too. Oh well." He made no further discussion until they reached their destination, which Rumil could discern judging from the burn marks on the normally pristine grasses.

Rumil didn't have the chance to count to ten before she heard the rumble of the approaching shuttle. Orion opened the sealed hatch once it set down, and Rumil and Dewin silently boarded. Orion was about to say something, but Dewin's disapproving shake convinced the Ubek to remain mum, and instead return to the pilot's seat.

It was relatively short flight back to the pirate cruiser, albeit extremely bumpy as they passed through the unusual ionosphere of the planet. Once the violent trembling stopped, the *Gallan* was clearly in view, and Orion began the docking procedures.

Justin was waiting for them in the shuttle bay, and Rumil was somewhat disappointed to see that Timothy wasn't with him. As she stepped out of the shuttle, she asked about the Solarian.

"He left in a bit of a hurry," Justin remarked, rubbing the back of his head with his right hand.

"That's what I wanted to tell you earlier," Orion said. "Timothy said he couldn't wait for the *Gallan* to depart. He said he had urgent business that had to be dealt with immediately. He prepped and took Shuttle 7 before I came down to retrieve you and the captain."

Rumil clenched her jaw, trying to hide her disappointment. "Well then, if he has more important things to do with his time, let him," she said flippantly. "I assume you have a destination in mind, Mr. Rio?"

"I do," Dewin answered, moving to the communications unit. "Bridge, plot out fold coordinates for Demod."

Chapter Five

"What… why?" Justin stammered when he opened the door to Dewin's safehouse to find the angry face of his wife staring back at him.

"That is so like you, Justin Feroz! You disappear without saying goodbye, leave me worrying about what happened… then I find these strangers at my doorstep telling me that if I valued our son's life, I'd pack everything up and follow them off Kiros without delay," Julianne grit out with a scowl, and Justin was certain small billows of smoke were escaping her nostrils.

Justin turned his head sharply towards Dewin, and the pirate grinned sheepishly. "You told me to keep an eye on your family. I heard tips that High Commander Feroz was preparing to take out his frustrations on your wife and son… so I had them sent here." This wasn't entirely true, as it was a subordinate that took the initiative of bringing the family there, but Dewin thought it best to take responsibility.

"And… you didn't think to mention this until now?"

Dewin shuffled nervously, and replied, "I figured you'd like the surprise."

"Daddy!" Jonathan suddenly shouted from the living room, slipping out of Fiona's grasp, and darting past his mother before clasping tightly to his father's legs.

Justin scooped up his son, and tossed him high in the air, catching the giggling bundle on its way down. "Hi there, little guy! Are you enjoying your vacation?"

Jonathan nodded vigorously. "It's nice, but Mommy and Fiona won't let me play outside."

"Well, that's probably for the best, Jonathan," Justin said. "Have you been a good boy?"

Once again, the young boy nodded, which Julianne scoffed at. "He's been the same little terror he's been well known for," she explained. "However, it is nothing out of the ordinary. So, in that regard, I suppose he's been good."

Justin placed the child back on the ground, and nudged Jonathan back inside the safehouse. Julianne made a mental count of heads then asked, "Where is your other friend? Was he not with you when you left?"

Rumil's right eyebrow twitched at yet another reminder of Timothy and his abrupt departure. Justin stepped in, and replied, "He had other things to take care of. He should be rejoining us later." In a lower voice, he added, "Maybe…"

Dewin then cut in, saying, "You know, as much as this is a wonderful day and all… many of us are still highly wanted outlaws. I'd like to get inside."

* * * * *

Dewin had been right. He had claimed that their hideaway had been cramped before, and now adding two people to the mix had only made it all the more crowded. Perhaps it had been a good thing that Timothy had moved on elsewhere… at least from a spatial point of view.

At that moment, Rumil leaned back in her reclining chair, and picked up her feet just as Jonathan crawled underneath, making a growling noise as if he was some fierce animal.

Nonetheless, Rumil would have given up another couple Tacks of personal space to get a chance to talk with the Solarian. The poor terms of their parting was somewhat due to its haste, and given time to decompress and rationalize things, she wasn't quite as angry as she had been. She still wasn't crazy about his hidden agenda, but she had decided to take Ghadri's words to heart, and at least give him a chance to explain himself if – no – *when* she saw him again.

"So… where did Timothy go, by the way?" Fiona asked from her right. The Feroz family attendant held two cups of steaming ducha, and offered one to Rumil. As Rumil took the mug, she nearly spilled it when Justin barged past chasing after his son.

"Okay, that's enough. I need to go outside. It doesn't matter if we're never seen if I wind up killing everyone," Rumil groused, and stood up.

Fiona smiled, and asked, "Would you mind if I joined you?"

Rumil motioned for Fiona to follow, and they slid outside into the night. The air was damp from forming dew, causing the air to feel slightly warmer than it was. They stood outside the doorway, sipping their mugs, letting the beverage warm them further.

Fiona finally mustered the courage to ask again, "Where did Timothy go, out of curiosity?"

Rumil shrugged. "I'm not sure. He left Dewin's ship before I got there. According to the crew, he said he had some people to contact, and from Dewin I got the impression that it wasn't anyone from Solaria."

Fiona paused. "I wonder if he was contacting Sentinel..." Then she blushed nervously, as if she had revealed something she wasn't supposed to.

"Sentinel?" Rumil queried sternly. "What is that?"

Fiona shook her head rapidly, "I'm not terribly sure, to be honest. I just remember my father being a member of it. As far as I have been able to glean, it is some form of organization, although I'm not certain just what they do. I just remember visiting my father a few staryears ago, and overhearing him talking about how the organization had managed to recruit a young, high-ranking Solarian Knight." She then shrugged, and added, "I just figured that since Timothy seemed that he wasn't communicating with his old sect... maybe he was the Knight my father was referring to."

"Oddly enough, that wouldn't surprise me if that was the case," Rumil noted. "I swear to you that Timothy's secrets have secrets."

Fiona chuckled at the comment. "Most people do... just some are better at hiding them than others."

Rumil cringed. "Please don't remind me. I'm just at the point where I'm not about to strangle a certain Solarian for what he hid from me."

"I won't pry, then," Fiona replied. Shaking her mug, and realizing it was empty, the portly woman asked, "Perhaps we should go back inside before someone chides us for blowing our cover."

Rumil quickly drank down the remaining ducha in her cup, and agreed. "Yes, I suppose it would be prudent before Dewin has a fit."

Inside, Dewin was indeed waiting. "Enjoy your little break?"

Fiona dropped her head somewhat shamefully, but Rumil was unrepentant. "I refuse to drive myself insane because you don't plan for proper contingencies. I figured getting some air was preferable to driving a cleaver into your skull."

"Okay… I'll grant you that," Dewin said with a resigned groan. "Justin's been prattling on about how we probably should be moving out anyway."

"Oh, is he now?"

Justin turned his attention towards the group, and explained, "In case you don't remember, there is a slightly dangerous situation brewing, and it isn't going to just solve itself." He then glanced nervously towards the hall, where Julianne was apparently putting his son to bed. "I think you know what I'm talking about."

Rumil sighed. "Maybe I do. But just what can we do about it? That thing was huge!"

"I know you probably don't accept a lot of my beliefs, but there is a weapon that supposedly was designed specifically for that purpose." Justin said in a hushed tone.

Rumil shook her head in disbelief, "Not this stuff again… believing in those archaic books is what got us in this mess to begin with. The last thing I want to hear is about your people's prophecies. Understand?"

Justin crossed his arms adamantly, and said, "All right, Miss Bonamede, just how do you propose we destroy that 'Great Seal' that we found?"

"Who says we need to destroy it?" Rumil floundered. "Outside of your doctrine, there is nothing that would prove to me that whatever we saw on that planet presents any immediate or substantiated threat to anyone."

To Rumil's surprise, Dewin answered the challenge. "I wouldn't say that… I could feel that Gate, or Seal, or whatever you want to call it, during my meditations here. Why do you think I came all that way to find you? I'm not always this benevolent, after all… but whatever that thing is… we can't count on it staying silent."

"You people just don't understand it at all, do you?" Rumil grumbled, turning away from the crowd, taking a deep breath to fight back a choked off sob. "I never wanted any of this, and I certainly didn't want you Erani ruining my life, not once, but twice. And most importantly, I don't want to care about any of your theological problems."

Justin regarded her choice of words with a sly expression. "But you do care about them now, don't you? Or should I say, you care about a certain person tied up in them?"

Rumil raised a fist in threat. "One of these days, Justin Feroz, you are going to wind up in more pain than you ever will want to imagine."

"Have you ever met his family?" Dewin quipped. "I have a hard time believing you could make it any worse."

The next half-tick passed in a sort of blur. It began with Justin suddenly snapping completely rigid, and diving across the room to where his weapon belt hung from one of the coat hooks.

As he pulled his plasma pistol from the belt, the door was kicked in by several heavily armored beings in black carbide and half-helmets with black-tinted visors, wielding various assault weapons.

There was the sound of glass breaking, and Julianne screaming, bursting out of Jonathan's bedroom with her child clutched firmly to her chest as she darted into the living area. Two more armored invaders were in hot pursuit, effectively surrounding the occupants of the safehouse.

No one moved immediately afterward, as the scene was frozen in a deadly and extremely one-sided stalemate. One of the armored operatives stepped forward, this one wearing a full helmet, lowering his plasma rifle slightly as he did so. "Stand down, and no one has to be hurt here. Gregor Krennan just wants to see some of you." His voice was heavily masked from the helmet, creating a muffled, almost mechanical sound.

Rumil blanched. "Why not just kill us here and save all of us the drama?"

"Apparently, he doesn't want anyone dead," he answered to Rumil. "We're under orders to bring you, Justin Feroz, and Dewin Rio to a meeting. Beyond that, I'm as clueless as you."

Justin didn't seem convinced. "And why should we believe you?"

"Because if Krennan wanted us dead, we would be," Rumil acknowledged. "He wouldn't waste time dragging us to Arcadia." With a resigned sigh, she stepped toward the squad leader and announced, "at least I'll be dealing with things that I have some comfort with. I'm the one Krennan wants, and I'm ready to leave whenever you are."

"I'm sorry, Bonamede, but Krennan's orders were very explicit," the leader said as impartially as he could manage. "All of you are required to attend, unharmed if at all possible. Don't make this any harder than it needs to be."

Silent glances filtered through the living area. Justin eventually turned his attention towards his wife and son. Julianne was utterly terrified, and rightfully so, while Jonathan seemed more enthralled by the strange invaders, likely oblivious to the danger. His mind was made up instantly after. There was no way he could risk a fight with them present.

"I'll go," Justin said, never taking his eyes off his family. With a softer whisper, he added to the pair, "I'm sorry."

Dewin also took stock of his situation. He had been dead-set on letting Krennan's goons have it, but his plans had hinged on the support of the Kiros Knight. Without Justin's considerable battle prowess and innate abilities, it would have been a slaughter. With a defeated exhale, Dewin nodded. "I'll have the *Gallan* prepared to follow. Just let me know when we're to break orbit."

"We're under orders to return to Arcadia as soon as we can," came the squad officer's tart reply. "You will come with us, and we'll leave coordinates for your crew to retrieve you when the meeting is complete. Any deviation from this arrangement will not be taken lightly."

* * * * *

Rumil recognized this meeting room all too well. Despite the expert patching job, she could still see burnt edges around the hole that Timothy had made in her first visit. Justin no doubt recognized it as well.

"It could not have been coincidence that Krennan chose this place," Justin said warily.

"Indeed it isn't," the media mogul replied, staring the trio down with a small level of disdain. "I just figured, considering our last appointment and all, that I'd rather not ruin yet another meeting room."

"Of course," Dewin remarked, unconvinced. "Although you'd have to replace the carpets after executing us anyway…"

"You really do have a grave misconception of our meeting today," Krennan said with a smirk. "No, I dare say I brought the three of you here because you all could be of great use to me."

"And just how would that be?" Rumil asked. She didn't like the way that Krennan was eyeing the three of them.

The hobbled man smiled conspiratorially. "I have had a dream for some time, and I think I finally have the means in which to fulfill that dream." He adjusted his position on his cane, and said, "I don't think this should come as a surprise to anyone that I hold very little love for the archaic ways of the Erani sects. Their religion pollutes common sense, decency, and any semblance of intelligent thought. Their draconian societies should have been cast away with the rise of manned space flight, yet it perseveres like a bloated pimple on the galaxy.

"Worse yet, their sanctimonious assertions of their religion and the superiority of their antiquated 'order' has destroyed far more than it has ever built. During their hegemony, they insulted the memories of generations of my people who had fought to free themselves from oppressive religious bureaucrats by imposing their religious law on us, regarding us as some sort of inferior peoples. The 'lesser races' was a term that was frequently used, if I recall correctly."

Rumil nodded in affirmation. It was an attitude that hadn't completely gone away either, judging from her experiences on Kiros and Solaria.

"Then, these sects actually massacred billions in the name of their holy war." Krennan's free hand was now clenched in an angered fist, his face tinting with his increasing rage. "To see Baramak from space… to see what the Erani did to it… and to know that to this day, that crime goes unpunished…" The media boss then stared down at his cane. "The Baramak Slaughter did more than incinerate almost one entire hemisphere of the planet. It affected a whole generation. By the time the radiation from the barrage was finally cleared, it was far too late for many… including myself. The sickness I acquired is what has warped me to what I am… with no chance of recovery. And each day the Erani people go on without answering for their transgressions against life itself… I've sworn I won't rest until they all pay."

Justin dropped his head, obviously uncomfortable with the story Krennan told. In that regard, Rumil differed from the wealthy businessman. She knew for a fact that most Erani had very little knowledge of that heinous attack, and that even more were largely oblivious to life outside their respective sect's influence. It was hardly fair to blame them all for the twisted machinations of a select few.

He suddenly blanched, and turned away slightly. "Do pardon me…" he eventually muttered. "My physician warned me to try and not get worked up."

Dewin grunted. "I'm waiting for the point where you start to make sense, and stop wasting our time."

Krennan scowled at the pirate, and said, "The fact is, with the three of you, I can finally strike back. Justin Feroz, I heard about your father's attempts on your family's lives. Surely you can understand that this must stop. Dewin Rio, I understand you too have issues with the Kiros. And I know Rumil is always up for a challenge. Together, we can make it happen."

"And just… how… do we plan to do this?" Rumil queried.

"I think I'll let my newest business partner explain the plan." Krennan then smiled playfully, "I suspect he'll also have a much better time convincing you of the merits of what I'm offering. Mr. Honore, if you may…"

From the south entrance, on the other side of the meeting room, a familiar figure dressed in black carbide stepped inside and closed the door. "Sorry about not introducing myself earlier…" Timothy said, his voice carrying a slight hint of apology as he strode to the center of the room just to Krennan's left, then removed his helmet. His eyes locked with Rumil's when he added, "but I wasn't sure how well I'd be received."

There was a stunned silence that followed Timothy's entry, and despite herself, Rumil was fighting the urge to punch him again. The Solarian seemed to recognize this, and said, "Rumil, I will allow you the pleasure of trying to strangle the life out of me when this meeting is concluded. Will that be acceptable?"

And to think, she had actually started to feel sorry for her actions on Mydor. "Fine, just get to whatever you want to say."

Dewin clicked his tongue on his teeth. "This is a bit of surprise, to say the least."

Justin seemed to agree, but he only managed one word. "Why?"

"I would think you'd already know the answer to that question, Feroz," Timothy said disapprovingly. "The leadership of the Solarians and the Kiros have grown increasingly dangerous since the Schism War. If their actions recently are any indication, I fear that the Baramak Slaughter might only be the first shot in a larger conflict. My father has been openly demanding war with the Kiros since my defection, and your father hasn't exactly been backing down from the threats either, especially since he declared you have been selling Kiros military secrets to the Solarians through me. It's why he was seeking to detain, and possibly kill, your family."

That was news to Justin. "That's preposterous. He knows that's not true at all."

Timothy regarded the Kiros with a bemused stare, as if he couldn't believe Justin could be that naive. "Of course he does. However, he's been looking for a reason to call the Solarian military on their threats, and nothing better than to make up his own reason. It's because of these recent developments that I've reached the conclusion that it has to stop, and quickly."

The idea of a full-scale war between the two Erani sects was enough to convince Rumil that something indeed had to be done, especially if the destruction on Baramak was at all indicative of what to expect. However, nothing so far had explained one very important question. "Just how do we plan to do this?"

"The first step is to divert the sects' attentions from war with each other. We're going to have to introduce internal issues that will delay further progress in their war efforts. I can think of two ways this can be done."

At some unknown cue, a small holographic projector lowered from the ceiling and the lights in the meeting room dimmed. A planetary map was projected in the center of the room, and Timothy continued. "In five cycles, the Ceremony of War will be beginning on Ub. As some of you might already know, about every twenty-five staryears, the Ubeks hold war games of sorts to determine which caste will control the Ubek people. Since the Schism War, the caste known as the Bluebloods has won this contest. What many have suspected, but not been able to prove, is that the Solarians have been tipping the scales somewhat in the Bluebloods' favor since they migrated to Solaria."

Dewin nodded. "The Bluebloods have always been the most supportive of the Solarians, and the ones most in favor of alliance with them. I assume that Solarian interference in the Ceremony is actually occurring then?"

Timothy frowned. "Do you honestly think that the same caste would consistently win the Ceremony of War without something going on behind the scenes? Even a fluke defeat would occur every so often."

Rumil shook her head, "But… the Galactic Alliance has investigated the Ceremony several times, and has always reported no evidence of collusion."

Krennan stepped in. "That is because it has been in the Alliance's best interest to say so. If the Ubeks were to ever break allegiance with the Solarians, it would shift the balance between the sects toward the Kiros."

"So then, why doesn't the Galactic Alliance do something about it now?"

"Because they are as blind to the danger as everyone else," Timothy answered. "They see this as simple posturing due to some damaged egos. We can't afford to take that chance. Now, obviously, a small group such as ours would be insufficient to turn the tables entirely, but with some proper planning, we could potentially level the playing field. Mr. Rio, your first officer… isn't he related to a matriarch of one of the Pale clans?"

Dewin was surprised that Timothy had been aware of that. "Yes, his sister is the battle leader of a large Pale clan in the city of Frazia."

"I think that we can convince her to accept our aid in winning the Ceremony of War. The Pales are the least inclined of the three castes to support Solarian alliance, and as a matter of fact, might actually be willing to renew… acquaintances on the field of battle. Needless to say, if the Solarians are trying to quell the leadership of the Ubeks, they won't be picking fights with the Kiros."

Justin acknowledged that, but interjected, "Yes, but as Krennan hinted to, that would just be opening the door for the Kiros to get even more aggressive."

"Not if they are fighting an internal battle of their own," Timothy replied, tapping at a projected key on the planetary map and changing the view to another world. "I'm sure that Justin recognizes this place; Feria, homeworld of the Ferian. Since even before the Schism, the Ferian have been under the yoke of a series of drugs that are supposed to quell their violent and animalistic natures. However, conspiracy theories have floated around that these medications are nothing but placebos, intended to generate a false dependence on the Erani, and more recently, the Kiros."

Justin nodded. "I had heard such theories in my day, but had never put much weight in them. However, knowing what I do now… I'm actually inclined to believe it."

"Well, the evidence I've managed to glean is that this is indeed the case. Needless to say, exposing this fraud for what it is could definitely hinder Kiros war plans as well. And if all goes according to plan, the internal strife would open up execution of Phase Three."

"Which is?" Rumil asked.

"Indisputable proof of the events of the Baramak Slaughter that not even the sects could deny. Sams Fidel, an Arcadian geneticist on Baramak, had an underground facility that might have survived the bombardment. However, no one had been able to precisely locate it… until now."

Timothy tapped the planetary projection one more time, and it switched to the half-charred topography of Baramak. From there, it zoomed in and flattened out a small section of the landscape on the ravaged hemisphere of the Arcadian colony planet. From there, a small red glow just underneath the surface caught the eyes of the gathering. "From information I've been able to gather, I have come to believe that Fidel's underground facility likely lies here. If it had survived the attack, like I think it has, more than likely it contains all the evidence we need."

"To do what?" Rumil queried.

"There's a reason that leaders of both sects want information on the Baramak Slaughter to remain secret. I suspect it is because they know what will happen if the truth is ever discovered."

"There would be a public outcry the likes of which we have never seen," Rumil deduced.

Timothy nodded. "It's also quite likely that elements within the Solarians and the Kiros themselves would find this absolutely unacceptable. Thus would emerge the situation in which the ruling elements of each sect would be fighting former allies, as well as trying to weather a political storm from both the Galactic Alliance and within their own spheres of influence."

Dewin caught on to the progression. "The resulting chaos would weaken the Erani nobility enough for the Galactic Alliance to push for the removal of the lifetime positions the monarchs hold. And without that position inside the Alliance itself, the monarchies would largely become irrelevant on the galactic scene."

Timothy then finished, "And hopefully any threat of war between the Solarians and the Kiros with them."

Dewin came to a conclusion of his own. "Meanwhile, my angle in all this is to use the Blood Hawks as a means to buffer Krennan from any connection to our actions. Seems like you have protected yourself quite well in case this all goes sour, Mr. Krennan."

Timothy cut off any further accusations. "At the moment, if it were discovered that Krennan was involved in what we are planning, we would quickly lose our base of operations and primary funding. Besides, I highly doubt you consider your score with the Kiros even."

Dewin sighed. "I suppose I don't. I know a lot of the Blood Hawks won't like it... but I suspect they'll come around."

"All we'll need is the *Gallan* and her crew," Timothy corrected. "The less people involved, the better."

"Understood."

Timothy then asked Justin, "Do you think you're up to this?"

Justin nodded. "I'm going to have to be, aren't I? Truth be told... maybe it's time for the old ways to finally be put to rest."

Finally, Timothy asked Rumil, "What about you, Bonamede?"

Rumil wasted no time. "I should ask if you think you can do it. I mean, some good friends of yours could wind up really hurt if everything goes as planned."

"I'm the one who dreamed up this whole plot," he said reassuringly. "I wouldn't be here if I wasn't ready to do whatever is necessary."

The answer didn't fully satisfy Rumil, but at the same time, she sensed something in Timothy's eyes. A feeling that, yet again, he wasn't telling everything he knew. She wasn't about to let him get away with it again... and there was only one way to insure that.

With a nod, Rumil replied, "All right then. I'm in."

Chapter Six

"We need to talk," Rumil declared simply as she imposed herself in the entry of Timothy's quarters on the *Gallan*, preventing the sliding door from shutting.

"About what, dare I ask?" the Solarian queried.

"About a lot of things," Rumil said with a sigh. "I think I might owe you an apology."

Timothy shook his head. "Well, we'll see about that. Come on in, make sure the door closes."

Complying with Timothy's request, Rumil stepped inside and looked back, confirming that the door had shut. With a deep breath, she muttered, "I'm sorry about hitting you."

Timothy smirked. "Perhaps I deserved it. You were right in a way. I had plans that didn't take your feelings into account. I won't deny that. My mistake was that I took your support for granted."

"Well, let me make this clear. My life is my own, and I don't want to hear any more about it, what you think I am or what you think I should be," Rumil said assertively. "I'm certainly no prophet of anything, and even if you disagree, at least respect my wish to stay out of the theological messes you Erani revel in."

Timothy nodded. "I can do that."

"Good," Rumil said. "Now, you can tell me what is really going on. I highly doubt that you suddenly decided that your people were so beyond hope that you'd actually sign up with Gregor Krennan."

"Actually, it is due time that things change among the Erani," Timothy acknowledged. "But in regards to Krennan, one would think you'd recognize a business arrangement. Krennan gets something he wants, and I get something I want."

"Okay... I know what Krennan wants... but something tells me it's not the same as what you're planning to get from this deal." Rumil paused before asking, "Just what are you expecting to get from all this?"

Timothy grinned playfully. "But, Rumil, I thought you didn't want to hear any more about my theological issues."

"Just spit it out," Rumil groaned, frustrated. "I want to know just what I'm in this for."

"My goal remains the destruction of that Gate we found," Timothy replied. "And to do that, it requires the use of an ancient weapon…"

"The Star Smasher again…" Rumil groaned. "Justin was droning on about it before you recruited us. I have only two problems with it. First, are you even sure that this great weapon, supposedly forged by your legendary 'ancestor,' even still exists? Secondly, how is Krennan supposed to help you find this thing even if it does?"

Timothy chuckled. "You know, if you spent as much time and energy accepting my beliefs as you do trying to convince yourself they hold no merit, you'd probably be the most devout person I ever met."

Rumil scoffed and observed, "That doesn't answer my question."

"Yes, I believe the Star Smasher exists. And I suspect that Krennan has actually already found it," Timothy said knowingly. "I have contacts who have informed me that about ten staryears ago, an Erani-style weapon had been recovered by Arcadian salvagers. According to the reports I received, appraisers made note that it was molded from the supermetal Durium, and judging from their analysis, it had been forged sometime around the Staryear 2600 to 2650 AW"

"Which I assume fits the timeframe of this weapon?"

"2648," Timothy answered. "Anyway, the weapon went into the black market, and was auctioned off for slightly under seventeen million credits."

Rumil interrupted, "Let me guess. The high bidder was Gregor Krennan."

"I knew you were a smart girl."

"Smarter than you know. Just where did you get this information? From Sentinel, perhaps?"

This caused Timothy's eyebrows to rise in curiousity. "And just where did you hear that?"

"Oh, so you can have your secrets, but I can't have mine?" Rumil teased with a hint of contention.

"I don't have nearly as many secrets as I thought I did," the Solarian commented ruefully. "But yes, that is where I got my information."

"In danger of being too bold, may I ask just what this Sentinel is? I'm sure it's probably something very exclusive and of the utmost secrecy and all…"

Timothy shrugged. "Sure."

The ease in which Timothy complied with the request startled her. "Did you just say… 'sure?'"

"Yes. It's nothing terribly guarded. It's just not something openly broadcast to the galaxy proper. Sentinel, at its core, really isn't anything more than a galactic information network. It doesn't even deal in information that is heavily top secret, just bits and pieces that members manage to scrounge up in their day-to-day lives. The strength of Sentinel is that it offers a quick way to gather and analyze information from several different points. What may just seem as a useless snippet on its own becomes much more valuable when put together with other snippets to form a larger picture."

He took a deep breath when he elaborated. "You can take my search for the Star Smasher as an example. In and of itself, Arcadian salvagers coming across an old twin-bladed sword wouldn't be worth much of note. Nor would an appraiser making a judgment on an old Erani relic from around the middle of the third millennium mean much on its own. Even the bit of Krennan purchasing an old Erani weapon in a black market auction wouldn't be terribly valuable, as he frequently makes such purchases."

"But when pieced together… it convinces you that Krennan came across a legendary relic constructed by a prophet of your people," Rumil finished with a slight frown.

"Exactly. And that rather brings me full circle to what I'm doing now. In exchange for helping Krennan's rather grandiose scheme, I acquire the Star Smasher, and severely hamper further influence from the Erani sects."

Rumil sighed. "I suppose I should tell Justin not to keep planning about how he intends to find the aforementioned Star Smasher. You appear to have everything well in hand."

"Why? Let Justin feel useful for a bit longer."

Rumil pondered that last statement before saying, "I'm going to assume that was meant to be funny."

"That would be a safe assumption."

There was an awkward silence that followed. Finally, Rumil asked nervously, "So… are you still going to be my little bodyguard?"

Timothy didn't even spend one demitick thinking about it. "While you may not believe in what you are, I am entirely convinced. I am no less interested in your safety than I was before."

On one hand, her independent nature was insulted by the implication that she couldn't take care of herself, and by his insistence that she was some divine messenger. Another, more subtle, part of her was cautiously relieved by his assertion.

"So… that's what it's all been about? Because you think I'm this Sixth Prophet and all?"

He closed the distance, placing his hands on her shoulders. "I'd be lying if I didn't say that was part of it. But what I told you as we fought through that sandstorm of Solaria is also completely true."

Timothy said something after that, but Rumil had no idea what it was. She was fading out again…

* * * * *

Instantly, Rumil had the feeling that this was one of the rare visions that felt as if she were seeing through someone else's eyes. Despite that, there were elements of this vision that were remarkably similar to the flashes of memory that plagued her every so often.

For example, it was dark, damp, and a little cold. She was huddled in the corner of what appeared to be some basement, rather well maintained judging from the stable masonry and neatly swept concrete flooring. She suddenly became acutely aware of a stinging pain in her neck, and she moved her hand over the source of the discomfort. She found herself relieved to note that she was no longer bleeding.

She slowly worked her way to her feet, and stumbled towards a partially shattered oval mirror in a rotating, tarnished gold frame. Instead of the varieties of her own face, the reflection that bounced back to her was a young boy's, with a mop of unruly black hair and shimmering blue eyes, one swollen shut from what looked to have been a nasty blow. She wanted to gasp, but no sound came out as she turned to examine the wound in the mirror; a deep gash along the neck and shoulder that promised to scar without prompt treatment.

That's when it all clicked. She had never even entertained the thought of Timothy as a child, but once she made the connection, it was unmistakable. She was getting a glimpse into his own past, his own memories, sneaking past the layers of secrecy he had surrounded himself with.

To her surprise, Timothy didn't cry. With great sympathy, she figured he was probably well-used to that sort of beating. Rumil could speak from relative experience that there comes a point where pain, be it emotional or physical, just isn't really felt. Not in a good way, though. In its place is just an empty void that in some ways is even more painful.

The sounds of voices through the north wall draws the young Timothy's attention. He creeps up to the masonry quietly, and presses his ear to the stone, trying to hear whatever the voices were saying. She couldn't make anything out, but it was possible that Timothy's slightly better hearing had managed to pick up something.

She could sense that he was curious and excited. Perhaps he hadn't known that there was a second room in the basement. Perhaps he was just feeling the rush of doing something that he probably shouldn't be doing, although the idea of Timothy being naughty simply for the sake of being naughty struck her as terribly incongruous with his character.

The voices died away, as if they had left wherever they had been. Timothy's vision turned up near the ceiling, where there was a ventilation grate about half a tack from the ceiling. It seemed abnormally large for the purpose, but a quick glance around suggested it was the only such vent in the whole basement, and thus would possibly explain its size.

Timothy reflected a hint of mischievousness as he started scanning the basement for objects he could climb on. An old child's stool, likely for feeding Timothy when he was still in his infancy, shows some promise, and is easily maneuvered underneath the grate.

His progress was temporarily interrupted by the sounds of arguing upstairs, although it appeared to be a rather one-sided argument. The loud bellows are clearly his father's, and the occasional timid interjections sound similar to his mother's voice, but the idea that she could ever be so meek was almost absurd. Then there was the sound of stomping that gradually died away. Rumil could feel Timothy grin, and a sense of relief wash over him. From that, she guessed that Niles Honore had left the manor. Apparently, Timothy saw this as just the opportunity he was looking for.

Yet once again, he had to stop as the door to the basement opened slowly. There was a slight flutter of happiness at the sight of Celine Honore appearing at the top of the stairwell, yet at the same time, she sensed a hint of resentment from the young Timothy. The slight resentment lingered in his mind like a subtle, pungent odor as Celine examined her battered son. The woman, who Rumil would have guessed was his older sister, had she not known better, began fretting over the lash wound on his neck. With a promise that Timothy's adopted brother was on his way, Celine shot back up the stairs and once again closed the basement door.

With that out of the way, Timothy went right back to work, making a couple experimental leans onto the chair to see if it could actually hold his weight. Satisfied that it could, he gingerly stood up, and grabbed the bars of the grate with both hands.

Displaying some of the strength that would make him a dangerous adversary and prominent Solarian Knight in adulthood, he grunted twice before pulling the grate loose from the wall, and setting it down quietly on the floor of the basement. Another show of strength and nimbleness allowed the boy to pull himself up into the open hole in the wall. It was barely a Tack to the other side, where another large grate awaited him. This one Timothy pushed outward, with his hands clenched around the bars to keep it from falling to the floor.

Timothy peered over the edge of the vent to see if there would be anything in his way, and was quite pleased to find a sturdy wooden desk just underneath him that would allow him to climb back up. It was almost obscene to think a child of his age could be that agile as Timothy pulled himself forward, bracing himself from falling by planting his feet firmly against the sides of the vent so that he could set the grate on the desk silently. From there, he clambered back up into the grate, turned himself around, and then crawled down onto the desk.

The second basement looked nothing like the first. As a matter of fact, this room looked like a private study of some sort, filled with bookcases and several glass-covered relics of days gone by. Clearly, Niles Honore used this room when he did not wish to be disturbed.

The giddy anxiety bubbling inside of Timothy was threatening to boil over, and she somehow knew he had a broad, naughty grin plastered across his face. He stealthily appraised the study, not seeing anything that terribly interested him, although he did give an awed glance to what appeared to be an antiquated pistol underneath one of the glass domes.

The awe in Timothy's breathless gasp amused Rumil, as she found it somewhat funny to think that Timothy was actually a child at one time. It just seemed so unlike him…

It appeared that he was about ready to end his little expedition, when he noticed something on the desk he had climbed down. It was the only object on the desk, save the vent grating that was propped against the wall, and had a bookmark of bright red velvet hanging out of the bottom.

Hopping into the plush chair in front of the desk, he found he had to sit on his knees to reach the book comfortably. Timothy pried open the old leather cover carefully, not wanting to damage it in any way and tip off his father that someone else had been in the study.

He whispered the lines of text that greeted him in big bold letters, and the sound of Timothy's voice at that young age once again amused Rumil. It was high pitched and childish, with a slight lisp, yet at the same time she could hear hints of what would become his almost song-like tenor as an adult. "The Prophecies of Bryan Honore…" Timothy frowned at that, and Rumil sensed his disinterest immediately. Clearly, the young Timothy was not an avid book learner.

Nonetheless, he didn't place the book aside, instead curiously opening the book to where the bookmark lay. Rumil almost immediately recognized the text on the page as the same passage Timothy had pointed out to her after her episode on Mydor. However, unlike Rumil, who had stopped rather quickly, Timothy seemed enthralled.

> *The Sixth is one of contrasts. I see little love in her life, yet she becomes the very focal point of the love that binds our race. She will live in hard times, yet she will be known for bringing a better life to all. She will suffer the slings of seclusion, yet her battle cry will be of redemption for all. She will dislike the esteem she is held in, yet through that esteem will she restore the ties that will soon separate us.*
>
> *Take care of the words I write. When the Sixth comes, there will be those that will wish to silence her. Do not let a lack of foresight cloud the greater future our people will have. Through her love, we will all be at last truly free.*

Apparently, that segment had a profound affect on the child reading it, and Rumil supposed that shouldn't be terribly surprising. The promise of love and freedom would be very appealing to a child that clearly had not experienced enough of either.

"Maybe she will love me," Timothy finally remarked hopefully to himself. "What if I find her? Will she love me like no one else does?"

* * * * *

Rumil jerked out of the vision, and noticed that Timothy was supporting her weight after she had apparently fallen victim to the vision. It didn't seem like much time had passed, since Timothy didn't seem terribly concerned.

"Another vision?" he asked.

Rumil looked up at the Solarian from where he held her to him. Suddenly, she was very disturbed by his closeness. She squirmed out of his grasp, and muttered while trying to clear her head, "No... this isn't right..."

Now Timothy looked worried about her state. "What isn't right?" He tried to close the distance between them again, but Rumil pushed away, backing towards the sliding doorway. She had to get away, to sort things out.

"Stay away... I can't do this."

"You're not making any sense."

Rumil then scowled angrily at the Solarian, her head finally clear. "I won't have this, understand? You need to ask yourself just why you are here, and what you are doing this for. Are you interested in me because of who I am, or because of what you think I am?"

"Don't be silly..."

Rumil cut him off with a warning finger. "Ask yourself that question, and seriously try to answer it. I meant what I said. I will not be used by anyone. I don't want any blind devotion. You need to ask yourself just why you are willing to travel with me. If you are going to be with me, I want it to be because you want to be with me." Without giving Timothy a chance to reply, she retreated from the cabin, leaving Timothy alone to wonder just what had happened.

Rumil rushed semi-blindly through the halls, making a rather long path through the *Gallan* towards where Justin had taken up quarters. She had some questions that she felt only he could answer.

She didn't bother knocking or pressing the call on the door, and it wasn't locked since it slid open as she triggered the proximity sensor. However, Justin yelped in surprised as he emerged from the bathroom in only a towel, apparently having just emerged from a shower. He leaped back behind the door leading to the bath and stuck his head around the side. "Don't you ever signal before you come in?"

Rumil, unrepentant, countered, "Don't you ever lock your door?"

"It's called courtesy!"

Rumil waved off the accusation. "Fine. I'm sorry. Now, can we talk?"

"Can I get dressed first?"

"Sure."

Justin waited for a few demiticks, then asked, "Then… can you hand me my clothes… they're on the cot behind you."

"Oh!" Rumil blurted, now beginning to feel genuinely intrusive. That would explain why he was walking out of his bathroom nearly naked. She gathered the articles, a black bodysuit and carbide armor that Krennan had supplied the two former Knights with. Handing the items in question to the Justin's extended arm, Justin ducked into the bathroom, and slid the door closed.

From behind the door, Rumil heard Justin ask, "So… what did you wish to discuss?"

Rumil tried to conjure different ways to ask her question, and failing that finally said, "Does your wife love you?"

"I'd like to think so…" Justin quipped, "Although sometimes I wonder."

"Why do you think she loves you? Is it because she likes you, or because of your position?"

"I don't hold that position anymore, I'd wager."

"Justin, I'm serious. Does she love you, or your standing?"

Justin grunted softly, and she suspected he was just closing up the bodysuit. "Well, we were arranged to be married because of my anticipated position. I'll admit that we could barely stand each other at first." She heard snapping sounds as Justin was closing the clasps of his armor plates. "However, I suppose we didn't have much of a choice."

"That's just disgusting. How can you actually live with the fact that you're married to someone who doesn't even care about you as a person?"

Justin emerged from the restroom, fully armored save for the helmet still sitting on the cot. "Can I ask what my relationship with my wife has to do with anything?" Nary a demitick later he groaned. "What did Timothy do this time?"

Rumil scowled, and snorted derisively. "Just answer my question."

"Of course Julianne cares about our relationship. She didn't waste much time leaving Kiros."

"Her life was in danger," Rumil noted. "Why doesn't it bother you that your marriage was one of convenience, rather that one based on love?"

Justin seemed confused. "How are the two mutually exclusive? Of course Julianne and I were married to strengthen psionic ties and to keep it within the family so to speak. As for love, she certainly didn't have to follow Dewin. I would like to think she followed because she hoped I'd be there at the destination."

"Her life was in danger, what else was she supposed to do?" Rumil repeated, somewhat upset that Justin wasn't more upset himself. "You have no proof whatsoever that she cares at all about you. How can you actually live with that sort of arrangement?"

"Listen, I'm not talking about my wife anymore, especially since I don't think she's who you're really talking about either." Justin crossed his arms, and said, "I look at the way Timothy reacts to you, the effect you have on him, and I have a very hard time believing that he's only interested in what he believes you are. As for proof… well there is rarely proof where emotions are concerned. You can only trust they are sincere…"

"And therein lies the problem…" Rumil muttered.

"I take it trust is something you have issues with?"

Rumil scowled. "I haven't had many reasons to apply such a concept."

"Well, if I may, I can speak from some experience. In the course of our travels, I have put my life in Timothy's hands more than once, and I suspect I will do the same several more times before my time on this plane of existence is concluded. At any point, he could have used those situations to be rid of me. He had every reason to, after all. I was a Kiros, the enemy of his people. The animosity between our sects runs very deep. Yet, he never did. If he can earn the trust of one of his ancestral adversaries... why is it that he can't earn the trust of one who clearly cares for him?"

When Rumil didn't retort immediately, he stepped past her. "I suspect we will be reaching Ub soon. If you don't mind, I need to take my leave."

"Very well..." Rumil waved him away, deep in thought.

Justin realized that he had to make a small reminder. "Rumil... this is my cabin."

The blonde woman flushed as she remembered that fact. Not saying anything, she bit her lower lip, and strode quickly out the door, turning left toward her own cabin. Justin shook his head in bemused amazement. It was moments like these that he began to see the advantages of having everything planned in advance. Love had a way of complicating itself.

Chapter Seven

"Are you listening to a word I am telling you?" Timothy scowled as Orion staggered away, the Ubek clutching his forearm painfully. "All the strength in the galaxy won't help you if you are not disciplined. It doesn't matter if you have the strength of a hundred men if your actions require a hundred and one."

The pale blue humanoid growled in frustration. "The methods you practice are deceitful and borderline dishonorable. Battle is a test of strength, to prove the stronger warrior."

Timothy's derisive laugh could be heard completely on the other side of the cargo hold. "My methods work. And battle is more a test of knowledge and intuition then of strength. The smarter warrior will defeat the stronger warrior almost every time."

Orion grumbled at the statement, but acknowledged, "I shall submit to your wisdom. You have proven my better, and I should be honored that you have agreed to teach me."

If either of them were aware that Rumil was watching them from the upper catwalk on the other side of the cargo bay, neither of them showed it. However, she was quite certain that Timothy knew… he always knew.

"The first thing you must learn is patience, until you master that, I can't progress any further with you," Timothy said calmly. "For example, I'll be perfectly honest when I say nine out of every ten blows I deliver I send with no intention of striking."

Orion's eyebrows furrowed, as if the very concept was utterly foreign to him. "Then why deliver them at all?"

Timothy tilted his head, somewhat disdainfully. "There could be any number of reasons. For example, to keep your opponent on the defensive. If he or she is wasting time warding off your attacks, it's keeping him or her from attacking in turn. Or, you use such blows to determine the weaknesses in your opponent's defense."

"How do I do that?"

"You first need to learn patience. With that patience, you can begin to analyze the fight as it happens. From there, the discipline to best any foe will follow. Now, defend yourself," Timothy ordered, and launched on the attack with a flurry of blows.

Even as he was delivering punches and kicks, spins and flips, Timothy was offering tips and advice as calmly as if he were discussing the weather. "Remember, look for the opening, and when it is finally there, then make your attack. Remember the indicators I taught you."

It was almost amusing to watch a large, hulking Ubek nervously backing away from someone half his size, uncertainly blocking and pushing aside the blows being thrown as the lecture continued. "Your instincts are no doubt sharp, and they will rarely fail you, but a person in control of his own abilities that can actually see the battle, rather than just be in it, will overcome any instinctive reaction," Timothy advised as he threw four alternating punches that ranged from Orion's right shoulder to just missing the Ubek's kidney. "The key is balancing your instincts with your knowledge… something that comes with patience."

Timothy had just finished speaking when Orion made his strike, lashing forward with a haymaker that seemed far too fast to come from his large, lumbering frame. Though Timothy had been distracted by his own talking, he bent over backwards with the fluidity of water as the massive fist cleared his forehead within a hair's breadth, then he pivoted and kicked out with his left foot, connecting soundly with Orion's chest. The Ubek grunted as the air was forced out of his lungs, and he collapsed on his rump with a thud.

"Very good," Timothy then said approvingly. "Now get up. We'll try again. Remember to exercise patience, watch for your opening, and then be prepared to repeat if necessary. Sometimes your intended strike won't connect. You need to be ready for when that happens."

Rumil had never been a fan of sparring or fighting. She had always deemed herself too sophisticated for that sort of violent behavior. Now, as she watched Timothy teach what he knew, she came to understand that to the Solarian, combat was something just as intellectual and calculated as science, but with all the grace and artistry of theatrical dance. Even to her untrained eye, she could see the coordinated synergy in his form, every muscle contributing in some part to even a simple jab.

Transfixed, she leaned against the railing of the catwalk, and continued to peer down on the two combatants as Orion slowly began to understand the lessons Timothy was teaching. She wasn't sure how long she watched the session, but she realized it had to have been a long time, judging by the progress Orion had made by the time they were finished. She had to admire their stamina – Rumil could barely run a TackMet before completely losing breath, much less punch and kick and block and jump around for what must have been at least two tenth-cycles.

"Well done, Orion," Timothy complimented. "You're truly a fast learner… but you're nowhere near where you could be. Eventually, with practice and, of course, patience, what you must right now actively think through will become almost second nature. Or, as it was once explained to me, it will become instinct to analyze."

"When should I prepare to meet you again?" Orion asked respectfully.

"Well, I suspect Miss Bonamede's presence here likely means that your captain sent her to inform us that we will arrive at your homeworld shortly," Timothy declared without even so much as looking in Rumil's direction. "I sincerely hope that it wasn't urgent."

Rumil gulped in embarrassment then called down to the pair below, "He just wanted to make sure that you were aware of the briefing you were going to give us at 3.25 LT."

Still refusing to make eye contact with Rumil, Timothy said. "You can inform Dewin that I have not forgotten. Unless I miss my guess, I still have another two tenth-cycles and ten ticks before it is scheduled to begin."

How Timothy would know that without consulting a timepiece, Rumil couldn't guess, but quickly checking hers, attached by a small chain in the breast pocket of her shirt, she realized he was disturbingly accurate. "That's… right. Well, since you're already aware, I'll be going now."

Rumil turned away to make her retreat, and she heard Timothy say something in parting to Orion, although she wasn't certain exactly what was uttered. She heard a slight whoosh from below, and then Timothy levitated up to the catwalk, dropping down in front of Rumil, blocking her path.

"What?" she asked testily.

"I would like to know just what is wrong with you."

Rumil grit her teeth. "I've already told you what's wrong, and I have a hard time believing you've come to any realizations in as short a time as you've had."

"I still don't understand why my reasons must be mutually exclusive."

Rumil stomped her foot, and shouted, "They just have to, all right! I'm not a pawn, I'm not some prophet, and I'm certainly not going to have friends that care more about my 'abilities' than me!"

"I don't recall ever saying that."

"But you haven't denied it, either. And you can't, because you know it's true!" Rumil anger was being fueled by Timothy's apparent lack of it.

"I still am confused why my feelings and my duties cannot coexist."

"Because they can't! I won't have it!" she screamed, and then pushed the Solarian with all her might. "Now get out of my way!"

Which the Solarian did, in a sense. Rather than resist Rumil's push, he toppled over the edge of the catwalk. Initially startled, Rumil quickly leaned over the railing, only to see Timothy gently floating down to the floor of the cargo bay, his eyes burning holes through her, clearly perplexed. Once she realized he was perfectly safe and in control, as she ruefully reminded herself he always seemed to be, she regained her indignant anger. In a mixture of embarrassment and fury, Rumil stomped out of the cargo bay, and made great haste to her quarters.

Two tenth-cycles later, she assembled in the conference room of the *Gallan*, which was nothing more than the Captain's office that Dewin never used, annexed to the bridge. What would have been the Captain's desk was replaced with a small, circular table of dark wood that saw little maintenance, judging from the deep gouges in the finish. Dewin and Orion were on one side, with Justin on the other, with two chairs separating the pirates from the Kiros on each side. Rumil took a seat to Justin's left and remarked, "So, waiting for Timothy, I take it?"

"Yes," Justin answered.

With a sigh, Rumil replied, "Figures. The man's late for his own briefing."

Unfortunately, the door slid open just as she said that, and Timothy strode through in full armor, with a dual-mobile PCU under his arm. "Actually, I am perfectly on time." Seemingly unperturbed, Timothy took his position in between the two chairs separating Orion from Justin, gently nudging both seats aside.

"So, what's the plan, fearless leader?" Justin chirped playfully.

Dewin interjected, "First, perhaps it would be important to note that our sensors have detected a Solarian Dreadnought in orbit around Ub's primary moon. Needless to say, if you expect the *Gallan* to sit around in the same relative orbit with that thing, you're in for a terrible disappointment."

Justin's eyes bulged. Whereas the Kiros military strategy was based on large numbers of speedy fighters and frigates supported by larger cruisers, the Solarians decided on a quality over quantity approach, helped by their immense superiority in raw materials. The Dreadnought was an example of this stratagem: massive mobile battle stations, the Class-D Dreadnoughts reached twenty TackMets in diameter. They could deploy and repair smaller cruisers on site, and boasted a weapons arsenal that rivaled most Kiros fleets. While latest intelligence had placed the numbers of those vessels to be around thirty, all it would take was one to severely alter a combat scenario.

"I figured as much actually," Timothy answered, jarring Justin out of his own thoughts. "It makes sense, when you think about it. The Solarians can watch, dictate, and coordinate the Blueblood's actions from the Dreadnought while sitting far enough away to claim innocence, especially as there is normally one such vessel around Ub at any given time." Seeing Dewin's increasing discomfort, Timothy added, "Fear not, I'm certainly not going to pit the *Gallan* against one of those monstrosities. You're going to fold into the upper atmosphere above Ub's south pole, drop off a shuttle including Orion, Justin, Rumil, and myself, then get out before the Solarians can react. I suspect we'll have about ten demiticks before the Dreadnought could get any effective weapons lock on the *Gallan*, so we should have plenty of time."

"We've got ten demiticks?" Dewin groaned. "Good Graces of the Creator, I'll start working on the necessary drills." The pirate captain stood up and with a slight slump to his shoulders left to the bridge.

"What about us?" Rumil asked. "They'll be able to track the shuttle, won't they?"

Timothy nodded. "They could, but if they were to act directly on it, it would go contrary to their claim that they're not paying any attention to the Ceremony. On the other hand, they are no doubt tracking the *Gallan* just as the *Gallan* is tracking them, and could act on this cruiser if they had the chance."

"And if they decide to act directly?" Rumil prodded. "You've already said it was in the best interest of the Galactic Alliance to conveniently look away."

"It's called 'plausible deniability.' Since the Solarians have been covert so far, the Galactic Alliance could feign ignorance. Something more overt would not go nearly as well."

"All right… assuming we get to the surface untouched, then just what is the plan?"

Timothy set his tablet down on the table, and said, "We obviously can't oust the Solarians through numbers… that means we're going to have to be crafty. We'll use Orion to gain support of his sister's clan. Justin and I will join her main battle party to help balance the playing field, so to speak."

"I can't imagine the Solarians will have assigned any of their Knights to this Ceremony," Justin nodded in agreement.

"Ordinarily not. Knights are just as valuable as a commodity to the Solarians as they are to the Kiros, and thus won't be wasted where they're not normally needed. However, considering recent events, I wouldn't be surprised if a few are assigned just in case. Nothing we can't handle, right, Justin?"

"Easily," the Kiros replied confidently.

"And what about me?" Rumil queried.

Timothy grinned, but his voice didn't reflect the change in his expression. "I assume that in your years, you've become just as skilled at incapacitating computer systems as infiltrating them, right?"

Rumil nodded. "That would be a safe assumption, yes."

"Your job will be possibly the most important of everyone's. You will need to remove the advantage that Dreadnought will grant the Bluebloods." Timothy handed her the PCU he carried, and continued, "On that unit is the technical layout of the hardware and software of the Class-B Dreadnought, the class of that craft orbiting Ub's primary moon. It should give you what you need to know to remove their interference."

Rumil smiled like a teenager given the keys to the family hover. "Heh, if things fall properly, I could go one better, and use those computers to give us what they plan to give the Bluebloods."

"Well, that would merely be an added benefit, it certainly won't be required." Timothy checked the time, and said, "We don't have much time. If I'm correct, the *Gallan* will reach Ub in twenty ticks. You'll need to have a couple changes of clothes packed and at the shuttle bay in ten. Move quickly."

Timothy had been right. The moment they had stepped out of the conference room, Dewin informed them that they had roughly twenty ticks before they were within orbital distance of Ub. Rumil darted to her quarters, quickly threw the first two matching outfits she could find in her satchel along with her PCU, and dashed out the door towards the shuttle bay.

She stumbled as the door to the shuttle bay slid open, and she staggered, hopped, and bumbled forward trying to keep her balance. She eventually failed as she was a couple Tacks from the shuttle, and fortunately Timothy and Justin righted her before she met with the floor.

"Graceful as ever," Justin teased.

She cuffed the Kiros, not quite in a manner that would be deemed playful, and said, "I'll show you graceful…"

"Hurry and get inside, you two," Timothy ordered, releasing Rumil and jumping through the port side hatch of the shuttle. "Orion's going through the startup right now."

With one more insulted glare, Rumil hopped the steps into the shuttle, Justin casually climbing in right behind. Timothy had taken the co-pilot's chair, leaving Rumil and Justin to choose between the four remaining seats in the rear. Justin chose the one directly behind Orion, while Rumil sat behind the Kiros, much to Justin's chagrin. All four strapped in tightly, and waited for instructions.

The shuttle hummed, then shook gently as power flooded through the systems. From the comm system, Dewin voice said, "Five ticks until we leave foldspace. We're going to start opening the bay doors now, and I'll give you the mark to release the magnetic docking plates."

Timothy then advised Orion, "Make sure we have the proper atmospheric entry vectors. If we have to pull up, we likely won't get another chance. Even if you have to go to manual, we need to get on that planet."

"I've been piloting the shuttles on the *Gallan* for about ten staryears," Orion replied. "I know what I'm doing."

Timothy backed off, with a respective nod. "Of course. I shall submit to your wisdom."

The pair then shared a short, rather warmhearted laugh at the comment. Orion turned his attention back to the piloting console, and waited for Dewin's cue as the bay doors began to open. Meanwhile,

Orion ran through his preflight checklist one last time, for understandable reasons. One factor overlooked, and they'd be in for one short flight.

"Ready?" Dewin asked from over the communications relay.

"Do we really have a choice?" Rumil grumbled sourly. She found stupid questions such as those to be extremely annoying.

"Dropping out of foldspace in five demiticks..." Dewin declared, then began counting down. "Four... Three... Two... One... Now!"

Taking the mark, Orion disengaged the magnetic landing plates of the shuttle just as the Gallan dropped out of foldspace, the white of ice surrounding Ub's south magnetic pole filling the view from the open shuttle door. Orion then fired the shuttles engines, and it sprung forward with a lurch and groan of metal.

Once the shuttle cleared the *Gallan*, there was another twist of tension as the engines fought against the momentum of the now retreating cruiser. Rumil could feel the conflicting forces as they worked through her teeth, and she clenched them together to keep from biting the inside of her mouth. From there, the typical buffeting of atmospheric entry rocked the shuttle, until it finally lost enough speed through the retrorockets to comfortably cruise through the atmosphere. Timothy deployed the air wings, and Orion pulled the nose up to level its flight.

"Gee... rockets, wings, nose," Rumil teased. "Who would ever imagine it would be that simple?"

Justin nearly growled in response, "Be quiet..."

"The Dreadnought doesn't seem to be making any move, but I'll keep an eye on it," Timothy said to their Ubek pilot.

"Wait, I thought you said the Solarians wouldn't expose themselves like that!" Rumil protested.

"I did... but things could have changed since I've been gone," Timothy said with a passive shrug. "One can never truly know."

"You know, for a man who supposedly is ready to die before he sees me harmed, you don't seem to have any trouble putting me in the line of fire."

"I thought you said you didn't want me acting that way towards you anymore," was the Solarian's prompt retort. "I am merely acting in accordance to your wishes."

"Ah, how I enjoy lovers' quarrels..." Justin said wistfully, "at least, when they don't include me." He was then the recipient of a dual-pronged staredown from Solarian and Arcadian eyes. He cringed instinctively, trying to decide which glare was more threatening, as both were quite fearful in their own respective ways.

"You two are lovers?" Orion asked in surprise. "I never knew…"

"I can assure you that we are not," Timothy answered.

"Yes, we can't be," Rumil sneered. "Think of how untoward it would be to defile a precious prophet in such a fashion."

Timothy sighed in defeat, and had his hands not been occupied with the console, he probably would have thrown them up in exasperation. "For a woman who didn't want to discuss that anymore, you seem to have no problems bringing it up."

"Are there ear plugs anywhere on this shuttle?" Justin moaned, once again drawing the ire of the arguing couple.

"Fear not, Feroz. We shall be reaching our destination in about ten ticks," Orion said.

"That's one small relief," Justin replied, then said angrily, "Will you two stop looking at me like that? I'm serious, the both of you are arguing just like Julianne and I do."

With a pair of simultaneous, disparaging huffs, Timothy and Rumil stopped talking, and for Justin, he came to appreciate what his… adopted father… had come to say when Justin was younger: *There is no more a blissful sound than silence.* Unfortunately, both Timothy and Rumil picked up on that casual thought. With a groan, Justin slapped his forehead with his right hand as they once again glared angrily at him.

"This is going to be an adventure…"

* * * * *

Helga Salazar was really losing patience with her clan. Since the start of the staryear she'd been having the same dialogue every day, reminding her clansmen about the responsibilities they had to their clan, their caste, and to the upcoming Ceremony of War.

Granted, she had to admit they had a point. The Bluebloods had been victorious in every Ceremony since the chieftain Horduth led his clan to victory more than seven hundred staryears ago. The fact that it coincided rather suspiciously with the arrival of the Solarians, who were heavily supported by the Bluebloods, has led many clans to believe that the Solarians were helping the Bluebloods win, and making sure that the Pales, who at times supported open war with the fey-like humanoids, were always at the bottom of the caste ladder. Many Pales openly questioned why they bothered fighting at all, since the outcome was predetermined.

Nonetheless, it had never been proven. Granted, there were some accusations of Solarian weapons and even Solarian forces directly interfering during the Ceremony when it looked like a clan from a different caste was about to win, but none could be conclusively proven, as the Solarians were more than capable of covering their tracks. Not that it stopped continued accusations.

Regardless, how could she convince her clan to fight with all their heart and strength, when her own brother had grown so tired of the Blueblood dominance that he had actually left the planet entirely, vowing never to return until he could ensure that the Pales had an honest chance? Last she had heard, he was a pirate, and likely had moved on, giving up any hope for his people. Even her mother and father had surrendered to the dismal future of their clan, having taken her brother's self-imposed banishment quite hard. Since the Ubeks forbade suicide, except if taken prisoner in battle, her parents had merely chosen a different path that Helga thought was just as cowardly, striking each other down in a choreographed training session.

Thus, Helga was left to lead her hopeless clan, a haggard group that was defeated before it had even begun the battle. At one time, blood had been a powerful bond between Ubeks, and while it was still strong enough to keep her clan together, even the most optimistic were merely only apathetic. The cudgels and bracers were half-heartedly made, and Helga often had to force the smiths to prepare them properly. Training was kept to a bare minimum, and only when Helga demanded it through strict punishment. Perhaps the winner of the Ceremony of War was already set in stone, but she was not going to allow her clan to assist in the forgone conclusion.

In her more distressed moments, she figured her clan would not last beyond this coming Ceremony. Already half of the Pale clans were not even attending, and a good many more were teetering either way. From what she knew of the Halfblood caste, things weren't much better. Eventually, no one would challenge the Blueblood dominance, and the

Ceremony would probably fade into antiquity.

She was in danger of fading into one of those moments right then, when she heard a voice that, while not necessarily promising hope, indicated that something, somewhere, had changed.

"Sister… I am glad to see you are preparing for the Ceremony."

Helga turned about to see the imposing frame of her brother standing outside her thatch dwelling. "Orion?" she said with a hint of disbelief. "You're…"

"I am here. I have returned." Orion's form carried all the vitality, pride, and power that an Ubek was supposed to hold. "As I had said when I left, I would not return until I felt I could balance the scales of the Ceremony of War." He then took one step to the side, and turned his body so that Helga could see the three figures behind him. Two were clearly Erani – one Kiros, one Solarian – but clad in deep black bodysuits and carbide armor. The third was a blonde-haired Arcadian with a battered suede satchel draped over her right shoulder.

Orion then confidently declared, "It may not seem like much… but these three will give our clan the fairest chance since Horduth led the Bluebloods to dominance seven hundred and forty-seven staryears ago."

Chapter Eight

Helga had initially possessed doubts that three apparently mismatched souls would be able to actually balance out what many had suspected was large-scale interference on the part of the Solarian sect. However, as the days before the beginning of the Ceremony passed, she had to acknowledge there was more to the beings that Orion had brought with him then met the eye.

The Solarian – Timothy, as she recalled – was clearly a master of Solarian battle tactics, and an extremely capable warrior as well, felling every challenger of her clan who had sought to test his abilities.

Justin, the Kiros, was no slouch either, as he was more than a match for any Ubek that sparred with him, and also seemed very knowledgeable in the areas of general battle strategy. Then, when she learned that the pair were more than simple former military, but skilled Erani Knights, that was yet another benefit to her cause.

Of the Arcadian woman, Rumil, Helga was less certain. Timothy had claimed that her role in the upcoming Ceremony would likely be the most important of anyone's, but she hardly looked to have any combat prowess, or any other tangible skills that would turn the tide against the Bluebloods. All she had ever seemed to do the last two days was tap diligently on the PCU in her lap, regarding the display thoughtfully.

Helga finally confronted the Arcadian, trying to figure out just what the blonde woman offered to the effort, but encountered a mess of display panels and seemingly disjointed language that was simply far beyond the Ubek's capability to understand.

"I'm probing the various surveillance satellites and broadcast buoys to determine weaknesses in the Solarians' computer network," Rumil then chuckled happily, "and I think I just might have found something…"

Rumil began typing again, and a small command prompt in a panel on the lower right corner of the display flashed with text. Three more incomprehensible lines followed, then the entire display flashed with an image of what appeared to be an overhead view of a scene that struck Helga as slightly familiar.

"What is that?" she asked, pointing at the screen.

Rumil smirked, and replied, "That's your camp."

Looking at it again, Helga decided that would be why it struck her as familiar. She was looking down at the thatch cabins built in tradition to the terms of the Ceremony of War, and could even see the movement of people around the camp in their duties, including two vague figures close together, the larger figure leaning over the smaller one, pointing at something in the smaller figure's lap.

"And that is… us?" Helga asked, pointing at the blurry image.

Rumil nodded. "Most likely. I could probably zoom in and clarify the image, but I'd rather not tip off our Solarian friends by playing with their equipment. I'll save that for the big day."

"So… how exactly will this help us?"

"Well, Timothy suspects that the Bluebloods are using satellites like these to discern the position and movement of their opponents. The advantage in that is enormous, as the Bluebloods can then coordinate their own tactics more effectively, or set ambushes and the like. It probably helps the Solarians decide just when and where to put their own forces for optimal deployment. At worst, I could at least block that transfer of information. At best, I could commandeer the Solarians' own equipment, and turn it against them."

"That seems awfully contrary to the spirit of the Ceremony," Helga said disapprovingly.

Rumil shrugged, and said slyly, "That hasn't been stopping the Bluebloods. If you really want to fight on an equal footing with them, you're going to have to be willing to do things that might not be what you deem honorable."

While Helga clearly wasn't happy with the concept, she was able to see the wisdom in it. "At one time, the Ceremony of War was an honest exhibition between castes for the betterment of the Ubeks as a whole. Now, it's seeped in deceit, shadows, politics, and modern warfare."

"I don't make the rules, I just play by them," the Arcadian woman said with another shrug. "What else can I do?"

"How goes the preliminaries, Rumil?" Timothy then asked from behind them.

Rumil twitched in surprise then cried out in pain when Helga, equally surprised, had instinctively clenched the Arcadian's shoulder. The Ubek woman apologized sheepishly, and stepped away, while Rumil rubbed the injury with her hand. "Think you can be a little quieter next time, Timothy? I couldn't hear the grass grow."

"It just comes naturally," Timothy answered with a smirk, "but I can certainly try to sneak up on you if you'd prefer."

Rumil scowled at the Solarian before turning back to business at hand. "Well, I've found a way to hack into the Solarian surveillance. Judging from the schematics you gave me, it should be a simple task to leapfrog from there into the Dreadnought's main computers. Once in there…" she grinned evilly, and rubbed her hands in anticipation, leaving the rest of the sentence unsaid.

It was probably fortunate she did, because Timothy would have interrupted her. His head snapped to the west, and he said, "We've got company, likely Bluebloods."

Helga followed Timothy's line of sight, but saw nothing. "How do you know this?"

"I can sense the psionic presence of a Solarian Knight. He'd only be here under the escort of Bluebloods," Timothy said. "I've informed Justin, he'll keep himself out of sight. You and I have to hide out for a bit as well. I'd rather not declare my presence here until absolutely necessary."

Rather than argue, Rumil consented to the Solarian's judgment and followed him into the nearest cabin, Timothy shutting the door behind them once she was inside. Sure enough, almost a tick later, she heard a large hover approaching. Curiosity getting a hold, she moved towards the window, but Timothy quickly pulled her away, back towards the center of the cabin.

Meanwhile, Helga confronted the visitors outside. Timothy had been right; they were Bluebloods accompanied by a figure in the brown carbide armor of a Solarian. However, these weren't just any normal Bluebloods, but the crown General of the current Ubek Grand General, with an escort.

"General Grodin," Helga said with as little venom as she could manage. "What brings such a noble Ubek to my battle camp? This is highly irregular and against traditions long held, even for the Utmost Caste."

Grodin laughed bitterly. "Let me assure you, I am not here to steal your plans. I am here to escort this investigator from the Solarians."

The Solarian then spoke with a light voice that Helga could both barely hear and yet could understand clearly. "I am Emmitt Fransisca, Commandant of the Solarian Knighthood. We detected a shuttle of Arcadian manufacture landing nearby, and were concerned of its occupants. We wouldn't want anything disturbing the upcoming Ceremony of War, after all."

"Of course not," Helga agreed, her tone of voice implying just how little faith she held in the Solarian's words.

"So then, who was in the shuttle that landed here?"

Approaching from the other side of the camp, Orion strode with all the speed his walk could carry. "That would be my shuttle."

Even with Orion's stature, he actually found he had to stare up at Grodin, who instantly recognized the newcomer. "Orion Salazar... so the wayward son returns," the Blueblood declared haughtily.

"I couldn't miss the Ceremony of War, could I?" Orion replied slyly.

Grodin's expression was equal to Orion's. "Funny... since that is exactly what I expected you to do. I certainly hope you don't expect to lead your clan... that would be terribly crude on such short notice, especially since your absence shows dire negligence to your people, and would never be accepted."

"I have no intention of leading the Salazars," Orion answered with a growl. "My sister has earned that right. However, I will take part as part of her battle clan."

"Very well. Perhaps it is best, since clearly your sister has shown greater strength in her resolve."

Helga was genuinely surprised when her brother did not rise to Grodin's continued baiting. Clearly, the training Helga had witnessed Timothy giving Orion had more of an effect on him than just his fighting skill. Rather than return the insult, he only assured, "You best pray to Ogath that we do not cross on the field tomorrow. Now might not be the time to break you like a cheap toy... but believe that I will not rest until I have done so."

"We shall see, won't we?" Grodin said dismissively, then with an aside to the Knight next to him, asked, "Are you satisfied?"

Reluctantly, Emmitt answered, "I suppose I am. I do have to return to Solaria as well. If you are comfortable with this investigation coming to a conclusion, I certainly won't complain." Nevertheless, his posture and eyes reflected a man who knew he was leaving something unfinished.

"I am more than comfortable," Grodin announced. "As a matter of fact, I am looking forward to tomorrow."

"You're not the only one," Helga added, not wanting to remain silent.

"Very well. Rather than extending long farewells or parting threats, perhaps we should just go," Emmitt said. "I wish you all the best for tomorrow." The Solarian Knight bowed, and strode away, stopping to glare at Grodin, who clearly was not moving fast enough for his taste. With one last growl, the Blueblood stomped off after Emmitt, climbed into the hover, and made all possible speed away from the camp.

Helga and Orion shared a sigh of relief, then both turned to Rumil and Timothy as the pair emerged outside again. Timothy looked more bemused than anything, then said, "Commandant, are you now, Fransisca? Quite a promotion for a man who was so uncertain of his future."

"I assume that is a position of some prestige?" Rumil asked.

"It was my position. It signifies the successor to the position of High Commander," Timothy said matter-of-factly.

"Oh," Rumil replied. She had never heard Timothy use the title even once, and perhaps that said something about the two Knights respectively. She had to admit, from what she had now heard, that Emmitt Fransisca did seem different somehow, just in his voice. Perhaps it was the confidence that came with his new position… or perhaps it had always been there, hidden under an uncertain façade. Something twitched in the back of her head, suggesting it was more likely the latter than the former.

"Well, I need to prepare for the ceremonial fire," Helga said with a sigh. "I just hope the Ceremony lives up to everything before it so far."

* * * * *

The following night was one of nervous anticipation, and even Rumil, who felt no real connection to the upcoming event, found it hard to sleep from the adrenaline that seemed to be radiating off everyone around her.

It seemed like she had barely set her head down on the pillow when Timothy was standing over her, throwing open the curtains of her cabin, sending the pre-dawn light of Ubek's sun into the small enclosure. As she sat up groggily, she noticed that he was holding two steaming cups of ducha. "Is one of them for me?" she said, motioning towards his hands.

Timothy gulped once, his eyes darting about nervously. "Y… Yes."

In all her time spent with the Solarian, she had never seen him stumble on a word so simple. However, in her still awakening state, the fact didn't grab hold as it normally would. "Then may I have it?"

He must have taken a few steps back when she sat up, because he nervously shuffled forward the equivalent of two strides, and leaned forward to hand her a cup. He quickly snatched his hand away once she grabbed the mug, and nearly jumped away again. He shuffled on his feet, his head moving to the side, and occasionally snapping forward as if his neck was fighting with himself.

"What is wrong with you?" Rumil demanded testily as she took her first sip. A small rivulet escaped her lips, and dripped down her chin. Wiping the hot liquid from her face, she noticed what must have been the problem. When she had sat up, the blanket she had covered herself with fell to her waist. She didn't see how it was that big of a deal however, as she was wearing a very functional and unflattering black undergarment over her breasts. She was hardly what she would consider indecent. "Oh, please…" she finally drawled grumpily after taking another sip of ducha. "You've seen me in precious little more before."

"But that… was different," Timothy managed to say, finally succeeding in turning his back completely to her. Even then, if his neck were able to contort fully backwards, she suspected it probably would.

"Because it was in front of two hundred people? Or is it because you were on a mission?" she queried. "I think you aren't nearly as free from your old traditional upbringing as you may think." She smirked triumphantly, glad to know that she could still have some effect on Timothy. She might not know exactly what his reasons were for following her, but he wouldn't be glancing at her so nervously if his reasons were simply theological.

"I just wanted to inform you that the Ceremony begins once the sun has completely cleared the horizon," Timothy said, regaining composure now that he wasn't looking at Rumil. "I'm not terribly sure how many preparations you need, so I felt it prudent to wake you now."

Rumil paused with her reply only to take another sip. "I thank you." She then took on an almost predatory look when she said, almost flirtingly, "I suppose I should get dressed now. Are you going to leave, or do you intend to watch?"

Timothy visibly cringed, and even though she couldn't see his face, she knew he was blushing. She could see even see a reddish tinge forming on his hands. He rapidly shook his head, and said, "That probably wouldn't be prudent. As a matter of fact, I probably have been lingering too long as it is for common decency's sake."

He waved in parting, and hastily left the cabin. With a relaxed sigh, she finished her ducha, tossed her blanket completely aside, placed her mug on the floor, and climbed out of her cot, moving across the cabin to where the clothes she had washed yesterday – by hand, at that – now hung dry on the wire that had been strung across the west wall. They were still somewhat damp as she plucked the various articles off the wire and began dressing for the day, but resolved to live with the slight discomfort for the time being. They would finish drying quickly enough.

When she emerged, Timothy was waiting just outside the cabin. As she suspected, being fully clothed calmed him immensely. She looked around the empty camp, and asked, "Where's everyone else?"

"Helga's clan has already begun the march to the field. The field consecrated for the Ceremony of War is well over ten TackMets away, and is usually two hundred TackMets square," Timothy explained. "As for Justin, he's over there."

Rumil followed Timothy's point towards the south end of the encampment. To her surprise, she must have overlooked him the first time she had looked about, since he was clearly in her vision once pointed out to her. He was sitting cross-legged with his back to her, his head bowed deeply to the ground, and his arms bracing his body from falling forward.

Timothy grabbed her arm insistently as she was about to call out to the Kiros. "I would recommend you not disturb him. It takes a great deal of time to do what he's doing, and I doubt he'd appreciate having to start over."

"What is he doing, if I may be so bold?" she asked a couple demiticks later.

"The Nerean Trance," Timothy replied, then realizing that probably wouldn't help much, added, "During the time of the Third Prophet, Groel, there was a bit of a civil war among the Erani. At that time, a Knight by the name of Hendrick Nerean discovered an underlying subconscious state in the psyche of the Erani people. This state removes the natural inhibitions inherent in the rational mind, making whomever is in the trance all the more effective as a warrior. The Nerean Trance has been taught to Knights of both sects ever since. Its only downside is that the meditation required to reach this state can take over a tenth-cycle or longer… thus it's really only effective when you know battle is coming well ahead of time."

"Oh," Rumil remarked, then queried, "Why aren't you joining him?"

Timothy frowned, and replied with an irked tint, "Because I'd rather not give my subconscious any more control than it already has."

Rumil accepted that reason easily enough. She had seen what happened when Timothy got especially angry, and if that was any indicator of what he'd be like in that Nerean Trance, she could fully understand why he'd shun the practice.

"By the way," Timothy said in warning, "when Justin comes out of his meditation, you may notice certain aspects of his personality will be… off. I can't be much more specific because the Nerean Trance affects each Erani differently. I can only say that he might not react to the same things in the same way he usually does… just to warn you ahead of time."

Rumil nodded, but said nothing further. She then took her place on the bench that she had commandeered for her workspace, and opened up her satchel while checking the rising sun to see how much time she had. Pulling out her PCU, she opened it and began plugging in her virtual interface. "So… what are you two still doing here? I figured you'd be with the battle party."

"We're going to wait until we see just how much information you can steal from the Solarians. If you can locate the forces that they're using, then I can bring the fight to them while Justin keeps an eye out for Helga. If not, then we'll take our place scouting for Helga's party."

"I see," Rumil stated, rather agreeing with the strategy. Most Arcadians followed the business philosophy of striking at your competitors before they could strike at you, a philosophy that Rumil agreed with in most circumstances. She once again turned her attention to the sun, wanting to time her attempt so that she hacked the Solarians systems just as the Ceremony started, giving them as little time as possible to react if she was discovered.

Finally, Justin stirred, slowly moving to his feet in one fluid, silent motion. He turned towards Timothy and Rumil, and for several eerie moments did nothing but look in their direction, as if he almost didn't recognize them at first. Then, with slow, deliberate movements, the Kiros closed the distance in a way that Rumil could only describe as… creepy. He said nothing in greeting, nor made any motion to acknowledge he was at all amiable towards them. When Timothy had said Justin might be different, he hadn't been joking.

It wasn't until Justin was literally face to face with Timothy that the Kiros said anything at all. Even then, the lighthearted tone was gone from his voice, replaced by an almost monotonous drone. Not the emotionless tone Timothy normally favored; that at least that had some substance. This was… empty.

"Are we ready to move?" The Kiros asked blandly. Rumil noticed the lively twinkle in Justin's eyes were gone. It was dark, blank, and cold rather than the energy that normally came when Justin so much as looked at anyone.

"We're waiting for the Ceremony to start," Timothy explained. "If Rumil can steal as much information as she claims, I think I'll take the fight to any Solarians, and you can scout for Helga and the Salazar clan."

Justin nodded, apparently accepting the strategy. "Makes sense. You'd be more familiar with the people you'd be attacking. You'd be the best to know the weaknesses you could exploit."

Normally, the following silence Justin would break with some lighthearted quip. However, such comedic relief was not to be forthcoming from the Kiros this time, and Timothy appeared to be quite comfortable with the uneasy quiet, nor was Rumil going to be the one to open her mouth, especially since her attention was focused on watching the sun that was now moments away from clearing the horizon completely.

Apparently, 'full sunrise' meant different things for different races. From the distance, the low, haunting melody of an Ubek battle horn floated into the camp, faintly sounding through the abandoned buildings. Despite never hearing such a sound before, Rumil instantly knew what it meant: the Ceremony of War had begun.

Rumil cursed, and quickly pulled the visor of her virtual interface snugly over her head, plunging her senses into the computerized world. She didn't even wait for the mesh grid to fully form, zipping along the connection represented by a belt conveyor rippling with yellow light.

She followed the connector to the Solarian satellite array, which appeared as a series of computer monitors. Quickly assessing to see what hidden protections were being used, she was not terribly surprised to discover the encryptions were rather simple. After all, they probably weren't expecting someone to be hacking into the array. Nonetheless, she disabled the trap warily. Computer programmers were wily sorts, often laying out one trap simply to lure a potential hacker into another.

Warping another of the security grids that manifested itself as a wire mesh along the room she was in, Rumil finally cleared a large enough space for her to slip through without breaking the grid. She slowly approached one of the monitors, which might as well have been in orbit above the other side of the planet from what she needed, neither did the next three monitors yield the desired result. She had figured that the Solarians would have turned several satellites onto the Ceremony, but she hadn't come across any of them so far. The fifth monitor was focused not on the battle, but on the battle party led by Grodin, and thus didn't provide what she was looking for. Clearly, the Solarians had decided him to be the winner.

Fortunately, the sixth had the information she sought. It was a direct motion satellite that recorded information in real time and in real video. It was even zoomed into precisely the aperture she wanted as well, showing the entire battlefield, with flags of different colors signifying the different battle parties. Judging from what she knew of Helga's position on the field, it seemed safe to assume that Blueblood parties were in deep blue, Halfbloods were likely the gray flags, and the Pales were white.

She opened a communications channel, and contacted Timothy, who was likely still waiting for instructions. "I'm in, and I've found a satellite feed that will serve our purposes nicely. I trust you still have the landscape stills of the battleground?"

"Yes," Timothy answered.

"All right… keep your PCU open, and connect to feed channel 661-330A. It'll give you the information from this satellite. That should be everything you need."

There was a short delay, likely as Timothy did as instructed. He then said, "It's coming through… good, very good indeed."

"Now, can I get to have my fun?" she asked.

"Yes, you may. Don't get into more trouble than you can handle."

"Yes, daddy." With that parting, Rumil ended the communication, and smiled. In her previous exploits, her actions required more infiltration than mass sabotage. She was actually looking forward to the change.

Pushing with her index finger in front of her, a yellow-lined cabinet door appeared. Opening it, she picked out an assortment of small vials representing some viruses she had been cooking the last few cycles, a scissored cutting tool for software links, a data decoder for areas that would be secured via passwords, and a large, two-handed axe… just in case her other weapons proved… inadequate.

With her new acquisitions, Rumil located the conveyor that connected the satellite array to the Dreadnought's computer systems. She whistled absentmindedly as she moved along the line, reminding herself to keep an eye out for more detection tools. One couldn't be too careful after all.

Back in the real world, Timothy glanced one last time at Rumil as she flailed about, her body mimicking the actions of her avatar inside the interface. In truth, he was worried that something would happen while she was playing at mass destruction. The computing scientists the Solarians had were no slouches by any means, and surely more than a few handfuls of such expert programmers were aboard the Dreadnought. He knew it was possible to severely harm someone physically through a virtual interface, and had little doubt that the Solarians would use such measures if she was discovered.

Fortunately for his sanity, actions on the battlefield began to draw his attention. Seven brown flags appeared on the satellite feed of his PCU, telling Timothy that the first group of Solarian military had reported in and were ready to make their move. Making a personal red note mark on the flag that Timothy knew represented Helga's battle party, he quickly determined which Solarian team presented the most immediate threat, and called up the landscape image that corresponded nearest to that team. Timothy slid the PCU into a holster on his belt, put on his helmet, and teleported into battle.

Upon appearing at his location, he quickly dropped to a prone position, and switched his visor to magnification to scout out his adversaries. The first thing he noticed was that these units weren't typical military, as he had suspected. From the unit patch on the shoulders of their armor, a black skull upon a light brown diamond background, he identified them as belonging to the Phantom Regiment, the covert operations specialists of the Solarian Military. No doubt the Ceremony of War would be a nice way to keep their skills sharp, serving as a real field application of the troops.

There were only twenty of them to this team, but then again, twenty would be all the Solarians normally needed in this case. The Phantoms' combat tactics generally involved quick strikes followed by quick retreats, taking a little bit at a time. Since their task was likely to whittle down their opponents rather than outright defeat them, smaller combat teams served the purpose more effectively.

Making a tight, faint psionic communication to Justin while maintaining his own cover, he informed the Kiros of his discovery. *Be careful, Feroz. We're dealing with the Phantoms. Keep your shields up and your senses sharp. There could be a lot more than have reported in, and they can come out of hiding anywhere. Just because they aren't Knights, doesn't mean they aren't dangerous.*

Acknowledged, Justin answered simply, and Timothy didn't sense any further attempts at communication. Thus, the Solarian turned his attention back towards the team, which was now beginning to move.

Timothy had heard it said that one Knight, with his psionic abilities, could have the same worth in battle as a thousand mundane units. That axiom was about to come to the test. He weighed his options for a moment, then decided to just have it out, right in the open. Even if he were to remove them stealthily, the Solarians would react the same, and logically conclude who was responsible. After all, there aren't many people in the galaxy who could take out twenty Phantoms without being detected, and those others would no doubt be accounted for.

So, without further hesitation, he stood up and waved, instantly drawing the attention of his opposition. "Fair warning, I'll kill if I have to. If you don't want to face death, I suggest you lay down your arms right now."

Seventeen plasma bolts were his reply. Sixteen of them would have been extremely painful and ten possibly even deadly, had they not been deflected harmlessly by Timothy's psionic shield. As he had suspected, the team instantly knew who he was, and the danger he posed, judging from their rushed communications back to their base of operations.

118

Timothy shrugged, and said, "Suit yourself." With a flash, he teleported into the center of the team, and despite the knowledge they had to have in regards to the abilities of a Solarian Knight, they were clearly taken off-guard as he engaged the specialist team with no prejudice or restraint.

Nonetheless, he reminded himself to be careful, as he drew his sword and cleanly severed the head of the nearest Phantom. The momentum of his slash spun him in position to take his pistol and fire two shots into the chest of a second. The soldier's carbide held against the shots, but not from the sword thrust that followed. The blade's hypersteel point punctured the armor plate, splitting the heart in half.

Realizing that their plasma rifles were useless against the psionic protections Timothy had placed around himself, seven of the remaining team pulled their combat knives from sheaths at their thighs, and the other eleven fell into retreat, likely to regroup with other forces in the area.

Timothy didn't worry much about that, or how many they brought next time. Nonetheless, he had to finish the skirmish quickly so that he could move on to his next objective. As the Phantoms circled him, Timothy sheathed his weapons, dropped his shielding, and focused his energy into one burst of psionic power.

Brilliant while balls of energy burst from his outstretched hands, quickly spiraling into their targets, hitting the circling Phantoms with concussive force. Each ball struck like a hydraulic hammer, crushing bones and ripping muscle before burning through flesh. One unfortunate soldier was struck by three such speeding orbs, the first tearing his right leg off just above the knee. The second slammed into his abdomen, splintering the plating of his armor before pulverizing his innards into a bloody jelly and burning completely through the back. The third connected right between his eyes, popping the optical nerves clean out of their sockets as it crushed bone and brain matter into a messy paste.

When the bolts finally fizzled, only Timothy remained, his breath not even the least bit affected by the exertion. He scanned the bodies, the smell of burnt and broken bodies filling his nostrils. He forced himself to look away, demanded his rebelling mind to focus on his purpose. He couldn't lose control of himself again… he was considerably stronger than he was just those scant staryears back on Canasa. If his emotions got the better of him, there was no telling what he would do.

He drew his PCU from his belt and acquired the data to his next destination, deciding to cut off the reinforcements the rest of the Phantom team appeared to be retreating towards.

* * * * *

Justin growled as he had to double back because he noticed that Helga's battle party had stopped. They had taken up a position along a forest ridge, and appeared to be making a splint for a fallen member of the clan.

"What happened?" Justin asked, clearly impatient.

"He fell into a sinkhole, and broke his leg," Orion replied, apparently serving as a lookout while the first aid was being applied. "Once the splint is set, he'll be escorted back to the camp."

"Or I can just teleport him there, save your team time and manpower."

"Absolutely not," Helga interjected, turning away from her injured clansman. "You and your friends are here only to balance the Ceremony, not to give us an unfair advantage."

"An advantage that I suspect the Solarians are already giving the Bluebloods."

Helga stood and tromped angrily to Justin, staring down in fury at the much smaller Kiros. "You just don't understand, do you? If we, the Pale *Ubeks*, are to win the Ceremony of War, it will be because *we* won it. I will not be the patsy of you or your little group, like the Bluebloods have sold themselves to the Solarians."

With a frustrated shrug, Justin turned about. "Fine. If I am not needed, I will return to scouting. Timothy should be able to keep the Solarians occupied, but the longer we sit idle, the more likely another party could catch you unawares."

"I thought you were supposed to be able to know where they all were," Orion said.

"I do," Justin said, glancing down at his belt where he was receiving the satellite feed of the battlefield, "but your leader doesn't apparently want me interfering in Ubek affairs. If a Blueblood or Halfblood clan comes upon you, I won't try stopping them or warning you."

Orion nodded. "Perhaps that is for the best. Let us try to win this on as fair of terms as you can manage."

Once again, the Kiros shrugged passively. "Whatever you want. You Ubeks just better not lose."

Without further comment or reply, Justin retreated into the forest, checking his PCU again to see if any more Solarians had popped up. There hadn't yet, but Timothy warned him that the forces that had been sent could be very sneaky. Nonetheless, the more immediate concern was a Blueblood party that was moving in on Helga's clan quickly, clearly already knowing where the team was.

With another frustrated grunt, Justin kept watching the display. He had not expected his role in all this to be so… boring. Judging from all the brown flags converging in the southwest corner of the battlefield about five TackMets from his position, the Solarians were clearly pouring all their resources into removing Timothy as a threat. Added to Helga's refusal of his aid against anyone else… what was there for him to do?

About five ticks later, he heard the battle cries of several Ubeks nearby and consulted his satellite display to confirm that the Blueblood battle party had moved in on Helga's clan. He silently dashed back to the ridge of the grove to check in on them. Despite Helga's wishes, if it looked like her squad was about to lose, Justin was going to step in. Too much was riding on their success for him not to.

Fortunately, once he reached the forest's edge, he was able to discern that Helga and her party were well in hand of the situation. As a matter of fact, the Bluebloods they were fighting looked increasingly confused and lost the longer the skirmish dragged on. Within ticks, fatigue was clearly setting onto the Bluebloods, and Justin could see the beginnings of a rather brutal rout about to occur. Clearly, these Bluebloods had assumed that the Solarians would be providing a great deal of assistance, and thus hadn't trained or prepared properly for the Ceremony. Already, he counted at least four Blueblood injuries that would not have occurred with proper conditioning.

It didn't take much longer for the considerably larger Blueblood battle party to be completely incapacitated. Justin was rather surprised when the defeated Ubeks dejectedly accepted the bright red paint markings on their chests that marked them as eliminated from the contest, as he had expected a more belligerent disbelief. Perhaps they were in shock, the reality of their defeat not yet sunken in.

Helga's party gave a loud raucous cry of victory, then jeered the defeated Bluebloods as the deep-skinned Ubeks marched towards the boundaries of the battlefield. Deciding he had nothing better to do, Justin decided to follow the losing party, just to ensure they didn't try anything duplicitous like having the marks removed and re-entering combat.

Emerging onto the clearing, he worked his way to Orion's side. "I'm going to tail those Bluebloods for a little bit to make sure they leave the battlefield." He handed the massive Pale Ubek a comm unit, and said, "Just in case you get attacked by any Solarians, contact me, and form a mental picture of your surroundings." Orion nodded in acceptance, and Justin asked Helga, "If those Bluebloods do try to re-enter the Ceremony of War, then am I granted permission to engage them?"

Helga nodded. "They will then be in violation of the rules of the Ceremony, and would therefore be beyond any moral objections on my part. If you think you'd be able to best that many Ubeks, then be my guest."

With a curt bow, Justin began his pursuit of the defeated Bluebloods, keeping enough distance so as not to be heard, and fashioning a psionic illusion to camouflage himself. Interestingly enough, the moment he began using his mental powers, he felt another psionic aura flare up, not even two TackMets from his position.

I assume you want to be found? Justin queried to the unknown presence.

How else would I have gotten your attention? came the rejoinder. *Now that I have done so, why don't you come meet me? I really dislike having conversations with people I can't see.*

Justin probed for any sense of deceit, and found a considerable amount, though none of it pertained to him or any pending meetings. Nonetheless, a mind as definitely well-trained as the unknown man's would have many mental shields as well.

Had I planned a trap for you, do you think I would have exposed my position to you? the unknown voice asked. *You clearly weren't expecting a Knight on Ub, and you clearly weren't looking for me. It wouldn't have been difficult to use that element of surprise.*

Justin had to concede that point, albeit reluctantly. He shouldn't have been so careless, especially since the man's aura was the same as the Knight's who had come to Helga's camp just the day before.

Are you coming? Oh... I do suppose you would need an image of where I am, wouldn't you? the unknown Knight assumed.

I'd rather handle it myself, Justin declined. *I have teleportation images of my own.*

The Knight sighed. *Very well… just don't take too long. I'd like to finish our meeting before the Ceremony ends.*

Of that, Justin could readily agree.

* * * * *

Another snip, another connection severed.

Rumil giggled gleefully as she very nearly skipped over to the next console connector, manifested by a series of wires along the corridor she was in. She didn't fear much for reprisal, as the technicians on the Dreadnought were probably spending the majority of their energy trying to restore the power grid she had locked up in the lower port section. By the time they got that up and running again, they would notice what she was doing now; severing network connections maintaining the hydroponics bay.

Another snip, another connection severed.

With each cut she made, she emptied part of the viral containers onto the severed links. Once some hapless fool reconnected the network, the virus would flood the entire Dreadnought, causing a bevy of power shortages and memory corruptions. A best case scenario would involve a reboot of the entire Dreadnought's computer systems, costing them valuable time and effort.

With that job done, she moved on to the big task: breaking the satellite uplink to the Dreadnought, thus cutting off their surveillance and ability to direct the Solarian and Blueblood forces on the planet's surface. She jumped back onto the conveyor, which was actually nothing more than the computerized director, and worked her way to her destination.

It stopped right at the uplink station, and Rumil hopped off cheerfully. The uplink station took the form of a high-domed enclosed room, empty save for a large steel-colored box about a Tack on each side floating in the center, with about thirty large cables of a rainbow collection of colors connected to it.

Unfortunately, she realized that a few others, five in fact, were invited to the party when their avatars flashed into existence, imposing themselves between her and the satellite uplink. This was not at all a part of the plan.

Before she could react, she was trapped in a neon green web mesh, the virtual equivalent of a forced system lock. She fell to the floor roughly, squirming ineffectively to get to the tools at her belt. With each motion, the web tightened, trapping her even further until she stopped her struggles. These Solarians knew what they were doing.

The five computer techs approached their bound quarry, and one of them knelt down in front of her, injecting her in the shoulder with a needle. From there, another bright green line shot from her position, and disappeared down the conveyor. Rumil cursed to herself, recognizing the trace command for what it was. The tech then stood, conversed with his colleagues, and then jumped on the conveyor to locate Rumil's physical position.

Of course, that was the least of Rumil's concerns as the remaining four began their interrogation. A line of five adhesive patches resembling electrical diodes were slapped roughly on her forehead, and finally one of the technicians, probably the senior officer, crouched down to look at her face. The man's smooth Solarian features suggested he was still rather young, with a short crop of brown hair and soft gray eyes, and while normally an avatar's appearance didn't mean much to the real person, something told Rumil what she saw before her was an accurate depiction of his physical form.

"I see that you have an avatar matching wanted hacker Rumil Bonamede. Would I be correct in assuming that is who you are?"

"Why ask me a question that you're going to know the answer to soon enough?" That statement was perfectly true. Once the tech tracing her worked his way through Rumil's path to her host computing unit, he'd be able to confirm all the details.

Her reward for that answer was a nasty shock which rippled through her body. "While that may be true, I will be the one asking questions, understand?" The tech officer said almost mockingly.

Rumil glared, but didn't reply.

Pressing on into the interrogation, the officer asked demandingly, "What is your purpose?"

"Now you're asking questions you already know the answer to."

Another shock blasted through her forehead, zipping down her spine, making her toes curl painfully. "Any more snide comments, and I up the Toules, understand?" Taking a deep breath, his attitude calmed again. "Then let's move onto a question I don't know. Who sent you?"

"You assume I'm doing this under anyone's orders."

Rumil was shocked again, and true to the officer's word, it sure felt like there was significantly more energy coursing through her body. Her jaw locked from the electric stimulus, as well as her limbs convulsing painfully.

"I'm not going to keep playing," the tech officer warned. "Tell us who sent you, or we'll have Knight Fransisca rip it out of your skull."

"Sir... Knight Fransisca left about two tenth-cycles ago," one of the subordinates reminded.

"When did you find this out?"

"Just now. I tried to comm him, and he said he was taking care of business on the surface. Perhaps it has something to do with this lady here."

The officer then asked, "Jensen, have you traced the source of this hacker yet?"

"I've discerned she's on the surface, and jumped here through a wireless connection into our satellite array," a disembodied voice answered. "From what I saw, it looks like she wreaked havoc on the systems in the hydroponics bay. I put some of our enlisted techs to repair it."

Apparently Rumil wasn't able to completely hide her triumphant smile, as the officer saw it and called out a warning. However, the warning came too late. There was a slight flicker in the virtual grid, then she noticed that the avatars of her captors were also starting to decompile, as well as the netting keeping her in place.

The virus infected the system rapidly, and the netting around Rumil vanished after flickering dimly twice, followed by the prompt departure of her opponents just as the virtual world around her vanished, bathing her in blackness. The grid was promptly brought back up as Rumil's computer restored her surroundings, since her computing unit had protections against the virus she had let loose. However, the Solarians wouldn't be so lucky. They'd have to reboot, then likely run diagnostic scans to make sure the virus wasn't still lingering in the system. By then, however, she'd have done what she planned to do.

Collecting her axe once more, Rumil set about trashing the uplink box, leaving the coding a mess that would take at least several tenth-cycles to repair. Then, she sprayed the contents of another viral flask into the room itself, one that would corrupt any backup programs the Solarians would try to use to replace the damaged uplink. As satisfied as she could be with the completion of her task, Rumil disconnected from her virtual interface, returning back to physical space. Instantly, she activated her comm unit and contacted Timothy.

"I've got good news and bad news," Rumil said nervously.

"Bad news first," Timothy said with a grunt. Over his comm she was rather sure he heard sounds of heavy plasma fire.

"Are you all right?" she asked, suddenly concerned.

"Nothing I can't handle," Timothy said through what sounded like grit teeth. "Now, are you going to spit it out? I'd rather not have to split my concentration much longer than I have to."

"The techs on board the Dreadnought were better than I thought. They locked a trace on me, and I'm not terribly sure how far they got. I had to break my connection. Sorry about losing the surveillance feed."

"That's fine, as long as you incapacitated their ability to do the same."

"Of course," Rumil replied with a hint of indignance. "It will take them several tenth-cycles to repair the damaged code, and even if they have backup uplinks ready, I'll have a nasty surprise waiting for them that would likely take even longer to sort out."

"Good. Justin and I will take it from here."

"Give me a few ticks, and I can have the feed running again."

"Negative," Timothy said insistently. "You need to get out of sight, and keep hidden. If the Solarians get their surveillance up quickly, then you can consider another jaunt. Outside of that, I don't want you endangering yourself unnecessarily."

"But what if you need to find more Solarians on the surface?"

Timothy grunted again. "Let me assure you that I have plenty for myself for the time being. If I need more, I'll let you know."

"All right… just… be careful."

"Always," Timothy replied confidently, and killed the connection.

Rumil began to pack up her PCU, then stopped. Patching into Timothy's comm unit once more, she said, "Oh… one more thing you might find important."

"What?" he said, his growing frustration evident in his voice.

"Emmitt is supposedly somewhere on the planet," Rumil said. "At least, according to the techs I overheard."

"Bannor take it all!" Timothy spat angrily. "He's right on the battlefield with… Creator damn him! I should have been paying closer attention to that man. Thank you, Rumil. Now get out of sight… *now*!"

"Yes, sir," Rumil quipped, saluting mockingly while scowling at the comm. Nonetheless, she complied, packing up her equipment as quickly as she could manage, and started looking around for a hiding space. She didn't want to take refuge in the camp's cabins, as they would be the first places the Solarians searched if they narrowed it down that far. She jogged to the edge of the camp, and scouted about, not seeing much except a tree line about a TackMet away. Deciding it was her best option at the moment, Rumil began walking.

* * * * *

Timothy found that he had several emerging problems at hand with Rumil's latest news. There was no telling if Solarian scouts would soon be scouring Helga's camp for Rumil, and from what he could sense, Justin was currently in direct contact with Emmitt Fransisca. That alone presented a set of difficulties, as Emmitt had proven quite crafty – perhaps more than Justin's limited experience could handle.

Nonetheless, there was precious little he could do about those problems because he was busy handling one of his own. The "thousand to one" axiom that many had paraded in regards to the Knighthood was proving to be somewhat… overrated. As it stood, Timothy was finding it hard to maintain his shielding against the assault of the two hundred Phantoms that had finally engaged him, much less attempt any sort of counterattack.

Several squads were on the move to cut off any route that Timothy might use to make a retreat, the remainder working on pinning him down in a grassy gully in which they could concentrate their heavier arms for greater effect. If they managed that, he had little delusions that even his undoubtedly strong mental prowess would hold out long.

As he continued to analyze his dwindling options, he again had to fight the stirrings of his dormant self. While Timothy was more than certain the outburst of energies that came from abandoning his control would easily dispatch every last one of his opponents, he wasn't nearly as certain that he would be able to rein himself in afterward, or what he would do after the Phantoms were removed.

Nonetheless, he was rapidly running out of choices.

The roar of several open-air engines caught his ears, presumably from incoming air fighters. Despite his curiosity, he couldn't afford to divert his attention away from keeping himself from being shot to pieces, but as the sounds came closer at great speed, they represented a threat that couldn't be ignored.

However, he noticed the Phantoms were turning their fire upward, indicating that they certainly weren't anything the Solarians expected. As he had guessed, the sound was a pair of fighters that now passed over Timothy's head, strafing the Phantoms with several bursts of fire. Timothy didn't recognize them until he saw the Blood Hawks insignia painted on the side of one.

"We saw that the little watchdog orbiting the primary moon was out of commission, and that you were entertaining some rather boorish guests," Dewin commented from Timothy's comm. "Hope that helped."

That it did. With the barrage momentarily broken, Timothy unleashed a storm of ball lightning that sent the Phantoms that weren't maimed or killed from the volley scattering in retreat.

"Sorry we can't stick around to help you mop up, but there's no telling how long that beast is going to remain under blackout. We should probably fold out to a safe distance as soon as possible," Dewin commented as the fighter envoy accelerated into the upper atmosphere, returning to the *Gallan*. "Just consider us even."

"For what?" Timothy finally responded.

"For the time you didn't cut me into strips," Dewin said with a hint of sardonic wit. "Anyway, we're about to dock back with the *Gallan*. Make sure you contact us when you all are done playing on the surface."

Timothy weighed the option of hunting down the remaining Phantoms, but decided that it would take some time for them to reassemble into anything that could be considered a dangerous threat to the Ceremony. Just as he had reached the decision to check in on Rumil, a burst of psionic power registered in his psyche. Clearly, the encounter between Emmitt and Justin had taken a turn for the worse.

Nonetheless, he felt the need to check in on Rumil outweighed his desire to immediately intervene. He knew both Knights rather intimately – Justin was at least able to handle himself for a while, and likely capable of besting Emmitt without Timothy's help. Rumil, on the other hand... he simply couldn't let anything happen to her, regardless of his reasons.

* * * * *

"Well, I see we finally meet face to face."

Justin stepped forward into the circular clearing that his counterpart had chosen for himself. "It would appear so."

The Knight gave a slight bow. "I suppose I am fortunate that I get to meet the former heir to the Kiros Knighthood personally." Noting Justin's reaction, he added, "Oh, don't be so surprised. It's simple process of elimination really. There are only two Knights that cannot be accounted for by the sects, and believe me when I'd say that I'd recognize Timothy's aura anywhere. Thus, it was safe to assume when I sensed your presence just who you were."

"Then you have me at a disadvantage," Justin observed. "You were on-planet yesterday, but I can't seem to recall your name."

"You wound me..." the Knight replied. "I would have figured you'd keep up with current events. I am Emmitt Fransisca, Solarian Knight, and Commandant of the Solarian Forces."

"Give me ten ticks, and I'll likely do more than wound you." Justin's sword arm started to hover towards his weapon as he made the threat, making himself ready for any act of aggression from his adversary.

"Yes... I can see that. I can only assume that you've entered a Nerean Trance in anticipation of the Ceremony of War," Emmitt sighed. "Now, I'm afraid you have me at a disadvantage. I'll be quite honest when I say I was not anticipating being ordered to remain on Ub, and had precious little time to prepare for any conflict. Besides, I'm here to talk, not fight, something I can't imagine you're in much of a condition for considering your current state."

129

"What is it you wish to discuss?"

"Timothy, more or less. I was a friend of his; we've known each other since our Academy training. There's something I'm trying to understand, and I was hoping you'd be able to enlighten me."

Justin's eyes narrowed, trying to sense if there was any truth in what Emmitt was saying. Not surprisingly, the Solarian man was keeping his thoughts closely guarded, but Justin did manage to glean a general curiosity in regard to what he claimed. Eventually coming to the conclusion that things probably wouldn't proceed much further without his cooperation, Justin began the process of dispelling the Nerean Trance. To be honest, he didn't like the Trance that much, as it seemed he lost a lot of his charming personality, from what people tell him.

Justin opened his eyes, and made a loud exhale of breath, he extended his arms, carrying all his normal playfulness, and said, "All right… here I am. So, let's get this chat started, shall we?"

"First of all… how's Timothy been? Still his same irritatingly pragmatic self?"

Justin shrugged. "I suppose. Trying to get him to talk about himself is as difficult as squeezing water from a rock."

Emmitt laughed. "Always about the mission, and his duty, and on and on…"

For a moment, Justin almost joined the Solarian, but reminded himself to be wary. "So, why the concern?"

"As I said, I've known him for a long time. We were in the same class in the Academy of the Knighthood in Centris. Since he was staryears younger than anyone else, I'd like to think he looked up me as a mentor of sort, then as a friend, but apparently not."

"Why do you say that?"

Emmitt sighed wistfully. "He was in my position before he left. He was in line to have more power and influence than most societies can muster. He had my loyalty, as well as the support of an entire generation of rising Knights. Bannor take us, we would have started a civil war if he had just given the word."

With a shrug, Emmitt continued, "Then… he just tossed it all aside. He returned from his mission hunting Bonamede, and he was different. For the first time since I knew him, I could see a passion in him that hadn't been there before. When I learned he made connections with the Kiros, I was mildly surprised, but not shocked, as he always had been one to take a different path. Then, in the span of less than three cycles, he just left… everything he had worked for, everything he had fought for… none of it mattered anymore. Then, when the reports came that you disappeared from the galaxy proper as well, I finally figured it out. You were the Kiros Knight he worked with in apprehending Krennan."

"I was," Justin replied. "And what is your point exactly?"

"In fewer than five ten-cycles, he saw something in you that he never saw in me or any of his comrades in arms and fellow trainees over nine staryears. I want to know what that was. What is so special about you that none of his own people had?"

Justin smirked, as he well knew just who Timothy saw something special in, and it certainly wasn't him. Nonetheless, Justin felt it prudent to let Emmitt maintain his false assumption. With a playful shrug, the Kiros joked, "Maybe it's my cheerful sense of humor."

Emmitt clearly didn't find it funny. He was trembling in fury, and his voice seethed in venomous ire. "All the plans you ruined… everything was in order… now the path is no longer in our hands… and for that, you will pay with your life!"

Justin's hand stopped drifting, and grabbed the hilt of his sword. "I'm not defenseless, I'll have you know."

"That's true," Emmitt sneered, "but you did foolishly give up the advantage. You see… when you released your Nerean Trance, you assumed I had done the same."

Justin gaped. "But you said you hadn't had time…"

"I lied," Emmitt replied with a cocky shrug which contorted into an angered tension. The man's draw and attack followed without another word, carrying such swiftness that Justin didn't even have time to draw his own sword in defense, having to lunge to the side awkwardly, and even then could only read and react to Emmitt's next attack, finally getting his sword free to barely block Emmitt's downward chop.

Fortunately, after deflecting that attack, Justin found time to regain his bearings and get a little distance from his opponent. Fransisca wasn't as powerful as Justin had been expecting the chosen successor of the Solarian Knighthood to be. The Nerean Trance enhancing his body and mind made things more difficult, but not beyond his ability to handle.

That is, if he didn't have any more epic lapses in judgment…

His train of thought was broken as Emmitt went on the attack again, forcing Justin back as he parried the collection of swipes and stabs. Finally, Justin saw enough of an opening to make a thrusting attack of his own, which Emmitt deflected, the Solarian bringing up his knee in counter. In response to this, Justin pushed with his psionic strength at Emmitt. The force was met by Emmitt's own mental aura, so it wound up having the opposite effect Justin intended, pushing him away from the Solarian since he wasn't as well braced against the ground. Fortunately, the effect it did have was good enough, thrusting Justin once again out of Emmitt's reach.

Upon gaining his footing again, Justin decided to go on the offensive. He began with a series of four crackling balls of fire that Emmitt managed to dodge or deflect, but that proved to only be a ruse for the intended strike, a swift precise slash that actually came but a hair's breadth from slicing Emmitt's throat open, and managed to rip a clean hole in the neck of his bodysuit with nothing but a thin line of blood that the Solarian healed quickly.

Emmitt regarded the close call with the indifference that came from the Nerean Trance. The Solarian ran one finger along the tear, then apparently gave it no further thought as he thrust himself into sword reach yet again, his blade poking and slashing, looking for a hole in Justin's defense.

Justin again jumped away from Emmitt, and rather fortunately too, as the flash of a teleporting Erani imposed itself into the gap between them. However, Emmitt was in mid-lunge, and so the blade moved directly towards the person stepping into physical space.

When the energy blinked away, Timothy was standing directly in front of Emmitt, his hands pressed against each other as if in prayer. In between his hands, he had actually trapped and held Emmitt's blade short of striking him. Even Emmitt and Justin, fully-trained and capable Knights in their own regards, were quite impressed with such a quick reaction.

"I take it my Phantoms were unsuitable entertainment," Emmitt said with a frown, then grunted as he pulled his sword out of Timothy's grasp.

"You could say that," Timothy replied. "I'm afraid to say that the chances the Bluebloods will retain control of Ub aren't nearly as good as they would have been."

To both Justin and Timothy's surprise, Emmitt didn't find that news terribly disturbing. As a matter of fact, he started laughing. "The Ceremony of War isn't of much concern to me, to be honest. My reasons for being here are merely personal."

"Is that right?" Timothy said dryly.

"Why did you leave?" Emmitt demanded. "Everything was going entirely according to plan... all we needed was a few pieces to drop into place, and then we could usher in a whole new galactic order! Why did you just toss that all aside?"

Timothy's eyes narrowed. "I found my proper calling... making sure that people like you don't fulfill your plans." His left hand gripped the hilt of his sword, and Justin had no doubt to his friend's intent.

"Kill me now... kill me later... don't you understand yet it makes no difference? You can't fight fate. You can't change what has already been foreseen," Emmitt scoffed, dropping his sword to the ground, and throwing his arms out to the side

"If that's the case, then why don't you stand still?" Timothy remarked coldly, and with a speed that Justin still found disturbing despite all the times he had seen it in action, Timothy's sword left its sheath and slashed upward in one fluid motion. However, Emmitt balked at the moment of truth, jumping backward to avoid the swiping hypersteel.

Timothy smirked triumphantly as if he had won some small victory in the exchange. "If it truly doesn't matter, Knight Fransisca... why do you fear death? Seems to me that you aren't as steadfast in your belief as you claim you are." With an air that came as close to dramatic as Timothy had ever shown to that point, he returned his sword to his sheath, and said, "Go back to Solaria... you aren't worth the supplies I would need to clean your blood off my weapon."

Emmitt's entire body shook with frustration, and a hint of embarrassment. "I suppose I have no choice, do I? Just bear in mind... you can't change anything. Those who challenge fate are fools."

"And those who don't are cowards," came Timothy's rejoinder, delivered in a backhanded fashion as he turned about to approach Justin. Emmitt left with a flash nary a demitick later, leaving Justin and Timothy alone in the glade.

"What was that about exactly?" Justin queried.

"Something that will take far more time to explain than we have at the moment," Timothy said with a hint of disapproval. "In case you have forgotten, there is a Ceremony of War going on right now."

"Well, I figured that dealing with a Solarian Knight on the surface would probably be rather important," Justin retorted. "Besides, it wasn't like Helga was letting me do much."

Timothy eyes narrowed, and he asked, "What… happened to your Nerean Trance?"

Justin started, and rubbed the back of his head nervously. "I… dispelled it to talk with your little friend…"

Timothy rolled his eyes, and turned his back to Justin. The Kiros then heard him mutter something along the lines of, "Sometimes I'm amazed you're still alive."

Justin felt like Timothy had just tried to stab him in the gut for a second, but had to acknowledge that he had done a rather stupid thing buying into Fransisca's ruse. "Yes, yes… don't give up any perceived advantage, and all that. I got it, all right?"

Timothy's now playful tone eased Justin's mood. "As long as you're learning. Now, let's move. While Helga may not want our help… she might need it."

Chapter Nine

"I haven't seen Justin in a while," Orion remarked, "and it appears that the sounds of battle to the north have quelled."

"Then we can hope that's good news," Helga said sourly. "Perhaps they've finished their tasks, and have left us to complete our duty in the way it was meant to."

"Sister, that has always been their intent."

She rolled her eyes at her brother's claim. "I have seen and heard too much about Solarian interference and practice to believe anything those point-eared waifs claim. You give them any foothold, and they take your planet."

"But Feroz is Kiros."

Helga shrugged, indifferent to the distinction. "A Kiros is nothing more than a Solarian with more sun."

Orion could do nothing but laugh at his sister's statement. No doubt Timothy and Justin could provide several tomes of differences between their respective peoples, many of which apparently were important enough to go to war over.

Then again, he could remember a time when he thought exactly the same way as his younger sibling. There was Ub, and there was everything else that really didn't matter. His exposure to the galaxy proper in his travels with the Blood Hawks caused him to see things in a much broader light.

Hard to believe it had been more than ten staryears since he left Ub in his self-imposed exile and found himself a member of a prominent pirate organization. He had initially signed on for nothing more than the money… then one event changed so much…

* * * * *

"Salazar! Pay attention!" Pilot Command Officer Dewin Rio hissed angrily.

Orion huffed at the scolding. Demodians were largely in charge of the Blood Hawks organization, and thus Orion reluctantly had to pay them the respect due to their position… but that didn't mean he had to like them.

"I fail to see what all the fuss is about," Orion said with a shrug, falling back against the rail of their rooftop lookout point. "It's one Solarian Knight. The crew of the *Gallan* is more than two hundred, yet we're the ones holed up like we're outnumbered and under siege."

"That may be true," Dewin acknowledged as he propped his elbows against the rusted metal rail, looking out across the street. "But Gallan's paranoid considering how close this fellow got on Altair. Besides… something's telling me that Knight is going to be trouble."

Dewin said that with such grim certainty that Orion grew just a hint more concerned. In the time he had served under Rio as a shuttle pilot, Orion had not known him to be overly dramatic or easily perturbed. "How do you know?"

"I've always had a sense for this sort of thing," Dewin replied, his eyes dashing back and forth across the condemned buildings on the other side of the street. "Never have been able to explain it, but I've always been able to tell when I'm in danger, or something really bad is about to happen."

"And you're getting that feeling now?"

Dewin nodded. "A whole lot of that feeling. Something's not right… and I can't shake the sensation that it's centered around that Solarian Gallan heard was tailing us."

"How would he even know we're here?" Orion queried. "Didn't we pull out to Canasa because *no one* knows we hide out here?"

"That's the idea… and I don't know how… but that Knight knows, and he followed us. I can guarantee you that," Dewin remarked. "That's why I want you on your guard. Things might get ugly in a hurry."

"Do you think he brought reinforcements?"

"Possibly… but if everything I've heard about the things a Solarian Knight can do are true, he likely wouldn't need much backup." Dewin stepped away from the rail, and warned once more, "Just… stay alert. He could be anywhere."

At that moment, Dewin comm bleated with Regis Gallan's voice, bordering on full-out panic. "Surveillance is picking up a small regiment moving towards us at a marching speed. All command personnel report to me, and all crew get to defensive positions."

Dewin regarded the report with a great deal of skepticism. "A regiment? Nonsense… we would have noted the arrival of a military vessel."

Orion then saw what certainly appeared to a large group of people about half a TackMet down the street, turning the corner from a nearby crossroad two blocks down. Pointing it out to Dewin, he asked, "Could that be what the Captain is talking about?"

Dewin dropped a magnification visor over his eyes, and replied, "No, it can't be… first of all, they aren't Solarian. Secondly, they aren't moving in any set step like Solarian regiments tend to do, and there are no ranks to speak of. They're probably scholars, studying the old Canasa mining fields."

Orion then pointed down towards the foot of the building, and replied, "Then someone might want to tell the assault team that…"

With a start, Dewin followed Orion's finger, and his eyes bulged, his hand at the same time ripping his comm unit off his belt, screaming into it, "Sir! Call off the attack squad! They aren't soldiers!"

"I know exactly what they are!" Regis replied feverishly. "They're undercover units sent by the Solarians!"

"Sir, they aren't even Solarian! You don't want to be responsible for this!"

But by that time, it was too late to convince the terrified leader, and the assault unit began firing, first with a volley of rifle-launched fragmentation grenades that landed with varying degrees of accuracy. However, with such weapons, close was all that was needed, the shrapnel shattering apart at almost sonic speeds, ripping through the touring collection of people. Those not felled from the first volley were systematically dropped by plasma rounds fired by snipers throughout the building.

"That godless waste of space…" Dewin grumbled in anger, before turning back to his comm. "Well, congratulations, sir! You've just killed over a hundred unarmed people!"

Orion barely heard his superior's words, his attention drawn to a storage facility across the street. It seemed to implode slightly, then burst into pieces as if detonated from the inside. In the rubble, he saw two small dots, the brilliant white light so intense that he could clearly see it

137

through the debris dust and the noonday sun above.

The dots disappeared in another flash of bright light, and almost simultaneously another flash occurred square in the middle of the assault team, followed by the almost hypnotic death dealing from the sword-bearing Solarian. For the first two unfortunate souls, they likely never saw death coming. The third might have had a chance to register a glimmer of hypersteel before it stabbed through his neck. The remaining seven members of the team no doubt saw their attacker, and yet that knowledge would do no good. They would die with the rest, quickly and efficiently.

"Salazar!" Dewin's voice screamed from Orion's comm unit. "Where are you? Get down to base level and help defend the building!"

Orion started, and whirling about rapidly, noticed that Dewin indeed was no longer on the roof, likely on his way to report to Captain Regis as he had been ordered. As he dashed down the steps towards the ground floor, his mind raced with what he had seen. While he had no doubt that he would prove to be more than a match for any Solarian face to face, he now could understand how they could be such effective fighters… more often than not, you never saw them coming, and even if you did, you were dead a demitick later.

And he didn't get a chance to meet this Solarian face to face either. As he reached the second floor, he could hear the sounds of battle, then from the bottom of the stairwell there was an explosion and a ball of fire that collapsed the stairs, sending him tumbling to the bottom followed by a large mass of rubble.

When Orion regained consciousness, and crawled out of the remains of the collapsed stairwell, the fight was already over. Judging from the carnage, what a fight it had been indeed. For example, he wasn't sure just how a hypersteel support beam had been literally wrapped around the head of one of the many bodies littering the floor, but it most certainly had an intriguing story behind it.

He followed the path of destruction towards the rear of the building, passing the empty smelting vats that the Blood Hawks at one time had stashed some of their heavier ill-gotten gains into. However, the vats had been broken in another feat that defied his imagination, shattered like glass, their contents spilled onto the sunken floor where molds would normally be placed. Ignoring the treasure for the moment, Orion pressed on, looking for any other survivors.

He passed through a hall that led from the smelting room to the shipping bay. In there he found the first of Regis's officers along the wall just to the right of the door, where the security officer was hanging a full Tack off the ground, a jagged piece of splintered metal sticking through his lower neck. Orion jolted from the gruesome totem, and tripped over Rydia Nabul, the communications officer. Or more accurately, her upper half that was lying on the floor, while her lower body remained stuck on a clamp attached to a ceiling conveyor. It wasn't a clean separation either, more like she had been torn apart with her attacker's bare hands.

In the center of the empty bay laid the body of the primary officer, Trev Ogral, the second-in-command under Captain Regis. He seemed normal enough at a distance, but once he was close enough to examine the man more thoroughly, Orion noticed that the body was bloated and dry, his clothes crumbling upon contact. The man's flesh was blistered and discolored, almost unbearably hot to the touch, as if the officer had been boiled alive from the inside.

He had given up almost all hope of finding anyone alive when he caught movement out of the corner of his eye. There was a mess of smashed and toppled packing crates, and one black-booted foot, gently twitching. Rushing to the crates, Orion started tossing the boxes carelessly over his shoulder to uncover a welcome sight, and a rare one as of late; a living being. Dewin was beginning to stir, and Orion initially snorted derisively, insulted that such a light blow as being tossed into a few wooden crates would knock the Demodian out, until Orion freed Dewin's other leg…

…to discover it was gone below the knee.

The wound seemed partially cauterized, as there was no great flow of blood that would normally occur from such an injury. However, it didn't have the same burnt smell that would normally follow a cauterization, just remains of a fine grey ash that stuck to the stump. As gently as an Ubek could manage, he lifted Dewin, and supported the Demodian against his shoulder as the pilot officer slowly gained his wits.

"Mr. Rio… I am glad to see you are still among the living," Orion said with as much relief as he could muster.

Dewin looked down at his missing limb, and remarked, "More or less…"

"Where is Captain Regis?" Orion asked, curious if Dewin knew the fate of their leader.

Dewin snorted in disgust, "I don't know... and I almost don't care. He ran off like a terrified child when that Solarian appeared, leaving us officers to secure his escape... not that we provided much resistance."

"Did the Solarian do this?"

Dewin rolled his eyes, and quipped tiredly, "No... we did this to ourselves."

They proceeded through the shipping bay, towards the rear exit that Dewin saw Regis retreat to. The door was open, suggesting the captain at least made it outside, but the signs of a short scuffle, followed by one set of Erani boot prints in the dirt, suggested that he didn't get far.

Orion began trembling in rage, partially because of what had happened, and partially because he had not been granted a chance to be part of it. "I will find that Solarian, no matter what it costs, and he will pay for every drop of blood he..."

"Stop it," Dewin chided. "Don't be foolish. There are more important things to worry about right now. I've certainly not completed what I sought out to do with this organization. And while I don't know your reasons for being here, I suspect you aren't finished, either."

Orion nodded... there was still plenty he had to do before he could return home... and he couldn't complete those tasks on his own. "So you plan on reforming the Blood Hawks? How?"

Dewin frowned, and replied, "I'm sure I'll think of something..."

* * * * *

"Brother, are you even listening to me?" Helga snapped.

"Sorry, Helga... I was thinking about something," Orion apologized.

"Well, the time for thinking has passed," she continued with a slight scowl, "because I do believe that is Grodin's party approaching us."

Orion had figured this moment would be coming. As opponents fell to the Salazar clan, he had little doubt that Grodin's clan would be doing the same to their opponents, and that conflict between the two would be inevitable.

As both sides charged the Modeghi Plain, the large stretch of flatland at the center of the battlefield, Orion and Helga were able to confirm what they already knew. Despite knowing there had to be several more clans still active, Orion couldn't help but feel that this coming fight would determine the champion of the Ceremony of War.

They both stopped at opposite banks of the shallow river that flowed through the plain. It was rather broad, almost ten Tacks from bank to bank, but even at its deepest point it was barely above the knees of an average Ubek. On the opposite bank, Grodin carried the confidence of a man who felt he had already won before the fight even started. Orion couldn't wait to see that confidence melt to concern when he discovered his support was dismally lacking.

"Well, I must say that I am glad to see you have survived this long," Grodin shouted from the other bank. "It will be an immense pleasure to eliminate you myself."

"As if you would have a chance without your 'advantages,' Grodin," Helga sneered. "Or do you think I cannot see that your clan's cudgels are not fashioned to the standards demanded of the Ceremony?"

Grodin regarded the weapon thoughtfully, and even from Orion's distance, he could see where the wood had splintered, exposing a gleaming hypersteel core. "Hmm... now that is peculiar..." he remarked. "I suppose I should have it replaced once I get the time..."

"Conveniently before your victory is investigated to determine legitimacy, no doubt..." Orion growled indignantly. He had never expected Grodin and his Bluebloods would be so shameless in their cheating and manipulation of the system. "Of course, why would you need to use illegal weapons when you can just get the Solarians to do your work for you?"

"I don't need the Solarians' help to win!" Grodin bellowed, clearly insulted by that accusation.

"Good thing for you, because I'm afraid your support won't be attending," Timothy's voice suddenly drawled from the east, grabbing the attention of both Ubek clans. He was standing along the Pales' bank of the river, arms crossed, Justin just behind him to his right. Orion was certain he had not seen either Erani as his clan had charged... but acknowledged that meant little.

Derailed by the news, Grodin turned to a comm unit clipped to his belt – another illegal item, Orion noted – and tried to contact his support, getting only static.

"The Dreadnought is out of commission at the moment. You weren't informed?" Timothy smirked. "I suspect they'll be active again relatively soon, but even then, the ground forces have been sufficiently scattered. I wouldn't count on any help, if I were you."

"Oh, but you intend to help your Pale friends?" the Blueblood chieftain complained.

Orion took one step forward, and retorted, "You are hardly the one to gripe about unfair advantages."

Timothy shook his head, and shrugged. "We have been requested by the chieftain of the Salazar Clan to not directly interfere in their combat. I see no reason not to respect those wishes. Nonetheless, we'll be watching you... just in case."

Timothy then motioned for Justin to fall back, giving distance for the two sides to engage. There was a newfound nervousness in the Bluebloods, as if they suddenly realized that nothing was predetermined anymore, and that they would have to really fight this one out.

"Well, this is what we've trained for, clansmen. If we lose, lose with the honor and the respect that we grant to those who are proven superior," Helga declared, and led the charge into the river, Grodin's battle party jumping forward into the shallow waterway.

Helga quickly moved to intercept her Blueblood counterpart, as she had a desire to square off with Grodin, but the Blueblood chieftain managed to shrug her aside into the waiting attack of two of his clansmen. It was clear that Grodin had targeted Orion as his opponent for this fight, and when Helga was able to think beyond her immediate opponent, she acknowledged that it was probably right. Grodin and Orion had never honored each other, and it was the condescending treatment Grodin gave to the Pales, and Orion specifically, that had caused her brother to depart those ten staryears prior.

But even as the two males squared off at the center of the melee, Helga wasn't sure how her brother was going to be victorious on his own. Grodin was an impressive specimen, even among Ubeks, topping Orion by a least half a Tack, and with a body that suggested he had not been idle in his training as his fellows appear to have been. Orion would likely need help, and thus Helga turned her attention into clearing a path for her to assist.

Helga wasn't the only one noticing that Orion might be in a bit of trouble, especially as the Pale Ubek started being forced backward by his opponent. Justin also noticed that Orion wasn't faring as expected. Grodin was swinging his reinforced club with a berserker flurry, but at the moment, Orion seemed not to receive any severe damage, turning aside several blows with his hide bracer, dodging several others with surprisingly quick moves for a being of his size and stature. Yet Justin couldn't be sure how long Orion could keep evading the Blueblood's attacks.

Timothy could feel Justin's mental aura charging, ready to give Orion a slight bit of assistance, but the Solarian reached back with a hand, psychically suggesting that Justin hold off on the effort.

You should know by now from watching me that battles aren't always how they seem, Timothy reminded cryptically.

Still, Justin grew ever more concerned as Orion was pushed out of the river and onto the Pale bank, his boots sinking slightly into the damp earth. Once again, Timothy held back the Kiros's intervention, and Justin could hear his Solarian counterpart mumbling, "Wait for it… wait for the opening… wait…"

Justin smirked, realizing that Timothy couldn't entirely help himself, quietly offering advice to Orion as if the Ubek could somehow hear him. Let no one say that Timothy did not become emotionally invested in his teaching.

Nonetheless, the Solarian was right. Just as the Knight had taught him, Orion's defensive posture was intentional, although when he felt certain of himself, he would occasionally make the exploratory swipe just to see how quickly Grodin could react while the Blueblood chieftain was recklessly attacking.

However, his main purpose remained fixed on what he had learned from Timothy; biding his time, waiting for the perfect opportunity to make his intended strike. Even Orion's still novice battle observation had identified several holes in Grodin's posture, but Orion's instincts told him to hold off, and keep waiting for an even better chance. As the Blueblood chieftain tired, the holes grew larger and more enticing, and no doubt would grow even more so as time passed.

Then Orion's chance came so suddenly that he almost missed it, then almost didn't act because of how broad the opening was. Grodin gripped his club with both hands, chopping downward as if trying to split wood. Orion bounced to the right, watching the blow as it set his Blueblood adversary off balance, giving Orion a clear shot at Grodin's defenseless back. Without any further hesitation, the Pale made his move, bringing a descending swipe that connected with a sickening crack of wood and bone along the back of the Blueblood's head. Orion's club split into two with the force of the blow, but it was doubtful Grodin even heard any of it. The Blueblood chieftain went limp the instant contact was made, his reinforced cudgel dropping from his hand, and toppling forward onto his knees and eventually face first into the softened earth.

The sight of Grodin falling served to halt the entire battle for less than five demiticks, but it felt like something just short of eternity that the Ubeks analyzed the change in the battle's momentum. Fighting started again intermittently, patches of Ubeks returning to combat until once again river water was tossed about wildly in the melee.

However, it became clear that the fight was largely gone from the Bluebloods. Things were not as promised, and the demoralized clan did not engage with the zeal for which they were known. Once again, Helga's battle party began to rout a foe that was superior in numbers.

Suddenly, Timothy's comm unit beeped and, curious as to who would be trying to contact him, he answered the device…

* * * * *

"Okay, this is getting boring." Rumil muttered. She slapped the side of the tree she was leaning into, feeling the bark crumble slightly under her hand. "If the Solarians were coming after me, they would have done it by now. I don't see why I have to stay here, and keep out of sight."

Timothy had demanded that she keep hidden in the forest until the Ceremony of War was over… but Rumil was not terribly good at following orders. Besides, what if the Dreadnought was up and running again?

With a smug grin, Rumil plopped down cross-legged onto the ground, and reached into her satchel, fishing out her hacker's gear. Nonetheless, she wasn't out to wreak havoc this time and now knew the threat her opponents posed, and so put her virtual interface back into her bag. At the moment, she only wanted to observe, and for that, she didn't need to cause any more undue attention.

Not surprisingly, she was able to link up to the Dreadnought rather

144

quickly, suggesting that they had finally restored systems. What she didn't like was that she was able to connect a little *too* quickly. Generally a transmission from her position to a lunar orbit would take a couple demiticks, even with subspace communication. In curiosity, she slipped into the vessel's navigation control, and sure enough, the Dreadnought had changed its position, moving from lunar orbit, into a geosynchronous orbit over the battlefield.

Initially, she decided that the Dreadnought had done so because of the damaged surveillance uplink, but then wondered why they would make such an overt move if the intent was merely to watch. Worried that the Solarians were preparing to dispatch more forces, she quickly spliced into the personnel system to try and get a grasp on what they had planned, then turned her attention to the armament controls when personnel turned up nothing.

Her eyes bulged as she discovered just what it was the Solarians were about to do, and it didn't have anything to do with shock troops. Her hand flew to her comm unit, and beeped Timothy as quickly as she could activate the speed connect.

"Timothy…" she began as Timothy appeared on her unit's display.

Timothy grumbled in exasperation, and scolded, "Rumil, I told you to lay low. What are you doing?"

"Listen to me for once in your life!" she said, barely restraining her panic. "The Dreadnought is preparing to drop a fusion bomb onto the battlefield!"

* * * * *

Unfortunately, Justin overheard Rumil's warning. "They're *what*?" he said in disturbed disbelief. "They can't possibly be thinking…"

"If they can't win… no one will," Timothy muttered. "It's the attitude that caused the Baramak Slaughter, and there was no reason to think it would change now."

Orion had been putting the finishing touches on Grodin's elimination mark when he noticed the two Erani were appearing quite agitated. He dropped the brush he was using, and began to approach Justin and Timothy as the former declared, "There's no way we'll be able to teleport this many beings in the time we have!"

"In the time we have for what?" Orion asked.

"The Solarians are preparing to fusion bomb the Ceremony!" Justin howled, then turned an inquisitive glare to the Solarian, "You could at least try to look concerned, Timothy Honore!"

The young Solarian didn't respond, his head down as if deep in thought. Justin was about to repeat himself when Timothy cut him off with a soft voice. "Justin… gather everyone around me in as tight of a circle as can be managed. Make it quick, as I don't know just how much time we have."

"What are you planning?" Justin asked, then dawning comprehension flipped across his face. "You're going to try and do something along the lines of what you did in our crash on Mydor. It almost killed you when you did that last time… and there isn't anyone here who could repair you if you overdo it now."

"It's not me I'm worried about," Timothy answered with a stoic candor. "I just… damnable Bannor, it doesn't matter. Just do what I ask."

Justin grimly went about on his chosen task. Understandably, many of the Ubeks had overheard Justin's ranting, and openly wondered just what Timothy had planned. Justin wasn't terribly sure how to answer them, and settled with a genial assurance that Timothy had something in mind.

It was an interesting sight, roughly fifty Ubeks all crouched down in a large circle around two Erani. Justin leaned around Timothy and peered up into the Solarian's face, seeing his friend and teammate deep in concentration. There was an interesting contrast of anticipation and dread tainting Timothy's psionic aura… an aura that was steadily building in power and intensity, quickly reaching simply preposterous levels, then extending beyond even that.

Demiticks later, there was the sonic burst that accompanied a large mass breaking into the atmosphere. Normally, an object in free fall would take a couple ticks to make landfall from planetary entry, but Justin knew the fusion bombs that both sects used were designed to reduce that time to a minimum.

Fortunately, the sound served to prompt Timothy to action. He spread his hands out, fingers crackling with blue-white sparks of energy. His eyes opened, and Justin could see two brilliant white beams cast onto the ground just in front of them, blindingly visible despite the daytime sun.

It started as a dull roar, but as the long, fiery fusion bomb burned downward towards its intended target, the sound of roaring engines and broken air became deafening. Justin began to see a twinkle in the sky, the super-heated nose of the missile-shaped object, and initially thought it was a lot closer than it really was. He then remembered that these bombs were absurdly large, with diameters over twenty Tacks, and lengths up to four times that. Granted, over eighty percent of a fusion bomb was in the plating that protected it from exploding prematurely in the heat of atmospheric entry - but they were still freakishly large and intimidating things to see up close.

And something told Justin that he was about to see it far more closely than he had ever wanted to...

From there, Timothy released the energy he had been storing, fashioning a dome of pure psionic energy, so dense that it was visible to the naked eye, casting everything inside it with a soft aquamarine glow.

Ten demiticks after that, the fusion bomb closed the remaining distance, striking the field directly in front of Justin's line of vision, colliding with such force that he was sure that whatever Timothy had done was not enough. He snapped his eyes shut, and his eardrums nearly ruptured from the sound of the concussive shockwave as it passed over him, followed by the incinerating burn of nuclear fire.

It wasn't much later that Justin came to the realization that if he was hearing those things, that he was most likely not dead. Gingerly opening his eyes, he beheld a macabre, yet fascinating sight. All around the psychic shield, white-hot fire danced and burned, then slowly funneled upward to the sky.

"I never imagined that Solarian Knights were capable of this..." Helga commented, awestruck to the point that her voice nearly betrayed her.

"They're not," Justin countered grimly, turning his attention to the man responsible for their continued living. Judging from Timothy's trembling form, he was clearly strained from the continued effort, but Justin didn't sense any indications that his aura was close to collapse or that another case of psionic shock was imminent. Even as the Kiros thanked the Creator for that, he was equally disturbed. Knights, regardless of pedigree, were simply nowhere remotely near the sort of power being displayed. Justin felt like a torch being held up to a star, and it took all the shielding Justin could generate just to keep from being overwhelmed by the dense, pervasive aura of the Solarian next to him.

147

Not wanting to disturb Timothy, Justin remained silent. The fire cloud was largely dispersed, but that did not mean that the danger was past. Temperatures outside the shield were no doubt approaching one hundred CelMel, if not more. A person exposed to that sort of heat wouldn't even burn… they'd just simply vaporize into a superheated gas state. As it stood, the ground all around Timothy's shield was reduced to a blackened, glossy mass, literally bubbling from the heat outside. The river that had hosted the Ubek's battle was no longer there; as a matter of fact, there was nothing for almost half a TackMet in any direction… nothing but the boiling black surface.

Not wanting to disturb Timothy's concentration, Justin sat down, and waited…

* * * * *

Rumil saw the detonation, then felt it, then heard it. The initial burst was so bright that Rumil had to turn her back to the battlefield, and cover her eyes with her arm. That was soon followed by the teeth-jarring rumble along the ground that caused Rumil to fear that some of the trees might topple and crush her. Finally the roaring fury filled her ears, and she cowered into as small a package as she could from the onslaught.

By the time she gathered enough courage to actually look back towards the battlefield, the cloud head from the fusion bomb's detonation was already billowing outwards, the plume towering above her, even though she was roughly twenty TackMets away. The truth of the weapon's incredible destructive power made any description she had ever heard seem outright pale, regardless of the accuracy in their reports.

And that was only *one* fusion bomb. She could only imagine what it must have been like during the Baramak Slaughter, where wave after wave of those weapons pounded the surface in the most outrageous display of overkill that she could ever conceive.

Her awe was followed with concern. She had little doubt just what, or more appropriately who, the Solarians had targeted with that weapon. Could Timothy, Justin, or anyone, for that matter, had survived the blast?

She tried to remember what Timothy had taught her about psionic power, how to focus and direct it to detect others… but she was having no success doing it herself. Then, it was as if someone flipped a switch in her brain, as the back of her mind started buzzing again… but with a force she had never felt before. The only time the sensation had been remotely this intense had been during hers and Timothy's escape from Solaria.

It was during this surge of energies buzzing and screaming in her mind that her vision began to haze, and the blackness of another episode started to overwhelm her. With a dismayed groan, Rumil succumbed to what she figured was inevitable…

* * * * *

She assumed that she was having another empathic vision, as the surroundings around her were nothing she recognized. It was a bright room – probably a kitchen, judging from the glossy panel floor and various cooking utensils hanging from the ceiling.

A pang in her stomach indicated that she, or more appropriately, the person she was seeing through, was hungry. The person opened her mouth, and Rumil was instantly stunned when instead of words, an infantile scream pierced the air.

Whoever this child was, he or she certainly had a strong pair of lungs, the first howling cry drawing out at least six demiticks. It was followed by a deep breath, then another wail that rivaled the duration and volume of the first.

From an adjoining room, Rumil heard a voice that almost sounded like Timothy's, but with an angry lilt that she had never heard the Solarian use. The voice demanded that someone "silence the brat." She then placed the voice; it was Niles Honore, and that the young infant in question was likely Timothy.

After a third and fourth cry, a figure finally entered the kitchen, and dropped down into Timothy's vision. He seemed to be in his teens, with flaming red hair and light brown eyes, a stark contrast to the darker-haired and deep blue eyes that the two males of the Honore family she had met possessed. She guessed that this was Timothy's adopted brother.

Yet, there was also a twinge of recognition when Craig's face filled her mind… as if Rumil somehow knew the young man. Her thoughts were rattled when there was another cry from Timothy, then a burst of brilliant white light…

The surge seemed to serve as segue to another, seemingly

unrelated vision. This time, she felt that she was herself, reliving another memory that she had at some point forgotten. She was sobbing for a reason she couldn't discern, being carried on the back of a man in brown carbide as they strode through a domed hall marked with flickering lights in a line along both sides. There was shouting, and the sounds of conflict from above. Perhaps that had been what was disturbing Rumil, because as the sounds grew louder, she began to cry more, burying her head in almost silken strands of bright red hair…

Then the vision was replaced with another… a scene of brutal carnage that initially swamped her with revulsion. A countless number of bodies of varying races were scattered about the run-down remains of what was some form of processing plant. She sensed a rage from the source of the vision, and looked as he held up two gloved hands literally dripping with blood from the bodies littered around him.

The vision continued, but Rumil was no longer able to follow it coherently, as at that time the two previous visions she had started to play through as well, like several clear animation screens being run one on top of the other, creating a confusing mess of images that made her head hurt trying to comprehend.

The images started whirling about, spinning and playing faster with each demitick. Coupled with the now violent buzzing in her head, it overloaded her brain, and she happily succumbed to the soothing darkness of unconsciousness that followed.

When she came to, a good number of tenth-cycles must have passed, as the setting sun was filtering in through the open window of the cabin she had been moved to. She blinked several times to clear her eyes and her mind, when she heard Timothy's voice say, "So, you're finally awake. When I told you to keep out of sight, I hadn't expected you'd fall asleep."

Rumil quickly sat up, her head ringing angrily as she did so, but she forced the pain back, turning her head to confirm what her ears had heard. Timothy was kneeling down at her bedside, his face level with hers, his features reflecting a degree of relief that she was no longer in her vision-induced slumber.

Without saying anything, Rumil threw her arms around the Solarian's neck, her unspoken relief that he was actually alive rather obvious even to those who weren't mind readers. As she pulled away, she noticed that her hands and the sleeves of her blouse were now stained by fine black grime, unseen against the similar color of Timothy's armor. She was lost in thought for a handful of demiticks… a sense of déjà vu… like she had seen this sort of dirt somewhere before… but couldn't quite recall where.

Once she had regained her composure, she asked, "So… did we win?"

Timothy smirked, and replied, "Helga's clan was the last one standing, yes, and promptly severed the alliance the Ubeks had with the Solarians. The situation on this planet could potentially get… unreliable."

"Meaning…?"

"Helga's already preparing for a potential Solarian invasion. We could be looking at a Second Ubek Campaign within cycles, especially if she keeps listening to Grodin."

"Grodin? I thought he was the Solarians' hand-picked leader. Why would he be advocating war against them?"

Timothy shrugged. "Apparently, almost being vaporized by a Solarian-made fusion bomb changed his attitude. Amazing how nearly getting killed by your allies will do that to a person. Besides, the pride of the Bluebloods is on the line now. They were basically betrayed by the Solarians, and thus it wouldn't surprise me if the Bluebloods led the charge in any military actions."

"So… then what are we going to do?" Rumil asked. "Are we going to stay on Ub?"

"No," Timothy answered with a shake of his head. "We have other tasks we have to complete. As much as I would like to help make sure that the Ubeks hold their own, what we can offer would be extremely limited in the terms of an all-out conflict. Our talents can be put to better use elsewhere."

Rumil didn't like the idea that they were leaving the Ubeks to fend for themselves after largely being responsible for starting the whole mess, but at the same time understood the truth in his judgment. "So, I take it you were waiting for me?" she finally asked slyly.

"Actually no… Dewin only recently returned. Apparently, some Solarians took offense to the *Gallan's* presence around Ub, and ran our pirate friends around the star system for a while before the Blood Hawks gave them the slip. However, since you appear to be none the worse for wear, I see no reason why we can't move on."

With a reluctant sigh, Rumil climbed out of her bed, and gathered her satchel from where it lay on the floor about half a Tack away. Running a quick inventory of its contents, and determining that nothing important was missing, Rumil made a sweeping motion for Timothy to lead the way out of the cabin.

Chapter Ten

Rumil beeped Justin's door, asking for entry, and when the Kiros didn't promptly reply, she called again… and a third time… and a fourth…

Finally Justin accepted the call, releasing the lock on the door to his quarters, the metal panel sliding away to reveal a considerably miffed Kiros man. From her position, she noticed that the lights to his quarters were off, with the variant flicker of candlelight from around the corner.

"Can I ask what is so important that it could not allow my prayers in peace?" Justin growled.

Rumil flushed nervously, "I'm sorry… I didn't realize that you were praying."

"One would have figured when I didn't answer your summons the first two times that it likely meant I did not wish to be disturbed."

"I'll come back later then," Rumil stated somewhat sheepishly. From what she knew of most Erani, they took their designated prayers very seriously. It was entirely possible that she had just insulted Justin in a very profound way.

Suddenly, Justin's eyes gleamed playfully, and his mouth turned upward in his trademark grin. "Actually, I'm already done. Get in here before we make even more of a scene."

With an exasperated sigh, Rumil followed, the lights to the quarters activating as the door slid closed behind her. The flickers had indeed been candles, eight of them on four-tiered holder, with the outer two candles on the lowest rung, and the two center ones on the highest. A book, presumably the Kiros Book of Prophets, lay closed in front of the candle holder.

"Normally, the Kiros don't use such items for prayer… but since I haven't been able to attend service since my departure from my kin, I've had to establish my own congregation of one."

"Why not ask Timothy?" Rumil asked. "Surely there is enough in common between your two sects to be able to perform something mildly passable."

"There is a lot in common between the two sects, but there are also marked differences," Justin answered. "Despite what I have learned, I'm still not comfortable taking guidance from Bryan Honore's prophecy, for example, something that Timothy would possibly insist on." Justin then rubbed the back of his neck, and added, "Besides, something tells me that Timothy doesn't exactly practice his faith the same way other Solarians do."

"Speaking of our Solarian friend, that's why I'm here."

"Oh no…" Justin moaned comically. "What did he do this time?"

Rumil bit her lower lip gently then replied, "Actually, I was hoping that you could tell me."

Justin's eyes narrowed, and he quickly guessed what she was referring to. "You want to know what happened on Ub when that fusion bomb hit."

"And… before we crashed on Mydor," Rumil amended, "because something tells me that something similar occurred."

Justin nodded, and sat down slowly on his padded sofa, Rumil taking a seat on the other end. The Kiros sighed, and confirmed, "You'd be right. Something very similar occurred in both instances. However, I'm not sure how I can help, because I'm still not terribly certain how to explain it."

He took a deep breath, then said, "I know you saw me under the Nerean Trance. Well, I could almost describe what Timothy did as something similar… except that whatever he did happened a lot faster than any Nerean Trance I have ever seen, and with far greater results."

He turned to face Rumil, his hands held out to illustrate his point. "You understand, the Nerean Trance allows Knights to utilize their powers to greater effect by removing our natural inhibitions. In that regard, we become more powerful physically and mentally. However, the time it takes to achieve that state is quite long… and the increase in our abilities isn't terribly drastic."

Justin then spread his arms wide, and said, "However, whatever it is that Timothy does… he can do it in a matter of demiticks, and the increase in psionic power is incredible. In that state, he can literally pull shuttles out of total free-fall, or shield a large party of beings from the effects of a fusion bomb at point of detonation. However, something tells me that power does not come without a price. When he did it on Mydor, the expense of energy put him into psionic shock. The second time…" His voice trailed off, and his eyes grew dark.

"What?" Rumil pressed.

"I… don't really want to say. It seemed so out of character for Timothy that I've almost convinced myself that I imagined it all. Helga's party, Grodin's clan, and I were waiting inside this shield that Timothy had constructed for him to decide it safe for us to move out. Suddenly, he looked at me… but not in the way that he normally does. First, his eyes were… it was like two burning stars where his eyes had been. It was literally painful to look at, so intense I had to look away from him as he turned to me."

"And?" Rumil asked, eager for him to continue.

"Secondly, he sounded so… disgusted when he spoke, and he said, 'You're fortunate I think you have something resembling value…' I had never heard Timothy speak in such a manner, and I'll admit he changed his attitude quickly enough. He turned away from me, and apologized… but… for that one moment… it's like he wasn't himself."

Rumil blinked in surprise. That did sound completely out of Timothy's character, as he had come across as so level-headed to the point of banality on occasion. She was about to remark on that when another trilling request came from Justin's door.

"It's open!" Justin called out, and the door slid aside to reveal the Blood Hawks captain, Dewin Rio.

"May I be so bold as to join you in this conversation?" Dewin asked.

"Do you even know what we're talking about?" Rumil retorted suspiciously.

"I suspect I do," the pirate captain answered. "You're discussing our Solarian colleague." He then added slyly, "It was rather obvious after all. It's the only reason I can think of that would prompt you to have a private discussion with Mr. Feroz."

"Do I have to scour my quarters for listening devices?" Justin accused.

Dewin smiled slyly, and said, "You can try… but you wouldn't find any." His features then flattened, the pirate deciding to get down to business. "Actually, I am here because I think I might have something to add to this discussion." He pulled out the desk chair from the other side of the main living space and took a seat in it backwards, his chest pressed against the backrest, with his head on his hands. "As I think you both have discovered, what happened on Ub was not the first time he has performed such unique feats of power… however, you might not know that neither was his actions during your unfortunate visit to Mydor."

Rumil already knew that. "Obviously. He had an episode similar to what Justin described during Timothy's and my escape from Solaria."

Dewin nodded, but replied, "No… the incident I speak of occurred even before your visit to the Solarian homeworld."

"You're talking about Canasa," Rumil deduced.

"Correct. Only on that occurrence, he acted on his violent urges. I had never seen anything like that before, or since. One man, killing over one hundred and fifty opponents, and we couldn't even so much as scratch him."

Clearly, this was not something easy for Dewin to remember, and his voice trembled as he continued. "I fell back with the rest of the officers to set up an ambush deeper in our hideout, but it didn't matter in the least. He shrugged off any and all weapons fire like we were children tossing pebbles at him."

"Trev was closest to Timothy, just inside the doorway, and tried to engage the Solarian hand to hand. Timothy grabbed him by the neck with one hand, and bent the metal door frame with the other. Right after, Timothy stuck Trev on the post, like skewering meat. Rydia was next, and Timothy ripped her in half with nothing but a thought… literally. He looked at her, extended one arm, and her top half popped off, then he tossed her lower body into the air. She likely lived long enough to see her legs dangling off the metal braces above her."

Rumil gagged sickeningly from the image presented, and even Justin, who had likely seen his share of grotesque imagery, was turning a rather ill color. Dewin's macabre grin promised the story wouldn't get much better. "Then he snagged Roget, the primary officer underneath Gallan. Timothy grabbed him by the edges of his uniform, and Roget screamed… His body bloated and discolored, and my guess is that Timothy literally boiled the man from the inside. I can't imagine too many more gruesome ways to move on."

"Weren't you doing anything?" Rumil asked.

Dewin scoffed. "At first… but as I said earlier, any efforts I made proved to be largely pointless. From my position, I couldn't run, and thus I simply waited for my turn to die. When he did finally turn his attention to me, I figured that was it. He teleported right in front of me, grabbed me by the sides of my head, and stared at me."

Dewin took another deep breath, rubbing his hands together anxiously. "That's when I saw what Justin described. His eyes were just bright white balls of light, so brilliant that it blinded me, the pain ripping through every nerve in my body; that is until I felt myself going numb. Then, as abruptly as he attacked, he stopped. As my sight returned, he released my head, and grabbed me by the front of my uniform, and tossed me aside like I was made of paper. As I flew through the air, I noticed that half of my right leg was gone... with clumps of gray ashen matter falling away." Dewin looked down at the leg he spoke of, and added, "I was able to get the limb regenerated... but it's never really felt the same, as if it shouldn't really be there."

Rumil turned to Justin, and commented, "That's eerily similar to what happened to the fellow who tried to kill me on Kiros, remember?"

Justin merely nodded, looking deeply disturbed with the revelations he had presented and received.

Rumil then stood, and replied, "Well, I do need to get going. Krennan expects a report from me within the tenth-cycle, and I've been holding it off as long as I can."

Justin nodded in acknowledgement, and Dewin waved in parting. Delaying briefly at the door as it slid open, she finally stepped outside the cabin, and let the door slide closed. She initially turned in the direction of her quarters, then after she took a couple steps, changed her mind, and whirled about in the opposite direction.

She found her quarry in the shuttle bay. He was practicing some form of martial routine with a wooden replica of a twin-bladed sword, sweat gleaming down his shirtless body, causing a gleaming sheen off the tightly toned muscles. Her attention was quickly taken away from the man by the practice weapon spinning tightly over his head.

Abruptly, Timothy stopped, made an unintelligible curse then turned his attention to what appeared to be a small book, likely a training manual, that was laying open about two Tacks from him. Suddenly, he asked, "Can I help you, Rumil?"

She was hardly perturbed by the question, finally used to the fact that he could know she was there without so much as looking. She approached slowly, but stopped at a safe distance to keep from interfering with his practice. "Nothing really... just didn't want to lock myself in my quarters, and Justin was praying, so I didn't want to bother him. Don't

Solarians pray?"

Timothy shrugged as he stepped away from the manual, and said, "Of course we do. We clasp our hands together and look down as opposed to looking up with palms pressed, but from what I understand, it's largely the same."

Rumil smirked playfully, and queried, "Do *you*?"

Timothy resumed his training, but still answered, "My feeling is that if the Creator God is as all-powerful, all-knowing, and all-present as I am led to believe, then I likely don't need elaborate rituals for Him to know what I'm thinking or desire." The period in the statement was punctuated with a shoulder thrust of his weapon, which apparently didn't please him from the way he scowled.

"Just what are you doing, anyway?" Rumil asked.

Timothy trotted back to the training manual, knelt down, flipped a page, and then started reading. "I'm trying to learn how to use a twin-bladed sword without the benefit of a master to inform me what I might be doing wrong."

"Oh… I can see how that would be difficult, I suppose…" Rumil then noticed that the book was actually a scanned copy of a text that was far older. She then asked curiously, "Is that in Middle Erani? I find it hard to believe there aren't more recent texts…"

"You'd be correct, that is Middle Erani, and no, there aren't any more recent texts. Twin-bladed weapons fell into disfavor just after the Schism War, and as carbide arm plating began using affixed shields as the standard. Added to the fact that I wasn't able to find a training text for my fighting style, I'm having to go off the text of the one that is most similar and edit as needed… it can be rather frustrating going."

Rumil blinked in confusion. "Then why bother at all?"

"I doubt you want to hear it," Timothy said, almost bitterly. "After all, it's theological in its nature."

Rumil sighed in exasperation. "Just try me."

"Obviously, I'm trying to learn how to use the Star Smasher effectively. I'm not sure just how familiar you are with the weapon's history… but there is a legend of sorts tied to the weapon. For reasons I cannot explain, the people who wielded it in the past wound up dying afterwards."

Rumil frowned. "Seriously?"

"From what the records of that time tell me," Timothy replied, "and I'd rather just take them for their word now than be unpleasantly surprised later."

"Fair enough… but why take on that responsibility with that sort of knowledge?" Rumil asked.

Timothy once again turned away from the manual, and as he assumed his combat posture said, "Because I suspect that if I didn't, Justin would try himself. I can't let him do that, especially with the responsibilities he has to his own family. I don't have such restrictions, it's much more logical for me to make that sacrifice."

Rumil had always lived her life according to self-preservation, and the idea of willingly bringing about one's own demise was a relatively foreign concept. Nonetheless, knowing Timothy's inherent protectiveness, it made sense that he would try to shield Justin from death.

"So… what's with all the questions?" Timothy inquired as he underwent another series of spins and swipes.

Rumil brushed away the implied accusation with her answer. "Because I want to know more about you. Is that wrong? You've been reading into my life and getting me to spill my secrets since we met on Altair, yet it takes a hydraulic tool to pry anything about you past your lips."

Timothy gave up his training for a moment, and set down the practice sword down next to the manual before sitting cross-legged on the floor of the shuttle bay. Rumil sat down as well on his left, but with her knees against her chest.

"I don't want to bore you," Timothy began. "There isn't much to say."

Rumil grinned playfully, and bumped his shoulder with her own. "Once again, you're making assumptions for me. How about you just tell me, and I'll fall asleep when I feel it necessary?"

Timothy returned a more rueful grin, and consented. "Do you want the abridged version, or should I give you the complete three-volume set?"

"Whichever you prefer."

Timothy thought about just what he was going to say. "Well, as you already know, I was born to Celine and Niles Honore in Centris, right on the Staryear 3400. No one can prove it, but my mother claimed I was the first baby of the staryear on Solaria."

"She would know... a mother always knows these things," Rumil teased.

"Well, as I am sure you also already know, my father hated me largely from the start. He spent the first two staryears of my life fighting against my legitimacy, and one of my first memories involved him screaming that I wasn't his son, regardless of my genetic makeup. The next staryear, I was sent off for my beginning Knight training."

"At three staryears?" Rumil asked. "Is that normal?"

"No, it isn't," Timothy answered. "Usually, children with Knighthood potential are sent to that preliminary study around six or seven staryears. However, with the Feroz family announcing that Justin had come into his potential at three, my father decided that his hand had been pushed, and thus sent me into early study as well."

His lips turned wryly, and he added, "I was sent to the last remaining master of the Solarian fighting style called Doten Gurido... it's an Old Erani phrase that translates loosely into Basic as 'Body Synchronization.' The philosophy is that every muscle, or more accurately, every part of your body contributes, even if in a small way, to every attack or defense you make. The style predicates on mastering every muscle group as well as bodily purity in diet and maintenance."

And you definitely have a very well maintained body... Rumil remarked to herself as she regarded the Solarian's toned and smoothly muscled form, then quashed the thoughts just in case she started telepathically transmitting. "There are multiple forms of combat among the Solarians?"

Timothy laughed softly at that. "Of course there are. There are over fifty unique fighting styles among the Solarians alone, and another fifty approximately that we share on some level with the Kiros. The one I was trained in had the reputation of being the most difficult to learn... as a matter of fact, the master I was sent to was the only Doten Gurido master in about thirty staryears."

Rumil was about to ask why Niles would send someone so young into such a difficult discipline, but answered it herself just as Timothy did.

"My father sent me into that master's training likely in the hope that I would grow frustrated with the training, and give up, giving him grounds to disown me, and any potential inheritance I would be privy to. But, at the time, I was still trying to gain his favor, and even at that young age, put myself wholeheartedly into the training. Grant – that was my master's name by the way – commented he had never seen anyone so young dedicate themselves to their mental disciplines so quickly. I grew physically fast enough that I was able to begin martial training by the time most children were just beginning to explore their mental abilities."

"For the next six staryears after that, when I wasn't training, I was studying my required educational classes, eating, or sleeping. My only goal was proving that I was worthy of the name granted to me. I think my father, and just about everyone else, was surprised when not only did my master deem I was ready for the Academy… but that I had just celebrated my twelfth staryear."

"I assume that's a rather young age to be in the Academy." Rumil quipped.

"Considering most potential Knights aren't mature enough in either their studies or their training to enter the Academy until they are seventeen or eighteen staryears of age… yes, I would consider that rather young. Fortunately, I was a bit of a freak of nature in that I was physically equal to most young adult Solarians even at twelve, and I had studied so dutifully that I was more than able to keep up with the academic courses."

Rumil placed her chin on the palm of her right hand as it rested on her right knee. "Were you still in the 'impress your father' stage at this point?"

Timothy regarded the question thoughtfully, "At first… yes. But as I progressed, I realized that my father was only getting more disapproving, and more intolerant, of me the more successful I became. Eventually what started as a desire to gain the favor of my father became a desire to spite my father by becoming as successful as I could be. By the time I graduated from the Academy, and was declared a Knight of the Solarian homeworld, my relationship with the man who sired me had gone so sour that I rejected everything I was entitled on the family estate, and made my own way."

He then continued, "Some of the more liberal Knights had claimed that my father sent me after Regis Gallan in the hopes that I'd get killed. However, I think I already told you that I volunteered for the mission… simply as another way to stick it to my father, to shown him what I had become in spite of him. While I didn't think of that mission as particularly successful, enough others did. With Craig dead, and my father reaching an age where his abilities were starting to decline, there was considerable pressure from the rest of the Honores, and the royal family itself, to name a potential successor."

Rumil once again interjected with a wave of a finger. "Don't get modest now... the pressure was for him to name *you* his successor. Which he apparently did."

Timothy nodded. "Even then, the title I achieved meant little to me, just another way to aggravate my father. However, I never actually expected to take my father's position." He suddenly grew a little nervous when he added, "I felt I had a... greater purpose... to fulfill."

"I noticed that you once again skirted over what happened on Canasa," Rumil said nervously. "Because... well... that's rather related to something I want to discuss with you."

"How so?"

"Well... Dewin, Justin, and I had a strange conversation earlier... I saw it on Solaria, Justin saw it on Mydor and Ub, and Dewin saw it on Canasa."

Timothy seemed to understand what she was talking about, but he asked anyway, "Just what is this 'it' you're referring to?"

"I don't know how to explain it... I was hoping you could."

From the entrance to the shuttle bay, they heard Justin comment slyly, "Rumil, I'm glad you brought it up and not me."

Rumil turned to Timothy, gestured towards Justin, and asked, "How long had he been standing there?"

Timothy shrugged. "Not sure. I sensed his aura about a tick ago... but he's gotten a lot better at hiding himself."

"Don't be worrying about me," Justin smirked. "Now, are you going to answer Rumil's query or not?"

Timothy took a deep breath and stood up. He took a few quick strides over to one of the fighters held in the bay, and leaned back, his elbows against the wing. Justin and Rumil followed like two children eager to hear a story, and Timothy did not appear to disappoint.

"Well, I suppose it is only fair, and that you both have the right to know about something this important," the Solarian acknowledged. "But bear in mind, I don't understand it much myself."

"I don't remember the first incident, but I had my first psionic episode when I was twenty-seven ten-cycles old. The burst of power I released apparently burned down the entire west wing of the main Honore mansion, and severely injured seven people, including Craig."

Justin rubbed his forehead, as if running through the math in his head. "No wonder you're so powerful." Seeing Rumil's perplexed expression, he explained, "An Erani's psionic power grows steadily from the time it first manifests until physical maturity. It's why Jonathan's potential psionic ceiling is going to be significantly higher than mine, even though he came into his ability only a few cycles before me. To have a manifestation at an age like Timothy's... I can't even perceive those heights."

Timothy continued, "I was put on medications that hampered the now active sections of my brain until I was actually aware enough to control my own actions. I developed normally throughout my training and Academy study, and so I began to believe what the rest of my family believed; that whatever it was that happened was just a fluke of nature. Then the Canasa Incident happened. I wasn't prepared for it then, and the results were... gruesome, to say the least."

"I came to realize there is a part of me that doesn't seem to be completely me, something that is tremendously powerful, and that continues to get stronger, even though I'm well past the point where my psionic power should have stopped growing. Every time I allow extreme emotion to get the better of me, or when I summon that part of myself, it gets harder to control and fight back. Judging from what I did on Canasa, I can't be totally certain as to what I would do if I ever lost it completely, especially as powerful as I seem to be now."

There was silence for a moment then Timothy finally said, "That's it. Now you know as much as I do. Now if you don't mind, I have some training to do."

Justin turned his head towards where the manual and practice weapon laid. "Yes... I noticed that. Planning on using a twin-blade in the future?"

"If it comes to that," Timothy answered. The pair didn't say anything further, their expressions carrying on a silent conversation.

Rumil read the two accurately. Both of them were prepared to take their own lives for the sake of the other. It was remarkably noble on one hand... and ridiculously childish on the other. She flipped her hand in farewell, and remarked backhandedly, "Let me know when you two grow up." Then with a quick turn, she walked away, out of the shuttle bay and towards her quarters.

Justin and Timothy watched her go, and once she was out of sight, Justin continued to question the Solarian. "Now that we've actually got a few demiticks, perhaps you can explain to me just what your little exchange with Commandant Fransisca was about."

Timothy nodded, and said, "There is a small school of thought among some Solarians that we should be the instrument of our own demise. In other words, these people are intentionally seeking out the apocalyptic vision at the end of Bryan Honore's prophecy. I have come to label them the Endtimers."

"And why on the Creator's high name would they want that?"

Timothy chuckled and replied, "Well… you see… *they* don't intend to be part of that final battle. They intend for everyone else to die, so that they can assume control of the Solarian, and possibly even Kiros, sphere and institute their new galactic order… an order of fear, intolerance, and general hatred of anything that doesn't worship the Creator the way they wish for Him to be worshipped."

"And your dear father chose one of those people as the successor to his position?" Justin mused. "I can only go on what little I know of him… but I can't imagine he's that extreme."

"My father likely doesn't even know. As a matter of fact, pinning anyone to that particular school of thought has been hard going. As far as Solarian intelligence has gone, they just know it's there. I have my suspicions as just to who prescribes to the theory… but I'll admit that Fransisca was not on my list."

Justin demanded, "Why didn't you tell me of this little threat before? It sounds like these people would directly conflict with what we're trying to do."

Timothy answered flatly, "Because at the time, the Solarians as a whole were in conflict with us. Now that they're by and large out of our way, we can focus on keeping tabs on that particular segment of Solarian theology, who likely aren't going to let some Ubeks halt their plans."

"What about Rumil? What if those Endtimer zealots reach the same conclusion that you and I have?" Justin asked.

At that moment, Timothy grew grave. "They likely already have. I have little doubts that your father and mine both acted the way they did because the two of them also reached the same conclusion. If the High Commanders of both sects have decided that Rumil represents the prophet who could destroy their perches of power, then it is safe to assume that this cult of sorts has as well."

"So, what do we do about it?" Justin queried.

"I don't think the Endtimers are necessarily an immediate threat to Rumil, after all, they need her as the catalyst to attain the events they desire… but I can't be entirely certain. It's in the realm of the possible that they'll try to remove her now, and establish their own 'prophet' that more suits their agenda. It certainly wouldn't hurt to be prepared for just about anything."

* * * * *

>>*364 over 260. I win again.*

Rumil smirked as she entered the gloating remark into the game, and laughed at the poor crewman's angry reply. Checking to make sure that the credits transferred into her account, she then proceeded to type.

>>*Anyone up for another round?*

Six of the twenty crewmen and officers declined, leaving the remainder to reposition themselves in the Multi-Jalte network game as the system dealt out the next round of cards.

Multi-Jalte was one of a multitude of card games played around the Galactic Alliance, and was probably Rumil's favorite. The rules were rather simple as most card games went, and thus a lot of beginners played, making them easy marks to lose some credits.

A Multi-Jalte deck consisted of sixty cards, with cards ranging in value from "1" to "10." Each round consists of several turns, in which a player is dealt a card and decides whether to bet or withdraw from the round. In the first turn, players are dealt two cards, which in Rumil's case this time was a "4" and a "6." She decided to make a bet, as did seven others. The second turn, players are dealt one card, as well as every following turn until they have four cards. Rumil received another "6" and happily bet again.

Finally, Rumil was dealt her fourth card, a "9." With that knowledge in hand, she quickly started adding up her card total. This was done by first taking the two "6" cards she had. Because they were a pair, the two cards were added together then multiplied by two, giving her 24 to be added with the "4" and the "9," giving her a total of 37. Had three cards been the same, the total of the three cards would have then been multiplied by three, and four cards all the same would have been multiplied by four.

37, all things considered, was a fairly decent hand, so she put out another bet. Finally, one last card was dealt in front of her face-down. This was the multiplier, whatever the value of the card was would be multiplied at the end of the hand if anyone matched the final bet.

This was where luck and skill really came into play. Even the most meager of hands could become very formidable with a high multiplier, and even a group of four "10" cards would be rather pathetic if the multiplier was a "1".

However, Multi-Jalte had several variants. One variant involved each player only being dealt two cards, with two more face-up in the center as a community to complete each hand. Some variants involved the multiplier being a community card. Yet another allowed a player to turn in any one card after all four were dealt. There was even one version of the game in which the lowest score was the one that won, and a version which also allowed bonuses for having sequences of cards.

In the variant Rumil was playing, every player that withdrew had to show the hands they had… which allowed the observant player to be able to get a pretty good idea as to what their multiplier was.

In Rumil's case, she noted that four of the "1" cards were exposed from withdrawing players. And judging from the size of the deck that remained from after all cards were dealt, the chances were that her multiplier wasn't a "1." Doing the same for every number, Rumil figured there were good odds her multiplier was something between a "7" and a "10."

With that knowledge in hand, she made a large bet, just to see who would follow. Two opponents did, and one actually raised her bid, forcing Rumil to take stock of her own hand. While what she had wasn't bad… it also wasn't what one would consider a lock. Nonetheless, she had a hunch, and equaled her opponent's bet.

166

Not surprisingly, the third player withdrew, revealing a hand of two "7" cards, an "8," and a "5." All multipliers being equal, that hand would have beaten hers. It was a good thing that he withdrew.

What *was* surprising, though, was when the opponent who initially raised the first bet... did so *again*. Taking another glance at the cards revealed, Rumil realized the possibility that whoever the person had a very good set of cards. No "10" cards had been revealed, and thus, the chances her opponent had one or two was rather high.

Rumil smirked though, testing the fickle nature of chance. She didn't get to be one of the galaxy's finest hackers by playing it safe, and the killing she had made in earlier rounds allowed her to cast a bit more into the fray, yet still come out well ahead. With that in mind, she decided to turn the tables on her opponent, increasing the raise the person had just made.

She grinned smugly when her final opponent withdrew, leaving Rumil the winner by default. The player revealed a "10," and three "8" cards, then flipped over the multiplier to reveal a "5," for a total score of 410. With the triumphant posturing of a woman who had just made the bluff of the round, Rumil revealed her own set of cards... and a multiplier of "3." She chuckled in a combination of relief and cockiness as her credit account reflected her latest acquisitions.

Suddenly, a personal message flashed in the corner of her computing unit. It belonged to the person she had just bluffed, and it said rather simply...

> >>*Just checking to make sure you weren't cheating, and to inform you that we'll be arriving near Feria in about five tenth-cycles. Justin wants to have a quick briefing in about twenty ticks.*

Then the opponent, who she now guessed had been Timothy, logged off the network game, leaving Rumil to extend her partings as well, rejecting the pleadings of the crew and officers begging for a chance to win their credits back. Sadly, duty called, and she could not be late.

* * * * *

Unlike Timothy before his briefing, Justin was actually the first one in the conference room, and had been waiting as the rest of the team filtered in. Once they had taken their seats, Justin addressed them.

"I wish I had as clear of a plan as to how we're going to handle the Feria situation as Timothy did with Ub, but I don't. To be honest, all I have to go on is that for several hundred staryears, the Ferian have been subjugated by a series of medications that hamper what the Kiros claim to be their base animalistic urges."

Justin then tapped the table with his knuckles, and said, "However, I was able to call in a few favors with some friends of mine, and they have connected me with an official of the Ferian homeworld who has been trying to run an investigation on the truth of these theories for some time. She'll be our cover while we help her get to the bottom of the accusations."

Turning to Dewin, the Kiros added with a smile, "And we'll be able to shuttle down to the surface normally. There will be no need to come up with drills to drop us off in ten demiticks or so. As a matter of fact, we're going to have Orion drop us off on the colony planet Horodin, then take a standard shuttle to Feria."

"That's a relief," Dewin muttered with his chin resting on his hands.

"However, our plan will require that we adopt disguises so as not to be... easily recognized."

"You're suggesting illusionary appearances?" Timothy asked. "That would be a stretch for us to accomplish, especially if the ruse has to continue for any extended period of time, or if we get separated."

"No... there is a strong Kiros element on Feria, after all, and they'd likely sense psionic illusions. I'm talking about something else entirely."

The "something else" Justin was referring to became clear later, just as Rumil was preparing to board the shuttle that would take the group down to Feria. A tanned, thin Arcadian man with closely-cut blonde hair stopped behind her, and frowned displeasingly. It wasn't until she looked closer that she correctly identified the man in question.

"Timothy?" she asked with a disbelief mixed with humor. Finally, she succumbed to her mirth, laughing enthusiastically.

"Glad to know someone is amused," the disguised Solarian said sourly. "This better not take long, because my ears are already sore."

That's when Rumil took a closer look at his ears. The pointed lobes of cartilage that would have been a telltale sign of his Erani were gone, folded back and held down by a cosmetic mold to appear Arcadian. It had the effect of making his ears look larger than normal, but would be passed over by anything but the most studious examination.

"Well, now you know how I used to feel whenever I had to wear those accursed undergarments that crushed my breasts together for dancing," Rumil said unapologetically. "Be a woman and get used to it."

Timothy scowled at her, and she smiled, refusing to grant the Solarian any pity. Justin then emerged into the shuttle bay, although she quickly realized that he had not undergone nearly the same sort of manipulation. As a matter of fact, Justin looked hardly any different, other than colored contacts, a longer hairstyle that was dyed red, and a small dusting of fake facial hair along his jaw.

"Alright, we all set to go? Looking good, Timothy, no one will ever be able to guess you're even Solarian, much less your true identity," he said cheerily.

Rumil decided to ask, somewhat in apology for teasing Timothy just a moment before, "I notice you don't seem quite as… altered as our friend here."

Justin shrugged. "Well, the original plan was to give him a Kiros appearance, but then I commented that he's tall enough to pass for an average Arcadian, and Lydia, one of the covert intelligence officers on board, went insane. It really wasn't my fault, honestly. I, on the other hand, really don't have the vertical blessings to make a convincing Arcadian… thus we gave my normal appearance some alterations. Since there are some Kiros who work for the Galactic Alliance, it should work."

From inside the shuttle, they heard Orion call out, "Why is it that no matter how early you three arrive in the bay, I always wind up waiting for you?"

Without further comment, the trio stepped inside the shuttle, taking positions similar to their descent to Ub, although Justin did make note that Rumil had moved to the seat directly behind Timothy's. He shook his head, as apparently the pair was again on peaceable speaking terms. On a tightly shielded thought, he bemusedly wondered how long that would last…

169

Chapter Eleven

Ferian were big, menacing, and nothing short of terrifying up close.

Rumil knew this… she had seen several Ferian face to face on many separate occasions. So it shouldn't have come as a surprise to her. Yet when the first of the Ferian envoy came close enough for her to see the dagger-sharp rear teeth that protruded from their upper jaws, she had to fight her instincts to jump behind Timothy. One Ferian she could manage… a planet full of the feline-like creatures was a little much for her rapidly dwindling courage.

Now that isn't to say that the Ferian are *intentionally* intimidating…because they aren't. There have been more than a share of times where after the initial shock to her system, the Ferian she had met were as friendly and outgoing as anyone else she had ever witnessed.

That didn't change her opinion that whenever a Ferian smiled, it looked like they were about to dive for her neck, however…

It didn't help that every single one of the ten-Ferian special envoy sent to meet them had such smiles on their faces, broadly baring every one of the fifty-two teeth that Ferian inherently possessed, the movement of their jaws causing their eyes to narrow, presenting a facial expression that was hardly disarming – more like one interconnected curtain of fangs and sinister-appearing expressions.

The Ferian on the left end of the envoy spoke, its Basic inflected by a natural predisposition to long vowel sounds and a throaty voice that sounded like someone was rubbing a grater over its vocal chords. It didn't help Rumil determine if the Ferian was male or female, as it all sounded alike to her. "Which of you is…" it began, and then looked down at the PCU it carried… "Lance Irons?"

Justin stepped forward, "That would be me."

The Ferian peered closer at his computing unit then back at Justin. Finally, the Ferian nodded, and said, "Advisor Ruun is ready to meet with you. We are to take you to the Administrative Complex."

"Then lead on," Justin said, with a gesture toward the starport exit.

Four of them led the way, with one flanking each side of Rumil,

Justin, and Timothy, forming a loose ring around the trio of visitors, while the remaining four took position behind them. Rumil instinctively crept towards Timothy's side, but managed to at least keep a straight face and stopped herself from grabbing onto the disguised Solarian as they left the starport.

The party came to a motorcade of four black hovers with deep-tinted windows. Justin climbed into the rear of the second vehicle, Rumil and Timothy right behind him in that order. The Ferian in the driver's seat looked back at them, and gave another one of those smiles that made Rumil irrationally question why it was driving. "It should not be long to the Complex… just sit back and enjoy the ride."

That was something Rumil doubted she'd be able to do.

The procession started to pull out into the roadway, and Rumil then noticed that Timothy was scratching his ears. She leaned over to him, and whispered, "Don't do that, you'll ruin your disguise."

He frowned, as if realizing for the first time what he was doing. "Thank you," he whispered back, and clenched his hands in his lap. "Ironic, I've been stabbed, burned, slashed, cut, shocked, whipped, shot, and otherwise battered without so much as a complaint… but glue my ears back, and I can barely sit still."

Playfully, Rumil ran a finger along the bottom of Timothy's ear, and when he shuddered from the touch, she whispered with a huskiness that even surprised her, "Have I found the weakness of Timothy Honore? This is a delicious piece of information, without a doubt…"

Justin then jabbed Rumil in the side, and muttered, "Stop flirting, you two. We have a job to do."

Rumil had actually almost forgotten that Justin was next to her, and she whirled towards him with a withering glare, partially from anger at being interrupted, and partially from the realization of what she had been doing. "You know, I have really had it with your little interruptions and quips, Mister *Irons*," she hissed, using his alias with a slight emphasis. "What I choose to do, and with whom I do it, is frankly none of your business, even if it were true!"

Justin cowered away from the sudden outburst, his hands instinctively moving to his face to ward off the angry woman. At that point, Justin began to see the light of wisdom, and decided maybe it wasn't a terribly good idea to keep prodding the two of them.

The Ferian driving didn't make any indication that it even

registered the short argument in the back, and Timothy clearly was more concerned with not scratching his ears than commenting. Thus, the cabin of the hover fell into silence for the remainder of the trip.

* * * * *

The Administrative Complex of Feria – both the capital city and the planet, as they share the same name – was not like what Rumil had expected, even though she probably should have. Governmental buildings on Arcadia were much like the Multimedia Towers in which Krennan held sway; large, multi-floored monstrosities that overlooked the landscape for TackMets around, with tinted windows and dark fiberwall that prevented much outside light from coming in, causing them to rely on interior lighting. The air in those buildings was heavily circulated and sterilized, creating a completely artificial atmosphere that seemed to turn anyone working inside into a mindless robot.

However, it was clear that the Ferian took inspiration for their building layouts from the Kiros, with spread-out complexes of several smaller buildings, often with no more than three or four levels apiece, and large courtyards with lush greenery. Windows were clear, wide, and frequently open, allowing the rich smells from outside to create a much more pleasant atmosphere to the eyes and nose.

Then Rumil remembered nearly becoming a violent crime statistic on Kiros, and the charm rapidly faded. Suddenly, every window became a shot line for a sniper… the air became a prime method of transfer for an airborne pathogen or gas.

She felt Timothy gently place a hand on the small of her back, and he whispered in her ear, "I don't sense any animosity in this building. I do believe you can relax. Besides, Madam Foran, your disguise is quite well-fashioned as well." He accented the point by moving his hand from her back to catch a few locks of her now midnight hair in his fingers.

"I still can't believe Justin pulled that stunt on us…" Rumil whispered back, referring to their aliases, which both Timothy and Rumil had learned on the way to Feria. Justin had given her the false name she had used trying to flee from Iomet, Rama Foran… but with one slight amendment, that being the title of Madam, implying that her alias was married. When Timothy ruefully noted that his alias was none other than Sir – rather than Mister, which implied a single status – Randall Foran,

Justin let them in on the joke.

"Well, the two of you already argue like a wedded couple. I figured I'd give you two the chance for a trial run," the Kiros had said jovially, smirking like he had just won some great battle.

Timothy's voice jerked her out of her memory. "I actually wasn't surprised... in fact, once he gave me my data to study, I figured as much," he remarked. "It just didn't seem important enough to argue over."

"Is that right?" Rumil said disapprovingly. That was not the answer she was looking for.

"I would have liked a name better than Randall, that's all," Timothy answered with a swift wink.

Rumil smirked disbelievingly, and replied, "Nice recovery. You'd make some lovely little Solarian woman happy after all."

"Don't you dare start talking like my mother," he muttered into her ear. Then he stepped back, and placed his left hand under her chin. "Let me warn you that it probably wouldn't be a good idea to keep teasing me."

Rumil found her lips parting involuntary as Timothy leaned forward against his better judgment, and her eyes also closed without any real thought. Thus, she never noticed the unwelcome hand until it tapped her on the shoulder.

"As good as it is that you two are in character and all... we have an appointment," Justin stated, jerking a thumb towards the stairwell behind them.

Rumil was about to punch him, but held back, thinking that Timothy was going to do it instead. At the same time, Timothy was about to punch him, but stayed his hand, thinking that Rumil was going to take the honor. Thus, neither punched him, and he turned about to proceed towards their destination without retaliation.

With a shrug, Timothy followed, once again guiding Rumil along with a well-placed hand. "One cycle, if you happen to find Justin taped up in a closet somewhere... don't help him."

"No worries there," Rumil answered as they took the first steps up to the second floor of the central building.

They found Advisor Ruun, Secondary Director of Interplanetary Relations on Feria, in the furthest office to the right on the second floor of the Central Administrative Building. The tan-furred Ferian with specks and splotches of deep brown greeted each of them with that same fearsome smile, and a hearty forearm grasp. Rumil was thankful the Ferian had retractable claws on their hands, which actually weren't much more than feline paws with extended pads and an opposable thumb.

"It is a pleasure to meet you... Mr. Irons," Ruun said with what Rumil assumed was a sly grin. "Sir and Madam Foran, I had initially been expecting two... unmarried investigators. Are you the same pair that I was informed of earlier?"

"They are," Justin answered for them, trying to ignore the accusing stares from Rumil and Timothy. "It's an unrelated issue, I can assure you."

Ruun merely shrugged. "I don't particularly care what you name yourselves. I just don't like surprises, especially when it comes to associating in a covert manner with a man who is wanted for high treason by the Kiros."

"That is understandable, Advisor Ruun," Justin said with an apologetic bow. "As for the charges of treason; you know me personally... and I would hope that you had greater faith in me in that regard."

"I would hardly call the chance meetings we had, 'knowing,' Mr. Irons," Ruun warned. "My goal is merely to seek the truth of the charges brought against the allies of Feria, whether they be honest or malicious."

"As it is ours," Timothy then interjected. "If we can discover no foul play, then we shall not bother you further."

Ruun regarded the heavily disguised Solarian. "Well, my opinion is that there are more likely falsehoods among the Kiros position than truth. While the history of Feria before the arrival of the Erani people is not well documented... I find nothing to believe that there ever was any danger inherent among us Ferian. That ailment doesn't seem to become a concern until many staryears after First Contact was initiated."

Ruun reached into one of the drawers under her black metal desk, and emerged with a small package about five Tackems each side that she handed to Justin. "Inside that package is a vial of the medication the Kiros and Ferian medical technicians formulate for us. I haven't been able to hire any outside analysis because of the attention I would draw, but perhaps you know someone who could arrange it out of prying eyes."

Justin then handed the package over to Rumil, and she stated, "I have connections who can do as you request."

"I don't know any place that would be certain to have answers to this mystery… but I would recommend two places if you can manage to avoid the aforementioned prying eyes of the Kiros," Ruun continued. "One is the ceremonial burial grounds here in the city. It contains the remains of several prominent ancestors from times before the First Contact of the Erani to recent leaders of our people. Normally, I would condemn the idea of defiling our honored dead… but there is a greater question that must be answered if the Ferian are to proceed into the future."

"The Solarians, and the Kiros I'd wager, have similar sentiments about the deceased," Timothy said solemnly. "The weight of your suggestion is not lost on us."

Ruun nodded appreciatively towards Timothy, and said, "There is another place you may wish to investigate. On the Murrra continent to the south is what is called 'The Reserve,' where the Wild Ferian roam. The Kiros claim this is where all those who reject their aid are found, and they also might hold some clues as to what is really happening to the Ferian."

"We thank you for your aid, Advisor," Justin said with another bow. "We shall strive to report our findings as soon as we are able. Unless you have further instructions, I see no reason why we cannot be on our way."

Ruun bowed awkwardly in reply, the rear-bent legs of the Ferian not up to accurately imitating Justin's gesture. "I wish you well in your endeavor. I will be awaiting your conclusions."

The three then left Ruun's office. "I suppose I can investigate the burial grounds" Justin suggested, "as the natives probably won't question a Kiros poking around as much. You two can take a look at the 'Wild Ones,' and try and find out what you can. The trip to the South could probably give you time to send the data on that medication to Krennan's analysis crew."

Neither Timothy nor Rumil had any objections to that plan, so Justin decided to progress with it. "Well, let's find our way to our dwellings, and make the necessary arrangements, shall we?"

* * * * *

Later that day, Rumil and Timothy were reserving a room for an overnight stay, both of them deciding that it was a little late to go charging through a reserve of violent Ferian. The manager of the hotel noticed their names and said, "I assume you will be desiring one bed..."

Timothy was about to decline, but Rumil caught him quickly, saying, "Yes... of course."

As the manager turned to acquire keys and call someone to help the pair with their luggage, Rumil explained, "We're supposed to be a married couple, remember? Don't you think it would be a little suspicious to request separate bedding?"

Timothy appeared ready to protest anyway, but stayed silent, his eyes darting over to the manager as he returned to the desk. The Ferian handed her a card that would grant them entry into their room, and said, "Arrtuuleth will take your luggage packs."

Rumil turned to see a "smiling" Ferian face just Tackems from her, and yelped in shock before falling backward into Timothy. The assistant was about at Rumil's eye level, but only because it was hunched over to collect the various packs. Timothy gave her shoulders a gentle caress, as if trying to calm her, as the Ferian stood, and said, "Follow me, I shall take you to your room."

Neither of the two seemed keen on taking the lead, but Rumil managed to get over her initial fright in order take step behind the attendant, Timothy reluctantly following, keeping a distance that Rumil determined to be barely friendly.

With a devious smirk, Rumil grabbed Timothy by the wrist, and before he could brace himself, pulled him to her side. "Now, love..." she teased, "I know we're on business, but that doesn't mean you have to keep an arm length away at all times," she circled her own arm around his waist for effect.

Timothy's glare carried very discomforting promises, but at least his body language followed her lead, as he gently draped his left arm over her shoulders, and took the lead following the attendant to the lift that took them to the required floor.

Their room was more to Rumil's style than it was Timothy's. It was a large suite with several rooms and enclaves for working and relaxing, like a bubbling hot spring tub near a panorama window of the outside, and a small kitchenette on the other end. The carpeting was a flat red with gold trim that matched well with the crimson velvet furniture, as well as brass polished hanging chandeliers with crystal lighting covers, which created a neat sparkling effect across the off white painted walls.

"How much was this room again?" Timothy asked as he leaned into the bedroom, then turned away nervously when he noticed Rumil was already undressing for the night.

Rumil noticed his discomfort as she pulled off her blouse, and remarked, "You really are such a prude. You could relax just a little."

"It has nothing to do with being a prude," Timothy denied from around the doorway.

"Is that right?" Rumil pressed the issue as she then stepped out of the long skirt she wore, "Is it because of the prophet thing again?"

"That's not it, either."

Finally, she popped around the doorway, and demanded, "Then what is it then? Stop being so irritatingly secretive and just tell me what it is that is bothering you!"

"You should know already," Timothy shot back. "I can't let myself act on the attractions I already have. It's too dangerous."

"Are you saying you find me attractive?" Rumil asked. Granted, she had suspected such, but at the same time had never been able to know for certain.

"I would have thought that was obvious," Timothy muttered, his eyes closed as if trying to stop himself from looking around.

"Well, just to let you know, you aren't nearly as obvious as you may think," Rumil said in observation. "So, if you're attracted to me… and you claim not to be such a prude… then why be so distant? Why can't you be a little more open, like you were on Mydor?"

"What I nearly did on Mydor would have been a potentially dangerous mistake," Timothy answered. "I've already told you what happens when I let my emotions get the better of me. If I were to do what you suggest… who is to say what would happen?"

Rumil gave pause to the thought. "You really think that would… I mean, it seemed that anger was the trigger every time you've… changed."

"Would you be willing to take that risk?" Timothy asked. "There's a danger any time that I allow my more emotional self to dominate my actions. Besides, I thought you were hung up on my reasons for following you. Just what do you want from me?"

Rumil smarted at the reminder, and slipped back into the bedroom, leaning back against the wall. "I… I guess I don't know anymore. I guess I understand what you're saying. And no, I suppose I wouldn't want to test your theory." She rubbed her forehead gingerly.

Timothy gently reached around the doorway, placing a hand on her forearm. "I would suggest we just let time sort out the issues we both have. Until then, that long sofa looks plenty comfortable for me."

She smiled, and accepted the slight contact as all that Timothy was going to allow her. Reluctantly, she admitted to herself that his reservations were likely valid, and added another complex facet to the on-and-off relationship the two shared. Perhaps he was right, and they should let time help them to understand what each of them expected and required from the other. "All right… I guess I can stop teasing… just for you." Her eyes crossed as she tried to figure out why that promise sounded so… oddly backward.

"I'm sure that must be quite the sacrifice," Timothy laughed. "I suggest you get some sleep soon. We might have a long cycle coming up."

She strode to her bed, gathered up two of the pillows and the top blanket, and stepped back into the main room. She handed them to Timothy, and said, "Here… you might need these." Then retreated to the bedroom before Timothy could again comment on her state of dress, smiling triumphantly the entire way, knowing the Solarian's eyes were on her.

The following morning, Rumil stepped out of the bedroom in one of the robes provided by the hotel. Timothy was already awake and active, performing some exercises while dressed in his full casual wear. "Okay… I'm willing to cover myself more appropriately so as not to ravage your tenuous emotional state, but why should I be punished in the same way?" she drawled playfully, stepping up to the room service tray that must have been recently delivered, judging from the steaming plates of food and blisteringly hot kettle of ducha.

"Just want to be fair and all," Timothy replied with a smile. "I mean, I don't want to seem that I don't empathize with your generous sacrifice."

She scooped some of the food onto one of the small circular plates provided, and poured herself some ducha into a finely crafted ceramic cup, adding sweetener and a candied flavoring with a small spoon before gathering both items, and taking a seat on the sofa. "Your empathy is duly noted..." she said, then smirked, "...but is hardly necessary."

"Very well," Timothy said with a shrug, tossing aside his vest, leaving him in his fully buttoned dress shirt and loose tan slacks, with the body suit underneath.

"You think you're so smart..." Rumil said with a roll of her eyes as she took her first few bites, but did not complain further as Timothy finished his exercises, and also gathered up food and drink, taking a seat next to her.

"So, has the analysis team reported in yet?" Timothy asked.

Rumil shrugged. "I only sent them the scanned composition of the medication a few ticks ago. It could take a full cycle before I receive any results from them. Besides, until we have all the information together, an analysis would be rather worthless I suspect."

"Which brings us to the task at hand," Timothy declared, unfolding his computing unit on the dining table in front of them. "Our cover is that we're investigating on behalf of the Galactic Alliance as to the general health and well-being of the Wild Ferian... for humanitarian reasons. As which, we likely won't be rather well received by the reserve staff."

"Justin and Advisor Ruun couldn't come up with a better cover?" Rumil asked. This entire plan was edgy enough as it was without unnecessarily angering reserve officers.

"Not one that would grant us the right to examine and take samples of the Wild Ferian," Timothy stated. "At least this way we'll have the reluctant support of the staff, rather than having to sneak around them."

"I suppose that's true enough..." Rumil said with a sigh. "I just wish I could have a run-in with officials that would be good-natured and genial."

"There is no such thing," Timothy answered wryly. "That's the nature of dealing with officials in any capacity. They're always going to resent you when you impinge on their authority."

"Perhaps..." She then placed her plate on the table, and stretched out. "So, when do you wish to leave?"

"Whenever you can burden yourself with getting dressed," Timothy said with an analytical glance at her robe.

Rumil stuck her tongue out at him then stood. "Very well... let me get prettied up, and we'll be on our way. Perhaps you can rent us a hover for the trip in the meantime?"

"Already done," Timothy answered smugly. "Then again... I awoke at a reasonable time."

His reward for that quip was a rather inaccurately thrown pillow from just inside the bedroom.

Chapter Twelve

"Sir and Madam Foran, I presume?" asked a Kiros man in a forest green uniform shirt and slacks, from the front gate of the Wild Ferian Reserve. "Officer Denis Hutner at your service."

Rumil huffed as she was passed over by the Kiros, who exchanged a forearm grasp with Timothy, who had to shift the rifle case on his back to return the gesture. She had almost forgotten the blatant sexual bias of Erani in general, and was not pleased at the sudden reminder.

"I'm not terribly sure just why the Galactic Alliance is concerned with the health of the Wild Ones," Hutner admitted, "but I'll do what I can to help you."

"Well, we just do the job... not ask why," Rumil cut in, hoping to force the reserve official into at least acknowledging her existence... which the Kiros man did... fleetingly.

"I suppose that is true," he stated, then turned right back to Timothy. "Is there anything you are looking for in particular?"

Timothy simply smirked as Rumil again answered the question. "We were told to get data on anything and everything. My guess is the science crews are trying to find anything they can make an issue out of."

"That sounds like the Galactic Alliance," Hutner replied with a fake laugh then turned right back to Timothy. "We'll take one of the offroad vehicles in... yeah, I know, it's not a hover, but there isn't any magnetic paneling for hovers on the reserve... and I'll escort you around to some of the more popular spots for the Wild Ones. With any luck, you should have everything you need by the end of the cycle."

"Sounds wonderful," Rumil remarked again, her voice starting to reflect her increasing annoyance. "Unless you two boys have something else to discuss, we might as well get on with our business."

Timothy again smiled, yet said nothing, willing to defer any discussion to Rumil. Whether that was because he acknowledged her irritation as valid or his nature to not engage in conversation without something to add, Rumil couldn't be certain... but she appreciated the unspoken gesture nonetheless.

The reserve officer finally took extended note of Rumil when Timothy deferred the front side passenger to seat to her. Like a disappointed child that wanted to speak his mind, yet not wanting to get punished for it, Hutner said, "Oh… I was expecting Sir Foran to… sit there…"

"Rama is the one in charge of this investigation, Officer Hutner," Timothy finally said, opening up the large black case he had brought with him, revealing a black long range rifle complete with several clips of feathered darts, presumably filled with sedatives. "I'm just the shooter."

It took a few demiticks for that news to sink in, as if the reserve officer only just began to contemplate the possibility. Rumil lifted her eyebrows in challenge, and allowed a smirk to slowly creep onto her mouth, as if daring the Kiros man to comment on Timothy's claim. The officer finally sank as low as he could into his seat, and Rumil reveled triumphantly in the man's discomfort… after all, he had it coming.

The magnetically sealed metal gate slowly opened to allow their treaded vehicle access to the interior of the reserve, the driver beginning to accelerate as soon as there was enough room for the vehicle to fit through. "Generally the Wild Ones keep away from the wall," Hutner explained. "It's electrified, and they seem to have the same implanted fear of civilization as other feral beasts. Fortunately there's over five thousand square TackMets of untouched wilderness so that they don't feel cramped or isolated."

"Just how many Wild Ferian are in the reserve?" Rumil asked.

The officer shrugged. "That's hard to say, actually. At last count from sat data and tagging, there was approximately two thousand, three hundred… but they have been known to breed, so there's no guarantee we've counted every single one of them as the new cubs wouldn't necessarily be tagged, and the dens they grow in could potentially block detection from satellites. However, I would say with all certainty that there can't be any larger than a population of about three thousand."

"I don't terribly understand why some Ferian would want to be feral," Timothy replied.

"I don't know either. There is a cult of sorts that calls upon its members to accept their beastly natures, but it's a very small group. Some just… I guess they just get tired of being slaves to drugs and the bustle of civilized life. The city jungle isn't for everyone, I suppose."

"You don't sound like you accept those theories," Rumil noted.

Hutner shrugged. "They make more sense than the conspiracy theories we can't get rid of. In order for those to work, the Kiros and the

Ferian would have to be in on the whole thing, and I can't imagine the Ferian actually doing that to themselves."

Timothy muttered something that Rumil couldn't hear over the sounds from the vehicle, but she figured it probably went along the lines of his experience with the Ubeks. If there was personal gain to be found, racial lines could be quickly forgotten.

It was half a tenth-cycle before they found their first signs that Wild Ferian were nearby… and it certainly wasn't something Rumil wanted to approach. Their escort seemed to have no such problems, pulling to a stop and jumping out of the vehicle to analyze the very fresh mountain of dung that was less than two Tacks from Rumil's shoe. She gagged and covered her nose from the smell with the collar of her shirt while the reserve officer seemed to take in the scent with little external reaction.

"Oh, this is a definite sign that some Wild Ones are nearby. This little dropping can't be any more than twenty ticks old or so. Let's take a look and see if the sats can pick some up…"

He jumped back into the driver's seat and cheerily tapped in commands on the vehicle's computerized panel located between the two seats. Rumil, on the other hand, simply couldn't take her eyes of the simply massive mound of feces that seemed to be getting closer the longer she stared. Because of her repulsed fascination, she barely heard Hutner declare happily, "Yes, the satellite's got one a little more than a TackMet away! With luck, we can sedate the thing and get what you need before it even knows we're there."

With that, the vehicle moved forward to Rumil's intense relief, albeit at a drastically reduced speed so as not to warn their quarry of their approach. Hutner called back, "Just how good of a shot are you?"

Timothy was quickly making a check of the rifle to make sure everything was set. "Good enough," was his reply. "Get as close as you feel you comfortably can, and I'll do the rest."

"Very well… just so you know; missing probably wouldn't be a good idea for our continued health. Wild Ferian are nasty sorts when they feel they are being provoked."

"I don't miss," Timothy assured.

The reserve officer looked over to Rumil, as if hoping to confirm Timothy's boast. Rumil had never actually seen Timothy use a long-range rifle before, but something told her not to doubt the Solarion's proficiency with the weapon. "He doesn't miss," she then agreed, hopefully without too much of a pause.

While Hutner didn't seem totally convinced, he continued driving, idling the vehicle's engines once the Ferian was in sight... barely in sight, but in sight nonetheless. To Rumil, all she saw was a reddish ball about half a TackMet away. "Is this close enough for you, Sir?" Hutner asked Timothy, who was already lying prone against the rear seat of the vehicle, his feet sticking out one end, his elbows propping the rifle firmly, the magnifying scope already pressed against his eye.

"Plenty close enough, Officer," Timothy drawled, instantly followed by a sudden pop of air as the rifle fired, the high-pressure dart zipping out of sight before Rumil even thought to follow its flight path. A couple demiticks later, their quarry suddenly lurched to its full height, staggered three steps, then collapsed back onto the ground.

"Good shot!" Hutner exclaimed, clearly impressed and relieved as he slowly accelerated to the site of the fallen Ferian, oblivious to the fact that the dart had been psionically guided, a fact that amused Rumil.

He then turned to Rumil and asked, "I assume you have the extraction tools, Madam?"

Rumil glanced down at her satchel, as if suddenly remembering that she did indeed have the kit and extraction needle to gather genetic material from the Ferian ... and that she couldn't use them from a distance...

"Are you sure it's... sedated?" Rumil asked nervously as the vehicle pulled to a stop in front of the fallen Ferian.

"Well, why don't you try and take a sample, and we'll see if he bites you!" Hutner declared cheerily, intentionally doing nothing to ease Rumil's slightly troubled state of mind.

"I'll keep the rifle trained in case one dose wasn't enough, lovey," Timothy promised with a playful grin. "Although judging from the sedative that was loaded into these darts, I can't imagine anything being able to get up from that."

Despite his assurances, Rumil didn't feel remotely close to secure, approaching the massive feline-like beast gingerly, worried that making too much noise would shake it out of its drugged stupor.

Half a tick later, she was leaning over the Ferian, the extraction needle Tackets from its fur... when Hutner crept up behind her, grabbed her shoulders, and emitted a very fake sounding roar in her ear. Nonetheless, Rumil screamed in terror and jumped backwards, tripping over Hutner's foot and falling roughly on the ground, panting in an attempt to catch her fleeing breath.

When her lungs once again filled with air, she scowled furiously, and kicked out, catching the officer directly on the side of the shin. She then turned a baleful eye towards Timothy to see if he also found the malicious prank humorous, as he didn't do anything to warn her of it. He simply looked back at her with a half smile, and gestured towards the sedated Wild Ferian, who still had not seemed to move.

Rumil was partially disgusted at the officer for pulling such an inane stunt, and partially disgusted at her response to it. Rather than shattering any sexist attitudes Hutner clearly possessed, she likely gave him another silly story to tell his friends that night; that of the scared little woman that buckled when given any sort of authority and cowered in terror before an unconscious Ferian.

Giving a murderous glare to the slightly wincing – but still chuckling – Kiros man, Rumil kneeled back down over the Ferian. She directed one more withering scowl to Hutner, then pushed the needle through fur and flesh, gathering blood and tissue samples when she pulled it out. The needle was detached, sealed in a vacuum bag, and then dropped in the hard plastic box with the rest of the extraction kit before Rumil placed the box back in her satchel.

"Now, provided we can avoid any more juvenile jokes…" Rumil sneered, giving the Kiros man her best look of warning, "we should be able to complete our task without any undue waste of time, and we can all return to business as usual."

A tenth-cycle later, they had collected three more samples, and Hutner decided it was time for a different target.

"I'm assuming you want a few females in your sampling as well," he commented.

"How do you know they're all males?" Rumil asked.

Hutner laughed at that, once again causing Rumil to scowl at what she perceived was another tidbit for the Kiros's bias. "Males are generally the only ones that you'll find solitary in the wild. Females are a lot bigger than any of the males, and are often surrounded by huge packs of males in a pride."

Then, the Kiros reserve officer surprised Rumil. He sighed then commented, "Sometimes makes me wonder... you start to rethink your ideas about the 'superior' gender when you see a Wild Ferian queen having an escort of twenty males or so. It's rather humbling in a way. By Bannor, their entire society is like that... the female is generally the one that's always had the power, and it's the men who have been fighting the status quo, trying to find some sense of equality in it all."

He flushed, as if embarrassed by the admission. "I know that doesn't sound terribly Kiros of me. I don't claim to be an expert on my faith... but when you're placing value on sheer chance, it just seems... out of place, no matter what some priest says... *there we go!*"

The sudden exclamation jarred Rumil, who was taken by surprise by the rapid change in the Hutner's mood. She noticed he was pointing at the satellite display in between them, and a large grouping of dots at which his finger was pointing.

"That's a nicely sized pride there," Hutner explained. "Has to be at least forty of them, and likely a queen with a few other females. Depending on how fast of a shot you are, Sir Foran, we could make quite a score here."

"You just drive... I'll shoot. We'll sort out the rest once that's done," Timothy replied, once again checking over his equipment.

With an energized whoop, Hutner pressed the accelerator to full, and the vehicle responded with a reluctant lurch as he made all due speed towards their next destination. "It doesn't pay to be discreet with a pride of that size," he explained, as if anticipating Rumil's question about the apparent change in tactics. "They'll simply attack if one of their number is threatened. What you have to do in these cases is to come in loud and scatter them, and make your shots in the confusion. As a matter of fact..." Hutner said thoughtfully, suddenly stopping the vehicle again, causing all three to jerk forward with the change in momentum.

Rumil stared at him questioningly as he unbuckled his harness, and dashed to the rear storage compartment of the vehicle. Rumil turned about to see what he was doing, and realized that he was piecing together a long-range rifle of his own. Noticing her and Timothy's attention, he explained, "Well, we increase our chances with two shooters, after all. That is... if Madam Foran feels she's up to driving."

Rumil's eyebrows raised as she registered the suggestion. "I've never driven a land-bound vehicle... actually..."

The rifle assembly complete, Hutner hopped around to the

vehicle's front passenger side, and said with confident persuasion, "Ah... there's nothing difficult about it, really. Just like driving a hover. That lever there is the velocity control... just push it forward to accelerate, and pull it back to brake. The further you pull the level either side, the harder the change in speed. This little beauty is designed with displaced treads as well, so don't get too worried you're gonna tip us over. It even has high-pressure thrusters so that you can maneuver a bit while airborne. Just pay attention to the windshield projection displays and if a warning pops up, just let the vehicle compensate for it. Not too tough at all."

"Think you can handle a device that does most of the work for you?" Timothy said bemusedly.

Rumil rolled her eyes, and muttered, "I think I can manage... yes." She took a deep breath, and climbed over to the driver's seat, allowing Hutner to take her seat on the passenger's side.

"Whenever you're ready, Madam," Hutner declared. "You don't have to go too fast... just enough to freak the Ferian out for a moment."

With another deep breath, Rumil grabbed the steering wheel – little more than a plastic circle with a handgrip on top of the steering column – in one hand, and the velocity control lever with the other. Then, her dangerous side took over. She looked back at the two men, and flashed a mischievous grin that caused Timothy to look slightly worried. He knew what it meant... and soon the unsuspecting Kiros next to her would as well.

Rumil licked her lips then thrust the velocity level to full acceleration, catching Hutner off-guard. However, the reserve officer recovered quickly, and it almost seemed like he was enjoying the thrill even more than she was as the vehicle bounced over ruts, divots, bumps, and hills.

The rush Rumil felt seemed to cloud her rational thought, because she never really registered the pride of Wild Ferian until the vehicle was almost right in front of them. She edged off the acceleration slightly as the pride scattered. Rumil couldn't hear the sounds of her companions shooting, but had little doubt they were.

"Loop around, and go after the ones that dashed off to your right!" Hutner shouted. "We should be able to catch up and tag a few more!"

Rumil pulled the velocity lever to an idle, and quickly whipped the steering grip to the right, feeling the heavy vehicle respond with surprising agility, turning approximately a hundred and twenty degrees in a tight enough radius that she worried for a moment that her harness would break from the strain.

Once the vehicle settled straight, it was back to full acceleration in pursuit of the fleeing Ferian that were still keeping a relatively tight formation. As she pulled even with the group in question, Rumil noticed that the one in the center of the group was indeed significantly larger than those around it, probably about two full heads taller than any of the rest. Rumil let off the accelerator again so as to keep pace, somewhat enthralled by the almost majestic creatures in flight.

"That's the queen… that's why those males are so bunched together around her!" Hutner said. "Pull around to the other side of them if you get the chance so that I can get a shot as well."

Timothy successfully shot one of them just before Rumil began to make the necessary adjustment in positioning. By the time the vehicle was on the other side of the group, he had sedated another in the rear of the pack.

"Tag the queen last!" Hutner advised. "Once you do that, all the males will scatter!"

If Timothy replied, Rumil didn't hear him. With that in mind, all she had to do was follow the pack as the two men picked off the pack, then finally the queen. Like all the others, the large female staggered and fell. With that, Rumil turned the vehicle about again, and approached the sedated Ferian… albeit considerably more slowly.

She stopped next to the Queen, and pulled the extraction kit out of her satchel. Hutner and Timothy followed, likely to stretch their legs.

"Well, I shot a few of the females in the pride at the initial site," Hutner claimed, "and I know you tagged quite a few yourself, Sir Foran. I suspect we probably can collect about fifteen samples just from this pride. How many are you looking to get, by the way?"

"Enough to determine we have an adequate cross-section of the population," Rumil answered as she took the required tissue and blood from the Queen. "If you estimate there can't be any more than three thousand, about thirty samples should suffice."

"Well then, we could probably hunt down another pride, and that should fill your quota nicely," Hutner replied, then suddenly his head jerked to the west, and his facial features reflected confusion. "What in Bannor…?"

Rumil looked up to notice that Timothy was looking in the same direction. Then she felt a strong buzz of psionic energy in the back of her head. Perhaps Timothy's occasional lessons helped her, because she felt she could identify who it was from the unique sensations it triggered. But how, or why, was Emmitt Fransisca wandering around on Feria?

Timothy reacted to something, jumping in front of Rumil, grunting as something struck him in the palm as he held his out in an attempt to ward off the attack. The psionic tingle disappeared soon after that, and Rumil stood up as Timothy pulled the dart free. Hutner grabbed the pointed injection needle, sniffed the tip, then grimaced.

"Good Creator, that's the fetish bait we use to attract Ferian for checkups… but this is really concentrated. This stuff could whip any Ferian into a frenzy," the officer commented. "But why would he—" Hutner was interrupted by the sounds of growling from where Fransisca had just disappeared. At the top of a rather large hill, a massive number of Wild Ferian started to appear.

Timothy scowled in anger, understanding Fransisca's plan. He sent a tightly shielded telepathic message across the planet, and when he got the reply he was looking for, turned to Rumil. "Quick, give me the extraction kit."

Rumil complied, keeping a nervous eye on the approaching Wild Ferian as they began to stalk forward slowly down the hill.

Timothy then addressed Officer Hutner. "A Kiros man, a Mister Irons, will be appearing shortly. Once he arrives, get out of the reserve as quickly as you can." Then he turned back to Rumil and said, "I'll return to the hotel as soon as I am able… I should be able to collect the remaining samples in the process." With that, he grabbed the fetish dart, and dashed away as quickly as he could, the Ferian changing their course to follow.

Finally Hutner blinked, opened his mouth while plotting out what he wanted to say, before finally managing to mutter, "What… just happened?"

Rumil shook her head and didn't answer. She wasn't sure she could in any meaningful way.

* * * * *

189

Until that night came, she still didn't get many answers.

Justin tried to brighten her mood, but it was clear that worry was fixed at the top of her mind, and it wasn't about to go anywhere until a certain Solarian walked through the door to their room.

"He's tough… he'll get here," Justin said with a smile. "He can shield himself from a fusion bomb, after all. Surely a few Wild Ferian are but child's play."

"Maybe," Rumil replied glumly. "But I doubt a fusion bomb hunted and stalked you both."

"Now, come on," Justin said in a playful chide. "You know those GalNet feature videos? The grand adventure things, where no matter what the odds, no matter the numbers of adversaries, no matter how close of range they're at… the hero always comes out alive?"

Rumil couldn't hold back the bitter chuckle that escaped her. "Holes in the plot you could fly a cruiser through, but nary a scratch on the hero's perfectly coiffed head."

"Timothy just seems to have that sort of ability," Justin continued. "Think about it… all the things we know he's been through, and survived… then realize that's probably only the half of it."

Rumil had to acknowledge the likely truth in Justin's arguments. It helped alleviate her concerns… if merely slightly.

Deciding that the sunshine routine wasn't entirely working, Justin decided to try to turn Rumil's attention to work. "So, have you heard anything from the team analyzing the medication we received?"

"That I did," Rumil replied. "They didn't find anything suspicious. Everything in that medication has been proven on their test simulations to calm portions of the brain that govern fighting and baser instincts in the Ferian brain."

"I see…" Justin muttered. That wasn't what he had hoped to hear.

"However…" Rumil continued, "They did find something… curious… in the samples you sent them."

Justin's ears perked slightly, and he asked, "That being?"

"Firstly, there was the presence of a synthetic hormone called ferazine in the tissues of some of the samples."

Justin tapped his forehead. "Why does that name sound like

something I should remember?"

Rumil tapped on her computing unit to bring up data on the chemical. "It was supplied by Arcadian dealers to the Ubeks during the Ubek Campaign. It's stimulates the release of inordinate amounts of adrenaline and other stimulating hormones into the subject's body chemistry."

"And this hormone was only found in certain samples?"

"Indeed. However, it only occurred in the earliest samples you acquired. The biological team surmises that it was potentially used to start the fear of 'Wild Ferian.' Then, the Kiros come in with their wonder drug to counter the effects… and instant dependency, here we are."

Justin nodded in understanding, "And the further forward in time we go, the more that time becomes hazy, and the easier it is to keep the myth going. However, that doesn't explain the current Wild Ferian. I can't imagine the Kiros being able to feed such hormones to the Ferian nowadays without someone noticing…"

Rumil then replied, "That's the other thing the team discovered. From what they can determine, there was a dramatic shift in the chemical and genetic makeup of Ferian around four or five hundred staryears ago."

"What does that mean?"

"Well, they can't piece it all together from what they have, but it appears that at that point, the Kiros started using a radically different medication. That would explain the chemical change… but not the genetic one. The genetic data is incomplete, but it appears that the genes that governed the Ferian's natural aggressiveness suddenly became drastically more dominant at that time. Not that anything can be determined conclusively unless Timothy returns with the more recent samples…"

"You mean, *until* Timothy returns with the recent samples," Justin corrected, determined to keep Rumil out of the funk that had just been plaguing her.

"Yeah… of course…" Rumil agreed half-heartedly.

Fortunately, Justin didn't have to do anymore cheering. To their surprise, they heard the sounds of light rapping on the panoramic window outside, and leaning against said window, looking rather haggard, was the vaguely unfamiliar form of Timothy Honore.

Rumil quickly opened the window to let him in off the balcony, and she quickly came to his aid as his right leg buckled out from under him. Contrary to the image Justin painted of the near-invincible hero, Timothy looked like he had been drug backwards through a wood chipper. His shirt was torn and ripped in several places, and spattered with blood. Judging from the gashes and cuts that could be seen, most of the blood was his. None of the wounds appeared terribly serious, until he staggered to the sofa, and she noticed that there were actually seven teeth embedded into his right leg.

"Accursed things are smarter than they look," Timothy admitted, as he handed her his belt pack, which contained all the samples that he had promised. "Thirty-seven, though I would have been smarter stopping at thirty-six. It seemed like I had shook them off, so I returned to where you had been to see if I couldn't collect some samples on the Ferian we sedated before they woke up. One of them I think heard me coming, and was pretending to be asleep. As soon as I got close enough, he tried to take a piece of my leg as a trophy." He then smirked maliciously as he added, "A few well-placed punches to the muzzle changed his opinion on the matter."

"Where did you get the rest?" Rumil asked.

"Well, let's just say the hunted became the hunter. I used the peculiar scent that Fransisca so lovingly granted me to draw Ferian to me, then quickly grabbed a sample before they could pinpoint where I was." He then hissed painfully when Justin removed his shirt to reveal the full nature of Timothy's injuries. "Although I wasn't quite fast enough to get away unscathed a few times."

"Why in the Creator's name didn't you use your mental powers to speed up healing?" Justin demanded as he began to do just that, the wounds on Timothy's body starting to close at a drastically increased rate.

"I'm supposed to be an Arcadian, remember?" Timothy answered. "I didn't want to take the off-chance that someone looking for me happened to sense me using psionics."

"I don't think you would have fooled them anyway," Rumil noted, pointing to the side of Timothy's head. The mold one his left ear had fallen off, exposing the telltale point at the tip. Timothy felt the ear with his hand then started laughing.

"Figures…" He guffawed wryly. "During all the commotion, I must have never noticed it had come loose." With a smug glee, he ripped the other ear point loose as well, and shrugged when Justin scowled at him. "It's not like it was going to be effective anymore."

With Timothy safe – relatively, anyway – Rumil's mood had brightened, which is to say, she was acting as she normally would. She closed the extraction kit again, and tossed Timothy's belt onto the table. "I better get these scanned and sent to be analyzed," she said, taking her computing unit, and disappearing into the bedroom.

Suddenly, Justin jolted. "Wait... you said Fransisca was here? Emmitt Fransisca?"

Timothy nodded. "Indeed he was. It's why I asked you to teleport over to watch Rumil just to be safe."

"You think he was going to try and do something to Rumil while you were occupied?"

"Actually, as I look back on it, I think I was his target from the start. He had a window in which he could have attacked Rumil had he wanted to," Timothy said thoughtfully. "I'm not really worried about that, since the idea of Emmitt getting me killed is almost laughable. I'm more interested how he could be walking around Feria casting an aura with seemingly no regard towards detection."

"Maybe the Endtimers spread beyond the Solarian sphere of influence..." Justin offered.

"That's not a pleasant thought," Timothy solemnly agreed.

Justin decided to change the subject quickly, "Well, the good news is by tomorrow we should be able to submit our findings to Advisor Ruun, and let everything else take care of itself."

"Actually, something a reserve officer said got me thinking," Timothy retorted. "Perhaps Ruun isn't the only one we should give this information to..."

* * * * *

"That was quick," Ruun declared as she met with Rumil and Justin in her office. "So, what were your findings, and where is Sir Foran, or should I say, Timothy Honore?"

"I think we can prove beyond a shadow of a doubt that the Kiros have manufactured the entire scare of the 'Wild Ferian' in order to maintain your alliance with the Kiros against any potential conflict with the Solarians," Rumil answered, "and Mr. Honore is currently finishing up some other business."

"Very well…" Ruun said with a hint of nervousness. "What evidence have you uncovered to prove your claims?"

"Well, the first thing we discovered was the presence of ferazine in some of the oldest remains since First Contact," Rumil said, then explained when she noted what she thought was confusion, "It's a synthetic hormone that had been found to enhance primal instincts in subjects of many races. It wouldn't be found normally in any being."

"Is that what has been going on?" Ruun asked.

"That was merely to start the fear," Rumil replied. "They played off stories of Ferian losing control of their primal instincts, and came forward with a medication that we figure was nothing more than a placebo, likely comprising of chemicals that were inert in nature."

"But if the medication was fake, how does that explain those who have stopped taking it eventually went wild?"

Rumil inhaled, and spoke again. "That's where the second phase comes in. Around four hundred staryears ago, the medication the Kiros provided radically changed into what you have now… an actual cerebral sedative that calms hyperactive sections of the Ferian brain. However, at that same time, the very genetic code of the Ferian *also* was altered."

Justin stepped in so that Rumil could catch her breath. "Somehow, the Kiros changed the genetic coding that controlled the primal urges of your race… somewhat of an evolutionary throwback, if you will. They also altered these genes so that they were dominant genes, so that it would spread itself through the population. With the rate that Ferian breed, it would only take a few generations for just ten thousand pairs of altered genes to become the majority of the population."

"How are you certain the Kiros did this?"

Justin replied, "All actions done at the genetic level leave signs of tampering… sort of a genetic fingerprint. Different races had, and still have, different methods that left different signs. The alterations performed on the Ferian matched the Kiros fingerprint at that time."

Ruun nodded, as if expecting the results. "I assume you have the data proof?"

Rumil handed her the data disc in question. "Everything you need is right here.

The Ferian Advisor smiled, but it wasn't a smile of good cheer. "Good… now we can be rid of you, and pretend none of this ever happened," she scoffed, and replied, "Oh, come now… don't tell me you were surprised. I, and the rest of the Ferian governing council for that matter, have known this for a long time. It was a perfect way to lure you all into our little trap. I already know that your dear friend Timothy has likely met a very untimely end at my hapless wild kin."

At that point, Rumil grinned knowingly. "Is that right?" She then glanced around the Ferian, who turned to see just what was so interesting… and saw the angry glare of Timothy Honore staring right back at her.

"Rumors of my demise were somewhat… exaggerated," Timothy drawled. "I actually was rather disappointed that I didn't realize it earlier. Once I learned your family line, it wasn't hard to figure it all out."

"Figure it all out… is that right?" Ruun replied, unconvinced, yet her eyes betrayed her fear.

"You belong to the 'Tawnee' line, am I correct?" Timothy asked then answered his own question. "Of course you are… the markings along your forehead and neck are proof of that."

Justin smirked, "The Kiros have always known that there were family lines of the Ferian that were predisposed to the Solarians from before the Schism War, and that many lines maintained sympathies for their expelled friends. The Tawnees have been one family line suspected of such."

"So sympathetic, in fact, to the Solarians that an advisor of the Ferian administration would invite the Commandant of the Solarian Knighthood to try and help eliminate a mutual problem," Timothy concluded. "I'm just curious how long you and Fransisca have shared the same ideal for the galactic future…"

Ruun scowled. "That is frankly none of your business. Besides, even though you have survived so far, do you honestly think you'll get off this planet alive?"

"Of course we will," Timothy answered smugly. "As a matter of fact, you're going to escort us off planet as heroes to the Ferian cause."

Ruun obviously didn't see how that was even remotely possible. She laughed, and smiled, but a smile that probably did bear all the malice they normally seemed to reflect. "And why would I do that?"

"Because that little data disc is only one such disc you hold. Several hundred more copies are ready to be sent to members of the Investigative Panel of the Galactic Alliance," Rumil smirked. "All I need to do is hit 'send' on my little PCU here, and everyone will know."

"It's in the Galactic Alliance's best interest to turn a blind eye to what has happened on Feria," Ruun said with a snort.

"You haven't been paying attention to current events, have you?" Rumil replied with that same confident grin. "The Ubeks have already severed ties with the Solarians, so I have little doubt they'd act on this information if only to try and maintain the balance of power between the Solarians and the Kiros."

Timothy then cut in, saying, "The way I see it, someone is going to get sacrificed over this. The only question you need to ask now is: do you plan on being the one sacrificed, or do you plan on being the one doing the sacrificing?"

* * * * *

"Nothing ever goes exactly according to plan with you three, does it?" Dewin said with a shake of his head as the trio related the story of what had happened on Feria.

"Not really... but the truly successful beings in this galaxy are the ones who can adjust their plans according to whatever wrinkles life throws at them," Rumil answered. "Besides, we did what we came to do. The Ferian, in light of the 'disturbing discoveries of deceit and abuse of goodwill' on behalf of the Kiros, have severed all diplomatic ties with the sect. As it stands, it's everything the Kiros can do to keep the peace with all the riots breaking out on the mixed colony worlds in their influence."

"So, it's on to Baramak, is it?" Justin said.

Rumil suddenly grew solemn, and nodded. "Funny how things come full-circle, don't you think? I mean, this is how it all started... with me trying to find out just what happened on Baramak fifteen staryears ago. Now here I am, getting ready to solve the mystery again."

"You're not the only one who's desired to know the events that led up to the Baramak Slaughter," Timothy commented. "I must say I'm looking forward to this as well."

"However…" Rumil said thoughtfully. "Before we get there… there's one thing I want explained to me."

Timothy blinked. "What would that be?"

"Just what Emmitt Fransisca, Ruun, and this 'ideal for the galaxy's future,' as you put it, have to do with anything. Normally, I wouldn't care much, but since you haven't even attempted to inform me about the connection, I've come to the conclusion that it must involve me in some way."

Her eyes narrowed in challenge, as if daring Timothy to try and dodge the question. "I will hack into this ship and freeze the engines if I have to, but we aren't setting foot on Baramak until I get some answers."

Chapter Thirteen

Rumil grit her teeth as the ship doctor pulled the needle out of her arm. "There you go, you're all set to enjoy the sights of the burned side of Baramak!" the blue-haired Demodian chirped, and as the woman stepped away with her hips in full sway, Rumil cattily thought that the doctor's hair color wasn't the only thing artificial about her.

"Oh, be sure to give the treatment about a full tenth-cycle to take effect," the doctor added absentmindedly as Rumil left the medical bay. Of course, Rumil already knew that it took time for the radiation treatment to flow through her bloodstream and shield her cells from the abnormally high radiation levels left after the Erani sects gave the planet a general sterilization bath.

Normally, the radiation from fusion bombs dissipates rather quickly, as opposed to its earlier thermonuclear ancestors. The radioactive level after the recent attack on Ub, for example, dropped to within habitable levels within four or five tenth cycles, and even then, the danger zone was barely ten TackMets in diameter.

However, even the most non-lethal weapon can become very deadly when fired at a target enough times. There had never been a very accurate account of how many bombs had been dropped on what is now labeled the "burned side" of Baramak, but it was enough to create such a concentrated radioactive field that fifteen staryears later, expensive radiation shielding injections are necessary to survive on the devastated surface. Even the civilians on the other side of the planet did not escape completely unscathed, as many suffered from the first large-scale cases of radiation poisoning in centuries. Because of that, the Galactic Alliance was unprepared to treat all the victims, and many were permanently harmed, like Gregor Krennan.

Those facts were never in debate. The question was why it happened; a question that, with any luck, she and her friends would answer soon enough.

Of course, that luck depended on many things. One, that the facility of Sams Fidel still existed. Two, that the facility contained the information they needed. And three, that those Endtimers Timothy told her about didn't bring the whole thing down on their heads before they left.

Surprisingly, Timothy told her about the rogue Solarian school of thought, what they stood for, and how it related to her, with very little pressure. The only thing about it all that bothered her were just how many people seemed to think she was this Sixth Prophet, and how many people seemed willing to kill her over it.

Figuring she had some time to waste, she decided to ask Justin if she could borrow the book that seemed to be the center of it all. She buzzed his door, and got no reply. See looked at the door status, saw that it was unlocked, and was prepared to open it when she remembered his chiding about courtesy. "Oh dear… my fragile memory. Amazing the things I forget in such a short time," Rumil said with an indifferent shrug, and entered Justin's quarters. He didn't appear to be inside, which made the fact he left his door unlocked ever more unusual, but she saw the book she was looking for on the sofa just in front of her, and picked it up. Surely, Justin wouldn't mind… and she could always tell him later.

Tucking the book under her arm, she prepared to leave, when she heard a soft thump from the closet. Curious, she stopped, and turned an ear in the direction of the sound, catching another thump. Slowly, she approached the closet door, growing increasingly piqued. Her hand floated over the pressure plate that opened the closet then finally touched the panel.

The door slid open, and Justin Feroz fell forward, wrapped from his feet to just under his nose in what appeared to be red packaging tape. She stifled a giggle as Timothy's bemused suggestion on Feria came to her mind, as well as her promise in regards to it. She put Bryan Honore's book on the floor, and helped Justin to his feet.

She then picked up the book again and held it in front of Justin's face, sweetly asking, "Can I borrow this?" Justin nodded, and mumbled something incomprehensible. She smiled and chirped, "Thanks!" then with her unique mischievous grin, pushed the increasingly panicking Kiros back into the closet, closing the door behind him as he fell inside. With an innocent whistle, Rumil left Justin's quarters, the book of Bryan Honore tucked under her arm.

Retreating to her own quarters, she tossed the book down on her bed, then jumped onto the mattress belly-down, kicking her feet up while she slowly opened the cover, so as not to damage the old text. After all, while she might not place much value in the book, her friends did, and for their sake she wanted to avoid mistreating it.

She quickly came to realize why young Solarians would dislike learning Bryan's Prophecy. Most of what he spoke of was as droll and slow-moving as she remembered from the recitation she heard on Solaria, and didn't say anything that people in modern times hadn't learned on their own.

For example, he wrote as if he had some great foreknowledge that the Erani were going to fracture, when most historians figure the rifts inside the Erani faith were forming before Bryan was ever born. He might have been the catalyst that finally made it happen, but anyone with any great amount of observation should have seen it coming.

The same was true with the cave paintings in the Boral Mountains of Kiros, which he contended were from a time before contact with the Se-Lan. Even the Kiros now acknowledged that, and many scholars and archaeologists were making the contention since the Staryear 2000 AW. With a frown, she started skimming through the book, looking for anything that might be something truly prophetic, or at least mildly interesting.

She finally stopped at the start of the Third Stanza, which Rumil recognized from her own brief exposure to the book, as well as what she had seen Timothy read in one of her visions. As she ran through the first page, she noticed that someone, likely Justin, had marked the upper right corner with a bright red bold stylus. Many pages from that point on carried that mark, and Rumil correctly guessed that they contained the passages that had been cut out by the Erani.

She also noticed that Justin had highlighted several passages, like the one describing the Sixth Prophet, which even Rumil admitted did sound remarkably similar to her in appearance and personal history. Justin apparently agreed enthusiastically, as in the margin on that page, he had written in black ink, "RUMIL!!!!" with seven handwritten arrowed lines leading from her name to portions of the highlighted text.

Turning the page, she found more highlighted text, this dealing with the two escorts that were to be the Sixth Prophet's guardians.

I mentioned earlier, the sixth shall have two sons of the Erani, one from each of the fragmented peoples. I also mentioned that they would each be of one parent, as one would not know his father, while the other would not know his mother.

The one that knew not his father would hail from

under the desert, and would be a reject among his kin. The
creator blessed him with a stature unusual among our
kind, with the strength of an Ubek, the hardiness of the
Ruma, the swiftness of a Ferian, and the mental powers
that rivaled the greatest among our kind.

He will carry a burden that none understand, not
even himself, and only time will be able to solve that
mystery.

In the margin, Justin had again scribbled with black ink, several
arrows pointing to the highlighted text from a note reading,
"TIMOTHY!!!!!" much as he had done to the segment that he believed
applied to Rumil. Again, there was an element of similarity… as Timothy
was born and raised underneath the Solarian desert surface, was indeed a
freak of nature among Solarians, and did seem at times to have the
prowess that Bryan Honore claimed. But Timothy actually did know his
father… probably knew him too well, in Timothy's opinion.

Or, did he? Timothy openly admitted that he had rarely spoken to
Niles much even while he lived in the family manor, and even less when
he had left. They could be thousands of TackMets away all while standing
in the same room. It was likely that Timothy barely regarded his father as
such beyond contributing half of his genetic material.

Rumil shook her head clear of the train of thought she had taken.
She was about to make the same mistake that every Erani theologian did
when studying the text; reading into the prophecy what wasn't really
there, allowing interpretation to overshadow the factual words of the
piece. Allowing personal insight into something as cryptically vague as
Bryan Honore's book of prophecy allowed the book to mean almost
anything, depending on the reader.

Confident she had regained an impartial state of mind, Rumil
returned to reading. She flipped another page to another heavily
highlighted segment…

The Sixth's second escort shall hail from two lands,
one well known, one known to us only in legend. Like the
first escort, he will come of age early, but his life of luxury
shall keep him from following in the first's path.

There is not much unique in this young man at first

glance… except that he is an orphan, neither parent who gave him life will see him past his infancy. Nonetheless, he will know a father, a lonely soul desperate for an heir. None, save the escort himself, will ever come to learn that there is indeed a family blood that binds the son to the father.

Until then, his life will be a secret to even himself, and it will seem to be sheer chance that will lead him to his past, and to a heritage that seems impossible. He will carry a blood stronger than any since the days of the Arrival, as he himself will bear direct lineage to the angel-kin.

Not surprisingly, Justin had noted in the margin, "ME!!!" With a sigh, Rumil understood how his knowledge would lead him to that conclusion. As much as she hated it, all the pieces, when put together, produced a reasonably accurate, yet still remarkably cryptic, description of herself and her friends.

"Why couldn't this prophet just end all the debate, and write in a manner that didn't lead to theological confusion?" she groaned, then flipped several pages ahead towards the next clump of red-cornered pages. She decided that she was more interested in what the Erani concealed from the general public than every boring word in the book.

On the date of the last day of the old ways, the split Erani shall converge on the planet of Mydor, the ancient home of the Se-Lan. On this ravaged landscape, on the fields of death and destruction in which the angel-kin first fought the demonic hordes, their descendants would take up the fight in the Second Battle of Mydor.

Rumil gulped, Bryan's description meshing with her own visions and experience. If Timothy and Justin were right, and that planet they crashed on truly was Mydor, then the place Bryan wrote of could very easily be the Dead Grounds Micha showed them. She rubbed her eyes, and once again chided herself, demanding she remained impartial, studying the text in and of itself.

On that terrible day, the Gate shall be cast completely open, and from that infernal pit shall be released a lieutenant of the Defilier himself, an Arch-Demon whose name I cannot mention without feeling ill from the evil it carries.

Rumil scoffed, recognizing the misdirection for what it was. Most likely, Bryan couldn't think of a fashionably archaic and evil-sounding name, so came up with that little excuse.

There are no words in the Basic language, or even my own native tongue, that can adequately describe the hideous visage of the foul lieutenant of Zaal. The towering creature had a hide of blood, with the size of ten Ubeks, and a mouth of fangs that would rival the collective maws of all the great Queens of Feria. It had eyes of blood and fire, and a crown of horns around its head.

This gave Rumil pause. Her breath went shallow and her mouth dry. Gooseflesh rose on her arms, and her entire body trembled. It felt as if someone had just turned the temperature in her cabin down about 20 Cel, yet a nervous perspiration began to pool on her eyebrows. Her determination to remain impartial failed. That simply couldn't be coincidence… there is no way that a man who lived over eight hundred staryears ago could possibly have known that face… that face that had haunted her for as long as she could remember… unless he had seen it himself…

Part of her wanted to close the book, and return it to Justin as fast as she could… or better yet, toss it in the trash bin and watch it as slid down the ramp to the closest incinerator. However, she couldn't, she had to read more… she had to know what he had seen…

The Sixth's Prophet's escorts will engage the beast while the battle rages all about them. It will seem to be a hopeless struggle, and the reality will not be much far off. No mortal weapon or agency can find purchase in the demon's hide, and as this truth comes to bear…

The next segment Justin seemed fit to not only highlight, but circle and underline repeatedly with the black stylus as well…

… one shall sacrifice himself for the other…

Rumil slammed the book shut, panting as if she had just run from one end of the *Gallan* to the other. As much as she hated to admit it, she was finally understanding why Timothy and Justin had seemed so certain that one of them was going to die. What Bryan had seen and recorded was too similar to her own experiences to dismiss it. There was no scientific or logical means to explain it all away… only her own experience – an experience that only she could begin to understand, much less explain with any accuracy to someone else.

When Timothy came to her quarters to inform her that dinner was ready in the galley, he found her huddled in the corner of the bedroom, rocking back and forth, with the book of Bryan Honore tossed in the adjacent corner. While her head was planted on top of her knees facing slightly down, her eyes were locked on the book. Considering her posture and facial expression, he had been half expecting to hear her muttering incoherent curses under her breath.

He gave her a slight tap on the shoulder, and it seemed as if she finally realized he was there for the first time. He gave her a wry smirk, and said, "Been doing some light reading, I see."

She replied, "Something like that."

He offered his hand, which she took, and helped her off the floor. "Just wanted you to know that dinner is ready in the galley. Considering that you look as pale as me right now, some food probably would not be a bad idea."

She nodded, and as she left, she looked back to see Timothy pick up the book. "Probably should return this to Justin, unless you're still reading it."

Rumil shook her head emphatically. She had already read more than she ever really wanted to.

"All right then, we'll stop quickly by Justin's quarters… he's out of the closet, by the way. Poor fellow couldn't get his hands free, so wound up resorting to an unfocused burst of heat to burn the tape off. It melted instead."

Rumil winced at the mental image that formed.

"It worked. He got free... though he no doubt had a few angry welts for a while." Timothy chuckled at that. "So, if Justin seems a little sour for a while, that's why."

* * * * *

After dinner, the *Gallan's* navigational officer informed the crew that they were approaching Baramak. Within a tenth-cycle, Rumil, Justin, and Timothy had convened in the shuttle bay, while Orion prepared the shuttle and Dewin provided final instructions.

"Orion will place you down at the Torous Starport; it's a small rural port outside a middling city of the same name, on the northeast coast of the 'untouched' continent. From there, as I understand, you plan to teleport to the 'burnt' side?"

"Actually, probably not," Timothy answered. "We'll likely rent a large sea craft and use that to get to the burnt side of Baramak covertly."

"Why?" Rumil asked. "I can understand why you don't want anyone to know we're here, but Baramak is a sparsely populated Arcadian colony. They wouldn't know psionics from cheap parlor tricks."

"If Emmitt Fransisca can rummage about on Feria… then I suspect he, among others, can do the same on Baramak. I'd rather not broadcast mine or Justin's presence until we have to."

Rumil acknowledged the point with a sideways nod. Any one of Fransisca's Endtimer friends could make things extremely difficult, and she supposed it wouldn't hurt to keep them out of the loop for as long as possible.

Justin set his foot on the shuttle ramp, and said, "I suppose we should get inside before Orion complains we're holding everything up."

"As long as you three know what you're doing," Dewin replied. "Be sure to contact us when you have what you need."

By the time Dewin left the bay, the shuttle had closed its door and departed the *Gallan* for their short trip down to the surface of Baramak.

Due to the *Gallan's* orbit, which Dewin had selected to keep them out of direct attention, the occupants of the shuttle were able to get a good view of Baramak's "burnt" side as Orion took a high atmospheric route to their destination.

Despite living much of her early life on Baramak, Rumil had never seen the damage done to the planet, let alone from the perspective she had now. The cloud cover was light and spotty, and the light of Baramak's primary, which would be approaching morning on the eastern coast of the burnt continent, allowed for a clear, dramatic view of the damage.

Much of the surface was dull black rubble, with a large range of what once were mountains, now pounded into a jagged, crater-ridden mess. The darkest scorched earth seemed to be centered on an area southward, just in her field of vision, that was completely leveled into a flat, featureless plain.

"That is where Fidel's main research facility was," Timothy said, swiveling his seat so that he could point out the window next to Rumil. "There is little doubt in my mind that it was the primary target of the barrage." His voice then grew grim as he added, "Hopefully, we can find out what so utterly spooked the Kiros and Solarians that they decided to torch everything else just to be safe. Fortunately, our target is underground in that region." He pointed to a small peninsula in the northwest, which did actually appear to have brown sections of earth.

Soon, the burnt continent disappeared off the horizon, and they were flying over the dividing ocean between the two hemispheres. Even the waters just off the burnt side were tainted with a sickly greenish hue. It was held back from mixing with the cleaner waters on the other side by an expensive series of shield buoys that used immense amounts of energy to generate a static shield around the poisoned segments. It was a project that had taken ten staryears, detoxifying most of the ocean and establish the buoys and network that managed it all.

Eventually, blue water and the relatively undamaged coast of the "untouched" continent came into vision, and the difference between the two hemispheres was almost as if they had folded over to an entirely new planet.

However, unlike most of the worlds she had visited, Baramak was not lit with the artificial lights of civilization. It had not been all that heavily populated to begin with… it was originally a mining colony that never really switched over to the high-technology civilization of the

Galactic Alliance era. After the Baramak Slaughter, anyone who could afford to leave the planet did, and thus all that remained was a very lower-class planet, like a neglected urban environment on a global scale. Homeless and unemployment rates often were around twenty percent, and at least twice a staryear the Alliance had to send peacekeeping forces to try and contain rioting. That's probably why the plan kept them away from the large metropolitan centers, as those larger cities were likely to break out into mass violence with little provocation.

There was a sudden jerk that jolted Rumil out of her observation, indicating that Orion had begun the shuttle's descent, and that the process of atmospheric entry would soon render sightseeing a pointless exercise.

* * * * *

"I hate it when everything is so quiet…" Rumil muttered to herself as she pulled the blanket Timothy gave her around her frame. The ocean air buffeting the sea craft was far colder than she liked, so even a slight breeze could be mistaken for the ominous chill down her spine that usually meant trouble.

"I like it," Timothy retorted, his eyes scanning toward the coast of the untouched continent as it receded beyond the horizon. "It makes it easier for me to sense potential dangers."

Since they were traveling relatively eastward, the solar cycle was passing by quicker than it normally would. As it stood, Baramak's primary was at midday height, and it would likely be the next morning before the sea craft covered the distance between the two continents.

"Rumil, have you slept since the last time you called it a night on the *Gallan*?" Justin asked from the pilot's seat. "It probably wouldn't hurt to get some down time."

"With the way this boat is rocking?" Rumil gestured, almost losing a hold of her blanket in the process. "You've got to be kidding me."

"Think of it as a hammock in a gentle breeze," Justin said wistfully.

"More like a parachute in a hurricane."

Timothy silenced them with an extended hand between the two.

"There's a sea craft approaching from the west. Likely peacekeepers."

Rumil went silent, and within three demiticks, she too heard the sound of an engine approaching rapidly, and a saltwater blue sea craft appeared to her left moments after that. Its color had blended beautifully in with the ocean, and it had gone largely unseen until sound gave it away.

Justin stopped his own engine, and allowed for the other sea craft to move in close. The gold emblem emblazoned on both sides of the hull identified it exactly as Timothy had figured; an ocean patrol for the peacekeepers stationed on Baramak.

"Good day to you all," the officer in the passenger seat said. "What brings you three out here?"

"Just sailing," Justin replied.

"Are you native to Baramak?" the officer said, suddenly suspicious one he examined the occupants closer. "No... you can't be. You're Kiros... and he's Solarian." Apparently, the officer was having a hard time wrapping his brain around the concept judging from the befuddled expression morphing onto his face. Finally his suspicion won out, and he had the pilot of his craft move close enough for him to board. Once finished, the pilot stayed on the peacekeeper's craft, within reach of the plasma rifle next to his seat.

"I'm just going to take a few ticks to search your craft here," the officer explained, causing Rumil to cast a nervous glance at her two companions, who didn't seem that perturbed. As a matter of fact, they followed the officer, and willingly opened every compartment and box for him.

When they came to the furthest aft component, Rumil slumped down in her seat, hoping that one of the peacekeepers didn't see her concern. She knew that was where Timothy and Justin had stashed their armor and weapons, and while it was hardly enough to be considered a potential cache of arms, she understood that peacekeepers often made arrests and seizures with very little provocation.

Justin opened the compartment, and instantly the officer's eyes focused on its contents. He started to reach for his comm unit when Justin said, "It a couple suits of carbide and small weapons for personal defense. As you yourself said, it's rough out here."

For a brief moment, the officer's eyes glazed, and his voice reflected a suddenly wavering mind. "Oh, no... I know your kind's mind tricks." Rumil knew the tricks for what they were as well, as she felt the buzz of psionic power in the back of her head.

Justin turned his head slightly, but not enough so that he could see the officer standing over him. "But, sir… I'm not even looking at you. How could I be influencing your mind?" The officer turned to Timothy, who was also looking down into the compartment.

Suddenly, his partner stood, and asked, "How many pieces do they have in there?"

Now confused with what must have been contradictory messages in his mind, the officer made a quick count and replied, "I see five… no, six. Two armor suits, two plasma pistols, and a couple swords."

"Then I highly doubt this is a smuggler," the pilot replied, barely blinking, clearly under the influence of some form of psionic suggestion. "We're looking for large-scale shipments, and sensors aren't picking up anything else."

"I suppose that's true…" the first officer replied, the admission allowing him to be convinced by what was no doubt some pretty significant leaning. Rumil had to admit the man's resolve to be quite formidable. "Although I would like to record your identification…"

"Do you really think that's necessary, peacekeeper?" Justin added, his voice carrying the musical lilt that normally accompanied telepathic coercion. "I mean, if you want the extra paperwork for something that clearly is rather irrelevant, I suppose we can accommodate you…"

Rumil noted the obvious clues, but was clearly confused. Neither Justin nor Timothy had yet to make any significant eye contact with either peacekeeper… unless they had made some form of link in the brief period in which introductions were exchanged.

Finally, the investigating peacekeeper fell to the suggestion completely. He sighed and said, "No, I guess that's not necessary… I suppose you aren't the sort we're looking for anyway. I just better not hear of any Erani running around causing trouble."

"It won't be us, I can assure you," Justin said with a smile as he and Timothy escorted the dazed-looking peacekeeper to the edge of their craft. As the officer stepped over the small distance separating the two vessels, Justin waved and added, "Have a fine day!"

"You as… well…" the man muttered, and soon, the peacekeepers were back on their way, Justin jumping back into the pilot's seat, and resuming course nary a tick later.

"Okay… how did you do that?" Rumil finally asked, curiosity overwhelming her. "Don't you need to make eye contact for any telepathic suggestion to work?"

Timothy and Justin laughed, and Timothy finally explained, "Remember the foil helmets the Arcadians liked to use early in their contact with the Erani, and how the Erani just let them believe they were effective? Similar principle – somewhere along the line someone assumed that we needed direct eye contact in order to make any psionic manipulation, and the Erani simply decided not to correct the assumption."

Justin added, "Truth is, while it's true that such suggestion has an extremely limited range due to the gentle amounts of energy that makes it most effective, whenever someone is within that range, we don't need to make any form of contact at all."

At that point, the fatigue from extended time without sleep began to affect Rumil, as she felt her eyesight start to blur, and her body begin to protest from being awake for so long. However, with her new knowledge, and another telltale buzz in her head, she realized with her increasingly drowsy mind that this fatigue was not completely natural.

"I'm sure you'll thank me later when you wake up," Timothy commented.

Rumil somewhat doubted that as she slipped into unconsciousness…

Chapter Fourteen

Once she did wake, she reached two conclusions. One, she *did* need the sleep after all. Two, Timothy was a jerk for "suggesting" she take it.

She scowled angrily at the Solarian was now sitting in the pilot's seat, and warned, "If you *ever* do that again, I will pop out your eyeballs then return them backwards so you can watch as I smash your brain in with a hammer."

"Thank you for the lovely image," Justin moaned. He had reclined his seat back, and apparently had been recently sleeping as well. "I'll stash it away for a future nightmare if you don't mind."

"Well, it's a good thing you're both awake," Timothy stated as if he hadn't even paid attention to them. "Because we're about to make landfall."

Justin pulled his seat to an upright position, then both he and Rumil leaned over to the front of the craft. They both had to shield their eyes from the rising sun, but there was indeed what appeared to be a tan coastline about ten TackMets away. It would have almost seemed perfectly normal, if not for the grossly off-color water all around.

Justin gingerly stepped across the rocking boat to the rear storage compartment, and pulled out a soft, brown leathery case. "Once we get on land, we'll take the booster shots just to be on the safe side," he said, speaking of a series of needles that contained second doses of the radiation-shielding chemical.

Timothy nodded in agreement as the distance to the shore dwindled rapidly. He checked the craft's sensors for any potential sandbars or reefs, then with about half a TackMet short of the coast, cut the throttle to one quarter, then soon afterward cut the engine entirely, letting the craft sail in the rest of the way.

Once they made landfall, Timothy and Justin began suiting up in their gear while Rumil made another quick check of her satchel's contents. She finished her tasks far quicker than her comrades, leaving her to examine her surroundings for what felt like the first time.

The landscape seemed uniformly bleak, a charred black wasteland... but the black was but a cover, a haunting sheet over the churned earth. It was what remained of the "black snow."

Almost a full day after the fusion bombardment, an eerie, fine black substance began to descend on the coastal regions of the untouched continent… quickly identified as carbon residue from the fusion reactions of the bombs, initiated from the heat of the Solarian and Kiros barrage. When rescue teams had finally mobilized and moved out to the burned half of the planet, they found the same horrific "black snow" covering everything in sight… a silent memory of the single most heinous attack in the recorded history of the galaxy.

She then recalled this same black dust had been on Timothy's armor after the fusion bomb attack on Ub, and was finally able to piece together why it had struck her as familiar. It would likely have been falling all about her and covering the ground as she had made her way through the aftermath of the barrage.

A hand dropping on her shoulder jerked her from her thoughts before any concrete memories could bubble up from the depths of her mind. Somewhat thankful for the reprieve, it faded as she saw Justin holding up a sheath of needles, filled with the booster medication that they would need if they wished to proceed any further into the "kill zone," the area in which radiation levels became lethal to anyone unprotected.

Rumil snagged one from Justin, and almost ruthlessly stabbed Timothy in his helpfully exposed forearm. He looked at her disdainfully, but said nothing as he rolled the sleeve of his bodysuit back down, while Rumil smirked playfully, considering them even for his earlier psionic lullaby.

"I hope it hurt," she quipped playfully, just in time to receive the gentle telltale prick on her own arm from Justin. She hadn't been expecting it, so she cringed, causing the needle to plunge a little deeper than intended, drawing a surprisingly fast trickle of blood. She yelped, and instantly Timothy was cleaning the wound with his bodysuit, then used his mental energies to knit the puncture hole closed before her eyes could blink twice. They then both stared at Justin with a pair of devious grins.

Justin backed away slowly, but their target was already chosen. Timothy handed Rumil the needle, grabbed Justin roughly by the neck, and bent him over. Rumil tapped her foot, tested the needle, and then jammed it right through Justin's bodysuit into the rump of the struggling Kiros.

Justin was still complaining about it a tenth-cycle later, after the Knights had donned their gear and the trio began their trek. "Did you really have to thrust half the accursed thing into my backside? Now I won't be able to sit down for a ten-cycle."

"Think of it as a favor..." Rumil replied in the teasing tone Justin used while on the sea craft. "Now you won't be able to sleep and have the nightmares you said I would give you over the next ten-cycle."

"I wonder what I'm doing with enemies. The friends I have are bad enough," Justin groused. He then abruptly changed the topic, and asked, "So, just how far inland was this facility?"

"About fifteen TackMets," Timothy replied, consulting his PCU to confirm it. "However, there should be an emergency exit within ten. I doubt we'd be able to find it though."

The words "emergency exit" triggered something in Rumil's mind. Worried at first that it was a warning of an upcoming vision, she was pleasantly surprised when she realized it was only something from her natural memory. She stopped, and turned about in a slow circle. "I remember this place," she then stated simply.

Justin and Timothy turned to regard her. "You do?" Justin asked.

Rumil nodded. "I'm not exactly sure how... but I remember being here." She pointed towards the next rise to the east, about a TackMet away. "That's where the black land starts, just past that rise... I remember this area because of that." She then pointed to the withered, dead remains of what must have been a large tree at one time. "It's probably the only sign of any living thing on this entire continent. I... stumbled up to here, and fell asleep. I remember being so tired... when I woke up again, I was in a medical hover... being taken across the ocean." She tried to fight back the memories that followed... those of utter chaos, being shoved out of the hospital and onto the streets to make room for wounded, then living in boxes and alleys until she was found and subjected to the different yet equal depravity of Krennan's orphanage...

She noticed her companions' questioning expressions, and it turned her back to the topic at hand. "The reason I bring it up is because... I think I came up to the surface from some sort of tunnel. Maybe it's the same one you're thinking of?"

"Why would you say that?" Timothy asked.

"Just a guess," Rumil said with a flippant shrug. She didn't want to voice the conclusion she was reaching just yet... that somehow her

213

past was tied together with Sams Fidel.

"Think you can remember how to get there?" Justin queried.

Rumil nodded, "I think so… I mean, we're going in that direction anyway, right?"

Timothy stepped to the side, and made a sweeping gesture with his forearm, "Then lead the way."

Rumil did so, and her first claim was directly on the mark. At the top of the rise, there was a jagged decline, and the beginnings of the rough, scorched black earth that marked the end of the bombardment. It was slow going to reach the bottom, and the loose rubble also hindered their speed.

"Are you sure you don't want to just teleport to the site of the facility?" Justin muttered to Timothy. "It could take us forever to get to where Rumil thinks she's going."

"Let's give her the chance," Timothy replied. "If she can find that secret way into Fidel's facility, that means we won't have to reveal ourselves to any potentially prying eyes at all."

"That is, if they aren't watching us already," Justin said with a few wary glances around the bomb-flattened plain. He cringed, then ruefully commented, "How did this happen?"

"How did what happen?"

Justin smirked. "Remember when we first were chasing Rumil together, how you were using your talents at a whim, and I was asking for a little restraint? Now, it's completely the other way around."

"Except…" Timothy replied, "I had a reason for my actions on all those occasions, as I do now."

"Hey!" Justin protested. "I had my reasons too…" He then frowned sheepishly. "Oh… wait… you're fooling with me, aren't you?"

"I might be."

Justin sighed. "You really should make it clearer when you're joking with someone…"

"Yes, I suppose I should."

Justin finally let the conversation die, still not terribly sure of Solarian's intent, but now certain he didn't want to find out.

Silence ruled the procession for the next tenth-cycle, Until Rumil stopped, pointed slightly north of due east, and remarked, "If I recall correctly, it should right about there, where the horizon is now."

Timothy again consulted his PCU and said, "That would match the rough distance and coordinates Krennan and I calculated. Keep going, you seem spot-on so far."

With a nod, Rumil again stepped across the blackened expanse, wiped her forehead, and took another gulp of water from the supplies they had brought along for the trek. The sun was now nearing its midday apex, and the black, ragged ground was absorbing and radiating immense amounts of heat. Considering how cold it had been out on the water, it was fortunate she had dressed in layers, her outermost clothing now shed and tied around her waist. She could only imagine what her two companions must be going through in their tight form-fitting black bodysuits and corresponding armor. Carbide might be rather light and provide good air circulation, but it still was a lot of weight, and sprayed with a very heat-absorbing color.

"How are you both faring?" she finally asked. "You two have to be roasting."

"I lived my entire life on a desert planet," Timothy remarked. "Most of my time on the surface was spent in armoring not much more comfortable than this. Have no worries about me."

"I'm not that bothered either," Justin stated. "While not exactly Solaria, Kiros gets awfully muggy and unpleasant quite frequently, so I'm also used to the heat to some degree."

"Of course..." Rumil drawled. "The unstoppable, untiring, unyielding Knights of the Solarians and Kiros. How could I forget?"

"It happens," Justin quipped, causing Rumil to roll her eyes incredulously.

Justin smirked, and asked Timothy telepathically, *Has she forgotten that these suits have full containment and climate control?*

Now, let's not ruin the mystique, was the Solarian's smooth reply, causing Justin to chuckle out loud. The sound prompted a suspicious glance from Rumil, but Justin waved her off with his right hand, and motioned with his other to keep leading on.

Half a tenth-cycle later, Rumil came to another abrupt stop, and spun about in place. "It has to be here somewhere... I don't recognize the area in front of us."

"How you can recognize anything is a mystery I'm not even going to get into," Justin remarked. "Besides… where is it?"

"The wind could have blown this place flat, covering anything and everything," Timothy answered before Rumil could reply. "Let's fan out and see if we can't find anything out of place. Rumil, you stay here so as to mark our position in case one of us loses sight of the other. Well meet up in a tenth-cycle."

With a resigned sigh, Rumil sat down and watched with a bored expression as the two Knights began scouring the area. A tenth-cycle passed, and it didn't appear that either of them uncovered anything of note as they returned.

"Well, that was an exercise in futility," Justin remarked.

"It was a bit of an off-chance to begin with, Justin," Timothy replied in defense of Rumil. "Considering how the surface of Solaria can change at a whim, I would have been surprised if the same hadn't held true here. We could feasibly be standing right on top of the exit and never even know it. Nonetheless, I don't want to spend any more time looking, especially since I don't want to mill about under this sun. We best be on our way."

Trying to hide her disappointment, Rumil shrugged and stood. "Well, guess you two should lead the way now." She stepped back to fall in line behind them when she stubbed her foot on something rather hard. She yelped and rubbed her foot trying to find out what it had been. "Gentlemen… look at this…" Rumil remarked, pointing down.

There was a thin lip of tarnished metal, barely visible and brushed with black dust. Judging from the imprint of Rumil's backside on the surface, it had been no more than a Tack away, and facing right at her.

Justin groaned in comic dismay as Timothy brushed aside some of the dust, revealing that the metal was a large beam, slanted into the earth… just like an underground tunnel would create.

"As I said… we could be standing right on top of it, and never know it was there…" Timothy repeated bemusedly. "Well Justin, I think we're going to have to use a little mental muscle to clear out this tunnel."

"That's assuming it hasn't filled completely in," the Kiros reminded. "Besides, what if the Endtimers are watching?"

"The only way to find out is to start digging," Timothy answered. "Besides, look at Rumil. I don't want to have to keep her out in this heat any longer than we have to."

* * * * *

It didn't take long to expose the entire exit, as it was barely three Tacks square, and the two Erani were able to push aside rubble and dirt with their telekinetic abilities at an impressive rate. While it had appeared that the tunnel had filled in partially, further digging revealed a thick inner hatch door that was partially closed, and the smell of stale air that implied a clear path behind it.

"Likely it started to shut when sensors detected that dirt was collapsing in," Timothy deduced, pointing at the hatch. "This could be a good thing actually. Since I doubt large amounts of earth were blowing and collapsing in immediately after the bombardment, this means that the facility still had power after the attack."

"Well, if there was power, it doesn't appear there is now," Justin said, peering down the underground pathway to where the sunlight failed to illuminate.

"Not necessarily," Rumil replied. "Most Arcadian facilities have an automatic backup generator if power fails, but the main generator has to be reactivated manually when that happens. It's to prevent overtaxing just-restored power grids with demands for power."

Timothy pulled free a palm-sized searchlight from his belt, and pulled the elastic strap over his hand and around his wrist. He activated the device with his other hand, and took the first step inside. "Well, it probably wouldn't hurt to let some air circulate before we move in, but we shouldn't dawdle long. The tunnel should also be cooler and easier going than outside."

While that was probably true, it was still a significant walk, especially as the tunnel wasn't exactly a straight line. Its course took a couple bends, perhaps around geological formations best left unbothered. The searchlight on Timothy's wrist provided an eerie glow to their surroundings, exposing ribbed rubber flooring and smooth cream walls with what would be orange guiding lights halfway up each wall, still in remarkable condition due to the relatively undisturbed air inside.

Timothy then stopped and turned his attention to what had been some sort of service closet. There had been several such small cubbies along the tunnel path, but what made this different was that this closet had been opened, with the dirty handprints of a small child visible on the interior side of the door, looking as fresh as they had been placed there yesterday.

Rumil gulped, the pieces of her dreams and memories falling into place. "I had been put there to keep me out of sight. The doors would have automatically locked, and this would be far enough away not to be searched as thoroughly. I was able to climb out when the power failed, and made my way to the surface…"

She leaned up against the wall, and slowly slid down the floor. Timothy crouched down next to her while Justin grabbed the searchlight, and casually peered down the corridor.

"It's making sense now… most of it anyway," Rumil said with a shrug. "I was here… I'm not sure why… but I was here, perhaps I was somehow related to Fidel… but I now know that for some reason, I was in this facility."

"The only way to find out more is to keep going in," Timothy said, trying to be assuring, offering his hand to help her to her feet. Once done, Timothy told Justin to keep the light and take the lead, allowing Timothy to keep a closer eye on Rumil in case more came to her.

Finally, another set of sliding double doors barred their path, but these were more the type that divided rooms, as opposed to the heavy blast doors they had encountered previously. Justin and Timothy pried them apart, opening the tunnel into a vast dome in which the spotlight gave little illumination. A large central column with computing consoles running along it, and a long circle of various machines along the outer wall was about all Rumil could clearly see with the lighting provided.

"All right… let's find the main generator, and see if there's anything left in terms of power," Rumil declared. "It will likely be with the main terminal, probably in the center."

Justin helpfully provided the light as she shuffled across the various consoles, until she finally stopped halfway around the column. "Here we go… I think this is it." Rumil then knelt down and popped open the panel along the column near the floor. Justin followed with the light, then Rumil reached inside the column, and flipped a red switch nestled in between two large pipes.

There was a groan of metal and gears, but five demiticks later, the series of lights covering the top of the dome slowly flickered before about half of them burst to life, providing dim but sufficient light. It turned out the dome contained little more than the circles of computing units they noted earlier, although the new lighting allowed them to note that there were four smaller rooms in each cardinal direction, sealed with decontamination and sanitation barriers, and another set of double doors to the southeast similar to the doors in the corridor they came from.

She then peered up over the keypad of the main console, and noticed that while the screen was active, there was nothing loading. Justin noticed this too, and said, "Looks like somebody wiped all the memory clean on the system."

Rumil pulled her computing unit out of her satchel, as well as several different cables and adapters. She unplugged some of the cables out of the terminal, analyzed the connections, and then utilized the proper adapters to connect her unit to the terminal.

"What are you doing?" Justin asked.

"I'm going to run a startup through my PCU – somewhat like giving a charge to a dead battery," Rumil answered as she began to type.

"Are you sure that little thing can handle a system like this?"

Rumil scoffed. "You honestly have no idea in regards to the advancements in computing technology, do you? This system can't possibly be any newer than fifteen staryears or so. It's possible my 'little thing' here has more processing power than the entire network of this facility."

As if in agreement, the monitors in the dome flashed to life with a replica of the operating system on Rumil's computing unit before loading up the hardwired programs each terminal was assigned. However, several errors began to flash, citing a lack of data to continue their functions.

"As I said, someone wiped the memory clean," Justin replied. "They clearly didn't want anyone getting any information that might have been kept here."

"Once again… you aren't entirely correct," Rumil shot back. "There is no such thing as a perfect wipe. Already I've recovered twenty percent of the data that was supposedly deleted."

Justin peered closer at the terminal screen linked directly to Rumil's, and noticed that there was a small window in the upper left corner with a progress bar and a percentage that was increasing at a substantial rate. Within a tick, it read forty percent, and within three,

Rumil's little computing unit had recovered over three-quarters of the data originally thought erased.

"That's about the best I can do… which I'll admit is a pleasant surprise. After fifteen staryears I'd expect the data to degrade considerably more than that. We could probably operate most of this facility if we wanted."

"We only need to access the information pertaining to what Fidel was researching, and perhaps some signs as to what prompted the Solarians and the Kiros to obliterate the entire continent," Timothy replied from his position on the other side of the column, his eyes constantly scanning their surroundings for any sign of trouble.

"I know that… I'm just saying we probably could," Rumil said testily. "By the way, Timothy, the console just to your right appears to be a slave interface directly connected to the main. You could probably run through the data I've uncovered while I am, and get through it all the quicker."

"Is there another interface so that I can help?" Justin asked, leaning over towards the terminals on both sides.

"Considering the ignorance you've already displayed concerning computing science, I wouldn't trust you with anything connected to my unit," she answered.

"So… no, then…" Justin quipped. If he was grievously insulted, he wasn't showing it. Instead, he crouched down behind Rumil, and peered over her shoulder while she worked.

"Let's see what we have here…" Rumil's voice died away as she began rummaging through the directory structure of the recovered data. "Research notes and progress documents… that sounds promising…"

The directory opened into a series of dated entries, the earliest dated 3395-22-6. She opened it, and started reading the text that followed.

I'm not terribly sure why I am keeping a log of what transpires here, as more likely than not I will be the only one who ever reads it. My mission here is a secret even to much of the Galactic Alliance. The secrecy involved is surely why Baramak was chosen as the site planet for this project.

I do not even know why Premier Tormay wants me

to study the nature of the psionic power used by the Erani sects. As I understand, not even the Erani fully understand its nature, but my position is not to understand why… merely to do.

The text went on to describe many of the staff that had been assigned to work under him, how he had worked with some of them in the past, which ones he liked and which ones he didn't, and his appraisal of the facility given for him to work with. Finding little more of use, she skipped to the next document. She kept reading through, even though most log entries were little more than empty updates on the lack of progress Fidel and his team was making, or puzzlements as to just what end the now former Premier Francis Tormay wanted the team to reach.

It wasn't until she came across a log dated 3396-1-9 that she found another useful tidbit of information.

I think I'm beginning to figure out a little more of Premier Tormay's plan. He has informed me that I and gene Experts Cahill and Sutland will be moving to an underground research facility built in the northwest of the continent. There he wants us to… artificially build Arcadians.

Rumil's eyebrows lifted in interest at the order. Shortly after the Schism War, Arcadian geneticists had successfully created the first "artificial humanoid" from synthetically building organic proteins and fashioning genetic material from them. Soon afterward, the Galactic Alliance forbade the process due to the influence of the Erani sects – who reluctantly allowed genetic science only to treat diseases in unborn children – and the inability of the other representatives to think of a good reason for constructing living beings. It was a decision that Arcadians decided wasn't worth the fight. So, why ask Fidel to do something that would possibly get the entire Alliance in some serious trouble?

The only thing I can think of is that somehow, Premier Tormay fancies that we will be somehow able to create Arcadians with psionic power. But why would he want to anger the Erani in such a fashion?

"He's right," Justin answered. "That would be an affront to both the Kiros and the Solarians. Both sects view psionic power as their exclusive birthright, and the knowledge that the Arcadians were trying to pursue it would agitate a lot of Erani." He then grew thoughtful, and said, "But... not enough for either side to blatantly attack an Arcadian colony."

"There's still a lot to read yet," Rumil said, pointing at the long list of documents. "Are you reading these things too, Timothy?"

"For the most part," was the Solarian's reply, but he seemed so deeply engrossed in whatever he was examining that Rumil decided not to bother him further.

Over the next staryear, Fidel's reports detailed the efforts he was making on both fronts. Apparently, the process of creating artificial humanoids was progressing considerably faster than the study of psionic power, as with the former, Fidel had previous study and processes to build on. Although, a log entry dated 3398-40-7 caused Rumil to go almost completely white...

> *My hypotheses were correct. With my advanced knowledge, I was able to determine just what made the artificial humanoids of the past so unstable, and why many failed to grow into viable beings, and I suspect why they all had considerably shorter life-spans than those born through more... conventional means.*

The next three screens of text were filled with the technical jargon of Fidel's trade, explaining just what he felt the flaws were in the old science, and what he had done to correct them. Rumil found very little interesting into it, until her eyes caught something that she couldn't believe was there. She scrolled back up, and reread the passage carefully.

> *Over the last staryear, I honed the process, making emergency adjustments to each developing embryo and fetus as potential problems emerged. Finally, the "masterwork" of the entire process, Subject #32, was self-sufficient enough to be removed from incubation.*
>
> *She is the apex of the artificial humanoid process,*

and I'll admit, I am rather fond of this young infant. I designed her genetic code to have an appearance similar to what I had always fancied my daughter would look if I had ever had the opportunity to have children of my own.

Perhaps that is why I find it difficult to keep referring to her as Subject #32. While it is rather wasting of my professional time to be thinking of names for beings that are largely going to be nothing more than test subjects, I can't bear to continue looking at this seemingly perfect infant without granting her some name.

My workday suffered terribly because I kept thinking and rejecting different names, but it finally came to me over dinner after my scheduled shift was complete. I do believe I will name her Rumil.

Upon confirming that she had indeed read the document correctly, Rumil wordlessly stood up, walked over to the far wall, and sat back down, ignoring Justin's queries as to her well-being.

Interestingly enough, her internal conflict wasn't about the realization that she was artificially created. Indeed, she was just as alive and viable and living as anyone else, so the idea that she might somehow be any less a person was simply laughable... had she felt at all amused.

The truth was that her thoughts dwelled on theological issues that she had been so determined on avoiding for so long. It couldn't be... it just couldn't be... could it? Bryan Honore's text spoke that the woman he had foreseen would not know any parents. Who else would have no father and mother than a being that was born from synthetic proteins, and nurtured in a machine?

If the visions that plagued her were any indication, it made a lot of sense... both how he could be so vivid and yet so vague at the same time. After all, the visions she received were always enough to get a clear idea of what was being seen, but without any real context or timeframe to make much of it.

It all made too much sense actually... especially considering she couldn't prove any of it...

In his concern, Justin had made a discreet mind probe of Rumil, and once he figured what was bothering her, he decided it was best for him to give her some time to sort it out. With that determination made, he walked around to the other side of the column to see just what Timothy was up to.

He was slumped over, his arms resting on the angled supports separating the terminals, his body trembling. Initially confusing it for grief, figuring he had learned his adopted brother's fate, Justin stepped closer. The Kiros noticed that Timothy's eyes were clenched tightly shut, his breathing was slow and deliberate, and his jaw was sliding back and forth not in sadness, but in anger, a pent up fury that he seemed he was barely able to contain. Finally, it erupted in a short white hot burst of energy that momentarily blinded Justin, and a telepathic message of such intensity that the Kiros was able to hear it, even though it clearly was not intended for him.

Mother, I know what you've done!

Considering the power that had accompanied the message, Justin had little doubt that the Solarian's mother, all the way on the other side of the galaxy, had heard. As it was, the energy Timothy expelled caused Justin's head to ring painfully, and the Kiros staggered back, trying to clear his mind.

Once his vision and other senses were clear enough for Justin to reasonably determine which direction was which, he slowly walked over to Rumil, who had clearly been jostled out of her thoughts by Timothy's outburst.

Nonetheless, when she looked up at Justin, her voice was still shaky as she asked, "What happened to him?"

Justin shook his head. "I'm... not sure. I didn't get a chance to look at what he was examining before he exploded."

Rumil uncertainly stood, and sat back down in front of her computing unit. "Well... let's see if we can't find out, shall we?" she whispered, flipping through the directory again, calling up a history of the slave terminal's actions.

Timothy had been scanning through an entirely different set of files, and had reached a log dating 3398-42-8. What had upset him became clear in short order.

My research into psionic power is going nowhere. Unlike the humanoids, where I had at least some background to examine, I am trying to find my way through unexplored territory. I can hardly request assistance from the Solarians or the Kiros, as that would totally destroy all the secrecy that Premier Tormay insisted I maintain, and it is doubtful they would provide assistance anyway.

However, just this morning, I received a most unexpected boon. I was called to a formal banquet to celebrate the progress made in abolishing genetic illness throughout the galaxy, a truly grand event attended by most of the representatives of the Galactic Alliance, as well as several prominent guests of said representatives.

During the gathering, I met a fascinating young Solarian woman by the name of Celine Honore. Since her name had not been on the list that Premier Tormay had told me avoid at all costs, I struck up conversation with her.

Apparently, she had learned of my study in genetic conjunction for couples who could not bear children, and that her husband, the very High Commander of the Solarian Military, was indeed sterile, as rumor had claimed for some time. She discussed the backward nature of her society, as well as her husband's problem. I agreed that modern science could repair the impotency that plagued him, but understood that the Solarians considered any genetic alteration of non-life threatening conditions extremely taboo. I explained to her I was under the impression that genetic conjunction was also against the mores of her people.

That was when she surprised me. I had been under the impression that women of the Solarian people were not allowed to develop any psionic potential they might have, but Celine quickly showed she was a special case. She explained that she had read my mind, and knew what I was doing.

Obviously, I was initially terrified of her exposing the secrets I had so closely guarded for so long. Once again, she surprised me. She explained she had no intention of telling her people of what I was experimenting with, and groused that they probably wouldn't even listen.

*Instead, she offered me a deal. She would
appropriate the research the Solarians had gathered, as
well as acquire hair or tissue samples of the Solarian
nobles she regularly met, all for my study. In exchange, I
would use her and her husband's genetic material to
conjunct a son for her.*

Rumil's eyes widened and Justin dropped his face into his hand in dismay. While it might have been troubling to the average Erani that Celine would have betrayed any psionic study to someone outside that race, Timothy was hardly average, and had shown little regard for most, if not all, of the social taboos of his people. Rumil concluded that something else must have angered him, and opened the next document in the search list to see if that held the reason.

*Thanks to the efforts of Celine Honore, my
research into the nature and source of psionic energy has
advanced further faster than I ever dreamed. I do believe I
have found just where the Erani come about their
extraordinary gift.*

*In the Erani genetic code, there are fragments of a
third helix of genetic material. The notes I have received
from the Solarians' research indicate that they have not
been able to isolate or identify the material in question…
but I have.*

*Using the various fragments of code that I was
able to extract from the tissue samples Madam Honore
acquired for me, I believe I have managed to complete the
phantom helix. After analyzing the protein structure of that
coil, I realized it followed no organic pattern that I had
ever encountered, and has a structure radically unlike any
other sentient species. If the Erani truly have ancestry in
some ancient alien race beyond recorded knowledge, my
suspicion is that this coil is from where it originates.*

*I will begin replicating and introducing this
element into some of the developing embryos, and perhaps
into some of the currently living subjects, and I shall see
what comes of it.*

Rumil then opened the next found document in the search...

Again, I have found success. Introducing the alien helix into the embryos caused every single one to die, to my dismay. Fortunately, the viable subjects in which I introduced the material merely seemed to reject the genetic material... with one exception.

My dearest Rumil, how I hated to put her through the painful augmentation process, how she cried as the tubes were inserted... it wasn't all totally in vain.

Rumil cringed. The vision she received when Fidel's name was first mentioned to her on Kiros... that had actually happened, and now she was certain the unidentified man who had looked over her was no doubt Sams Fidel himself.

Rumil, unlike all the other subjects, retained about five percent of the helix, the alien material twining with her genetic code just like it did in the Erani samples Madam Honore had given me. It is too early to discern if she will develop psionic powers like the Erani, but I would like to schedule future augmentations to see if I cannot get more of the phantom helix to twine itself.

In the meantime, I have begun work on my part of the bargain. Knowing how the Solarians value the fighting prowess of their Knights, I have decided to conjunct a warrior that will truly give honor to the Honore family line.

I have a fantastic pedigree to work with. As much as I loathe the restrictions that the Solarians put upon themselves, and the dangers that come with breeding too close, the material I have been given to work with is almost flawless in and of itself. However, I have put my expertise into the fields that random chance usually inhabits. I've granted Celine's son with the greatest physical attributes that I can compute, and to my amazement, the entire alien helix wound into the boy's genetic code without so much as even a single protein out of place. All things considered, I suspect that Celine's son will truly be a Knight above all others.

"Without question…" Rumil muttered, and Justin agreed with that sentiment with a quick nod. Looking around the column quickly to see if the Solarian was about to erupt again, she acknowledged that Sams Fidel certainly did a fantastic job, even if Timothy might not agree. Nonetheless, she still didn't see just what had so angered the Solarian. However, since only one last document remained in the search, Rumil figured whatever it was had to be in that log entry, something that the date of the entry confirmed…

3406-16-4… the cycle of the Baramak Slaughter…

Well, I finally discovered Premier Tormay's plans… far too late to do anything significant about it.

His plan all along was to use my research to create a threat, then use that news to get the Solarians and the Kiros to attack each other. He actually told each side that not only had I successfully created Arcadians with psionic power, that I have given that genetic code to various people all over the continent so that they would pass those genes on to future generations, in the hopes of building an army of psionics to take to war against their peoples. I knew he hated the Erani, but I never imagined he would go so far as to sacrifice billions of his own people for his own political vendetta.

If I believed in a hell, I would damn him to it.

I already can hear the bombs the two sects are using to exterminate every living thing on the surface, and they have already stormed this facility once. But even in this despicable act, one Erani man demonstrated the nobility that their kind professes to act with. The irony is that once again, the Honore family has come to my aid.

Craig Honore had quickly identified the sham for what it was, but unfortunately had no authority to stem the attack. Instead, he was willing to kill his own comrades in arms, and take my darling Rumil somewhere safe. He seemed convinced she would not be found, and that she would survive the onslaught. Apparently, they had been told this facility was actually a secondary building, where nothing more than the data was kept. Clearly, Tormay wanted to recover the information stored here, and use it to destroy the influence of the Erani once and for all.

Now Craig waits in this central chamber with me, knowing that soon the Erani will pour inside with full force, and that neither of us will survive.

However, with these last moments, I will deny Premier Tormay the end he desires. I intend to erase all my research, all my logs, all the data I have compiled; everything. No one will be able to prove anything about anything that happened here, and thus will that lying, corrupt politician be denied his precious victory. My name, and even Craig's name, will be forgotten… and sadly that is the way it must be to prevent an even greater atrocity than the one committed.

As a matter of fact… why am I even dictating this log? I guess it has become such a habit to record my every coming and going in this facility that even now, on the verge of deleting everything, I make one last statement.

I suppose such is the way of fools…

Justin pounded the column with his fist, apparently understanding now the anger that had to be flowing through Timothy. Even Rumil could not believe the callous nature of people in power, and the lengths they would go to achieve even the smallest of victories, and often for nothing more than pride and ego.

And now she understood Timothy's anger and the guilt by association that came with it. His mother's actions… the valuable data and materials she had gathered for Fidel's use… had almost directly caused the Baramak Slaughter. At the same time, his adopted brother, the man who he most admired, gave his life to keep Rumil safe.

"You must hate me now," Rumil said with downcast eyes and a heavy heart.

She hadn't expected a reply from Timothy, but he said, "Why

would I hate you? You certainly aren't responsible for the actions of a dense doctor and a selfish woman who wanted a child regardless of the cost."

"I mean... what Craig did..."

"My brother lived and died just as Fidel quoted, with all the honor that my people are supposed to have. It was the only thing his code, and the faith he followed dutifully, would allow him to do... save the lives of the innocent even at the cost of his own. It is the very essence of the creed every Knight, be it Kiros or Solarian, make when they commit to the Knighthood."

"I will be the shield of the defenseless," Justin recited softly. "I will be the sword of the powerless. I will be the stalwart for the helpless... until my dying breath."

Rumil abandoned her computing unit, and moved around the column to speak with Timothy face to face. "It's your mother, isn't it? You think she caused all this."

Timothy finally turned away from the terminal, and shouted, "Of course she did! The information she gave Fidel allowed all this to happen! She is responsible for the deaths of over four billion innocent lives because she wanted to have *one*!"

"Too many people played a part in the Baramak Slaughter to put the blame on one person," Rumil shot back, not backing down. "The former Premier of the Galactic Alliance cooked up this entire scheme, it was Sams Fidel who made it happen. It was likely your father and Justin's uncle who made the order to bomb everything to oblivion. How could you blame one woman who just wanted to have the same treasure that almost every other woman could enjoy?"

"Had she not given the necessary information and materials to Fidel, none of this would have happened! Her short-sightedness cannot be simply dismissed!"

"Had she not given the necessary information to Fidel I might not even be here right now," Rumil remarked, and that managed to give Timothy pause. "I have the feeling that Craig felt the same thing you felt when you first met me."

"Craig would have sought to save your life regardless," Timothy retorted.

"Very well, then I survive. Then who is to say that you come to the aid of a normal Arcadian woman being accosted by some thugs? You yourself admit you felt a compulsion to protect me… something you attribute to my special abilities."

Timothy's mood darkened even further; something Rumil almost didn't believe was possible. "How dare you insult my decency and my honor by suggesting that I would not have rescued you from those pirates?"

"You're right. I don't doubt you would have. But what then, when you cornered me on Altair? I would have been nothing more than just another hired hacker. You would have used me to capture Krennan, then would have gleefully handed me off to your superiors to have me imprisoned for life or even worse. Or are you suggesting you would have even come to my aid then?"

Timothy had one final, if feeble, argument. "Actually, those things would have never happened at all, since I would never have been born."

"I know… and for that, I'm glad your mother did what she did, even considering all that happened because of it. Because, despite the tragedy that happened, I honestly think this galaxy is a better place because you're in it. I know my life is better… and I think Justin could say the same."

Even though neither could see him, Justin again nodded in agreement.

Rumil gently put her hands around the Solarian's waist and gave him a tender embrace, dropping her forehead on his chin. "I can't believe I'm about to say this… but I'm certain there is some higher power governing this universe… and that he has his reasons for everything. I think I now know his reason for the Baramak Slaughter. With what we now know here… we can put an end to all the atrocities committed by all those in power. We can truly make a lasting impact on this entire galaxy for the better… and in that regard… four billion lives is a pittance to pay. I must believe that whoever is guiding the events that transpire has granted a special recognition for those that died… and that recognition is that we let the truth be known… and never let it be forgotten again."

She pulled away slightly so that she could look Timothy in the eyes. "What do you say? Think you can forgive your mother?"

Timothy regarded Rumil, his rage dispelling. If there was even the tiniest shred of doubt that she was the prophet Brian Honore foretold of, it was completely gone now. He gently broke away from her, and pointed through the column to where the main terminal would be. "Why don't you quickly gather up the restored data so we can get out of here? We do have a job to finish."

Justin tried to communicate with the *Gallan* to inform them they were about ready to depart... but found the Blood Hawks flagship was no longer in range. He tried again, and had the same result. "Curious... Timothy, try contacting the *Gallan*..."

Timothy did as requested, and also failed. "That's absurd," the Solarian commented as he stared down at the error message. "These comm units have a range larger than this entire planet, even if there is radiation interference. I'm going to try contacting Orion. He might already be on the surface waiting for us."

Fortunately, Orion was, but he had a bit of a tale to tell. "I had figured that Dewin had contacted you three directly..." There was then the sound that must have been the Ubek slapping himself. "That's right... he told me to tell you... and I forgot."

"Tell us what?" Timothy demanded.

"He had to leave... someone I didn't recognize from Demod had contacted him, and he left me with instructions to take you to Arcadia when your business was completed."

"Why did he leave?"

The Ubek grunted. "I don't know. If I had to guess, it probably had something to do with that Diviner he had been visiting."

* * * * *

Despite Orion's slightly less than keen skills of deduction, the Ubek was correct. Taesha's mother had frantically contacted Dewin to tell him that the girl was in dire straits. Some men had forced their way into the temple, and blackmailed the young Diviner with the lives of everyone inside if she did not divine something for them. By the time Dewin had arrived, Taesha's energies had nearly withered away entirely, and Dewin had just been able to pull her away from the depths of the abyss. He had no doubt as to what the intruders had asked Taesha to find. He wanted to know who... and why.

Finally, the young Diviner stirred, and started to regain

consciousness. Once her vision cleared enough to see the face of her rescuer, she buried her face in his neck, and sobbed the tears of a terrified child who had seen the most horrible nightmare of her life. "They made me, Dewin… they said they'd kill everyone if I didn't take them and show them where you had gone. They made me follow your path… and took that place from my mind…"

"Who did?" Dewin demanded.

"They were… Solarian, I think," Taesha said. "Yes… they had to be Solarian… they were too pale to be Kiros. Their leader… he was the worst of them… I could barely look at his face without feeling ill."

"The Endtimers…" Dewin hissed, remembering Timothy's little briefing on that group of Solarians.

Taesha's mother interjected, "The man matched the description of a man who visited the temple just before you left last time. The guards reported that he talked to you then hovered about the garage level for a few ticks before leaving himself."

Dewin remembered the face… and could wholeheartedly agree with Taesha's impression.

"It was so cold… so dark… I couldn't get away… If you hadn't come… I would have been swallowed whole by that… that… thing…"

Dewin was clearly torn between consoling Taesha, and leaving… but as much as he wanted to make sure the young Diviner was well, he had no choice but to leave. "Taesha, I have to go."

Her pleading, terrified eyes looked up at him. "Why? I beg you… don't go…"

He couldn't allow himself to be swayed by the pathetically troubled girl. "If I don't… we could possibly wind up in more trouble than what you just struggled through, as unbelievable as that may sound."

She fortunately realized that Dewin meant it wholeheartedly. With a resigned sob, she said forlornly, "I suppose you must then, if you are certain."

"I truly wish I could stay," Dewin said in parting. "Just stay well… I'll return as soon as I can."

Dewin dashed out of the temple, and contacted the *Gallan* in orbit. "Has Orion reported in?"

"Yes," the acting primary officer replied. "He collected Knight

Honore, Knight Feroz, and Miss Bonamede literally just a few ticks ago, and are on their way to Arcadia."

"Good… plot coordinates for Arcadia immediately. I want to depart the instant my shuttle locks in the bay."

Chapter Fifteen

Krennan gleefully took the data disc containing some of the information that the trio had uncovered on Baramak. "Is this everything?" he asked.

"Everything relevant to your case," Timothy answered.

Krennan was clearly too excited with what he had in his hands to ponder the somewhat duplicitous answer Timothy gave. He inserted the disc into the console at his desk, and ran through the log entries quickly, cackling with glee. "Yes… yes… this is everything I desired."

"I believe we had a deal as well," Timothy stated.

Krennan started, as if suddenly remembering. "Oh yes, that we did. Very well, come right this way."

Timothy and Justin began to follow, then Timothy stopped and said to Rumil, "Stay here. Things might get… unpleasant."

Rumil snorted as Krennan and the two Knights left down the rear door of the media mogul's main office. Once they were out of sight, she promptly ignored Timothy's advice. She hadn't seen a vision, but she somehow knew that something was about to happen and that that the pair were going to need her help.

She quickly sat down in Krennan's desk, and subtly hacked into the surveillance system in Krennan's study. From there, she looked into her satchel to make sure her PCU was activated and receiving the data being transmitted. Confident that the stage was set, she strode into the hall after the three men.

* * * * *

"There it is, gentlemen," Krennan declared as he pointed inside the small room just off his main study. "I hope it is what you were looking for."

In the center of his trophy room was an ornately designed and forged twin-bladed sword, resting on two prongs that held the weapon at the end of each side of the half-Tack long hilt. The hilt itself was wrapped in gold gripping foam and concaved in precise places, in the manner of a weapon designed for the hands of a specific individual. The hand guards were both decorated with a single diamond flanked on each side by two sapphires, and then two rubies. The blades gleamed with an almost platinum shine, but the metal they were forged from was infinitely harder than that precious metal. They broadened from the hand guards until they abruptly narrowed at the points with a smooth curve. On the flat of each blade were etched the words of Bryan Honore, declaring this weapon to be born of his vision and the unparalleled craftsmanship of his friend, Julius Feroz.

"What do you think?" Justin asked, but even he already knew.

"You'd have to be psychically dead not to feel the energy radiating from it," Timothy replied sardonically. "There is no question in my mind that's the Star Smasher."

"How fitting that the weapon that is supposed to drive you Erani to suicide is the weapon that will cause your deaths," Krennan cackled from just outside the doorway.

Timothy and Justin whirled about, but before they could make any move, the media boss raised a small black device with a display and a red button. "I'd be careful. I've put an energy shield around that little room, and this device is measuring your psionic energy outputs. I'll press this button, and pour enough radiation to cook both of you to cinders if you so much as… think wrong…" He laughed almost insanely from his little joke, then paced back and forth across the doorway separating the room from his study, looking down at the display. "I do so love irony. To think that I will kill you religious little bastards in the same way you nearly killed me."

He stopped, and crowed, "I knew you wouldn't be able to resist getting that little weapon behind you. You see, I'm quite familiar with the story. Oh yes, I've read that charming little fairy tale, and once I kill you, I'll send the information you so lovingly gave me and destroy any Erani influence in the Galactic Alliance. The scandal should be the death knell for your theocratic dominance, ending your fairy tales and myths once and for all." Now on a roll, Krennan couldn't resist the fun of gloating as he delivered the punchline. "It's almost unbelievable that your kind ruled this galaxy for as long as you did. I mean, you little brainless believers are so easy to manipulate. Tormay knew all he had to do was send Sams Fidel on a fruitless exercise, then give some bogus and well-timed reports to get the Erani to completely hang themselves."

236

"So the plan was never to create Arcadians with psionic power," Timothy noted.

"Of course not!" Krennan scoffed. "That's what would make the Baramak Slaughter all the more damning. They killed and maimed people that had no ties to Fidel's hopeless project. Once I learned of the plot... I almost forgave Tormay for starting it and doing this to me. The plan was sheer brilliance after all."

Timothy and Justin looked at each other knowingly, now gaining the full scope of the plan for Baramak... and that they knew something Krennan didn't.

Krennan didn't notice the silent exchange. He was too busy howling with vicious glee. "It doesn't even start there either. All the way back to Gregor Tan... he saw the rifts forming in the Erani, and correctly pegged Bryan Honore as the piece that would shatter the puzzle. Another piece of sheer brilliance... he had Bryan Honore killed, the prominent families would start arguing with each other... mix well with some well-placed misinformation... and you have one fine Schism War that Tan could then negotiate peace for, and become a galactic hero!"

This was news to both Erani men. There had been rumors that somehow the Arcadians had played both sides during the war that severed the Erani people, but neither of them had figured just how deep the Arcadians' fingers had dug in.

"Nothing to say?" Krennan finally sneered. "Come now... surely you must be trying so hard not to think of all the ways you could kill me. I'd like to think I'd done a better job of taunting you than that."

Finally, he got the response he was looking for, as his display flashed with detection of growing psionic power. However, the source wasn't coming from inside the trophy room. His eyebrows furrowed in confusion as he turned about to see just what was generating the energy... and saw Rumil, her arm outstretched, palm up, with blue-white prongs of electricity crackling around her hand.

The maimed Arcadian's eyes bulged with dawning comprehension, realizing in an instant what it all meant and where he had gone terribly wrong.Unfortunately for him, he didn't get much longer to think about it, as the energy leapt from Rumil's hand in a long splintering bolt, striking Krennan in his chest. He was already dead when his body slammed into the far study wall with a loud crack, knocking down two expensive paintings. Then he slid sickeningly to the floor, folding over himself so that his head rested between his feet.

She numbly strode over to the wall connecting the study to the trophy room, picked up Krennan's device from where it had fallen, and deactivated the energy shield. She hardly felt Timothy's arms move about her, barely heard Justin's thanks and awed amazement at what she had done.

She hoped that she never was granted the power to do that again. In all her life, in all the crimes she had committed, she had never directly hurt a person, much less killed someone. Even as much as he probably deserved it, she still felt… dirty. She simply couldn't comprehend the soldiers and the Erani Knights like Timothy and Justin, who were willing to kill those who might have nothing more to divide them than a few religious practices. She was certain she never wanted to understand them in that regard.

Justin took a hard plastic case lying on the ground near the far wall of the trophy room, correctly assuming by its size to be the case Krennan had used to ship the Star Smasher. Using a shroud that was quite possibly priceless in itself, he covered the weapon and set it inside the case, pulling the shroud away, then closing the case, programming a locking combination on the digital keypad.

"Well, we have the Star Smasher now," Justin said. "I do believe we have a Gate of Bannor to destroy."

Justin's comm unit then beeped. He pulled it off his belt, checked the sender data, then flipped it open and activated the display. "Dewin, nice to see you made it. What was with the detour?"

"We've got a serious problem," the pirate captain said hastily. "Your Endtimer friends just busted their way onto Demod, and forced one of the Diviners there to reveal the location of the Gate you found."

"Do you know who?" Timothy said.

Dewin shook his head. "All we were able to figure out was that they were Solarians. But I think it's a pretty safe guess who they answered to."

"The Endtimers." Timothy muttered to himself.

"It might not hurt to make all due haste," Dewin replied. "Even without meditating, I can sense something happened to the Gate even from here. And I think it's a safe bet that whatever is happening, it's not good."

Rumil, Timothy, and Justin regarded each other with a sinking dread, already knowing what had happened. The sounds of the guards finally breaking through the lock Rumil had placed before leaving Krennan's office also spurred their decision.

"Want to make another exit, Timothy?" Rumil asked, even as Timothy quickly gathered the energy to do so. If they were right... they had to get to Mydor as fast as they possibly could... and hope they weren't too late.

Chapter Sixteen

"Horace, what are we doing here?" Emmitt hissed demandingly. "We should be remaining on the Dreadnought, and letting the final cycle unfold!"

"Circumstances here require our attention at the moment, Knight Fransisca," High Priest Hightower said calmly. "Let me assure you the plan has not altered in the slightest." He cut off all further conversation as they entered the hearing range of others.

Not that the parties in question would have even heard the private discussion. The monarchs and highest nobles of both the Solarian and Kiros were in heated argument, angrily shouting at each other over petty disagreements and a general sourness towards each other that they probably couldn't adequately explain.

Horace smiled, knowing that by the end of the cycle, those insignificant differences would soon be over… the old ways would soon be ground into the war-torn earth beneath their feet…

"How did you learn about the location of the Gate?" High Commander Honore demanded of the collected Kiros.

"Like we would divulge our sources to you," snarled his counterpart, Kiros High Commander Joseph Feroz.

The argument quickly devolved into an incomprehensible mess, and it took great effort on Horace's part to get their attention.

"I am afraid the Kiros learned of this planet's location from me, High Commander," Horace said, and fending off the accusations of treason from his fellow Solarians with a wave of his arm, replied, "The destruction of the Gate is the desire of both our sects, and in the spirit of the Creator who breathed life into all of us, I felt it was prudent to invite the Kiros."

"Well, I'm glad you decided to perform such an action without consulting me, or anyone for that matter," King Frederick said slowly, his eyes boring into Horace, trying to pry a way into the High Priest's mind. Horace smiled, knowing that the monarch would not succeed.

"I deeply apologize, I did not mean to seemingly deceive you. Time was of the essence, and I acted quickly," Horace said softly, bowing to his King respectfully. "Nonetheless, finding and destroying this Gate should be a grand event for all Erani born, whether we come from Solaria or Kiros. Please do not let our differences overshadow the greater goal."

That speech lowered the intensity among the gathering to a deep simmering mass of angry glowering and scowls. Horace was deeply disappointed. If they maintained such deep resentment for much longer, they would fall too quickly.

"You said you had the means to destroy the Gate," Frederick then commented.

Horace nodded emphatically. "I do. I can proceed now, if you wish." He turned to the Kiros contingent, and bowed respectfully. "If you feel I need an escort, you may provide one."

Despite Horace's openness towards them, the Kiros leaders remained wary. King Lionel, as was his way when he was uncertain, preferred to keep his people close. High Commander Feroz also had a tendency to keep his forces in formation whenever he was unsure of a developing scenario. Thus, Horace knew they wouldn't do such a thing as he had suggested, and they didn't disappoint.

"You'll be in sight… I see no reason to send anyone to follow you," Feroz declined.

"You've been the most honest Solarian towards us since the Schism War," Lionel said. "I see no reason to watch you like a child. Just as long as you destroy that Gate before it opens."

"Of course," Horace replied with a nod. At the same time, his mind mulled with tightly-guarded thoughts. *Of course you want the Gate destroyed before it opens, because you know what it means when it does.*

Horace moved past the leaders, and down the open corridor separating the Kiros ranks from the Solarians. Soon, he was past the lines, in the neutral zone between the soldiers and the crater in which the Gate of Bannor resided.

Horace! What are you doing? We need to get away from the Gate… not toward it! Fransisca's insistent telepathic voice rang through his head.

You are free to try and leave any time Emmitt… although I suspect your attempt would be noticed, and punished accordingly, Horace replied with a smirk.

Emmitt went silent. Horace suspected the Knight was starting to realize the High Priest's true plan, but it bothered Horace little. It was already too late, and everyone would know the truth soon enough.

Horace stood at the crater's edge, and looked down upon the carved onyx circle. He savored the dark energy that flowed into him… so much stronger, so much purer than anything he had ever felt. This was what he had been called by his Creator to complete… to be the instrument of apocalypse… to bring the end of the old ways.

He knelt down, and began quietly reciting the ancient incantations he had learned through his studies into hellish lore. He paused just before speaking the final syllable, and stood back up with a smile.

He turned to the gathered armies, and used his psionic powers to enhance the volume of his voice. "Perhaps there is one thing I should explain. Most of you don't know that this has all been preordained by our Creator. We are all truly here to fulfill the Creator's will… a will that is to have us all… eliminated."

The gathered Knights and enlisted soldiers began talking amongst themselves, and even though he couldn't see them, he was sure the leaders of both sects were in a panic… trying to decide whether to intervene and prove Horace right, or to continue the ruse.

Finally, High Priest Horace Hightower revealed the purpose that he was destined to fulfill since he was first exposed to the true prophecy of Bryan Honore as the successor to the former High Priest, the first life Horace had taken in service of his Lord and Master. "I am not here to destroy the Gate of Bannor… I am here to *open* it!"

Horace then shouted the final syllable of the ritual, then began laughing in triumph as the ground began to tremble, and the disk sealing the Gate shattered like glass, the shards tossed upward in an eruption of dark red and black energies, fire and shadow entwining in a plume of power a TackMets high.

The armies initially broke down in confusion and shock before their leaders restored discipline, launching the first volleys of weapons fire and psionic energy in the hope of killing the High Priest. However, the energies from the gate had swelled, surrounding Horace in an impenetrable shell, stalling any and all attacks.

From just behind him, Horace heard the sound of the first demonic hand finding purchase on the edge of the crater. He never saw the creature that killed him, the blow from the demon's clawed hand ripping through his left shoulder and down through his chest, tearing through the priest's flesh like a razor through paper and literally cutting

Horace into several diagonal slices.

The first casualty of the Second Battle of Mydor had been made…

* * * * *

Rumil jerked in her seat, nearly falling out of the chair that she had taken in the galley. She must have nodded off, and no one bothered to wake her. Inactivity had caused her PCU to go into standby mode, but she hardly noticed it, abandoning it in the galley in her haste to leave. She had no doubts anymore that she had seen a vision of events unfolding on Mydor – they would not arrive in time to stop High Priest Hightower.

Right outside the galley, she met Justin, leaning against the wall, his head down. "We're already too late…" she muttered. "The Gate's open."

Justin didn't seem at all surprised by that news, and didn't even bother looking up. "I figured as much. Everything Bryan Honore had foreseen is coming to pass."

"You aren't at all worried?" she gaped. "I've read that book… I know what will happen to one of you… either you or Timothy…"

"Will die… yes, I know."

"Timothy intends to be the one who… doesn't come back," Rumil stated, even though Justin knew that fact as well as she.

"I'm sure he does," Justin answered, still not moving his head at all. "However, it's not his choice. The Creator deemed who would fall long before either of us were born. Only time will tell who that will be."

"So… that's it. We're just pawns… we had no choice but the path we are on."

"Our choices led us down this path regardless of who had seen it happen. I don't even pretend to understand the nature of prophecy, whether it is predestined or self-fulfilling, and to be honest, I don't care. It is not my place to wonder why…" He finally looked across the hallway to Rumil. "That would be yours."

"I don't even understand it," Rumil admitted. "I honestly fear I will go insane with it all, in fact."

"Things will change by the time the next cycle begins," Justin said as if he hadn't even heard her last statement. "You may never have the chances to do what you wish to do again. I suggest you take that opportunity now if that is what you desire."

While his words could have meant anything, the mental image he supplied her told her exactly what he was referring to. "*That* isn't your place, either," she said, insult warring with embarrassment as a flushed heat crept up her cheeks.

"Maybe not…" the Kiros admitted. "But you know I'm right." Justin didn't give any partings as he pushed off the wall, and walked away, leaving Rumil to her thoughts.

Half a tenth-cycle later, Rumil buzzed Timothy's door. "I must be insane," she muttered. "Now isn't the time to be doing… this…"

Rather than giving a vocal command to unlock the door, Timothy did it manually and waited on the other side. The sight he presented caused Rumil to think that maybe now was the perfect time for such things…

After all, Timothy wouldn't need much time to prepare. He must have either been getting ready to sleep – if not already sleeping – as he was wearing nothing more then a pair of loose shorts. His normally long, straight hair was wet and unruly, as if it was still drying from cleaning. He made a boyishly cute, and strikingly alluring, figure.

"Are you going to tell me the reason for this visit, or did you stop by just to stare at me?" Timothy groused, his voice heavy. He must have been sleeping, and Rumil suddenly felt guilty for coming.

"I didn't mean to wake you… I can… always… come back…" Rumil stammered, he momentary courage broken.

"Don't worry, I was asleep anyway," Timothy muttered, rubbing his eyes, possibly trying to adjust to the light from the hallway. "Come in."

Rumil gulped as she followed into the dark quarters, a dim light soon illuminating the simply furnished area, just as Timothy seemed to like it. He walked around a corner into the sleeping area, and said, "Let me get dressed."

"Don't bother… I won't be here long." Rumil said, thinking that if she didn't get her act together, she probably wouldn't be. She'd likely run out of the quarters in a panic.

He emerged back into the living area, the sleep almost completely out of his face and voice. "All right then, what is it?"

Rumil knew what she wanted to say... but her mind wouldn't allow her to put it together without sounding disgustingly crude. After all, just how did a woman go about broaching such a subject?

You know, Timothy, since there's a half chance you won't be alive come this time next cycle, wanna have a quick tumble in that bed over there? Something told her that wouldn't go over well.

Timothy, just in case you die down on Mydor, how about a goodbye wild dance? Right...

Hey, wanna sleep together? Sure, before she died of embarrassment.

Timothy, remember what I told you on Baramak? How I'm glad you're in this galaxy and in my life? I wasn't totally honest. I've come to need you in my life... so badly that the thought that you might not come back seems to be killing me already. Just in case... can I have this one memory, this one moment, something I can have just in case the worst possible thing in my life happens? Rumil wondered if the higher power that was giving her these visions decided to help her out by giving her that little speech, but since it fit so well and captured her feelings so perfectly, she decided not to question it.

However, when she opened her mouth... it didn't come out, as if her own vocal chords had disappeared without letting her know they were leaving. Thus, the only sounds out of her mouth were incomprehensible "ah"s and "um"s.

"I was sleeping." Timothy said testily. "I'd like to get back to it if I may."

Rumil blinked, not totally comprehending his words as she was still too busy trying to figure out why her voice wasn't working. Finally, she managed to spurt, "Can... I... use your... restroom?"

Timothy pointed to the small room connecting to his sleeping area, and said, "Be my guest."

She shuffled quickly into the room, sliding the door shut behind her. What was wrong with her? She had spent almost a full staryear seducing men, dancing around and exciting their hormones... yet now she was stammering like some shy little girl asking her neighbor's son for a kiss.

That's when it occurred to her. Men hadn't cared what she said

245

before… she hadn't even spoken at all, for that matter. She decided to forgo trying to talk her way into the mood, and instead let her actions talk for her.

She stepped out of her shoes and stockings, then quickly discarded her blouse and slacks, leaving her in a set of blue undergarments, remarkably similar to the articles she had worn the first time she had met the object of her affections. She had purchased them while waiting for their shuttle to Feria after learning of Justin's little name game, figuring that maybe she would get a chance to get totally into character. Of course it hadn't turned out that way…

Even though that wasn't even a ten-cycle ago, it seemed like an eternity. So much had changed… and so much was going to change in less than a cycle. Justin was right; she wasn't going to have this chance again. Taking one deep breath, as if the air in the room was laced with courage, she quickly exhaled and opened the door.

"Are you ready to tell me what is on your… oh…" Timothy began then stopped abruptly. Even in the dim light, she could see his eyes darken, a reaction she recognized all too well. Emboldened by it, she stepped out of the doorway, her movements slow, deliberate, and intentionally suggestive.

She finally found her voice, and her words were equal to the language her body was speaking. "I wasn't sure how to approach you. I know this may seem horrifically inappropriate, but I know that you yourself didn't seem totally opposed to the idea before…"

He didn't reply; his eyes were fixed upon hers. She would have thought he was trying to read her mind, but she didn't sense any significant increase in his mental powers. His expression didn't change, but she somehow felt that she was going about it the wrong way… it didn't seem quite as right anymore.

When she spoke again, her voice and her words were even softer. "I'll admit it… I'm scared. I'm scared of what is going to happen on Mydor. I'm scared that you aren't going to come back. I'm scared that I'll never get the chance to tell you… that I'm scared of losing you."

Timothy closed the distance quickly, pulling her against him, dropping a feather-light kiss on her forehead before propping her chin on his left shoulder while doing the same on her. He still didn't say anything. He just held her, and she took comfort in his closeness, in his presence. In that short time that they didn't say anything, the full enormity of their relationship came to bear on Rumil... as passing strangers... then as a hunter and criminal... then as tenuous allies... then as friends... and now finally this... whatever this was. It was love, Rumil noted, a passionate love that yet somehow... didn't seem quite like what she had expected it to be.

She had read romantic stories, had seen a few romance serials on the GalNet. The hero fights through all odds, whether they be fantastic or mundane, rescues his damsel, he kisses her deeply on the lips, and the story ends with the two confident in their passion, to live life happily ever after together.

This was hardly a happy moment. There was a fifty-fifty chance Timothy would die. And what she felt right now was so much fuller than anything she had ever read or watched. She honestly couldn't say if the news that Timothy was gone ever reached her ears, that her own life wouldn't just spontaneously fail her. It was such a depressing weakness that at the same time made her feel so strong... so alive. It seemed as though that she was literally a part of him, and if he were to go, part of her would go as well. It was something that went beyond a physical relationship... something that made her initial plans seem very insignificant.

"I just don't want to be alone right now..." she finally whispered in his ear.

"I'm not sure I'd be able to control myself," he whispered back. "You know that."

"I'm not talking about that anymore. I... just don't want to be alone..."

* * * * *

She felt comfortable and completely safe for the first time since... well... ever.

Rumil snuggled closer, once again nestling her head on Timothy's chest and neck, letting her hands run along his well-toned arms. She didn't want to wake up yet, but the navigational officer had just come over the intercom declaring that they would arrive in orbit around Mydor within one tenth-cycle.

Timothy seemed to agree with her opinion, as he coiled his arms around her back tighter, his fingers unintentionally slipping under the strap of her top undergarment for a moment. For another tick, they laid there awake, yet reluctant to admit it.

"You realize that everyone is going to think that we… well…" she mumbled shyly.

"Let them think what they want," he replied. "I really don't care."

"We probably should get ready."

"Yes… we should…"

* * * * *

When the pair finally emerged onto the bridge of the *Gallan*, no one was in a mood to muse on what had been occurring. Instead, their eyes were transfixed on the cruiser's viewscreen, where a Solarian man in full Knight's uniform was waiting.

"I assume you know this person, Timothy?" Justin asked, gesturing to the screen.

"Knight Datson," Timothy said in reply and in greeting. "I figured you would be on the surface. What's this communication for?"

"I see that all of you are rather disturbingly aware of recent events," Datson answered. "As for being on the surface, your father stationed me here in charge of the fleet, although if things get much worse, I'll probably be called along with everything but a skeleton crew. As for the communication, we detected your craft, and I figured you were on it. I just wanted to warn you that High Priest Hightower—"

"Was likely the leader of the Endtimers movement, and has opened the Gate of Bannor," Timothy finished. "As you said earlier, we are rather up to date on the events."

"I wish I knew what this was all about honestly. Hightower was ranting about how all of this was destined, and foreseen by the Fifth Prophet, but it certainly wasn't anything I had read…"

Timothy smirked. "If we both get through this, I'll let you in on the secret. Unfortunately, at the moment, I don't have a ten-cycle to explain what has happened and the consequences of said happenings. We're about seventeen ticks out of orbit at this moment. You can inform my father that I will be arriving shortly, and that I'll be bringing something that could help."

Datson turned to the side, and laughed. "Apparently, my primary officer already informed the High Commander of your pending arrival. Your father wishes to let you know that your arrival is most fortunate, and that he'll need every little bit of assistance you can provide." Robert laughed again in bemusement, "I honestly never thought I'd ever hear those words come out of his mouth."

"Knight Datson…" Justin interceded somewhat nervously, "if it's possible… could you inform the Kiros High Commander that Justin Feroz will be arriving on planet as well?" He then regarded Timothy's dark scowl coolly, as if daring the Solarian to challenge his desire to take part in the battle.

Robert blinked, and uncertainly tapped out a few commands on the console in front of him. "I've passed a text message along to the Kiros flagship, and I suspect they will notify their High Commander."

"Thank you," Justin said with a polite bow.

"Anyway, we'll be awaiting your arrival," Robert said, winding down the meeting. "We'll hold the line as tight as we can until you do."

The screen went dead, and nobody needed any further instruction. Justin and Timothy rushed towards the shuttle bay, Justin's hands clenched tightly around the handle of the case carrying the Star Smasher. They would check their equipment one more time in the bay, and make their descent onto Mydor within a tick of the *Gallan* dropping out of foldspace. Meanwhile, the rest of the crew would remain in distant orbit, safe from immediate harm.

Rumil didn't like that plan one bit.

"I'm going," she stated.

"Going where?" Dewin asked, even though he had a sinking feeling he knew just what Rumil was referring to.

"Down. To the planet," she replied, turning about to leave.

"I never knew you were trained to pilot a shuttle," Dewin reminded.

"I'm not."

He tapped his chair casually. "Then who is flying you down to the planet? I doubt neither Timothy nor Justin is going to allow you on their shuttle."

"If I have to fly it myself, I will." While Rumil definitely seemed to have changed since visiting Baramak, she could be as stubborn as ever.

"Oh, you could definitely *try*," Dewin remarked coolly. "But I doubt you'd actually *succeed*. It took me three ten-cycles of training before I was ready to perform atmospheric entry maneuvers, and I was a fast learner."

"I'm leaving, even if I burn to a cinder trying."

"You're clearly not getting the point…" Dewin began, then stopped when Orion suddenly surrendered the helm, and moving towards the exit.

"You are incorrect, Mr. Rio. She gets the point entirely," the hulking pale blue humanoid said darkly. "I will fly her down to the planet."

"Even if I order you not to?" Dewin asked. He didn't necessarily mean it as a threat, but more of a means to determine just how seriously both of them wanted to proceed.

"There is a battle occurring on that planet as we speak, and if I assume correctly, it is an epic battle that casts a great shadow on all the wars of history. Never before has an Ubek ever stood aside from combat and let others fight in his or her stead… and I do not intend to be the first."

Dewin sighed, knowing he should have figured that Orion would drag his racial honor into the argument. To be honest, Dewin didn't want to sit in the captain's chair and watch the carnage either. That Gate had haunted him for some time, its presence like an annoying blot in his vision that he couldn't get rid of. He merely didn't want to be the one who suggested abandoning their posts for a suicidal visit to the front lines.

"Actually, I'd rather like to see this Gate up close myself, and last time I checked, I was the captain of this vessel," Dewin reasoned with a sly grin. The Demodian then rose from his seat and attempted a majestic stance – his feet apart, fists on his hips, chest out and chin raised – but in reality his slight frame made him appear unfortunately silly. "Mr. Salazar, lead Rumil to munitions, I'll meet you shortly."

* * * * *

If Timothy had not been looking directly at the sight before him, he would never have believed it.

No, not the scenes of battle as the Erani – buoyed by the aid of newly arrived Se-Lan survivors – clashed against the demonic hordes in an attempt to drive them back into the Gate of Bannor. What struck Timothy was the look of utter relief and gratitude on his father's face as the High Commander saw him emerge from his shuttle.

Joseph Feroz also reacted kindly to the appearance of his adopted son as Justin climbed down the ramp, with a long, gray weapons case in his right hand. The two dashed towards the assembled leaders, who were about one half-TackMet short of the battle line.

After extending abrupt greetings, Timothy ruefully commented, "This has to be the first time two 'traitors' have ever been welcomed into the fold." He exchanged a long, thankful forearm with King Frederick, genuinely grateful to see his old friend once again.

"Desperate times often call for such measures," Niles replied.

Meanwhile, Joseph had placed a hand on Justin's shoulder warmly, and looked down at the case the younger Knight carried. "Is that what I think it is?" Joseph asked.

"Probably," Justin answered a little coldly. "And this case won't leave my hand until absolutely necessary," he added when he noticed how his uncle was looking rather enviously at the case in question.

"So, you intend to destroy the Gate with the Star Smasher before the rest of Bryan's prophecy can come to pass," Niles deduced. "Why? You've never liked much of our society and what it stood for. I'd figure you'd want to see us all destroyed."

Timothy turned his eyes towards Justin, and said, "I have my reasons." Turning his gaze back to Niles, he continued, "Do we have enough manpower to break a hole in the demons' line? If you can do that, I can do the rest."

Niles rubbed his hand through his hair, and said, "I'm not sure. These Bannor-forsaken fiends have been pushing us back steadily since it all started. We can barely even slow them down, much less press them."

"I don't need a large opening," Timothy answered, levitating up briefly to take a scope of the battle, dropping back down before he drew too much attention from the demonic forces. "They don't have a second line, and they're more interested in fighting rather than defending the Gate." he observed. "If you can press into the demons, and give me enough of a break that I can fight the rest of the way through, I should be able to destroy the Gate before they can retaliate. But we have to move quickly."

Timothy didn't need to explain why haste would be required. Niles nodded, and called over Joseph to make the necessary plans and deliver the orders needed. Timothy pointed to the battle line, indicating that he would be taking his position. Niles nodded in approval, and Timothy turned to Justin, hand out. "Give me the Star Smasher."

"As I told my uncle, this case will not leave my hand until absolutely necessary. Besides, I'm the only one who knows the combination," the Kiros retorted.

The pair exchanged a dark glance. "I know what you're trying to do… I can't let you do it," Timothy finally muttered.

"And I'm supposed to let you instead?" Justin answered. "I'm not giving this to you unless I have to, and I don't think we have time to argue. How about we let the Creator make the decision rather than trying to do His job for Him?"

Timothy scowled, but surrendered to his haste and perhaps acknowledging part of Justin's argument. "Fine, but let's move quickly."

Chapter Seventeen

Rumil yelped in pain as Orion buckled the clasps of the carbide armor breastplate along her back. Now she understood why Timothy and Justin wore nothing more than form-fitting bodysuits underneath their armor, as the molded metal left little room for anything else underneath.

"Sorry…" Dewin remarked, seeing her grimace of pain. "The carbide molds haven't been used in a while, so it's possible the calibration is a little off."

"No… it's my fault," she replied, "I'm still wearing my undergarments. I should have figured since I had to strip down to get molded, that I would probably need to do the same to put the stuff on." As it stood, the plastic clasp of her undergarment top was digging painfully into her back.

"Would you like to remove them?" Orion asked.

Rumil shook her head. "We don't have time. Timothy and Justin are probably already on the surface. I'll just have to live with it."

"You realize Timothy probably isn't going to like it when he sees you on planet," Dewin chided.

"Well, he's just going to have to live with *that*."

"I suppose it's fortunate Timothy is as even-mannered as he is," Dewin said with a light voice and a shake of his head. "Any other man would have been driven mad trying to watch after you."

"Why?" Orion asked in confusion. "Rumil is a strong woman, even if her strength does not lie in her muscles. She does an honor and a credit to anyone she considers a friend."

"You've served under me for ten staryears, right?" Dewin asked.

"Yes, Mr. Rio."

"Then you should know by now that not everyone thinks like an Ubek."

Orion smirked playfully. "Maybe more people should." He then buckled his arm plates into place, and reached into the weapons locker, pulling out a large plasma rifle almost as large as Rumil, slinging it over his shoulder before coming out with a pair of smaller pistols that he handed to Dewin and Rumil.

Rumil looked over the weapon uncertainly, and Dewin said, "This little end is the handle, and this is the firing coil, and that's the trigger…"

"I know that!" Rumil snapped sardonically, putting the weapon into the holster at her waist. With a sheepish voice, she added, "I just… I'm not used to killing."

"Are you sure you want to go down, then?" Dewin asked. "Because I suspect there's going to be a lot of death both before and after we land."

"Actually, I suppose I don't really want to," Rumil admitted, "But… I have to. Something in my mind is telling me I have to be down there, that I'm supposed to be down there."

Dewin shrugged. "I'm not going to argue. Just as long as you are certain you need or want to do what we're doing, I'm not going to stop you."

Orion then handed them close-combat weapons, a brightly polished curved sword for Dewin, a short, thin stiletto-like dagger to Rumil, and a heavy hypersteel battle hammer that looked like it could put a hole in the *Gallan's* hull for himself.

On top of that, the Ubek loaded himself up with a harness of plasma grenades, a large detonation charge pack which he slung over his other shoulder, three combat knives he sheathed in his armor belt, another pair of plasma pistols, and a long belt pack containing various plasma shell magazines to rearm their pistols and his rifle.

"Orion, I think the Solarian and Kiros armies can supply themselves," Rumil quipped.

"If the battle is truly as vicious as we have been hearing, we might need every single weapon I'm bringing," Orion replied seriously. "Now, if you both are ready, I had one of the reserve helmsmen start up a shuttle for our departure."

Rumil nodded, figuring she was as ready as she ever was going to be… the longer she waited, she more she realized how insane she was.

* * * * *

Timothy and Justin awaited only the order to make their press, the front line fighters trying to break as far into the demonic forces as they could. Hopefully, it would be enough for the two to punch through the rest of the way.

At that moment, Timothy heard over the open communications channel that another shuttle from the *Gallan* was entering the atmosphere. He put a hand over the ear of his helmet to hear the repeated update from his headset more clearly, and immediately glowered in disgust. He turned his head to Justin, who shrugged.

"How much do you want to bet Rumil is on that shuttle?" Timothy said in defeat.

"That's a bet I know I'd lose," the Kiros answered. "Is there enough time for her to ignore us again?"

As if on cue, they both heard the order come through for the stealthily-gathered joint forces of the Solarians and Kiros to begin their push. Timothy figured that was a more effective answer than anything he could have given, and joined the surging Erani and Se-Lan forces with Justin right behind.

The charge took the demons by surprise, as Timothy and Justin were halfway through before they had to draw their own weapons. The first adversary to confront them was a hideous creature barely larger than a Ruma, with misshapen fangs, a sickly crimson brown hide, and seven horns – three on its head, two on its left arm, one sticking out its back, and one small one on its left knee. It had managed to duck under the front charge, only to have its head cleanly lopped off by Timothy's sword.

The Solarian discovered everything he'd heard about the enemy's otherwordly resilience was no exaggeration. It felt like he had been trying to cleave through a stone with his blow, and despite the demon being decapitated, Justin yelped in surprise as the creature's fanged maw snapped at his feet as he passed.

From there, the push slowed to a crawl, and had the demons reinforced their line to counter the attack, Timothy and Justin would have probably never broken through. Fortunately, the hellish denizens seemed to be fighting rather haphazardly, with no order or discipline, as the old stories of the Archangel War suggested they were prone to do if a strong leader wasn't present. Timothy could only hope they would destroy the Gate before said leader made its appearance.

Timothy had almost broken through when three demons crowding the back of the horde noticed him, and saw their chance to get involved in the fighting. Like the one he had hacked earlier, they were smaller specimens, which was probably why they were in the back rows, unable to force their way through their larger kin. He readied his sword to engage them, learning from other soldiers and his own experience that plasma rounds did barely anything to them other than knock them backward a little. But before he could make a move, he stepped aside, sensing something large barreling in from behind him.

The massive form of Orion Salazar charged past, plowing through the demons. A swipe of his hammer was directed at one with such naked ferocity that an onlooker might think he intended to send his victim into low planetary orbit. The creature flew about ten Tacks into the midst of the demon hordes, likely ripped apart and trampled to death soon after.

"He's been itching to fight something since he saw the battle firsthand," Dewin remarked from behind him as Orion methodically cleared the rest of the path, while more demons noticed the break in the line.

Timothy quickly changed the topic. "How could you let Rumil come down here?" he demanded, as he made an overhead chop that split one minor demon from the top of its head to its belly.

"I didn't *let* her do anything," Dewin commented, parrying away an attacker himself. "If I didn't take her, she would have killed herself trying to fly down on her own."

"I'm surprised the Solarians or the Kiros didn't try to kill her the moment she disembarked."

"They're too busy understandably fighting these things to really notice me," Rumil remarked from behind him, seeming unperturbed by the chaos around her, effectively shielded by a ring of combatants. "Besides, I doubt anyone would recognize me in this gear."

He afforded a quick glance back towards the woman. Considering that she was in full carbide armor with helmet, and the fact that her psionic aura was once again suspiciously absent, Timothy agreed that her assessment was likely true.

"Nonetheless, this is not the place for someone like you to be!" he hollered, making his point by incinerating a charging demon that marked Rumil as an easy victim. When the vile monster kept coming, Timothy slashed off one arm and kicked it backwards, where it collapsed into a heap against two other charging demons.

"It's not as if she's helpless out here, anyhow," Dewin remarked wryly. "You should have seen the way she triumphantly bested that demon head you mistakenly left unaccounted for. It was truly an epic battle."

The image that statement generated almost got Timothy chuckling in spite of himself. Rumil grunted angrily, and replied, "In case you hadn't noticed, it was still biting at people."

"Less chatter, more moving!" Justin shouted, pointing just ahead. "It looks like our Ubek friend is about to give us the opening we need."

Sure enough, Orion's larger, stronger frame was having an easier time with the demons, swatting them away with each powerful blow, and it did seem that he was knocking them back faster then they could reinforce the break in their line. Timothy decided to assist the effort by supplying a small stream of concussive energy balls with a thrust of his left arm. Zipping around and over the Ubek so as not to inadvertently strike the massive humanoid, they didn't do much damage to any of the creatures, but did send several of them flying or tumbling, creating exactly the hole needed.

They finally broke through the rear of the horde, dashing through at a sprint. Once clear of the melee, Timothy stopped as he again held out his hand, and said, "Open the case, and give me the Star Smasher." Noticing Justin's reluctance, Timothy shouted, "I don't have time to argue. Give it to me!"

Rumil pointed to the crater, and said, "Actually, go ahead and argue… I think we're a little too late."

The rest of the group turned to see what Rumil was referring to, just in time to see a second massive, meaty, black-clawed hand grasp the edge of crater. A third and a fourth followed, then with one powerful heave, a creature bigger than anything they had ever seen leaped about twenty Tacks in the air, landing with an earth-shaking thud in front of the crater that actually knocked over most of the rear row of demons.

Rumil had seen the Arch-Demon in her visions, Justin and Timothy had read about it in Bryan Honore's prophecy, and Dewin had felt this evil's presence rather closely, so none of them figured they'd be terribly shocked if they saw it in person.

They were wrong.

The giant demon exhaled so deeply that they felt the blast of air, a thick plume of black smoke rushing out and billowing from its flat, wide nostrils; the scales overlapping its face quivering. It licked its lips, fingers of flame escaping its maw as it did so, followed by more wisps of acrid, ebony smoke. It drew itself to its full height, at least four times that of Orion – and likely fifty times heavier – stretched all four of its arms above its horned head, and issued a bloodthirsty roar that seemed to carry pure fear, momentarily paralyzing everyone within its range, demon and mortal alike.

"No way…" Justin mumbled. "We're supposed to fight that thing?"

Timothy gulped, and for the first time that anyone present could think of, his voice was laden with nervousness. "You're the one who wanted to put our lives in the hands of fate. No backing out now."

"Literally," Orion quipped, noting that the demonic line had sealed once again, giving the group nowhere to run. The rear demons were cackling, merely content to seal off escape and allow their master the pleasure of the kill.

Timothy took a deep breath, and dipped his head, slowly regaining his wits. Once he gathered his composure again, his orders soon followed. "Justin, let's go. Keep your head on a swivel, and stay sharp. We'll have to strike quickly, and not worry about making a kill, if a kill is even possible. Perhaps if we can force it back into the Gate, we can keep it from returning."

"Oh, sure," Justin answered. "And after we've done that, we can find a nice mountain to move a few Tacks."

"Wasn't it the Prophet Nicolai who commented that with even faith as large as a grain of sand such was possible?" Timothy said, smirking under his helmet.

"Actually, I'm quite certain it was Groel," Justin answered, the banter helping him find his courage. "Alright, let's meet fate, shall we?"

Timothy turned to the other three, and ordered, "Dewin, Orion, if those demons decide they want part of the fun, I'm counting on you both to keep Rumil safe."

The two pirates nodded, and Timothy turned back around, striding purposefully towards the towering Arch-Demon, who was looking down at them bemusedly as they approached. Then, the creature's eyes locked on Timothy, and they narrowed as if suddenly concerned.

"Is this the best that the Se-Lan could bring against me?" the creature said casually with surprisingly perfect Basic, but even its casual voice carried as much volume as a shuttle take-off. It then sniffed, and added, "You aren't even Se-Lan at all, now that I look at you. You are… those Erani creations, aren't you? Odd, I never knew you were given powers of the angel-kin. Nonetheless, you are both rather puny, aren't you?"

"One would think that your apparent previous encounters with those of the angel-kin would tell you that size doesn't necessarily tell the whole story," Timothy answered, his voice carrying a confidence that Rumil was certain he could not have felt.

"That is true," the Arch-Demon spoke again with an evil chuckle, "But I was actually referring to the power you two possess. The Se-Lan have truly fallen since the sealing of the planes if they are sending mortal-born to face me." Its voice became candid, and it said, "Now, could you indulge me with your names? I would feel truly awkward if during our little… skirmish… I were to call you 'victim one' and 'victim two.'"

"You'll be calling us off in ten ticks," Timothy threatened, his hand gripping his sword tightly, gathering his mental prowess at the same time. In the back of his head, his other self began clawing at his mind… the righteous fury that started to bubble to the surface.

Again, there was a moment of what appeared to be concern on the Arch-Demon's face as it seemed to try and quickly analyze Timothy, as if trying to see inside the Solarian's armor. The look quickly vanished, and it laughed heartily, "Why do I sincerely doubt that?" The giant creature then growled, "I am the Arch-Demon the Se-Lan call Chau-Fagn. When I rend you to pieces, I want that name to be foremost on your mind."

For a creature of its size, Chau-Fagn struck faster than either Knight could have expected; and while they managed to jump away from the overhead swipe, the concussive force that followed when its hand slapped the ground caused both of them to fall on their backs, rolling to their feet in anticipation of a second blow that didn't come.

Instead, Chau-Fagn laughed again. "Truly pathetic," the Arch-Demon growled, then launched itself into a series of savage attacks against his significantly smaller adversaries.

Rumil noted that the Arch-Demon was spending much of his time attacking Timothy, almost ignoring Justin entirely save for the occasional swipe to keep the Kiros off balance. One of Chau-Fagn's strikes seemingly caught Timothy off-guard, but instead struck the Solarian's invisible psionic shield, and to her surprise as well as Chau-Fagn's, the protective dome held. The demon's momentary disbelief allowed Timothy one clear shot with a jagged spear of ice he had fashioned from the water vapor in the air. However, the projectile literally vaporized before ever reaching the Arch-Demon.

Justin also took the opportunity to make an attack of his own, trying to stab with his sword into Chau-Fagn's calf, but the point of the blade literally bent, then shattered, rather than piercing the demon's flesh. Chau-Fagn's counterattack was brutal, as Justin looked down at the jagged hypersteel, and was cuffed by a hand that hit him in the head, shoulder, and side all at once, shattering his carbide breastplate, and driving one shard deep into his side. The Kiros screamed painfully as he was tossed into the air, and landed on his injured side, pushing the broken carbide even deeper.

With Justin incapacitated, Chau-Fagn could divert its entire energy against Timothy, pushing the Solarian back with a series of swipes and slaps. The Arch-Demon then gathered its own mental powers so quickly that Timothy had to react on pure instinct, leaping back with a psionic-induced jump that just barely cleared him from the ten tack radius that suddenly immolated into a plasma state. Unfortunately, his jump took him a little too close to the demon ranks, who raked at him with claws and snapped with their teeth, forcing Timothy to roll to the side, and right into the grasp of Chau-Fagn, who grabbed the Solarian in one gargantuan hand, and began squeezing.

Justin was jerked to alertness by the sound of Timothy's scream, and the Kiros struggled to his hands and feet. In his pain-hazed vision, he saw what was happening, and wondered why Timothy was holding back his power. He understood that Timothy was afraid of what he would do if he ever lost control, but they were running out of options.

Finally, it seemed Timothy realized that. The Solarian's aura burst, enough for him to force the demon's hand apart. Timothy fell to the ground, panting for breath, and Justin realized the move was merely one of desperation, not a conscious decision. With an angry roar, Chau-Fagn kicked, sending the Solarian through the air, landing awkwardly on his neck, his head bouncing off the ground twice before skidding to a stop.

Surprisingly, Timothy managed to stagger to his feet, despite being clearly dazed from his landing. Chau-Fagn also appeared to be growing tired of playing, and was preparing to simply be done with the Solarian.

Justin quickly reached the conclusion that the only chance anyone had was if Timothy stayed alive, and just who would have to make the sacrifice Bryan spoke of. He had figured it for some time, ever since the events on Ub, but couldn't be entirely certain. Now there was no question, and that meant Justin had to move… now.

Chau-Fagn lifted its upper right hand, as if gloating, letting it stay there until Timothy could look up and see his doom before death was dealt. That stay was what Justin needed, dashing with what remaining strength his wounded body had, yelling to draw Chau-Fagn's attention.

Which it did. The Arch-Demon reached out with its lower left hand, grabbing Justin in a similar death grip as the one it held Timothy, but Justin knew that he didn't have the hidden power to break the hold, nor would he have had the energy to use it if he did.

The shard of carbide burrowed deep into the center of his abdomen, but Justin didn't even cry out as he felt his shoulder blades compact and crush from the increasing pressure on his body. In that moment, just before death claimed him, he understood what had driven his ancestor, Julius, to give his life in exchange for Bryan's to destroy the First Gate on Solaria. It had been an act of selflessness for the sake of his best friend, with the knowledge that his friend was someone truly special, someone who had a far greater destiny than to die that day.

Justin smiled, now numb to the pain of his body being crushed to a pulp.

With his last coherent thought, he made one telepathic request to Timothy. *Take care of Jonathan, will you, Timothy? I can't think of anyone else I'd rather have to tell him about his father, and train and teach him the way a Knight should be.*

The message complete, Justin Feroz's vision went black, and the Kiros was no more.

Timothy had cleared his head just in time to receive Justin's last request, and looked up to see the Kiros's blood flowing from between the Arch-Demon's clenched fingers, carrying with it small pieces of bone and internal organs. With one final squeeze, there was a sickening pop as Justin's torso was pulverized in a burst of blood and gore, his limbs fell away, and his head flew up into the air. Chau-Fagn's maniacal laughter mixed with that of its minions as the severed cranium tumbled about ten Tacks from its remains, and landed with a dull thud right in front of Timothy. Justin's face was turned towards the Solarian, his cold, blank stare contrasting with the serene, peaceful smile on the mouth.

He heard the thud of a helmet, and Rumil vomiting from behind him. He didn't blame her, he might have done so himself had he not decided to deny the Arch-Demon the pleasure of seeing his disgust.

The seething, brilliant rage that Timothy had been trying to keep reigned in surged, and this time the Solarian didn't fight it. Chau-Fagn wanted scorched earth; then let the demon have fire...

* * * * *

An eerie silence followed the death of Justin Feroz; then ten demiticks later Rumil felt the rush of pure power that made the buzzing seem like it was going to burst out of the back of her skull. The pulsing pain would have made her vomit again, had her stomach not already been emptied.

Once her mind adapted to the overwhelming sensation, she looked back towards Timothy, who had straightened into a defiant posture, though his head tilted downward, allowing the telltale beams of white light to cast down on the ground beneath him; telling her precisely the source of her current discomfort.

But this time, his eyes weren't the only thing that changed. From the back of his shoulders, the carbide plate bulged, then shattered. Two long wings of a brilliant silvery-white color with metallic, bladed feathers burst from his back and unfurled majestically.

From there his entire body burst with a brilliant, white hot nuclear plasma, bathing the entire area was bathed in a blinding light. Any that didn't look away quickly, both demon and mortal, were reduced to ash and scattered with the solar wind generated by the Solarian, with one exception.

Rumil was transfixed, unable to look away, but unaffected by the consequences that had befallen others who did the same. To her surprise, she was able to peer through the blinding light, her mouth agape as she witnessed the transformation taking place.

She looked in awed horror as Timothy clawed into his own right arm, ripping the skin off like a long glove, and letting it drop onto the ground, leaving a brilliant white metallic surface underneath. The other arm soon followed, then both hands gouged into his face, revealing more of the bizarre flesh.

Finally, a second burst disintegrated armor and clothing, leaving nothing but a shining humanoid figure. From the nuclear inferno, energy congealed into matter, taking the shape of platinum-colored plates, latching onto Timothy's liquid metal skin, each piece covering the light radiating from beneath. At last, a helmet formed over his head, and the metallic flesh was fully contained save for the two small, blazing pinpoints of light where his eyes were exposed. The armor resembled the bodysuit and carbide armor of an Erani Knight, but was made of something beyond modern science, the plates adorned with luminous light blue script that Rumil had never seen before, yet somehow understood.

It was a warning to whoever beheld this terrific creature; telling the tale of its history, its many battles, equal victories, and that this armor was not for its protection... but for the world around it. A shell for a monster that could break reality itself if left unshielded for any length of time.

The light receded, and everyone could safely behold the results of the transformation. Niles Honore had levitated up to get a better view of the battle with the Arch-Demon, and saw what he had feared almost since Timothy's birth.

He had suspected this since Timothy's first psionic episode, barely a half-staryear after the child had been born, and had been terrified of what it meant. He tried to stall the events he knew would unfold by trying to ruin the child's life, but fear of his faith and defying his Creator's will prevented him from completely destroying the child… one fear had warred with another, and caused him to do things that would have been unthinkable before.

Seeing it now, the majestic being of metal, clad in Durium, the armor of the Angelic Host of Annor, with the holy runes of the angelic tongue etched onto the impossibly strong material, he knew that he had been right. He remembered the promise that Bryan Honore made in the prophecy, that when everything seemed lost, this would happen. The heavenly being that had led the armies of Annor during the Archangel War before recorded history had been born on the material plane, to appear at precisely this moment.

The Archangel Mican had emerged from the mortal shell of his son.

* * * * *

The demeanor of the Arch-Demon radically changed once it recovered from the blast of energy. Despite being over ten times larger than the being in front of it, Rumil could see the concern, and perhaps a little fear, in Chau-Fagn's eyes.

"So, you've finally woken up," the monstrous demon said coolly, but his voice betrayed him ever so slightly. "Good… I had been wanting a real fight on this plane."

The metallic figure simply glanced upward, and Chau-Fagn instinctively stepped back slightly, growling at its involuntary display of weakness. It looked for a moment that the figure was going to speak… but then turned about, as if completely ignoring the Arch-Demon. With one flap of his wings, the Archangel glided the distance between him and the three almost paralyzed mortals inside the circle of demons.

"Open the case," he said in a voice that seemed remarkably similar to Timothy's, though it carried more powerfully and had a curious quasi-echo effect. His eyes turned down to the weapons case at Dewin's feet, where Justin had put it before going into battle.

Dewin knelt down in front of it and reached for the latches, then realized sheepishly, "I don't know the combination." Quickly adding, "No worries, I know exactly what to do…"

Apparently, the Archangel wasn't in the mood for waiting. He held his hand out above the case, and the weapon burst through the reinforced plastic, sending bits of the inner foam spraying in a small plume, and his hand clasped expertly around the hilt.

Dewin fell back in surprise, landing roughly on his rump, then finally managed to blink before squeaking, "I suppose that will work also…"

"Will you need assistance?" Orion asked, although it somehow seemed more of a rhetorical question.

The metallic being regarded Orion almost disdainfully. Despite the fact he was exactly Timothy's size, he somehow seemed to look down on the Ubek. "Let me assure you I have everything well in hand."

His gaze drifted to Rumil, and his voice softened. "I do have an important task for the three of you, however. I need you to deliver a message to the Erani High Commanders. Have them gather the Se-Lan survivors and all non-noble military and get them to evacuate the planet. I think you all know the reason why."

"That's all well and good..." Dewin said skeptically, once again on his feet, "but something tells me they aren't about to let us leave." He pointed his thumb back to indicate to the horde behind them.

The Archangel paused, and with an invisible hand he almost flippantly swatted away a massive fireball from Chau-Fagn, who mistakenly believed the divine being was presently distracted. He then turned his attention to the surviving circle of demons, who had closed their ranks once more despite having lost close to half their number during Timothy's change. One outstretched fist, followed by a flip of his fingers, sent an entire section of the line twirling in the air like scraps of paper caught in a hurricane. After that display, the demons weren't nearly as eager to form ranks again.

"I think you'll be fine," the Archangel quipped flatly. "Now go."

None of the three felt it was in their best interests to disobey, dashing down the cleared swath towards the Erani side of the battlefield. Confident they would obey his order, Annor's general turned back towards the Arch-Demon Chau-Fagn, and said, "I must agree. I too was hoping to get a good fight here on this plane. Sadly, it appears we both will be disappointed."

* * * * *

Niles Honore's face went even whiter than it normally was when he saw... that woman... running up to him and the other assembled leaders of the Erani. One part of his mind figured he had the perfect chance to eliminate her and change his fate right then, as did many others, he wagered. However, as the first sounds of battle between the two extra-planar beings rang through the Dead Grounds, he decided not to make his sins against the Creator he claimed to serve any worse.

"Tim..." Rumil began, then corrected herself, wondering just how much of what Timothy had become was still him, if any. "Mican... that silver angel thing... whatever he is... wanted me to tell you that he wants the Erani forces to gather up and evacuate all the Se-Lan and standard enlisted Erani from the planet."

King Lionel balked at the idea. "That's impossible! Scans of this planet revealed there were almost twenty million Se-Lan living here!"

Joseph then scratched his chin, and replied, "No... actually... it's quite possible, I think. High Commander Honore, your Dreadnoughts carry a standard allotment of around one hundred thousand personnel, right?"

Niles nodded. "Yes... when you include those stationed on the secondary cruisers the Dreadnoughts carry."

"Would it be safe to assume that you could actually fit about four or five times that amount on the vessels, along with a crew to operate them?"

Niles quickly consulted with Knight Datson watching over the fleet, and then answered, "It would be tight, make no mistake, but we could."

"How many Dreadnoughts did you bring?"

"All thirty-four of them, loaded with just about every Knight in our influence."

Joseph did some quick math, then said, "Well, that's about thirteen or fourteen million right there, and I suspect that between the Kiros fleet, we could make up the difference."

At that point, Niles had an epiphany. "But only if we reduce the necessary crews to a bare minimum, likely with the enlisted personnel. We'd have to call down just about every Knight to the surface."

Monarchs and nobles looked at each other in realization. It was finally Frederick who declared with great determination, "Then our plan is set, and we need to get about completing it without delay." He ordered Niles, "Call down every Knight save one for each Dreadnought in a command role, and have them bring every available vessel capable of landing with them. Arrange for them to land at places to maximize the evacuation process, and split up any available Knights on the surface to assist. I'll give you a tenth-cycle to have everything in order."

"I'll have Knight Fransisca get right on it," Niles answered, turning to his comm unit, but received no reply.

"Emmitt was... one of the Endtimers that started this mess," Rumil explained as Niles shouted angrily into the communications device. "He probably ran off when he saw the opportunity, and we don't have time chasing after him."

"She's right," Lionel stated almost humbly, "Let's move quickly, and at least perform one proper action for our Creator…"

Suddenly, there was a huge succession of blasts, then silence before a deafening demonic roar rushed past. As the sound faded, the demonic line fell into chaos once again, some attacking each other while they dropped into a full retreat, either diving back into the crater that held the gate or winding up dead at the hands of other demons.

Within a tick, the Archangel dropped down nimbly onto the gathering. "The Gate is too large for the Star Smasher to destroy. I will have to take drastic measures," he said simply. "I trust the plans for evacuating the Se-Lan are underway."

They nodded, the awesome presence of the angelic being rendering them unable to do much of anything else. Realizing he wouldn't get much of a reply, he slung the Star Smasher, still dripping with the brownish red blood of Chau-Fagn, over his shoulder, and said, "I will return to the Gate and make sure the demons realize the foolishness of making a second attempt to gain purchase on this plane."

He turned away, serving to jolt Rumil out of her stupor, and she said, "Wait! I'm wondering if you could answer something for me…"

The Archangel turned his head, as if waiting expectantly for her question. Rumil's courage once again failed her, and she mumbled. "Never mind… it's not important."

He shrugged, then took to the skies again, his gleaming wings flapping occasionally, carrying him back to the crater. Rumil dropped her head, hoping no one could see that her face was flushed. She couldn't bear to ask the question, fearing the Archangel's answer, dreading that it would confirm her deepest fears.

Dewin tapped her on the shoulder, and asked, "Perhaps we can help them in the evacuation effort?" He asked more in an effort to get her mind on something other than what was clearly troubling her.

"Actually, I think there is something we can do…" Rumil replied, the distraction working as her eyes lit up.

* * * * *

He never really understood just what lying truly meant until just now. Of course, he had lied before, or at least never told the full truth, but it was only now that he really appreciated it for what it was, now with his change, now that the full extent of who he was and the purpose for which he imposed himself on the material world became clear.

For the mortal-born, it came naturally… to tell another person something that they knew was not the truth, a conscious decision that even the most truthful and honest could make with relative ease. It was a part of the mortal condition, and likely not something they could fully grasp. But to him, he saw what such a simple act truly meant. It was an exercise of free will, an expression of freedom by denying that which would normally be immutable. It was rather refreshing.

Truth being, the Star Smasher was more than capable of absorbing the power of the Gate and sealing it shut. But the Gate was hardly the only thing that needed to be disposed of. There were many secrets and ancient knowledge that still resided within these dead lands, things that he could not allow the Erani, or any mortal race, to know.

So, he had lied. And now he stood before the culmination of plans thousands of staryears old. His power grasped at the invisible threads of the universe and pulled it together, forming the means in which he would dispose of everything that could become a nuisance in the future.

* * * * *

The *Gallan* was about ready to make the jump to foldspace when the sensors picked up something… odd…

"Sir, we're detecting two unexplained masses of dark matter forming along both poles of Mydor," the secondary helmsman of the *Gallan* stated.

"Is there some form of magnetic anomaly occurring?" Dewin asked, knowing enough quantum science to be aware that dark matter doesn't start congealing without provocation.

"No sir. The dark matter is literally forming. As in, out of pure energy, likely psionic, from the analysis I'm getting."

"The amount of energy needed to forge that amount of any type of matter is beyond the combined efforts of the Galactic Alliance, much less any psionic," Dewin scoffed.

"Not unless you're an Archangel of Annor," Rumil interjected dourly.

The pirate captain turned and asked, "You mean to tell me Timothy is doing this?"

"I'm not sure he's Timothy anymore," Rumil answered. "And yes, I know the Archangel is responsible. I've seen it... I already know what is going to happen."

"Sir... the masses almost equal the entire mass of the planet," the helmsman said in awe, turning on the main viewscreen despite not being ordered to. The image of Mydor filled the monitor, and he pointed, "You can actually see the planet itself being pulled apart from the gravitational forces. Sensors are detecting earthquakes planet-wide that have an intensity ratio over two hundred."

"What is going to happen?" Dewin asked, barely registering his helmsman's running commentary.

"That," Rumil said, pointing to the viewscreen.

Mydor, which had been bulging at the equator, suddenly started to squeeze inward, as if the dark matter was starting to press into the atmosphere. Then within about five demiticks, the planet could no longer withstand the strain, and exploded with a shockwave that rattled the *Gallan*, despite its position far out of orbit.

Micha yelped in horror, having just been explained to on the shuttle trip up to the Blood Hawks cruiser that the tiny ball in the window had been her home. Rumil would have tried to comfort the distressed Se-Lan woman, had Rumil herself not been so melancholy as well.

Silence ruled the bridge for slightly longer than a tick, before the communications officer broke the moment with a polite cough.

"Sir... they're at it again..." she declared with a roll of her eyes.

"Who is?" Dewin asked, wishing his officers wouldn't be so annoyingly cryptic.

"The Kiros and the Solarians. I tried to patch in to negotiate plans for when we returned to the galaxy proper, but they're too busy arguing over who is responsible for what just happened." The officer opened the channel to the bridge speakers, and a cacophony of accusations and insults soon filled the bridge.

Dewin groaned in disbelief, slapping his hand onto his face in frustration. Because of that, he didn't immediately see Rumil trudge over to the communications station. She gently nudged the comm officer in the shoulder, and quietly asked if she could step in. With a passive shrug, the officer surrendered her chair, and allowed Rumil to sit.

Rumil forlornly tapped out a few lines of code on the terminal, sending a screeching feedback through the communications system that caused Dewin to cover his ears from the obnoxious noise, and likely doing the same to every vessel in the immediate vicinity with an open channel. She let it play for about three demiticks then cut it off with a violent keystroke. Dewin was about to comment about her methods when he noticed she no longer had the dejected expression of moments before. Now, she just looked angry; completely, fiercely, and violently irritated.

"Now that I have all your attention…" she began with saccharine sweetness, then bellowed in a way that made the nearby officers jump, "Will you all just listen to yourselves for a tick!"

She gave the subjects of her derision a few demiticks to let her accusation sink in, before going into her rant once more. "I almost can't believe all of you! You just survived likely the most hellish moments of your life this cycle, and you *still* fail to see who, or what, the real enemy is! Those… things… you just encountered, *that* is what you are called to fight, not *each other*! Those creatures don't care one iota about how many Prophets you decide to count, or how you hold your hands when you pray, or what you want to label the damn stupid war both your kind fought *eight hundred staryears ago*!"

Right then, Rumil's face and voice almost instantly changed from righteous anger to a heart-wrenching sorrow. "Just how many of you Erani do all of you think died today? How many of you can think of friends that you'll never see again? I had two friends when I came here… one is dead, and the other one probably is as well. All they wanted was to try and bring their respective peoples together, like it should be…" From there, her voice again regained its anger, yet the sadness remained as well. "I cannot believe you would dare to insult their memory, or even the memory of everyone from both sects who died. Those who fought side by side against a truly devastating evil, the way you all should have been from the start! None of you thought of that, did you? Of course not, you were all too busy tossing accusations at each other, when you really should be blaming yourselves!"

The woman looked like she was about to physically and emotionally collapse as her forehead dropped onto the console. "I can't help but think that if all of you bastards had been on the same page when Justin Feroz and Timothy Honore downright gift-wrapped the chance to restore ties, that they'd still be alive today." As if expecting protests from the statement, she quickly added, "And don't any of you say that wasn't your decision to make, because hearing what I did just a couple ticks ago, I have no doubt you would have made the exact same decision as your leaders."

"Wake up, and see reality for once!" Rumil pleaded. "Half the galaxy doesn't even believe in your mission… the other half only follows it out of intimidation. And judging from what I saw today, we can't afford you morons fighting each other. We already have a tough road ahead, and none of us can afford you short-sighted imbeciles making the struggle all the harder!"

"I'll be keeping this channel open, just in case some of you decide to finally come to your senses," she snapped in conclusion, "but something tells me I shouldn't wait with expectant hope."

With that, Rumil finally went silent, exhausted both in body and mind. She had no idea just where that rant had come from, but she was glad she was able to say it, as it allowed her to vent the emotions that had been fermenting and boiling inside her. Now, she was simply tired, and was certain that she was about to fall asleep at the communications station.

Then the first voice broke the silence. It belonged to the Knight Robert Datson, who apparently had been one of the few noble-born spared to command the refugee vessels. "On a selfish level, it is somewhat hard to accept words of wisdom regarding our religion from an Arcadian woman, but I would have to be both blind and deaf not to understand them for what they are. Thank you for putting my own feelings into words I never had the courage to say."

Another voice, one she didn't recognize, spoke next with a hint of a sarcastic sneer, "Since you seem to have a pretty good grasp of things, perhaps you have some ideas as to the problems that started this argument?"

With a tired sigh, she muttered, "What would those be?"

Datson then interceded, in case Rumil went off again. "One problem is where we are to take the Se-Lan refugees. Their Elder Councilor seemed totally adamant about not taking residence on either Solaria or Kiros."

A demitick later, the voice of the Netrian Elder Councilor Pius came over the comm with his broken Basic. "Greetings once again… Rumil. Let me… extend my regrets… as I know your… loss well. I lost a… grandson at the… moment you lost a… friend."

"Thank you. But what exactly is wrong with the suggestions the Solarians and Kiros have made?"

"We… do not wish… to be a… burden… upon someone else's… home. We would like a… planet… we could call our own. Someplace where we could… live without worry of… upsetting the… balance of… things."

Rumil pursed her lips, and a bolt of inspiration struck her. "I have an idea. What about Baramak?"

Datson seemed a little skeptical. "What? Are you serious?"

"Of course! It's perfect, when you think about it!" she suddenly said brightly. "The untouched continent of Baramak is barely populated as it is, so the Se-Lan wouldn't have to worry about displacing anyone, and Creator knows that upsetting the balance of that place might just be a good thing. The Galactic Alliance has been trying to get people to move there, and we have twenty million beings that need someplace to set down."

"This… Baramak… sounds like a… un-good place," Pius commented.

"I'll admit, it's not pretty. Half of the planet is a nuclear nightmare, and the part that isn't ravaged by radiation is rather… undeveloped by the standards most planets judge themselves," Rumil admitted. "However, considering what you have been making do with, it's practically a paradise. I have no doubts that you and your people would quickly set order to the place, and make it into something we'd all be proud of."

Datson then added, "There are a lot of other undeveloped planets out there though, if they don't care about the amenities that the rest of the Alliance enjoys…" He then added with a hint of trepidation, hoping not to insult Rumil, "…places a lot better than Baramak."

Pius regarded the arguments, and said, "What do you… wish, Rumil dear?"

Rumil smirked, and said, "I'll admit, my reasons are rather selfish. Baramak is my childhood home of sorts, and I'd like to be able to make a home worth returning to. Perhaps with your help, I could make that happen."

"Very well… I understand your feeling. When my people… just emerged… from the Great War… some left to find… other places to explore and live. My ancestors… and the ancestors of all my people… stayed to build our old home back. I would be… honored… if we could do the… same for yours. I will… discuss with the other… Councilors… but I am sure they will not… object."

Datson seemed uncertain of the decision, but didn't argue it any further. "Alright… Baramak it is. I'll spread the word to plot fold coordinates."

"Now, what are the other problems you're having?" Rumil asked, emboldened by her first small victory.

"Nothing that cannot be dealt with at a later time. Right now, let's get the Se-Lan to their new home, then we can discuss other issues when we have more than a few Tackets of personal space."

Chapter Eighteen

The following ten-cycles would prove to be hectic at best. As she had expected, the truth of what happened in regards to the Baramak Slaughter sent shockwaves through the Galactic Alliance. Every senior member of the previous executive administration was arrested, including over forty of the Galactic Council, more than half of them tried for "heinous crimes against the Alliance." Unfortunately, former Premier Francis Tormay disappeared without a trace, but she knew that he wouldn't stay gone for long. After all, she had foreseen it.

The fallout was so terrible in fact that the current Premier of the Alliance was pressured into resigning because of his ties to Tormay, even though it had been proven that he had little association with those responsible for the Baramak Slaughter. Thus, the entire Alliance was in stasis while those that remained in power figured out the process they were going to take in selecting a leader and representatives, replacing those that had been removed from office or convicted. This also didn't surprise her, as she had foreseen that as well.

She kept close contact with the Solarians and the Kiros, quietly helping them negotiate the terms to end their theological and militant feud once and for all. As the truth of what Bryan Honore had seen in his visions proved to be more accurate than any could have imagined. Only the most hardcore minority of the Kiros could deny that Bryan was indeed a great prophet of their people. The Erani people came full circle two ten-cycles ago, as the remaining Priesthood of the Kiros overwhelmingly voted on an edict to accept Bryan Honore's prophecy as official canon.

In conjunction with the surviving elements of the Solarian Priesthood, the joint Erani clergy made several decisions regarding the future of their faith and their people, including the decision to construct a great monument to those that had fallen in the Second Battle of Mydor, as well as finally paying tribute to the innocents that died in the Erani's grievous error on Baramak. The battered planet was chosen to be the site of the epic monument, consecrated as holy ground for both Erani peoples just a ten-cycle prior. That, she had also foreseen.

For the Se-Lan, they were fortunately able to receive special permission from the Galactic Alliance to become citizens of Baramak before the governmental body ground to a halt from the scandal plaguing it. As she had expected, the Alliance was more than willing to bequeath almost the entire untouched continent to the Se-Lan. Despite the dogged resistance of corrupt planetary leaders and a fearful reaction from ignorant, desperate citizens, the Se-Lan progressed on their new mission with astounding grace tempered by a sheer immovable determination to make their new home the best it could possibly be.

Already, half a staryear later, Baramak was as peaceful as it had been since the colony planet's inception. The new administration, which the Se-Lan graciously opened to many of the original denizens of the planet, had taken great strides in balancing the technological prowess of the Galactic Alliance with the rustic, earthly ways of the Se-Lan. The effort yielded many breakthroughs, including policies to finally clean up the burnt side of the planet, rather than just contain it. Funding the project proved to be a small problem, until geological surveyors, assisted by the psionic abilities of the Se-Lan, discovered several veins of the metals used to form amorphous alloys, like carbide and hypersteel, which were as pure as anything mined from the depths of Solaria. Then again, she had foreseen that as well.

She had also foreseen the arrival of the visitor that had just appeared on the doorstep of her home, built by the Se-Lan and the Erani in thanks for what she had done. It was a rather simple, two-level construction, without many of the luxuries that most people of the Alliance considered necessary, but with enough of them that she could stay in the know, as well as spare room for her housemates: the Feroz family, their attendant Fiona, and three special friends, Micha, Ghadri, and Pius, all of whom didn't have much family left, and so were assimilated into her ragtag family of strangers.

"Greetings, Miss Bonamede," Robert Datson said with a polite bow when she opened the door.

"Greetings to you as well, Knight Datson," Rumil replied, gesturing for him to enter. Winter on Baramak wasn't as harsh as some planets, but it was still rather cold.

"That title is rather inappropriate, I'm afraid," Robert answered as she closed the door behind him. "I resigned my commission about three cycles ago."

"Why would that be? The Solarians need leaders like you to rebuild in the way that does justice to their people."

Robert shrugged. "There are plenty enough to do that already. I wasn't the only one with reservations in regards to the old ways, after all. Besides, unlike most of the survivors, I was close enough to the truly powerful elite in the Solarian hierarchy that I should have known the truth as to what was happening. I guess I felt guilty by association."

"Too many decent people have fallen victim to that plague already, Robert," Rumil said with concern, extending a hand in invitation to take one of the beautifully hand-carved wooden chairs in the parlor. He did so, as Rumil sat down across from him with her right hand on her cheek.

"The only leader the Solarians and the Kiros truly need is you," Robert replied, his eyes locked on hers. She leaned back innocently in her chair as Robert said, "Don't be coy, Miss Bonamede, it doesn't suit you. I know as well as all the other negotiators in the Erani peace accords that you directed it all from the background, allowing us to take the credit while you slipped out unnoticed. I also know enough about what Bryan Honore truly saw now to recognize you for who you are. You are the Sixth Prophet he told of, aren't you?"

Rumil shrugged. "I can't say for certain. I know that I have visions of the past and future that come from a power I cannot totally comprehend, and that this power seems to be calling me to act on those visions the best that I can. Is it the Creator that you worship? I'd like to think so, but I can't prove it. I can only assume on faith that it is. However, even if I am correct, I suspect that Bryan expected something out of me that I really am not."

"Is that right?" the former Solarian Knight said. "He said you would come to rebuild the ties between our peoples, which you have, despite what you might say to the contrary. The Erani would not be where we are without you."

"But I'm not a leader, Robert. I couldn't take the pressure and the responsibility that came with a position of power. It's almost more than I can bear trying to deal with these visions I keep having. I can't go outside my front door without worrying that I'm suddenly going to be overwhelmed with some message and I'll collapse in the middle of the street. There are points where I am certain I am going to go mad trying to cope with them."

Robert nodded. "I suppose I can understand that. Nicholai had apparently said something similar. I'm not sure why all the prophets before him could handle the duties of leadership and prophecy, and all those since could not. Perhaps the nature of those visions had somehow grown worse as time as passed, or maybe the first three were mistaken in taking up such mantles. But I also cannot make any judgments on them, as I can't begin to relate. I suppose you would know what is best for you, and I certainly don't want to push you into more than you think you can handle."

There was a momentary silence, and Rumil then noted, "There's something else that is bothering you."

Robert twiddled his fingers. "It appears my name has emerged as one of the candidates to take up the vacant seat of Premier in the Galactic Alliance. I'm not sure how, but apparently enough of the remaining councilors remember me from the occasional events I attended with the monarchy, and supposedly the peace accords have garnered me accolades among the general populous as well."

"That's wonderful!" Rumil said with amiable cheer.

"Is it?" the Solarian man questioned. "It wasn't even me who made the peace happen, and my time before the fall of the monarchy was spent in blissful ignorance. Everything they are lauding me for I either didn't deserve, or should be reviled for."

"Nonsense," Rumil said with a dismissive wave. "Contrary to what you seem to believe, you did spearhead the peace between the Solarians and the Kiros. I merely gave you the courage to move forward in the way you always wanted to. As for your 'blissful ignorance' as you call it, ignorance is only dangerous if you do not learn. I suspect you have. I have no doubt that under your watch, something as terrible as the abuses of the Solarians and the Kiros, or the Baramak Slaughter, will never happen. And that is what is important, to remember the crimes of the past, so that they never occur again."

She leaned forward and put her hands on his shoulders, and said, "Look at me." When he complied, Rumil continued, "It's not only the Solarians who need leaders right now. The galaxy needs someone who can restore faith in the eyes of the populace, and to lead with dignity and honor. They need someone like you."

Robert was silent, probing her eyes with his own, and she could sense that he was probing her innermost thoughts to try and detect any pandering or well-intentioned deceit. She let him search her mind, let him see that she truly meant every word she had uttered. Finally, with a resigned sigh, he stood, and Rumil quickly followed him back out to the entry.

"You honestly think I should accept the position if it is granted to me?" Robert asked, as if he hadn't just read her intentions as plain as writing on a page.

"I can't think of anyone better to take it," she assured him as he opened the door, and walked back out into the Baramak winter. She kept the door open, watching him as he stepped clear of the home, then teleported away. She stood at the threshhold for several ticks, staring out into the falling snow, thinking that he would indeed overcome any obstacles in his path and become one of the finest Premiers the Galactic Alliance had ever known.

After all, she had foreseen it.

But as night fell, and she sat at the desk in her bedroom trying to write down what she had experienced and what she had seen in some remotely accurate manner, she would soon receive a small message from a man she feared was as dead to her as the names on the memorial she could see from her balcony...

This was something she had not foreseen...

Epilogue

The cloaked figure nodded, and replied, "Of course I know those things. After all, I was there, wasn't I?"

"I wasn't sure," Rumil admitted. "After all, after you… changed… I wasn't sure just how much of… Timothy… was left, if anything at all."

"Was that the question you were going to ask me on Mydor?" the shrouded man queried, his voice slightly tinted with amusement.

Rumil nodded. "I wasn't sure I was ready to know the answer. I'm still not sure if I am. But, I can't run away from it. I just want to know… you're still… you… right?"

The man didn't immediately reply, first throwing back the hood of his cloak. Rumil's breath caught in her throat as, instead of the shimmering metallic features that she had last seen on Mydor, she saw the same smooth pale skin, and shining sapphire eyes, that she had looked directly into just before that fateful cycle in which everything had turned upside down.

"I am still the one you remember… just a little bit more now. That's all."

She happily threw her arms around his waist, and he returned the embrace for a short while before releasing her and replacing his hood. When she looked at him questioningly, he explained, "I don't want too many people to see me just yet, and eyes have an annoying tendency to appear at most untimely moments."

"Why?"

"Because I'm still sorting a lot of things out regarding myself," Timothy answered. "Even though I have a better idea about the power that I have, I'm still not sure how, or even if, I can control myself while using it. I want to make sure I can answer the questions that some people would have for me satisfactorily before I make public my return. The idea of a man floating about the galaxy with the ability to destroy planets and not be completely certain he can control himself probably wouldn't settle well with many."

"I suppose that's true," Rumil acknowledged reluctantly. "So I take it you're going to leave again?" He had just come back to her, and now it appeared he was going to leave her alone to worry once more.

He didn't answer the question, instead looking up towards the pearl-colored monolith that marked the center of the circular monument. "Nice speech, by the way."

Rumil momentarily looked over the text carved onto the obelisk. She had given the dedication to go along with the ceremony that had consecrated the area as holy ground, and a special-order engraver had performed the task last cycle when it was voted to be included. The negotiators of the Peace Accord had demanded that she say something, and she chuckled when she remembered how most of the gathered dignitaries and audience had no idea who she was.

It had been a very short speech, in contrast to the tenth-cycle-long addresses of the many negotiators that had brought peace, and the three-tenth-cycle sermon that the newly appointed High Priest of the Joined Faith had given just before it. Nonetheless, there had not been a single dry eye in attendance when she had finished, not even her own. "You should have been there. Apparently, it was quite powerful in person."

"I was," Timothy answered. "And it was. I would dare say it was... divinely inspired, to say the least."

Rumil blinked. "I didn't see you... and I didn't sense you either."

"I know you didn't, but I was there nonetheless. That's the point, actually. You asked me if I'm going to leave again... but I had never left. I was watching you as you helped the Solarians and the Kiros reach peace. I was there as you watched them build your new home. I was there when you convinced Robert to pursue the nomination of Premier."

Noticing her confusion, he gently grabbed her shoulders, and placed a light kiss on her forehead. "That's my answer. I'll always be around... you just might not know it."

Timothy stepped away, then just seemed to fade into nothing, only his footprints on the snow indicating that the man she had seen was more than a ghost or illusion.

She scanned her surroundings with her eyes, investigating her peripheral vision for a ripple or anomaly that indicated Timothy was simply floating about, invisible and shrouded from detection. "So, are you here now?" she asked, the only reply the soft slap of wet snow on her head and nose. Suddenly realizing how cold it was outside, she pulled her jacket tighter around her, and turned around to return to her home. As she did so, her eyes caught the speech she had delivered on the monolith, and she paused for a moment. "Divinely inspired" Timothy had called it, and perhaps he was right. She wondered if even he felt a little moisture in his eyes when she had finished speaking.

I did. Timothy's voice, like the whisper of a gentle breeze, floated in the back of her head. With a smile, Rumil turned away, and retreated back into the warmth of her home, where Ghadri waited in the doorway, berating the younger woman for going out into such a cold night without properly dressing first. Ghadri demanded to know what had possessed Rumil to walk out in nothing but a nightgown and jacket, but Rumil wasn't sure how to answer the Se-Lan woman, and thus simply smiled apologetically.

Meanwhile, a lone man, invisible to the eye and mind, read the names that had been engraved in the outer wall of the memorial, stopping at the name of Justin Feroz. His unseen hand traced the name, and he silently vowed to always remember and honor the name of his fallen friend. From there, he turned to the monolith, and read the text carved into the monument as small droplets of water seemed to appear out of thin air, leaving small marks on the snowy ground.

We are here today to dedicate this place to those who had died in defense of their faith and honor against a menace beyond the comprehension of simple words.

Many will scoff, and likely many already are, at what we are doing here, but it is a position born out of ignorance and misplaced pride in the fragile limits of mortal knowledge. We should not blame them for this, however. After all, we failed in the purpose we were called to do, and it is going to be a tough mountain to climb in order to regain that trust, if indeed we ever had it.

That is also part of the reason why we are here today; to recognize where we failed, and to reaffirm ourselves, to ready ourselves to correct those failures. It is the only right thing to do in accordance with what we believe to be true, what we hold faith in to pursue.

Every one of you assembled here will meet a time where it seems like you are accomplishing nothing, that the hearts of those you profess to will be harder than stone. Most of you will encounter that frustration frequently, and some of you will encounter that barrier more times than you will be able to count.

When you do, remember the words I have spoken here. You will merely be sacrificing your reputation and your pride in following this cause. The souls we honor here today have given their lives. They gave their lives in the hope that you wouldn't have to. They fought with the desire that you wouldn't be required to do so.

But more importantly, they died. They died for those they called friends. They spilled their blood for those they cared for. They sacrificed everything for the thousands upon thousands they loved, and for the billions upon billions they would never know.

The End

Appendix: Guide to Time and Measurement

Time

Though the worlds and societies of the Galactic Alliance maintain their own measure of local time, particularly days and years in accordance with the movements of each individual planet, a standard measure of time is a clear necessity for an interstellar civilization. The *cycle* is the fundamental unit of time in the Alliance, its span being an average between a Kiros day and an Arcadian day. Ten cycles constitute a *ten-cycle*, and fifty ten-cycles (or five hundred cycles) equals one *staryear*, the largest unit of time commonly observed. For approximate comparison, a cycle is roughly 20 Earth hours, a ten-cycle is 8.3 Earth days, and a staryear is 416.7 Earth days.

Cycles are divided into two sets of ten *tenth-cycles*, the first set labeled the Early Ten (ET) and the later set the Late Ten (LT). (This means there are actually *twenty* tenth-cycles in a cycle, which is somewhat counter-intuitive. Apparently the habit of dividing daily - or cyclical - time with a meridian is one thing that a pan-galactic society simply can't break.) Finally, each tenth-cycle is then divided into fifty *ticks*, which are themselves divided into fifty *demiticks*. As further comparison, a tenth-cycle is almost identical to an Earth hour, a tick is 1.2 minutes, and a demitick is 1.44 seconds.

The format for noting the calendar date is done from the greatest denomination down…

3406 AW (staryear), 16th ten-cycle, 4th cycle.

In the case of cyclical time, the shorthand is often used as such…

5.34.16 ET (meaning the 5th tenth-cycle, 34th tick, 16th demitick of the Early Ten).

Measurement

Base units of other measurements were devised by Erani, who used these units since their Industrial Age. Because of its simplicity and ease of conversion between units, this system became the standard throughout the Alliance, almost completely supplanting local traditional measurements. Each form of measurement has a base unit (which is always capitalized), and suffixes are added to indicate exponential increase or decrease by a factor of ten.

Met: *1000
Mel: *100
Mem: *10
em: 1/10
el: 1/100
et: 1/1000

Noting the presence of the capital "M" in the suffix is essential; it's the signifier for whether to multiply or divide the base unit.

Length: The base length is called the Tack. 1 Tack is approximately 0.85 meters. Scientific studies also make use of larger units such as the L-Tack (the mechanical term for a light-staryear) in astronomical distances, and the Tackeg and the Tackeu (1 Tack$*10^{-20}$ and $1*10^{-25}$ respectively) in nuclear science.

Volume: The base unit of volume is the Drup, which is about 0.85 liters.

Mass: The base unit of mass is the Humm, and is approximately 0.85 kilograms.

Temperature: The base unit of temperature is called the Cel. 0 Cel is the equivalent to the theoretical temperature of Absolute Zero, while the freezing point of water is 2 CelMel (or 200 Cel.)

Energy: The most common label used for energy is the Toule, but is a bit more complex than what it would seem on the surface. It is generally misused as a measure of energy output, but while for most rudimentary usage it suffices, such a label is inaccurate.

All energy sources of the same size and composition have the same potential energy while within the same medium. The Toule registers the efficiency of the mechanism to transfer that potential energy into its designed purpose. The higher the toule rating, the less energy is wasted in an unusable form.

While initially a pure 0-100 scale at its coinage in the early days of the Erani Industrial Revolution, as technology improved and changed the understanding of the base potential energy of most sources, Toule measurements merely starting registering values over 100 than alter the values of everything else prior. The current level of technology has generated a confirmed record Toules of 109.3, though even that is subjective considering that different energy sources have different potentials.

Toule measuring has become most popular in determing an Erani's psionic strength, after intense study revealed that all Erani have, with minor deviations, the same size "battery" of psionic energy to tap into, but the difference in relative strength amounted to how efficiently the psionic used that available pool.

In reality, measuring energy is a messy thing with several different units depending on the scale and type of energy being measured. As a result, the Toule has become attached to something akin to electrical watts by the rank and file, even if using such labels around an engineer will get you a stern lecture or a roll of the eyes.

The Head of the Beast

I am willing to wait for a great many staryears to see my plans come to fruition, but that does not mean I am a particularly patient person; especially when I am scheduled to be somewhere, and am waiting in a dingy, dark, secluded alley in the heart of Centris for a man that I am not fond of. It has made me impatient.

For I now stand on the precipice of a new age for Solaria and the worlds under its influence, and proud of my accomplishments; not proud of myself, but of how far we have come in such a short time.

It was a scant twenty-four staryears ago that I put the cogs in motion, that I took control and shaped the movement that would topple the old ways, and bring our people into a brighter dawn. A society no longer controlled solely by family blood, no longer discriminating by gender or wealth. A society where the destitute are no longer locked in cages where they could be conveniently hidden and eventually forgotten. A society that offered as much 'freedom' as can be truly granted when ruled by a governmental body. That was my vision, that was my dream.

I will never claim to be proud of what I have done, the people I have hurt, and even sent to die, in order to change the world around me. Good men, as well as wicked men, were a mass sacrifice that had to be made. It was what had to be done, for even the good men were part of the slowly consuming disease that threatened the whole.

Change had to happen. The pillars of Solaria had to be ripped down while there was still a foundation that a new era in our society could be built upon. That meant everything had to be purged, all had to be erased, even those with true nobility in their hearts. As long as they lived, my people could never move forward.

It honestly did not take much to shape the path that history would take. Our society was already on the inexorable path laid out in Bryan Honore's prophecy; I merely needed to shift the rails ever so slightly to reach my desired end. Setting the events of the Baramak Slaughter in motion, then helping to expose Solaria's role in the tragedy, guaranteed that what few Knights remained after the Second Battle of Mydor would be rendered impotent, hounded by the crimes of their superiors and unable to form a bloc of power that any Solarian would follow in large numbers.

My every slumbering moment is haunted by the cries of the

innocent dead; lives snuffed out in a wave of nuclear fire. Faceless ghosts that steal the sleep from my eyes, and leave me on the verge of tears when exhaustion finally overcomes me.

I have done all I can in the two decades since to not learn anything about the people who died in the Slaughter; the few names I had no choice but to learn and already knew already weighed down my soul as it was. To learn more might cause such regret that I'd take my own life, and I can't afford that... not yet. While I have no doubt that one day my penance will come for me, it is a sentence I must stay as long as I can. There is far too much for me to do.

Yes, I used and indirectly sacrificed many people, turned their own dreams towards mine, even those who thought they were serving a far greater good than any mortal agency. Perhaps I regret using those who thought they were bringing the end of the old ways as the Creator's will. Those dreams served no will but mine, their sacrifices, both in time, money, and even their lives, certainly did not reach anything divine.

There's a part of me that feels somewhat sorrowed for a man like Horace Hightower; he devoted his every fiber of his being to bring forth the end of Bryan Honore's prophecy, truly believing that he was performing the role destined upon him by the Creator. He earnestly believed in his role, and that a greater blessing awaited him. Misguided as he was, as depraved as what he thought the perfect Solarian Empire was, all he did was in service to a higher power, with little thought of his own wants. There is something of a nobility in that, and I somewhat regret using it for such dirty mortal designs.

There were some, however, who knew of the true purpose of the cult known as the Endtimers, and followed my design in the hopes of merely replacing the tired system that was slowly failing. For those people, I have no sympathy towards, no regrets using and bleeding their usefulness until there was nothing left, at which point I discarded them. They were no better than the corrupt, dying system they railed against, and would have done nothing good for the society I strove to better.

I am about to meet one of those people now.

Creator have mercy on his vacant soul.

Alex Datson was a sandscrub of a man; a hanger-on at best, using his family name as an easy access through life, even as his mediocre skills in both mind and body should not have afforded him much more than any layman.

He was short, even for the smaller stature of the Erani, and gangly. It was obvious why he did not survive the knighthood training, and wouldn't even now. His dark brown hair was oiled back so heavily that the sheen was visible even in the dim light of the alley I had chosen for this meeting. I'm not sure why or how Alex thought he should be seen looking like that.

His name made him useful, however, able to gather information gladly and candidly that would never have been granted to me even with my influence. My public persona was so above the board and proper that I would have been immediately distrusted, and none of the people I was searching for would respond to my alter ego at this point.

He was also remarkably stupid, so eager to attach onto any circle of power that he wantonly ignored all the warning signs about me. A person who had turned on the Knighthood of old, the cult I had formed, and the very crown of Solaria itself, would have no problems turning on the stale crust of a crippled noble family.

"Greetings, master. I have some of the information you requested."

"Some?" I ask, the displeasure in my voice evident. "I did not ask you for 'some', I asked you for 'all.'"

"I'm sorry, master." Alex says, whimpering like a beaten dog. "I did all I could. The Endtimers in SIA were very clever in covering their tracks, I learned of three of them, but it seems they were abandoned by the rest when they were compromised."

"No doubt under Emmitt Fransisca's instruction." I mutter disdainfully. Whether by cleverness, blind self-preservation, or dumb luck, Emmitt had escaped the Second Battle of Mydor with his life, and had the influence of the old ways to draw together the more secretive elements of the Endtimers, men that not even I had been able to identify when I had taken control of the cult.

"Did you at least determine if he was the one who stole my recording?" I query.

It really wasn't so much *my* recording, more that it had been in my possession. Just the fact that I had it at all could potentially be disastrous, much less how I went about acquiring such an ancient and potentially valuable recording from the non-progressed world that it had been hidden on.

I'm not sure how the Endtimers had even known where to find it, but they had considered the site sacrosanct. Learning that I had arranged for Nicolai's resting place to be defiled would not sit well with the Endtimers, or *any* agency for that matter.

Alex nods, "It would seem so. There was rumor floating around that he had... acquired... something of considerable value that 'changes everything we know about the faith.' Does that sound like what was on your recording?"

"It does." I reply. It doesn't matter what I reveal at this point. Alex has outlived his usefulness. Now I know Francisca possesses Nicholai's secret prophecy, and that he thinks he'll be able to do something with it. He promises to be a thorn in my side, but not a fatal one. His anger and ire is turned towards the Sixth Prophet... and that is not a fight he is going to win.

"Will this be a problem, master?" Alex wonders. He doesn't like uncertainty... but then very few people do. It's why Solaria clung to its outdated structure thousands of staryears longer than it rightfully should have. The comfort that came with familiarity was more important than not being abused and mistreated.

"No. Of course not." I answer. While the truth, it's meant to placate him in his final moments. A tense, panicking mind is not easy to kill silently, a subtlety I need at this moment.

"Very good." Alex says, the worry dissipating. "We're just so close... you say the coming High Tenant is on board with our ideals?"

"Indeed she is." I afford myself a knowing smile.

"To think, a mere staryear after all Solaria thinks us broken and lost to history... we will have in fact attained everything we sought!" He crows, and I swear I hear a giggle and snort escape his lips.

There is nothing to cheer in what has come to pass. It was necessary, not a victory. That Alex Datson thinks there is only gives me all the more reason to terminate him. I'm at the point where I no longer need to hide my disgust. "You seem to have a mistaken estimation of your worth in the eyes of this new world." I at last say, the darkness in my voice only partially masked by the alteration program. "We have attained *nothing*. *I* have shaped this new world. *I* will be the one who guides it. *You* have no part in it."

Alex, of course, was stunned by this betrayal, but he would not say another word before I silenced his existence with the threads of energy I had linked to his vital functions. He could not have had any inkling I knew such a technique, and thus the only reason it worked. Even the most feebly talented Erani could resist a Threading assassination if they suspected it was coming.

It was reserved generally for the highest ranking assassins in the SIA, never recorded and only taught orally, and one of many I had taken from the memory those unaware of what I was capable of. It would leave a man now identified as an Endtimer (due to the information I had leaked to peacekeepers earlier), and show no signs of foul play. It would be dismissed as a suicide by Peacekeepers with more important things to do, and no one else will give it much further thought.

I consult my PCU and determine that I need to move quickly if I'm going to be back where I'm supposed to be before someone comes to check on me.

I do not need to move far, which is to my advantage, as I really cannot move quickly in the heavy clothes I'm wearing. There are many capable psionics around, and I do not want to make too much "noise" for them to hear.

I turn to the back of the building, discarding my heavy robe and dropping the PCU onto the weighty black material. It feels good to be out of that ridiculous outfit, but it needed to be absurdly heavy to be laced with the metallic fibers that blocked technological and psionic scans.

But this is where it gets tricky, because I don't have those protections, and I'm going to need my power to dispose of the evidence.

I move quickly, folding the robe and the PCU on top of it into planetary orbit to get lost in the clutter. I wish I had the strength to fold it all the way into the sun's gravity well, but this would suit enough... anyone crazy enough to think I would be discarding evidence into the pre-interstellar travel clutter in high orbit would not have much luck either getting anyone to help search or find anything even if they did.

The next step is even more worrisome; because if someone happened to be looking in just the right way, they'd sense a fold coming from the direction of my suite, and that would prompt several questions I am not keen on answering. But at the same time, delaying would only increase such a chance. I close my eyes, and focus on the inside of the bathroom through the open window I had used to leave.

A couple of my guards had cocked an eyebrow when I had chosen the suite I did for my preparations. I had told them I still was a fairly modest personality and didn't want a bathroom looking out into the street.

291

They had accepted that rationale as far as I could discern. It also didn't seem I had been detected, as there wasn't a cadre of armed Solarian Knights barging in looking for an intruder.

Comfortable that I had slipped back in safely, I focus on fixing up my appearance, smoothing out my hair, then the collar and waist of my blouse, as it had come free from under my skirt when I had shed my robe. I am satisfied that I once again look the part of a modest Solarian woman as I sense that someone has entered my suite. It is such a unique presence that I instantly know who it is before I even re-enter the living area.

She is the reason I took the initiatives I did when I first learned of the prophecies of Bryan Honore that had been deleted. The words of this woman's coming had given me the hope that I had needed to begin this long, arduous process.

Rumil Bonamede, the Sixth Prophet.

"You were in the restroom so long that your guards were getting worried." Rumil said, her smirk reflecting her amusement. "I offered to come in and check on you when it was clear they were worried they'd catch you indecent."

I sigh forlornly. Some attitudes clearly still needed some adjustment, even if it was of benefit to me in this case. "Well, as you can see, my dear. I am quite well. Just fussing over my hair."

"You look great." Rumil answers with a roll of her eyes.

It's easy for Rumil to say, she looks lovely wearing anything and in any style. Women such as myself have to work at it.

I genuinely like Rumil and respect her. I truly do. In many ways, she is everything I wish Solarian women to be one day: strong-willed, independent, capable, and able to rise to any challenge, be it something mundane as assisting in a factory to being a political leader. I am honored that was able to play a significant part in what has led her to her rightful place as the spiritual leader for the Erani in this new world that has been created, and would do anything for her to keep it that way, even if it meant my own life.

"Anyways, I suspect the guards were getting anxious because it is almost time for your confirmation." Rumil says. "Shall we?"

"After you, my dear." I answer, taking step behind her, only to shift to her left side once we left the suite and into the protective circle of Solarian Knights.

"Nervous?" Rumil asks me quietly.

I shake my head. "It's not like I've effectively held this position since the Second Battle of Mydor. The official title changes nothing."

She laughs half-bitterly at this. "I wish I had your courage."

"You just think you don't." I answer, then change the topic. "I'm glad you are here, by the way. Your presence tends to give my words legitimacy."

Rumil's laugh this time is far more genuine. "Like you need me on that score."

I then fake some regret as I speak next. "I'm just... disappointed that Timmy isn't able to see this."

Broaching this topic was not accidental, nor was its timing. Rumil had carefully guarded her thoughts on this particular issue ever since that fateful battle, and gave me little to confirm what I already knew. This time, however, she was not prepared for the invoking of his name, and her reaction wasn't nearly as rehearsed. It takes a demitick too long for the practiced sorrow to form on her face as she assures me that he probably can.

She knows exactly what I do... that Timothy Honore is not gone from this material plane, even as the rank and file of the Erani believe he has returned to Annor with his mission complete.

I know that it isn't, and I wonder how much Rumil does. It can't be much... I can't imagine Rumil having that knowledge and accepting it, especially if much of what Nicolai had foreseen comes to pass.

I personally have an understanding most don't, so I am not inclined to try and ruin his designs. I know far too well that sometimes things must change, even if such change hurts at first. I, and fifty generations past mine, will be long gone when those plans come to fruition. My concern for my people has its limits. If the Erani are strong enough to survive the turmoil of the distant future, they will.

We reach the end of our short jaunt, just backstage behind a thick red velvet curtain that hides us from the podium at the center of the stage. The stage itself is much like the real world; behind all the carefully crafted appearances there is a dark, damp, and sometimes smelly underbelly where function trumps form and where everything that happens in the light really gets done.

I've lived in both worlds, but mostly only as an observer, and despite my confidence I projected to Rumil, there is an invisible line I'm about to cross; the point where I officially make my announcement that I am going to be more than an observer. I am going to be someone who takes action.

I hear my name called, and an applause that could not have come only from noble hands follows.

Rumil smiles warmly, and gestures for me to take the lead this time. "Are you ready, Madam High Tenant?"

I return the smile. I've been ready for this for twenty-four staryears. "Absolutely."

I step past the curtain, and cross the invisible line. I am now High Tenant Celine Honore, and I have a duty to perform.